DISHWASHER

DISHWASHER

JOEY TRUMAN

WHISKEY TIT

VT & NYC

Published in the United States by Whisk(e)y Tit: www.whiskeytit.com. If you wish to use or reproduce all or part of this book for any means, please let the author and publisher know. You're pretty much required to, legally.

ISBN 978-1-952600-28-9

Cover design by Michael Jung.

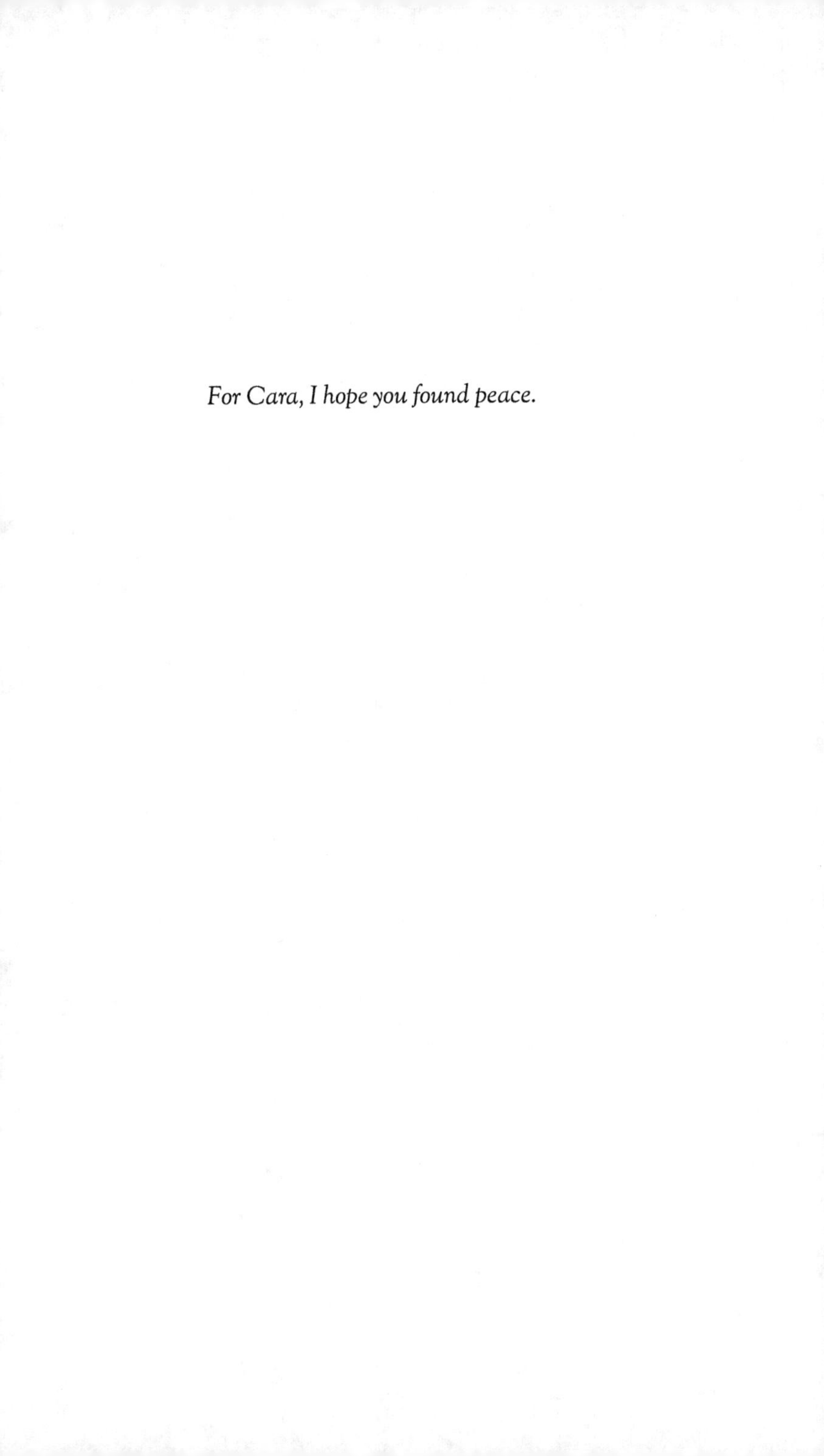

For Cara, I hope you found peace.

I

———

"You got your soakers, your scrubbers, the scratchers, the sinkers, the big soakers, the leavers, your scrapers, your glovers, we got *this* guy (who can't be described), we got the fast silverware, the slow silverware, the oddies, the triple ladles, the flip greasers, the three-inchers, the boilers—we don't do giant glasses though, remember that, it is very important, those go out to the girls, 'specially Lisa, she knows the drill the best—you got the dinner ones, the lunch ones and the breakfast ones, you see these salad guys? These are important. They break easy, so be careful. You got the veggie tubs, the salad tongs, all the dressing bottles, the milkies, the strainers, the big skillets, the tiny pineys, the apple trays, you got the half pans, the cookie sheets, all the pokers, you got the bottom lids and the top lids, you got this little guy that you can't lose—it goes here, see the sign? It says, 'Don't Lose.' Put it there. Don't lose it. You got the easy soakers and the hard soakers, when I get a second I will show you the difference. We got the whisk army, which usually comes in after the eight pans, but that depends on the night, Ronito will usually bring you those, that way you'll know where you are with the night—if Roger brings you those that is not a good sign, you might want to call your wife and tell her you'll be late for dinner, yeah ha! You got the leaners and the unos, the *impossibles* that I usually leave for last but this other guy I used to know, he was crazy, he would try to do them first thing, sometimes you just gotta laugh, yeah ha! I guess that kind of covers it. I'll be here the whole time so there's no need to be scared, don't be afraid to ask for help, it can get pretty intense, you're the third new guy this week. I am beginning to think they hired me to just train new guys for them to send off to the Altitude Too. Nah, I'm just joking. You don't want to work there. The guy like me over there is a real stick in the mud. I used to know him. Surprised they still keep him around. From the things I hear, yeah ha! You got any questions? Last requests? Just joking, this isn't a firing squad, yeah ha!"

"So I spray stuff here, and then I wash the stuff in that thing?"

"Were you even listening to me just now? This job is going to eat you alive if that's your attitude."

"Look, man. The scholarship people said I need to work two nights a week. They sent me here. I'm not trying to win any awards. Between you and me, this is a load of horseshit."

"I'll pretend I didn't hear that. Put that hairnet on."

"But I already have this stupid paper hat."

"It's regulations."

[*Mumbling*] "I'm gonna kill that fucking finance fucker."

"What's that?"

"Nothing."

"Okay. Let me show you the cardboard. See, if you hold it against your stomach like this and just push the side in, the tape comes free and you can just peel it back. A good dishwasher doesn't even need a knife. Not if they know what they're doing."

"But you got the knife, why not just use it? Look at your fingers, man, I think you're bleeding."

"Oh, that's just because I had the last two days off. My fingers just crack sometimes."

"Are you serious? Man, fuck this job."

The college boy took his apron off. His paper hat off. His hairnet. Wadded them up into a ball. Threw them to the ground. Lit a cigarette. Smiled at the Dishwasher and said: "Good fucking luck, man." And walked off down the alley.

The Dishwasher stood there with a cigarette in his mouth. Watching the college boy walk away. He looked down at the box, half-folded in his hands. A piece of lettuce was stuck to the packing tape. He shrugged. A bit of smoke got into his eye. He squinted. Looked up. The train tracks and the viaduct were right there. The sun was setting. He finished folding the box. The pile of other boxes still needed to be broken down. The dumpster was getting pretty full. He reached down and grabbed another box. Pushed it into his stomach and pulled the packing tape back. It was true that his fingers were bleeding, but that was nothing new. The bigger problem was that he was once again alone for the night. He didn't understand why these college kids kept quitting before he had a chance to fully train them. If they stuck around, they would understand how good the job was. How very satisfying it became. It was hard work and the pay was not the best, but if you worked enough hours you would be able to pay rent. You could get a couple days off sometimes. The people were mostly nice. You got free meals. Plus, you got to see all the people from all over the place. Like that family from Florida. Or the Vietnamese family that came in tonight. They hardly even spoke English. How wild was that?

The Dishwasher broke down all the boxes. Got into the dumpster. Jumped up and down until the boxes fit better. Crawled back out. Went back into the kitchen. Through the large prep area, past the front line, taking a left into the dish room. There was a pile of dishes waiting for him. He got right to work. Scraping plates into the trash. Running water for the soaking sink. That would take a while. He squirted some soap into the stream. Looked around. Saw that he wouldn't have the luxury to do much soaking, so he turned the cold water on, in addition to the hot water. He could hear yelling coming from the kitchen: "We need ovals, stat!" The Dishwasher spun around and opened the Hobart. The cycle had finished while he was out back breaking down boxes. He pushed the green plate rack through the other side. He stacked all the ovals and brought them out to the front line. Stacked them behind the cooks. Ronito said, "Thanks!"

The Dishwasher looked at the ticket carousel. It was already full. The dinner rush was early for some reason. He was kind of glad the college boy had ditched. He didn't have the time to be training somebody at the moment. Tonight was already looking like a nightmare. He went back into the dish room. Slid the two soupers into the Hobart and shut the door. The machine kicked in. He put a plate tray next to it. The one with the little fingers sticking up. He sprayed plate after plate. Standing them up as he went. When the Hobart turned off, he lifted the lever that opened the door. Steam came out. He used the dish tray to push the tray with the two soupers out. He shut the door. Someone in the front yelled, "We need silverware!"

The Dishwasher had a silverware washer ready to go. He reached under the sink and grabbed a flat tray. Put the silverware washer on it. Plus two metal bowls that were used for salads. Mixed salads. He scraped more plates. Checked the water on the soaker sink. It was ready to turn off. He plugged the middle sink and ran some tepid water. Testing it with his hands. He added a tablet. From a bucket next to the sinks. For health purposes. There were chemicals in the tablets that killed germs. The Dishwasher didn't know what was in the tablets, but they didn't smell like bleach, so it must have been something else. He turned around. Opened the Hobart. Steam came out. He pulled the plates out. Went to the other side and pushed the silverware and the salad bowls in. Shut the door. The machine kicked on. He stacked the clean plates and brought them to the shelves behind the front line. He looked down and saw a medium metal bowl that needed washing. He reached for it. Ronito yelled, "Don't even think about it!"

The Dishwasher pulled his hand back and scurried to the dish room. He picked up the plate tray and put it under the Hobart. He opened the door. Pulled the tray with the two salad bowls and the silverware out. Let them steam. He went over and started scraping plates again. Then he looked at the middle sink. It was ready to be turned off. He bent down and picked up a stack of plastic bowls that had been sitting under the sink since the salad station finished. He dumped them into the middle sink. He turned around and bent down. Picking up a plate tray. He became frustrated because he should have just put the plate tray from before in the secondary slot to begin with. He must have been distracted. Which was not a good sign. His mind started to race. He started seeing flashes of light. Anxiety started to kick in. His arm hairs started to stand up. All he could think of was the word *distracted.* Which he kept rolling around over and over in his head. Changing it into *dish-tracted.* He tried to ignore it. But it kept coming. *Dish-stracted.* The little lightning bolts on the edge of his vision. He was sure he was dying. He ran out of the dish room and into the dining room. People were eating. The girls at the front were running back and forth. Getting drinks. Giving people food. Taking orders. The Dishwasher bumped into a waitress he didn't know. She said, "What the hell are you doing?"

The Dishwasher could only focus on a very yellowish and heavily made-up pimple on her face. He tried to smile. He didn't know what to do. He spun around and went back into the dish room. He started scrubbing a large pot that was burned at the bottom. The potato soup had been in there. He tried to ignore his mind. The thing that was coming.

A loud noise came from the dish room window. He looked over. The new waitress had dropped a stack of plates. This stopped his brain from going into overdrive. He rushed out and started picking up broken plates. The new waitress said, "I'm sorry." And left.

The Dishwasher forgot all about his brain and scraped the food from the short carpet with his bare hands and put it in the hole that led to the trash can under the window. He was glad that the migraine hadn't come to fruition. His arms were back to normal and he was able to truly focus. He went back into the dish room. Washed his arms and hands in the middle sink and went back to work, scraping dishes and stacking them up. Rinsing them. He remembered the silverware. He took the holder out to the waitress station and filled it up. Someone said thanks. And patted him on the buns. He scurried back to the dish room. Confused by the buns pat. But also energized by the buns pat. Then someone from the front line yelled, "Salad plates!"

The Dishwasher started stacking salad plates as fast as he could. Not wasting any time spraying them down until they were vertical. Ranch dressing droplets went everywhere. His midriff was soaked. Sweat pouring down his face. There was no distinction between his body and the sinks and the Hobart and the trays. He was in his element. The din of the dining area. The classic rock coming from the prep area. The yells from the front line. Asking for small skillets. It all made sense to the Dishwasher. He didn't even know himself in these moments. When time practically stopped. When the lips of the waitresses stopped making sound. The heavy bags of food trash, light as a feather. The glass after glass of soda pop sucked down to ice. Eyes filled with sweat. The steam of the Hobart punching him in the face. The decision to grab a flat tray or a plate tray, just knee-jerk. The soakers filled with water and put down on the ground. The half pans stacked on the very edge of the conveyor. The triple run of silverware with a stack of nearly all the spatulas, because the new guy in the prep area forgot about them. The Dishwasher that night remembered hardly any of it. In a sense, he blacked out. The only thing that stuck with him was Ronito yelling, "Where the fuck are those spatulas, Disher! We need them yesterday!" And then nothing.

The Dishwasher was aware again standing next to the dumpster in the alley. Pulling a box into his stomach. Yanking the tape back. A cigarette resting between his lips. The smell of old and rotting oil. Frying oil. Slippery footing on concrete. Cold silence. A couple of drunks pissing down the alleyway, talking about a girl from Chicago that had some big ol' tits. He was worn out and starting to get cold from his sweat. Fall was coming. The two drunk guys walked by him. One of them said:

"Yo dude, you got a smoke?" The Dishwasher pulled some cigarettes out from under his apron. "Squished, eh?" The

Dishwasher squeezed a cigarette out. Handed it to the drunk. His friend was swaying. Trying to stay upright. "Light?"

"You want me to smoke it for you?" the Dishwasher said.

"What was that?" The drunk guy took the lighter. It took a few times but he managed to light it. He handed the lighter back, "Hey, bud, you know where the Buckhorn is?"

"That way." The Dishwasher pointed in the opposite direction. Up the alley. The other drunk guy, the one that seemed like he might fall over, said, "Fuck that." The first drunk guy said, "Oh shut up, we told those guys we would meet them there. Thanks, man. Keep up the good work." They stumbled down the alleyway. Towards the Buckhorn. The Dishwasher watched them for a second and then went back to breaking down boxes. There was a lot more to do. Before he was finished for the night. He thought about the college boy as he dropped his cigarette onto the ground. He looked over at the metal bean can that was filled with cigarette butts, next to the door. He thought that he should clean that up when he got a second. Then he walked back inside. Thinking about the trash and the Hobart drain.

2

____

When the Dishwasher got back to the dish room, he found a stack of rubber skidders on the floor. He was a little surprised by this. Either he was running late or everyone else was running early. He peeked around the corner to catch a glimpse of the cooks. Ronito had a beer and Roger was putting plastic on the cold sauces. "Fuck," he thought. He looked at the clock. It was a quarter past eleven. "It's not late. What's going on?" It didn't matter. He still had his work to do. This didn't change anything. Still, it confused him. He got to work on the late soakers and what remained of the dinnerware. He couldn't run the mats through the Hobart until the very last thing. They made a huge mess and gummed up the works. In an emergency he could wash them, but then he would have to clean the Hobart before using it for other things. This wasn't an emergency. It just meant that he now had to work on top of an eight-inch stack of rubber, exactly in the middle of his work space. He scrubbed all the late soakers and ran them through the Hobart. When he took them back to their stations, Ronito and Roger were no longer in the kitchen.

There was one guy left in the back. This guy Norman who seemed a little bit stoned all the time. He seemed to be finishing some prep thing that should have happened hours ago. The Dishwasher had a look-see. To make sure he wasn't using any fresh dishes that would need to be washed. Norman looked up. He looked confused. He smiled at the Dishwasher. The Dishwasher just frowned. Norman had all sorts of fresh dishes. Knives, plates, sheets, what looked like a burnt frying pan. The Dishwasher sighed and went back to the dish room. He cleaned all the sinks, knowing that he would have to use one of them again when Norman was finished. There was nothing to be done about that. He cleaned the spray zone, where the waitresses put their dishes. The sink next to the Hobart. He sat there for a second, looking. There was no point in doing any of this yet. He would just have to wait for Norman.

He was about to go harass him when Lisa came into the dish room. She was in charge of hiring people. She was the head waitress. She ran the front of the restaurant. Ronito ran the back of the restaurant. The owner, Laura, was also the manager. She didn't come around very often. Only sometimes. To hang out in this kind-of-secret back room—to do what, the Dishwasher didn't really know. She came around to get money mostly, and to yell at people. The Dishwasher enjoyed when she came around. He was never the focus of her abuse. Plus, the people she yelled at usually deserved it. Plus, she was pretty and smelled nice. Lisa was okay. She was pretty too. In an adult kind of way. Whatever that meant. That was just the way the Dishwasher would describe her. If for some reason he was going around describing people. She was kind of tall and had black hair. She had a nice demeanor. Never seemed too frustrated with things. Kind of understood that things were always pretty lousy. Which was a good thing, the Dishwasher decided. Because it meant that she wasn't always going around yelling at people. Not like Laura and Roger. Both of whom yelled a lot. Ronito and Lisa were kind of the same style of people. Pragmatic. They didn't yell unless they had to. Which made their yelling more effective. If you were to ask the Dishwasher, that is. Lisa said:

"How did Marty do tonight? You already let him go?"

"Who's Marty?"

"The new guy."

"Oh, the college boy? He lasted about ten minutes."

"Oh, Disher, what did you do?"

"I didn't do shit. Don't pin this on me."

"Well, did you do your whole *these are the soakers and these are the rinsers and don't you dare forget about those boxes at any time or the sky will fall in* routine?"

"You mean, did I train him? Yeah, I showed him the job."

"C'mon man, this job isn't that hard, you got to stop scaring these kids off, that's the third one this week."

"Have you thought about bringing in somebody that isn't a college boy? Maybe somebody that actually wants to work for once?"

"Like who? Who the hell wants to do this job?"

"You could pay people better, to start with. I rather enjoy this job, for your information."

"Pay them for what? This job is unskilled labor, anyone can do it."

"I would like to see you do it. It's not as easy as you think. You know what's easy? Writing down somebody's food order and bringing it to them. You think that is somehow skilled labor?"

"That's not the point, Disher. We just need people to stick around. For your own sake. Don't you want help?"

"It's not my fault this job sucks. Why do you keep blaming me?"

"I'm not blaming you, I just think it would help if you weren't so intense sometimes. Like maybe let them do some work for a little while before you start with your nonsense ."

"Well, you could train them yourself, say, like on Sunday."

"I am very aware of the days you refuse to work."

"Refuse to work?"

"I didn't mean it like that, you know what I mean."

"I don't know anything, ma'am, I am just an unskilled laborer keeping this business going."

"Don't be dramatic. All I am saying is, if we can't get anyone else in here to work these shifts we are kind of fucked. I can't spend so much time hiring people only for them to not work out."

"How is that my fault?"

"Well, when I talked to Marty he seemed pretty excited to get to work, and then it took all of ten minutes for him to think otherwise?”

“Have you thought about not hiring college boys?”

“That is all there is, you know that.”

“I don’t know that, I am not a college boy.”

“Okay, then how do you think I should go about it?”

“Have you tried paying people more? I mean, I could use a raise.”

“It doesn’t work that way, you know that. I can ask Laura for *you*, but aside from that we can only do the minimum for new hires.”

“Because it is unskilled labor.”

“You know it is. You have to admit that.”

“I don’t have to admit shit. I worked my ass off tonight, and you guys think it is just some vacation in the park where anyone can come in here and wipe rainbows off of unicorns all night long with nothing but orgasm utopias.”

“The job is pretty simple, dude. You wash the fucking dishes. End of story.”

“Oh, yeah? Do you know what I am doing? Right now? I am waiting for fucking Norman in the back there, with his glassy-confused-stoned-bone eyeballs, trying to figure out how many fucking biscuits to put in the bins for tomorrow. And when he figures that out, I have about thirty more minutes of cleaning up to do, all because he spent his break in the alley hitting his one-hitter until he couldn’t see straight.”

“What? Norman is doing what?”

“Oh, nothing! What I mean is...”

Lisa went into the prep room. The Dishwasher suddenly felt like a huge asshole. He didn’t mean to rat on Norman. He was just trying to make a point. He started to pick up the rubber skidders and fold them. Putting them on flat trays. Getting them ready to run through the Hobart. He could hear Lisa talking to Norman. He couldn’t catch the exact words, but he was getting yelled at.

The Dishwasher broke out into a sweat. This was not good.

He had violated an oath. The unspoken oath of not ratting his fellow coworkers out. He really hoped that Norman wouldn't get fired. He started to run the rubber skidders through the Hobart. Knowing he would have to clean the machine again before Norman's dishes came into the dish room. This was a penance of sorts. He would work harder as a way of saying sorry to Norman. Not that Norman would understand or appreciate it, but because it was the right thing to do.

When Lisa came storming back by the dish room, she didn't stop to give the Dishwasher any more grief. A few moments later, Norman came into the dish room and dropped off a bunch of dishes. He said:

"Thanks for selling me out, you fuck. I hope you choke on a ladle."

The Dishwasher's skin went cold. He got a knot in his stomach. His butthole clenched. He couldn't look up. He just sprayed the rubber skidders, pretending he didn't hear Norman. Norman just stood there. Staring. After a while, after the Dishwasher didn't look up from what he was doing, Norman left. The Dishwasher heard some noises in the prep room. Things banging around. Then he heard the back door slam. The Dishwasher waited a second. Went into the prep room. There were piles of black pepper on top of the metal tables. They spelled the words FUCK YOU.

The Dishwasher's heart sank. He knew that Norman had been canned. And it was his fault. The Dishwasher's.

He panicked. He ran into the dish room and grabbed a rag and ran back to the prep room and wiped all the black pepper into a bowl before anyone else saw it. He grabbed the rest of the fresh dishes and brought them to the dish room. Then he went back and finished doing Norman's prep work for him. Which was just putting some biscuits into plastic containers and putting lids on top of them. For tomorrow. The job was quite easy. It took him five minutes. He went back to the dish room. Finished running the rubber skidders through the Hobart. He put them back where they came from. Originally. On the line. And in the prep room. And behind the bar. He went back to the dish room and ran the Hobart a few times. To clean it out. Then he rinsed the drain. Cleaned the catcher. Ran the machine a few more times with chemicals. Rinsed it out. Emptied the water. Refilled it. Ran it a few more times. Then he was able to run Norman's fresh dishes. The skillet he had burned was soaking in the middle sink. The Dishwasher would have to just leave it for the morning crew. Whatever was burned onto it was really caked on. He ran the Hobart a couple more times. With nothing in it. Left it open. To steam out. Drained the water. Wiped down all the metal surfaces. Took a look around. The dish room was clean and ready for the next guy. Aside from the soaking skillet, the Dishwasher had left the room exactly like he would have liked to have found it. Not that anyone ever did that for him. But he had principles.

He went into the back. Next to the door. Took his apron off. Threw it in the hamper. Threw his hat and hairnet in the trash next to it. Found his time card above the hamper. Punched out. Put his time card back. Went over to the coat hooks. Found his black hoodie. Put it on. His crotch was wet. His stomach was wet. He smelled like a dirty wet sock. A dirty wet sock soaked in fryer grease. He made sure he had his cigarettes and keys. His wallet, which he took out of his back pocket and put into his front pocket. His lighter, which he took out of his front pocket and put into his back pocket. He opened the door onto the alley. The chilly air hit him. He shivered a little. He squeezed a cigarette out of the smashed packet. Bent it into something straight. Lit it. Blew smoke.

It was after midnight. He couldn't decide if he should just go home or go to the Buckhorn for some beers. It was band night so the place would be super busy. He didn't feel like going home, though. His roommates were getting on his nerves. They were terrible about doing their dishes and they had been eating all of his food without asking. Plus, rent was due and he didn't have it in him to ask them for it again. He decided to at least walk by the Buckhorn and see what was happening. Maybe someone cool would be there. Like Blinddog Smokin'. But that would mean they were charging a cover. "Whatever, it's like five bucks," he thought. He walked down the alley. His crotch drying in the cool air. The cigarette as flat as a pancake.

3

The back door to the Buckhorn was actually a side door. The front of the bar faced the street. The side of the bar faced the alley. There were two dumpsters, one on either side of the door. Which meant that drunks would come outside to piss. It was easy to hide their dicks because of the arrangement. Plus, you could see any cops coming. It was also a good place to hide if you wanted to sneak into the bar. Someone would come out to piss and you could just walk in. Which didn't do you much good if you were underage. They would card you anyway if you tried to get a drink. And if they were charging a cover they would give you a stamp. So if you got caught without a stamp they would kick you out. And if you didn't have a stamp and tried to drink, even if you were of age, they would kick you out. The place was kind of lawless, except that if you got caught breaking the law, they would just kick you out. Which was pretty effective. But the alley door was a way to bypass the front door if you needed to. For whatever reason. Maybe you needed to talk to somebody but didn't want to pay the cover. Or you were running from the cops and you didn't want the bouncers to see you come in. Or there was an ex you were trying to avoid and you saw her smoking a cigarette out front. None of it really made sense. But some nights, when it was very busy inside, the logic was sound. Usually if you were using the side door it was because you were already drunk and didn't want the bouncers to kick you out before you got in. Then again, you would usually get found out pretty fast, because you were drunk, and you would get kicked out anyway.

The Dishwasher walked past the alley door. There was a guy pissing behind one of the dumpsters. He said, "Hey!" to the

Dishwasher. Then waved his flaccid dick at him. Piss streaming out. "You want some lemonade, faggot?" The Dishwasher just kept walking. The guy said "Fag," and kept pissing.

At the corner, where the alley met the street, the Dishwasher paused before going around the corner. To see who was standing outside. There were a few people he was avoiding at the moment. None of them were standing in front of the bar. He walked slowly towards the entrance. The bar had a wall of giant windows looking onto the street. You could see in and people could see out. It was kind of a trap if you weren't paying attention. The place was crowded. The Dishwasher knew quite a few of the people standing around drinking cans of beer. Yelling over the music. There was a sandwich board that said that the band was indeed Blinddog Smokin'. The hottest band in town. They played covers. Mostly. They had a few original tunes that nobody liked. They mostly played mostly blues and funk songs. The cover was five dollars.

The Dishwasher couldn't decide if he wanted to go in or not. He had seen the band a million times before. And it was late enough that everyone was already quite drunk. He saw a couple friends near the pool table. Drinking beer. Moving whenever a guy with a stick would come over to take a shot. He never understood why they didn't just shut the pool table down on nights like this. His theory was that it created a bottleneck for the bouncers to exploit. Like, it gave them some space to maneuver if anyone got unruly. Which happened almost every time they had bands playing. Or, really, any night of the week. The bar was a college hangout as well as a hangout for locals. So tensions were always pretty high. Not to mention, they hired very large Black men, who were also college students, as bouncers, which made the locals very nervous. Which meant most of the trouble started when a local drunk-and-racist asshole said something very racist to a bouncer. The drunk asshole would start some shit. The bouncer would tell him to leave. He would resist. Then everything would get really intense. Then the asshole would be physically removed. Everyone would let out a sigh of relief and then mind their business. Bringing things back to normal.

The Dishwasher decided to go inside. He took out his wallet. Opened it. The bouncer asked for ID. He showed it to him. The bouncer handed it back. The bouncer said the cover was five dollars. The Dishwasher paid it. He put his wallet back into his front pocket. The bouncer stamped his hand. Stepped aside and let the Dishwasher in.

He went straight to the bar. There were two bartenders. Everyone was drinking, but they didn't seem to be busy. Mostly because all anyone was drinking was beer, or beer and shots. The Dishwasher ordered a beer. The bartender asked to see his stamp. The Dishwasher showed it to him. The bartender got the beer. The Dishwasher paid the bartender. Took the beer over to his two friends standing by the pool table. It was very loud. The band was playing in the back room. There was no stage. The back room was as crowded as the front. Some people were watching the band, but mostly people were just screaming at each other. Chugging beers. Nodding their heads with the music. The Dishwasher held his beer up to his friends. They knocked their beers against his. He watched the band for a second, then a guy playing pool tapped on his shoulder so he would move, so the guy could take a shot. He watched the guy take the shot. He missed. The guy walked away. The Dishwasher moved back to where he'd been standing. The music stopped. Suddenly the air was filled with loud voices. A few people clapped. Somebody yelled, "Fuck yeah!" The band leader said, "Alright, we're gonna take a break." The band removed their instruments and walked away from the equipment. This caused the crowd to relax and the Dishwasher and his friends moved over, closer to where the band had been playing. Country music came on, over the speakers. Loud, but not as loud as the band.

The Dishwasher had known Dong Smells and The Slippery Wrist since middle school. They were both going to college.

Dong Smells worked at the Altitude as well. As a line cook. He yelled:

"How'd it go tonight?"

"Same shit show. I think I got Norman fired."

"No shit! What'd you do?"

"I didn't mean to! Lisa was giving me shit and I let it slip that he had been smoking pot on break. I thought she knew."

"How couldn't she? That dude is slower than hair. Was he pissed?"

"He wrote 'FUCK YOU' in pepper on the tables and stormed out."

"Holy...!"

"What's that?" The Slippery Wrist got into the conversation.

"This guy we work with, Norman, Disher got him fired and he lost his shit."

"I didn't get him fired! I just accidentally ratted him out."

"Was he pissed?"

"He spelled out the words 'FUCK YOU' in black pepper on the tables, then stormed out," the Dishwasher said.

"That's fucked," The Slippery Wrist said, not totally understanding what that meant.

"He's not here tonight, right?" the Dishwasher asked.

"I saw him earlier. He might still be around, I guess," Dong Smells said.

"Shit." Suddenly the Dishwasher was paranoid. He really hadn't meant to rat him out. And he really didn't want to have to talk to him right now.

"You're fine. What's he gonna do? Just tell him it was all Lisa's fault," Dong Smells said.

"But he knows it was me."

"We got your back, Disher," The Slippery Wrist said. The Dishwasher could see that The Slippery Wrist was drunk. He was usually very peaceful.

"I'm not that worried about it. I really didn't do anything. It was all just a misunderstanding."

The Dishwasher was actually quite worried about it. He kept scanning the crowd looking for Norman. Norman, who was stoned almost 100 percent of the time and would forget what he was doing while he was doing it, also had a bad temper. The Dishwasher had seen it before. When he would get frustrated during the busy parts of the night. He would start throwing things. Then Ronito would have to go to the back and tell him to calm down. And Norman would say stuff like, "You're not my mom!" And Ronito, who was used to dealing with chaos, would say stuff like, "Norman, you have to calm down. If you can't do your job, we are going to need to get someone who can." And for whatever reason this would calm Norman down. He would come into the dish room and ask for the Dishwasher's help cleaning up his mess. And he would help him and everything would be alright for a while. Norman had some issues. The Dishwasher was afraid of what those issues were. He half expected Norman to come out of the blue and brain him with a pint glass. The Dishwasher knew nothing personal about Norman. Whether he needed that job or not. What his home life was like. All he knew about him was that he loved to smoke pot and get angry. For all he knew, Norman liked to get really drunk as well, and start fights with coworkers who got him fired for smoking pot.

They stood there looking at stuff for a minute. The Dishwasher was getting more nervous by the second. He said:

"I don't know what to say. I think I'm getting out of here. Anyone want this beer?"

"I hate to see it go to waste," Dong Smells said. The Slippery Wrist just smiled.

"Later, dudes. If you see Norman, tell him it was an accident."

The Dishwasher pushed his way out the front entrance. The cool air hit his crotch like a wet rag. There was a nice silence outside. Just a few people smoking and talking. He decided to just go home. Maybe there was some beer in the fridge. It was too late to get some from the store. Hours too late. He could have gone back into the bar and bought some to go, but the idea of running into Norman was not a good one. Of all the people the Dishwasher thought he would have to be looking out for, Norman would be the last person on his list. Until now. Now he was the first person on his list. He walked the couple blocks home with his head down. He didn't even smoke. He could do that at home.

He got to the apartment building. Opened the door to the building. Walked up the carpeted steps. Opened the door to the apartment. It wasn't locked, so he assumed his roommates were home. They weren't. All the lights were on. The door led into the kitchen. The kitchen was a mess. The sink was filled with dirty dishes. The trash was full. He walked into the living room. Which was a tiny little room with a loveseat and a blue beanbag chair. A television that was connected to a video game console.

There were two bedrooms. The Dishwasher lived in one. The other two roommates lived in the other. There were three mattresses. One in the Dishwasher's room. Two in the other room. All of them just lying on the carpet. The place smelled like cat shit. Not because a cat lived there, but because of the carpet and the fact that they smoked inside. The Dishwasher went into the roommates' bedroom. To turn off the light. The two mattresses didn't have sheets. Just a single blanket and a single paper-thin pillow each, with dirty pillowcases. There was an ashtray on the windowsill, and a couple empty beer cans. The Dishwasher got depressed looking at it. He turned the light off.

He went back into the kitchen. Opened the fridge. There was an 18-pack of beer in it. Half-empty. A thing of ham slices and some sliced white bread. This also depressed him. He took a beer out of the 18-pack and closed the door. He stood there in the kitchen, looking at the mess. The floor was linoleum. There was dirt everywhere. He thought about starting to clean up, but he got too depressed. He opened the beer. Set it on the counter. There was a little bit of space next to the sink. Took his cigarettes out of his pocket and pinched one out. He straightened it. Lit it. He was annoyed by the soft pack. He would have to go to that store by the highway that sold those Dave's cigarettes in hard packs. They were supercheap as well. He would just have to make a point of it.

He stood there smoking. Ashing ashes onto the dirty dishes piled in the sink. He was not happy with the roommates he had. Not that he could get better roommates. At least these two paid the rent on time, kind of. They were college boys so they had money. But the Dishwasher was starting to wonder if it was worth it. He could afford all the rent. If he wanted to. But only kind of. He was pulling in 300 dollars a week. If he worked eight hours a day. Which he didn't. It was more like six hours a day. Which meant he was bringing home about 180 dollars a week after taxes. Which was about 720 dollars for the month. And if you took rent out of that, he was making 320 dollars. Take away bills and food. He was not doing so well. It was a little surprising he was even still alive. It was no wonder that all he had was a mattress and a garbage bag full of clothes, and two roommates that ate all the food he brought home and didn't do their dishes and whose only contribution to anything was a shitty 18-pack of beer in the fridge that would probably run out by the time the night was over.

The Dishwasher stood there, smelling smells, smoking and drinking beer. He needed to shower, but he couldn't bring himself to do it. The only towel in the bathroom right now was an old T-shirt that didn't absorb anything; it just wiped water and mold smells onto your body. Plus, they had run out of soap, so the only thing to wash with was dish soap. Which only really worked on pubic hair.

He stood there drinking beer and smoking, pacing around in the little kitchen. Trying to think. He needed to go to bed, but he didn't have the courage to do that yet. His mind was on fire. He really did feel bad about getting Norman fired. He hadn't meant to. And these roommates were not working out so well. He expected them to show up at any time. Half-drunk and loud. About to spend the entire night playing video games and yelling at the television. He managed to choke down four beers before he calmed down. Then he went into the bathroom. Looked at the

T-shirt hanging from the towel hanger. The pure filth of three men living together without cleaning up after themselves. He brushed his teeth. Which was the only thing he had control over. Nobody abused his toothbrush. In fact, he didn't even know if his roommates ever even brushed their teeth. A thought went through his head that *they used his toothbrush.* But then he pushed it back. Decided that was impossible. Spat into the sink. Put the toothbrush in the holder. Shut the light off. Turned the lights off in the living room and the kitchen and went into his room.

His room was just a mattress on the floor. No sheet. With a single blanket. A flat pillow. A plastic bag of clothing. Carpet. A cigarette tray on the windowsill. A bare-bulb light. Nothing on the walls. No art. Or posters. A pile of dirty clothes in one of the corners. The room smelled like deep musk. He took off his hoodie. Threw it on the ground. He pulled the velcro strips on top of his shoes and kicked them off. They were covered in dish-room debris. He removed his wet socks. Threw them in the corner where his dirty clothes were. He looked at his pruned feet. White as a smothered wound. He pulled his pants down. They were still wet. Jeans. He draped them over his plastic bag of clothes. To dry. He took his shirt off. Threw it into the corner. He could smell his armpits. He had a clean shirt in the plastic bag for tomorrow. He stood there naked. His body skinny, and hairy in some places. His penis stiff and cold, pointing down at his walnut balls.

He shut the door and turned the light off. The light from the streetlamp was shining in. Or, more precisely, the light from the train tracks was shining in. There was no reason for a streetlamp to be behind the building aside from the trains coming and going. He didn't have any curtains to keep the light out. He just had to deal with it. The light.

He lay down on the bare mattress. He could smell the dish room on his body. Not quite mold, and not quite rotten food, but somewhere in between. He shifted the flat and nearly useless pillow until it held his head. He played with his penis until it became erect. He thought about Lisa yelling at him. He could imagine her tiny breasts heaving. Her little butt, tight in the black nylon pants that she wore. He pictured her saying, "You know what I think you need to do to make this right? Come with me." And then they were in the walk-in freezer. Lisa was spread-eagle on top of the boxes of lettuce. And then, that was it.

The Dishwasher wiped himself clean with a dirty sock he could reach. He wrapped himself up inside his blanket. Wadded his pillow up with his hands. And fell asleep.

4

____

The Dishwasher slept well for a little while. Then he was awake. His roommates had come home. They must have dropped some pots or dishes because he could hear them cleaning things off the ground and stacking them up again. The Dishwasher found this very irritating. He knew he was about to be harassed. He knew he was about to be harassed because he always got harassed whenever his roommates showed up drunk at what had to be four in the morning. He lay in bed waiting. He had to piss. He was about to get up when he heard the clock tower chime. It was indeed four in the morning.

He stood up and put his still-damp jeans back on. They stank. He needed to wash them. He'd never understood why all the other people in the kitchen were given checkered pants to wear, but not the dishwashers. He had an idea of why, and that was that none of the dishwashers ever stuck around. The management didn't want to have to hunt down pants whenever somebody got fired or quit. In their defense, the Dishwasher would have just used the checkered pants as regular pants and wouldn't return them either if he had them. But still, he would have liked to not have to ruin his own jeans for work purposes. Maybe when he had worked there long enough he would get the courage to ask for checkered pants. At this point he was considered a new employee still, even though he was the top dishwasher of the night shift. Whatever that meant. He didn't see himself working at the Altitude for any meaningful amount of time, but he had already been there for over half a year. As it was, he had two white button-up shirts and that was it. Those two shirts came out of his first paycheck. He owned them. He could sell them back, or exchange them. Which he often did, instead of washing them. But they belonged to him. They'd cost him twenty dollars. Which was a huge amount of money. Considering how small his paychecks were.

That first paycheck nearly made him quit. When he saw how little it was, combined with the twenty removed for the "uniform." He couldn't imagine what they would have taken out if pants were involved. So in that sense he was kind of glad they didn't give him pants, but as time went by he was starting to realize that the scam they were running was a long scam. That his jeans would be ruined before too long and he would have to buy new jeans. Which would cost more than checkered pants. He made up his mind to get up the courage to get Laura, the manager, to give him some checkered pants. Even if it meant paying for them out of his measly wages, having extra pants to wear to work would be better than ruining his good jeans.

The Dishwasher buttoned up his damp jeans and went into the kitchen. He looked at the mess in the kitchen. It was depressing. He walked to the bathroom door and looked into the living room. The two roommates were drunk. Playing video games. Smoking. Drinking beer. One of them looked up. He said:

"Yo Disher, how come you don't bring food home no more?" He stopped looking at the Dishwasher and stared at the television. They were both sitting on the floor. Leaning against the couch. The other roommate said, "Yeah, Disher, what the fuck?" The Dishwasher went into the bathroom. Pissed. Flushed the toilet. Walked back out. The first roommate said, "You didn't answer the question, we're hungry. Don't they let you take food home anymore?" The Dishwasher stood there. He didn't answer the question. He said, "You mind turning that down a little, I am trying to sleep." The second roommate said, "What do you care, you don't have to work till five tomorrow." The Dishwasher said, "What the hell does that have to do with anything?—turn it down, you jerks." The first roommate said, "We're the jerks? You leave us starving all night long, and we're the jerks?" The

Dishwasher said, "Don't be an asshole." The first roommate slid over to the television and turned the volume up. Then he looked at the Dishwasher and yelled, "DOES THAT HELP?"

The Dishwasher went back to his room. Took his damp jeans off. Laid them out to dry. Got back into bed. Wadded his pillow under his head and tried to sleep. The sound of the video game was clear as could be in his room. He could hear laughing. Then the sound of neighbors pounding on the wall. A few moments later, there was a pounding on the door. The video game sound went away. The Dishwasher's heart was beating fast. He was starting to hate his roommates. Now he was worried that the neighbors would complain to the landlord. Which was not good news. He wasn't even on the lease. He had inherited the apartment from a friend. The lease would run out in a few months. He was hoping to get onto the new lease when the time came. It didn't help that things like this were happening.

The Dishwasher lay in bed thinking of ways to kick the roommates out. That would mean getting a second job. He could barely stand the one job he had. He could work double shifts, he supposed. That would mean getting up at 9:00 a.m. and working until midnight every day. That was just too much work. He decided against getting a second job or working doubles and instead just lay in bed with his eyes closed, fantasizing about getting rich and famous from some science thing that nobody understood. Listening to the trains roll through town.

Around eleven the next morning, the Dishwasher was awake. He'd slept decently. He ran through a series of sexual adventures in his mind. He found the same dirty sock from the night before and wiped its crusty skin up and down his loins. He threw it on the carpet and stood up. He put his jeans on. They were still damp and smelled like mildew. He rooted around in his plastic trash bag until he found a clean T-shirt. He put it on.

He went into the kitchen. The mess depressed him. He wanted some coffee but there was none in the house. He was hungry, but he didn't want to eat a sandwich. He opened the fridge to see what was inside. The ham was gone. The bread was gone. The cardboard box of beers was still there, but it was empty. He shut the door. He decided enough was enough and started stacking the dishes so he could clean them. When he was about to start washing them, he couldn't find a sponge.

He went into the bathroom. There was no sponge in the bathroom. He looked under the sink. There was only a green cardboard cylinder of cleaning agent. And one yellow rubber glove. He went into the kitchen. Looked under the sink. There was exactly nothing. Not even a bug. He dumped all the disgusting water out of the pots that were in the sink and finally found the sponge. He wrung it out. It smelled like a fart wrapped in a pile of puke. He rinsed it and rinsed it. The smell didn't change. He went into the bathroom. Took the cylinder of cleaning agent and tried to pour some of the contents on the sponge. Nothing came out. He had to whack the thing a few times on the side of the sink. At that point one of his roommates yelled, "Hey, Asshole! We're trying to sleep!" He ignored them. He poured some of the powder out. Onto the sponge. He got a mouthful of it. He coughed. He ran hot water on the thing. Rinsing and rinsing. Eventually the smell of farts and vomit was gone. Now it just smelled like chemicals.

He went over to the shower and grabbed the bottle of dishwashing soap that doubled as bathing soap. It was getting empty. He needed to shower. For a second he thought about what to do. He decided to take a shower first. Just in case. He shut the door and turned the water on. He took his jeans off. His shirt off. He got in the shower. He washed his body and his hair. Using as little soap as possible. Then he got out. He took the T-shirt that was the towel and smelled it. It smelled worse than the sponge. He used the clean shirt he'd been wearing before to dry off. He put it back on. Then he put his jeans on. He went into the kitchen. The dirt on the floor sticking to his wet feet. He went back for the dishwashing soap. The sponge was sitting on the edge of the bathroom sink. He grabbed that too. He went back into the kitchen and started washing dishes.

There was no place to dry the dishes so he just stacked them in the corner. On the counter. Thinking he would then rinse them, then figure out what to do. Maybe just put them in the cupboards wet? Halfway through, the first roommate came out to go to the bathroom. He said, "Dude, what the hell? You can't do this later?" To which the Dishwasher said, "Yeah, sure, I will do your dishes at your earliest convenience. Don't you have class or something?" The first roommate said, "Ha! Not anymore, we dropped out, dude. By the way, we don't got rent." The Dishwasher said, "What's that?" The first roommate said, "It sounds like I said it, *no dollareos por rentos*, dude." The Dishwasher said, "So, when can you pay the rent then?" The first roommate said, "What part of we dropped out of college don't you understand? No college, no rent. You really are a boner, man." The Dishwasher stopped washing dishes. The first roommate went into the bathroom. The Dishwasher's heart sank. The first roommate came back out. He said, "Man, that T-shirt you use for a towel stinks! You should probably do something about that. Keep it down, we are trying to sleep." The Dishwasher said, "Shut your door, then." The first roommate said, "Dude, you know there ain't no door on that room, think." The Dishwasher said, "Oh, right." The first roommate put a finger to his head, tapping on his skull. The Dishwasher just stared at him.

This was horrible news. Rent was due and the roommates weren't going to pay their share. The Dishwasher had just barely enough money in his bank account to cover it. And then what? There was exactly one week as of yesterday before he would get paid again. One week without any money at all. One week without beer or smokes. The bills also needed to be paid. This was a nightmare. The Dishwasher left the dishes and took his wallet out. He had twenty-three dollars. He was pissed that he spent all that money at the bar last night. The five dollars at the door and the four dollars for beer. Three dollars for the beer, one dollar for the tip. That was three packs of smokes right there alone. Maybe he would have to start working doubles. Just to cover the rent. He couldn't wrap his mind around it, though. The idea of paying the rent for his roommates. Just because they dropped out of college. He needed to think.

He went into his room and fished around in his plastic trash bag of clean clothes. He was out of clean socks. He rooted around in the pile of dirty clothes in the corner and found two socks that weren't covered in cum, or smelling like death. Or both. He'd found a couple that were wadded up in a way that suggested they weren't work socks. He smelled them. They smelled okay. He put them on. Put his velcro shoes on. Strapped them tight. Looked outside. It looked warm—there was sunshine, but because it was the beginning of fall he couldn't be sure. He put his hoodie on. Made sure he had his wallet and his keys. Went into the bathroom and brushed his teeth. He couldn't be sure, but the toothbrush seemed wet. He really was starting to think his roommates were using his toothbrush. Either that, or they never brushed their teeth. Both things could have been true. He decided to stash his toothbrush and toothpaste in his room. Hiding them in his garbage bag that held his clean clothes. Then he thought about it. He moved them under his mattress. They were likely to check his clean clothes first. They wouldn't look in his dirty-clothes pile. There was no way they would check under the mattress. He hid the jar that he kept his change in, in the closet. He put it in the corner that was closest to the closet door. On the right. They might look in there, but it would take a little work to crane their necks to see the jar. For security, he put some dirty clothes on top of it.

The Dishwasher left the apartment. Making sure to lock the door behind him. He ran into a neighbor on the landing of the stairs. Coming up. Carrying groceries. The guy must have been the guy that banged on the door last night because he said:

"Man, you gotta keep it down at night—we got families living here."

"Hey, man, I'm sorry, it's just these roommates..."

"I don't want to hear it, next time I'm calling the cops."

"Yeah, okay, I'm sorry."

"Yeah. I don't want to hear it."

The Dishwasher was now sweaty. What a terrible morning. He just needed to think. To figure out what to do. His roommates had to go, but then what? How the hell was he going to get new roommates? That place was a sty. The roommates he had kind of come with the apartment. When the guy he got the apartment from moved out, he told the Dishwasher his brother was moving in and he had a friend. And that was that. He said he could have the place on one condition. That his brother and his friend could live there. This was how it turned out. Did he need to call the guy? Tell him what was up? Ask him to pay the rent? Or was that it? The Dishwasher now just paid all the rent? Did this mean that when the lease was up the Dishwasher didn't have a chance to take over the lease? Was he now homeless unless he kept these jerks around? Did it even matter? Could he kick them out and just ride the lease out until the end and see what happened? Could he call the landlord himself and tell him what was happening? Or did he just have to take it? Let them eat all his food, not pay rent or bills? Drink all his beer late at night while they were playing video games? Burning holes in the carpet with their cigarettes when they passed out? The Dishwasher had paid a deposit. He knew he wouldn't be seeing that again. Yet he had no desire to be homeless in a few months. And all this when he still didn't know if Norman was cruising around looking for him, wanting to rough him up for getting him fired. Even though it was all just a misunderstanding. Not only that, but he had some other things on his mind that were just as pressing. He walked down the stairs.

When he got to the street, he took his soft pack of cigarettes out. He peeled the paper back and saw that he had three cigarettes left. He took one out. Bent it straight. Lit it. It was as flat as a pancake. He really needed to get hard packs from now on. But they always sold the soft packs at a discount for whatever reason. He needed to go over to that place where they sold the Dave's. He decided that was where he would walk. The air was nice. Kind of brisk. He was glad he put his hoodie on. Soon it would be cold. Really cold. His coat was sitting in a pile behind his bedroom door. The pile with sweaters and his long johns. Still dirty from last winter. From back in May when he stopped using them and just put them on the floor, thinking, "I should wash these soon." But never did. He walked quickly. Looking at his shoes. Trying not to make eye contact with anyone on the street. He lived in the downtown area. There were people on the street. Buying things from stores. Clothing and university memorabilia. Restaurants and businesses.

The Dishwasher got to the main road. Walked a couple blocks. A large truck pulled up at the light and the passenger yelled, "Hey, fag, you thirsty?" and dumped his drink out the window. Catching the Dishwasher's leg with pop. The truck peeled out. The Dishwasher ignored it. Shook his leg off. Crossed the street. Took a right. A couple blocks later, he came to the place that sold the Dave's. It was a pawnshop. It was closed. The Dishwasher looked at the red sign that had the hours. Closed on Saturdays. It was open Sunday at noon, but this didn't help him at all. He turned around. Crossed the street before the crosswalk. When there was a lull in the traffic. He made sure the guys with the truck weren't coming back to run him over. He ran across the street. Went back to the street with all the businesses. Walked to where the street met the overpass. Went under it. Came around the other side. Walked back towards the main road and went to the mini-mart there. Walked inside. Stood in line for a second. Behind a guy buying a hot dog and some chewing tobacco. Stood at the counter and said, "Lights if you got them, hard pack please."

The guy behind the counter said, "We only got softies, sorry."

The Dishwasher said, "Such is life."

The guy sold him the cigarettes. The Dishwasher put them

in his pocket. He walked outside and just kind of stood there. Things were not going so well. He went back inside the mini-mart and got a cup of coffee. He was pouring dry creamer in the cup when the guy that had thrown pop on him came into the store. He said to the cashier, "Can of Copenhagen. You ever see so many faggots in your life, man?" The cashier just shrugged. "Thanks, man—don't fag the place up."

The Dishwasher put a lid on his coffee. Took it to the counter. The cashier looked at him. His fingernails were painted black. He said, "It's on me, man."

The Dishwasher said, "You serious?"

The cashier said, "Don't worry about it."

The Dishwasher made sure the truck was gone before he went outside. He stood there drinking his coffee. Feeling safe for a second. Then he became worried that another truck would show up, so he walked to the underpass to drink the coffee in peace. Uncertain how he would spend the next few hours before he had to go back to work.

5

The Dishwasher drank his coffee in peace under the overpass. This made some *things* happen that suddenly became very urgent. He made his way back to the apartment. He cursed himself when he realized that he forgot to grab some napkins when he was making his coffee. There was no doubt that the roommates had not bought any toilet paper. The Dishwasher had been meaning to steal some from work. He forgot every time he was done with work. Mostly because he was either too exhausted to be bothered, or he had something else on his mind. He tried to remember if he'd seen any napkins on top of the toilet when he was in the bathroom earlier. He couldn't remember. Even then, there was no guarantee that the roommates hadn't already used them up, if there were any to begin with.

He was kind of panicking. Thinking if there was somewhere he could stop on the way to either buy toilet paper or find some napkins. He thought about the Buckhorn, but that would mean buying a beer. Plus, it was early enough that he wasn't even sure it would be open. He had never gone into the bar during the day. He assumed it was open during the day, he just wasn't sure. He hurried home. Crossing his fingers.

When he got to the apartment, the roommates were gone. He rushed into the bathroom. Nothing. He went around the apartment looking for anything remotely akin to toilet paper. He found nothing. He decided to wing it. He went into the bathroom and quickly used the toilet. Then he sat there thinking about what to do. There was the disgusting shirt that doubled as a towel that he could use. But then what?

The only real option was to rinse his buns off in the bathtub.

He stayed squatted and maneuvered his buns over the edge of the bath. Turned the water on. The parasol was up; water started shooting out of the showerhead. He got sprayed with water. He nearly fell over. He was able to reach the parasol and push it down before he got soaked. The water was now running out of the faucet. He reached into the water and scooped some onto his buns. He used his fingers to probe clean the important parts. Then he rinsed his hands. Stood up. Grabbed the disgusting shirt that doubled as a towel. Wiped his buns clean. Hung it back on the towel rack. Pulled his jeans up. Buttoned them. Flushed the toilet. Went into the kitchen. Used a little bit of the remaining liquid dish soap to wash his hands. He felt much better. Clean, even.

For the next couple hours, he just lay in bed reading. At one point he fell asleep. Then the roommates came back. The first one came to the door of his room and said, "We got another 30-rack, dog." The Dishwasher said, "Did you get toilet paper?" The first roommate said, "We're out? I thought that was your job?" He turned around and left.

The Dishwasher decided to get ready for work. He found the cleaner of his two button-up work shirts and put it on. It smelled like death. He would have to change it out tonight. He thought about this for a second. He took the shirt off and put his T-shirt back on. Then he put the button-up work shirt over his T-shirt. In his mind, this would help matters. But what those matters were was kind of unclear.

He put his hoodie on. Went into the kitchen. He looked at the mess that he had started to clean up. He had time to finish the job, but he didn't feel like it anymore.

He went into the bathroom. He took his toothbrush out of the toothbrush holder. He put some toothpaste on it. He started brushing his teeth. Then he paused. He realized that his roommates *were* in fact using his toothbrush. Not only that, but they'd gone into his room, rooted around, and found it under his mattress. He was more grossed out than he was upset. He stopped brushing his teeth. Took the toothbrush over to the toilet. Was about to rinse it off in the disgusting toilet water. Then he stopped himself. *Then what?* He thought this would teach his roommates a lesson, but it would also mean that he wouldn't be able to brush his teeth until he got a new toothbrush. The Dishwasher was at a loss about what to do. He had a fantasy about going into the living room and holding his roommates down and shoving the toothbrush up their asses and then brushing shit onto their teeth. Then he calmed down. He decided to just end it. He snapped the toothbrush in half and threw it in the little trash can under the sink that was full to the brim with who the hell knew what. He would figure out what to do about it tomorrow. At worst, he would have to brush his teeth with his finger. It wouldn't be the first time. At least his roommates couldn't brush their teeth either.

He left the bathroom. His roommates were drinking beer and playing video games. His heart was filled with hatred towards them. He made sure he had his keys and wallet and cigarettes and lighter. He started to walk out the door when the second roommate yelled, "Don't forget to bring food home tonight! See if you can get us some of that chicken thing you got a few nights ago!" The Dishwasher ignored him. As the door closed he heard him yell, "Disher! Did you hear me!" He walked down the stairs to the front door. He opened it. As the door was closing he heard the second roommate yelling from the open apartment door, "Disher! You asshole! Did you hear me!"

The Dishwasher looked down the street. At the clock tower. It was 4:30. He was going to be early. He walked slowly. Looking in the business windows as he walked by them. All the things they were selling held no interest for the Dishwasher. It was all cowboy shit. Western things that only tourists bought. Tourists and locals that had a point to prove. A lie that they were cowboys or cowgirls or whatever. Overpriced bright riding shirts, or boots, or tight-fitting jeans. The Dishwasher found it repugnant. It hurt his feelings for some reason. It made him feel like society was not his friend. That the world was out to get him in some way. He wasn't wrong. He wasn't exactly right, either.

By the time he got to the alley door of the Altitude, he was in a very bad mood. He opened the screen door and went to the stacks of clean button-up shirts. Found one his size. Took his hoodie off. Put it on top of the clean button-up shirts. Took the dirty button-up shirt he was wearing off and put it in the hamper for dirty aprons. He took his T-shirt off. Put it on top of his hoodie. Tried to understand why he had put his T-shirt on in the first place. It didn't make sense. The Dishwasher put the clean button-up shirt on. Buttoned it. Took his hoodie and T-shirt to the hooks where they hung their jackets. Hung his T-shirt up. Hung his hoodie up. Put his wallet in his back pocket. His lighter in his front pocket. Took the new pack of cigarettes from the pocket of his hoodie. Thought twice about this. Took them out. Put them in the front pocket that didn't hold the couple remaining cigarettes in his nearly empty pack. He needed to remember to hide his smokes somewhere in the dish room. Otherwise they would get ruined. He found a clean apron. Put it on. Found a hairnet. Put it on. Put a paper hat on. Clocked himself in. It was 4:45. The Dishwasher walked into the prep room.

The Dishwasher's heart stopped.

Norman was standing right there. Cutting potatoes. He stopped cutting and looked up at the Dishwasher. He said, "Well if it isn't Benedished Arnold. Thanks for selling me out last night, fucko. You're lucky we are at work, or I would cram this potato so far up your ass you would be washing dishes on Mars, you faggot."

The Dishwasher kept walking. There was nothing he could say. His skin was crawling. Half of his stomach had seized and the other half had gone liquid. He hadn't felt like this since high school. When one of the school bullies had made fun of him for being in the poor-people line at lunch and everyone standing around just laughed at him. It was all very confusing. The bully also used the poor people's line. In fact, he'd been standing in it at that very moment. The same went for Norman. The Dishwasher did not sell him out. Norman sold himself out. The Dishwasher just accidentally said the wrong thing at the wrong time. There was nothing he could do about it.

The Dishwasher was lost in thought by the time he got to the dish room. He was stunned to see Lisa, the head waitress, training a new dishwasher. The kid looked like he was about twelve years old. He smiled at the Dishwasher. The Dishwasher frowned. Lisa smiled as well. She said:

"Hey Disher, this is Mike, he is the new dishwasher."

"Hey, Mike. That's cool, I can take it from here, Lisa."

"Yeah, about that—I think I will train him in."

"How is that?" The Dishwasher made a face.

"Now, c'mon Disher, you know what I mean. We talked about it last night."

"We did not talk about it last night, you just told me I was not doing my job right, that isn't talking about it."

"Well, I just thought I would show the guy the ropes a little bit before you scared him off is all."

"Well, have at it. By all means."

"What the hell does that mean?" The Dishwasher could tell that Lisa had been preparing for this showdown. Which kind of hurt the Dishwasher's feelings. Why did everyone have to hate him all the time? He tried to calm down about it, but it didn't come out right.

"Well, what I mean is, I know you have good intentions, but there is no way you are going to train this guy in, you just don't have the ability."

"Oh, right. Dishwashing is hard work. Nobody understands it but you. Look, Disher, it's Saturday, this is the busiest night of the week, I don't want to hear it."

"That is exactly what I mean. There is no way you can run the front and also train a dishwasher in. I don't care how good your intentions are."

"Watch me—Mike, look at this. The plates go into this tray like this, you just spray them down and slide it into this thing here and pull the handle down like this and then wait for the things to get clean. Then you take them out over there. See? It's simple." Lisa turned around and smiled at the Dishwasher, very proud of herself.

"And then I just do it again?" Mike was trying to learn the job.

"Exactly. Just do that again and again and the job will get done. There's nothing to it."

"Touché." The Dishwasher said. He looked around for a place to put his new pack of cigarettes so they wouldn't get ruined. He found a space at the top of the pot rack. Next to the largest pot, which never got used aside from holidays. He went to work cleaning the prep sinks. Filling up soaker pots and filling them with ready frying pans. The Hobart stopped running. Lisa opened it. Went to the other side. Pulled the tray out. Pushed a new tray in. Pulled the lever down. The Hobart started. She said:

"See. Nothing to it. Now don't let Disher here give you any gruff about how complicated this is. It is all very simple."

"Well, if that is the case, maybe I should just take the night off."

"Don't be an asshole, Disher. I am just being honest with this kid."

"Oh, you want honesty? Listen Mike, this job sucks, the pay is shit, the hours are garbage, you smell like a manure pile for days on end, the only redeeming quality is that you get free food and all the pop you can drink."

"Disher! I told you."

"I am just being honest."

"You're not helping! Now Mike, look at this. You take the dry dishes and—" Just then a waitress came from the front and said:

"Lisa, you are needed in the bar, there's a problem with the credit card machine."

Lisa looked at the Dishwasher. Her lips were pursed. She couldn't ignore the waitress' demands. She said, "One second." She stopped telling Mike what to do and walked to the door of the dish room. She hissed at the Dishwasher, "Just don't fuck this one up." The Dishwasher smiled. He said, "Sure thing, boss."

Lisa hurried away. The Dishwasher looked at her tiny little buns in her black nylon pants. For later. He was attracted to Lisa in an inappropriate way that would never go anywhere. Like the way that he wore his T-shirt to work. There was no reason for it. It wasn't that he was ambitious. More like, he existed somehow on the fringes of society in a way he couldn't comprehend. That for some reason, he still held out hope for. Like he wouldn't be this way his whole life. Like maybe there was still a chance. What that chance was, was anybody's guess. Still, the Dishwasher had ideas. Those ideas came to him in weird and fantastical ways. That, or he was just a pervert that liked to look at ladies' buns in tight black nylon pants that he would think about later when he was masturbating. Either way, he felt guilty objectifying Lisa. He couldn't help it, though. He turned around to find Mike staring at him. A dumb look on his face. Waiting to be told what to do. The Dishwasher took Lisa's advice and tried to make it seem like the job was worth doing. He said:

"Look, Mike, you're pretty young, yeah?"

"I'm nineteen."

"Okay, good. Look, this job is okay. It is a lot of hard work. If you want to, you can work hard and eventually you will get promoted to the prep room. After that, you can work your way up to the line. After that, who knows? You can get a job pretty much anywhere in Laramie. The Cowboy, Two Lights, Gringos, even the chain restaurants. Does that make sense?"

"I guess so."

"That being said, let me show you the ropes.

"You got your soakers, your scrubbers, the scratchers, the sinkers, the big soakers, the leavers, your scrapers, your glovers, we got *this* guy (who can't be described), we got the fast silverware, the slow silverware, the oddies, the triple ladles, the flip greasers, the three-inchers, the boilers—we don't do giant glasses though, remember that, it is very important, those go out to the girls, 'specially Lisa, she knows the drill the best—you got the dinner ones, the lunch ones and the breakfast ones, you see these salad guys? These are important. They break easy, so be careful. You got the veggie tubs, the salad tongs, all the dressing bottles, the milkies, the strainers, the big skillets, the tiny pineys, the apple trays, you got the half pans, the cookie sheets, all the pokers, you got the bottom lids and the top lids, you got this little guy that you can't lose—it goes here, see the sign? It says, 'Don't Lose.' Put it there. Don't lose it. You got the easy soakers, and the hard soakers, when I get a second I will show you the difference. We got the whisk army, which usually comes in after the eight pans, but that depends on the night, Ronito will usually bring you those, that way you'll know where you are with the night—if Roger brings you those that is not a good sign, you might want to call your wife and tell her you'll be late for dinner, yeah ha! You got the leaners and the unos, the *impossibles*that I usually leave for last but this other guy I used to know, he was crazy, he would try to do them first thing, sometimes you just gotta laugh, yeah ha! I guess that kind of covers it. I'll be here the whole time so there is no need to be scared, don't be afraid to ask for help, it can get pretty intense, you're the fourth new guy this week. I am beginning to think they hired me to just train new guys and send them off to the Altitude Too. Nah, I'm just joking. You don't want to work there. The guy like me over there is a real stick in the mud. I used to know him. Surprised they still keep him around. From the things I hear, yeah ha! You got any questions? Last requests? Just joking, this isn't a firing squad, yeah ha!"

"I think I understand."

"Well, good. Let's get started, then."

By the time the Dishwasher had given his speech to Mike, the dish room was in chaos. The Dishwasher did almost all the work while Mike just kind of stood there drinking pop and looking stupid. The Dishwasher used him mostly to take glasses to the bar and plates to the front line. Plus anything that needed to go to the prep room. The Dishwasher didn't want to have anything to do with Norman. When there was a lull in the rush, the Dishwasher took Mike out back to deal with boxes. He removed his nearly empty pack of cigarettes from his pocket and squeezed one out. Straightening the thing into something smokable. He lit it. It was flat as a pancake. Slightly bendy. He said, "See, you hold the things like this, against your stomach, and just rip the tape back." Mike imitated him. He did a good job of it. The Dishwasher said, "Okay, you do that, I am going to take a little break."

The Dishwasher stood there, watching Mike. Smoking on his pancake. Mike didn't smoke. Or at least he wasn't smoking. It was chilly outside. Already dark. The Dishwasher thought about toilet paper and his roommates. About Norman.

Norman came out. He was sweaty and had a bad look on his face. He lit a smoke and walked a few feet away. The Dishwasher could see he was thinking about something. The Dishwasher wished that Mike would just hurry up and be done. He was about to abandon him when Norman turned around and said:

"Dude, that shit really fucked me up. Why don't you mind your own business, faggot?"

"Hey, man, I didn't do shit. It's not my fault you got caught smoking."

"Oh, yeah? Nobody caught me smoking, loser, I wasn't even smoking, it's just these allergies." The Dishwasher laughed on accident. Norman said:

"What was that?"

The next thing he knew, the Dishwasher was on the ground wrestling with Norman. The concrete and asphalt. Greasy and slippery with rancid fry oil. Norman was yelling, "What the fuck did you say!" The Dishwasher was yelling, "I didn't say nothing!" An elbow went into Norman's guts. He farted. The Dishwasher accidentally laughed. "You think this is funny, you fucking faggot!" Norman somehow managed to punch the Dishwasher in the face. The Dishwasher went limp. Not because he was knocked out, but because there was no point.

Norman stood up. He was crying. His paper hat was still on

his head. It was comically askew, though. He looked pathetic. Somehow he was still holding his cigarette. It was broken in half, still burning. He threw it on the ground. Said, "Let that be a lesson to you!" Then stormed into the building.

The Dishwasher just lay there on the ground. The concrete and asphalt felt cold on his back. He managed to stand up. He put his hand to his nose. No blood. He looked at Mike. Mike looked scared. The Dishwasher frowned. He said, "Don't worry about it. Are you about finished with those boxes?" Mike looked down. Went back to work. The Dishwasher took his package of cigarettes out of his pocket. Squeezed one out. Bent it straight. Lit it. It was as flat as a pancake. He brushed himself off. He was covered in rancid grease. One of his velcros was off of his heel. He bent down and ripped the velcro back. Righted the shoe. Strapped it down again. He looked at Mike, who was done breaking down boxes. He said, "Go back inside and run the short glasses. I'll be in shortly."

"Okay."

"Hey! Don't forget to drain the Hobart first. Then run it empty once."

"Okay."

The Dishwasher stood there smoking. He thought, "That was certainly shitty." That was about it. His face hurt and his arms were scraped up. He finished smoking. Went back inside. He couldn't look at Norman when he went through the prep room. Norman didn't look at him either.

When he got back into the dish room, it was chaos again. Mike had no clue what the Dishwasher was talking about. The Hobart was trying to run without any water. Which made it make a horrible noise like it was dying. The Dishwasher stopped it running. Ran water into the system. Told Mike to get out of the way. Spent the next hour getting everything back in order while Mike just stood there, incapable of helping. When things got right again, he had Mike go get them a couple more pops.

There was a slight lull in the mayhem. The Dishwasher took

this opportunity to empty the prep sinks and wash them out. He was refilling them when Dong Smells came into the dish room carrying three large frying pans. He said:

"You want these?"

"Drop them in, it's ready."

"Holy shit! What happened?" Dong Smells had a look at the Dishwasher's face. It was beginning to bruise.

"Oh, nothing, stupid Norman."

"You okay?"

"I'm fine."

"Dude, I meant to talk to you. Last night after you left—I guess you already know."

"Yeah, I don't know what to say. How did the rest of the night work out? Anybody get clocked?"

"You sure you're okay? That's quite the shiner."

"I'm fine."

"Fuck that guy." Mike showed back up with pops. The Dishwasher told him to deal with the trash. Mike left the dish room to deal with the trash. "Man, you're glad you left. Toby showed up looking for you."

"Fucking hell."

"She said she might come here tonight."

"Fucking hell."

"Just a heads up."

"Thanks."

Somebody yelled from the kitchen, "Yo, Dongs—today!" Dong Smells said, "Gotta go!"

This put the Dishwasher in a very foul mood. First the roommates, then Norman, now Toby. When would it end? Luckily the night went haywire and he didn't have to think about anything for a couple of hours. Just dishes and how to soak the dishes and how to scrape the dishes and how to wash the dishes and how to deal with trash and boxes and people yelling at him for more plates and more pots and more utensils. Mike was working out just fine. He actually seemed to be committed to the job. Whether that would last or not was anybody's guess. He seemed willing to take the abuse. The Dishwasher wasn't sure if he was a college boy or not. He assumed so. But if he could make it through a Saturday, then he would have no problem with the rest of the week. The Altitude was slow on Sunday and closed Monday. Maybe on Tuesday he would show back up again. Ready to demean himself for peanuts. Because the kid was new, the Dishwasher sent him home at eleven. When the kitchen closed. He could teach him how to close some other time. For now, he would just get in the way.

The Dishwasher felt bad for the kid when he let him go. The look on his face. He didn't know if he was coming or going. He was covered head to toe in debris. His nose was running, and the Dishwasher could tell he was hungry. The Dishwasher went onto the front line and asked Dong Smells if he minded making a couple cheeseburgers with fries. If it wasn't too late. Dong Smells said, "Of course, shit! I forgot to ask." Ronito said the same thing. It was just such a super-busy night. The Dishwasher said, "No worries, guys." A few minutes later, Dong Smells brought two to-go containers to the dish room. He put them on the drying rack. Said, "Here ya go." Then went back to cleaning the front line. Mike took his container of food and walked out the back. The Dishwasher yelled, "Don't forget to clock out!" Mike yelled back, "Okay!"

The Dishwasher spent the next hour finishing. At one point Norman came in to drop off his last dishes. He said:

"Look, man. No hard feelings. I didn't mean it." The Dishwasher wasn't mad. He understood. He might have even reacted the same way if the tables were turned.

"Hey, we are all in this together." This pissed Norman off for some reason.

"You know what, man, fuck you."

"What?"

"I don't know why you think you are some hot shit around

here, fag. All you do is wash dishes." Ronito showed up with a steaming grill cleaner and scrubber. He interrupted the exchange:

"C'mon, dudes, relax. None of this is important, where do you want these, Disher?"

"Just there is fine. Fuck Norman, man."

"Fuck me? Fuck you!" Norman stormed off.

"I really don't know what I did, man." The Dishwasher said.

"He's just pissed because he had to apologize is all, let him burn some steam off."

"But I didn't do shit, this is bullshit!"

"I don't know what to say, avoid him for a while, I am sure he will calm down."

"Hot stuff coming through!" Dong Smells came in with two hot skillets smoking. The Dishwasher and Ronito moved to the side. Dong Smells dropped the skillets in the soaking sink. That was the end of it. Ronito went back to cleaning up. The Dishwasher brooded while finishing his work. He lived in a world of babies. There was nothing to be done about it. When the line cooks brought their slip mats into the dish room, the Dishwasher asked Dong Smells what he was up to later. Dong Smells said:

"I was going to drink my shift drink and then shoot some stick. The Slippery Wrist said he might drop by. Haul ass."

"Yeah, okay."

"Dude, that shiner."

"Fuck that guy."

The Dishwasher finished all his jobs. He was about to shut the lights off when Lisa came into the dish room. She was wearing her jacket. About to leave. She said:

"Damn! What happened?"

"Nothing."

"Tell me what happened."

"I won't."

"You have to tell me."

"I slipped on a banana."

"Like hell you did, it was Norman, wasn't it?"

"Don't do this to me."

"Fucking Norman, I told Laura to can his ass—he is the son of the college president, you know."

"I know all about it."

"How did Mike do?"

"He did just fine. I think he might stick around."

"Oh! Good. Look, Disher."

"I don't want to hear it."

"Look, though, we like you here."

"Money says big words, Lisa."

"That's not up to me, you know that."

"Yeah, I know lots of things."

"Well, don't hold that shit against me."

"I'll try not to."

"Well, thanks."

"You got it."

"Okay, see you on Tuesday."

"See you *next* Tuesday."

"Don't be an ass."

"Later days, Lisa."

Lisa walked out the back. The Dishwasher couldn't help it; he checked out her ass in the tight nylon black pants. For later. She really did a number on him. Mostly because she was sincere. He doubted that she couldn't actually get him a raise. But to what degree she had any control over the matter was unknown. He knew that she had a family and took this job seriously. Maybe she didn't want to compromise it for something so menial. However, the idea of the Dishwasher making as much as everyone else didn't seem so menial, not to the Dishwasher at least. But he knew people were lazy and scared of employers. The Dishwasher was just the same. Afraid that at any moment his job would just go away and he would be broke and homeless. He had no savings. He could barely afford rent. His roommates were bailing on him. Norman was an asshole. And now, supposedly Toby was coming around later to give him the grief. In the grand scheme of things, everything was a mess. The Dishwasher had no real idea of who to blame for it. So instead of blaming anybody, he just blamed himself. He deserved this. This was his lot in life.

He sprayed the skidders down. Ran them through the Hobart. Put them back where they came from. Ran the Hobart a few times. To clean it out. Pulled the drain. Made sure the doors were open. Shut the lights off. Went to the back. By the alley door. Took his paper hat off. His hairnet. Put them in the trash. Put his apron in the hamper. Clocked out. Took his buttoned-up white shirt off. Put his T-shirt on. Put his buttoned-up white shirt back on. His hoodie. Took his wallet from his back pocket and put it into his front pocket. Walked back to the dish room. Got his new pack of cigarettes. Put them in his hoodie pocket. Walked out into the dining room and ordered a pint of beer. He didn't have to pay. It was his shift drink. He said thanks and walked up the two steps to the side room where the pool table was. Dong Smells and The Slippery Wrist were in the middle of a game. Dong Smells looked up from the shot he was about to take and said:

"Yo Disher! Glad you could make it." He banked the ball and sunk it into a side pocket. The Slippery Wrist shook his head.

6

————————

The Dishwasher and Dong Smells and The Slippery Wrist played pool for a couple beers. He told them about how lousy his roommates were being and what happened with Norman. It was after midnight and the beers seemed expensive. Dong Smells was feeling generous and said that he could put some beers on his tab. Which was an indication that Dong Smells was getting drunk. The Dishwasher was feeling anxious. He assumed Toby would show up at any moment. Which he was not in the mood to deal with.

The last time they were together did not end well. She had gotten so pissed off at him after the fight they'd had, about something very trivial, that she watched him fall asleep and then just stared at him until she got even more angry, at which point she punched him in the face while he was sleeping. He woke up so confused that he knee-jerk punched her back. Which created a whole thing that meant they stayed up until dawn screaming at each other. The neighbors must have been out of town because nobody called the cops and nobody banged on the walls or came to the door. He couldn't remember what the roommates were up to. Probably passed out or still drunk, laughing about it all. Or maybe they were out of town too. If he remembered correctly it was a holiday weekend. But what holiday happens in the summer aside from the Fourth of July?

He couldn't recall the circumstances, just that the relationship ended that day. Or, so he thought. As far as he was concerned, it was over. But the rumor going around town was that she still considered herself his girlfriend, even though he had avoided her on purpose for over a month. A thing that was no easy feat.

And, like in all ill-fated love affairs, she was circling around him like some bipolar buzzard, waiting for him to let his guard down. Then she would swoop down and start the thing all over again. The Dishwasher loved Toby as much as he could. But she was not well. And the relationship had been doomed from the start. However, like in all passionate things, the second they saw each other things would reset and go right back to square one, where they had wonderful alone time together followed by tragic misunderstandings and very hurt feelings. It didn't help that Toby had some brain chemistry issues that exacerbated things. The Dishwasher really wished he could help, but was unable to. She needed to want the help herself. She was sadly not someone to help herself.

At one point they went out back to smoke. On the way back in, the Dishwasher grabbed his cheeseburger with fries. From the dish room. He ate all of it while watching Dong Smells and The Slippery Wrist play pool. Dong Smells was getting trounced. He always got trounced. He was no good at pool. Neither was the Dishwasher. But the Dishwasher didn't care. Dong Smells did. For whatever reason. He would get really upset when he lost. Not in a way where he would throw things and scream at people, but you could tell that it hurt his feelings. However, the more beer and shots of whiskey he took, the better he got. The opposite happened with The Slippery Wrist. Which was too bad. In a way. This change in dynamic made Dong Smells feel better, but it made The Slippery Wrist feel worse. It was kind of an emotional shift, when it happened. That was part of it too, though. The Slippery Wrist got his nickname from being good at pool and being good at foosball. More so from the foosball than the pool, but he had the special touch. They also called him The Greasy Limb when the nickname Slippery Wrist became stagnant.

The night was going pretty well up until this point. Tomorrow was Sunday. Which meant the evening would be the slowest night of the week. Then they would have Monday off. Which meant it was a good night to let loose. A hangover tomorrow wouldn't be too bad of a thing. That is, until Toby showed up.

Toby showed up with her friend Lindsay. They were both drunk in a salty and giggly way. Toby was wearing her work outfit. From the Cowboy. Which was a short western skirt. A western button-up blouse. Cowboy boots. The worst possible outfit for the Dishwasher's resistance. The second he saw her, he knew he had lost. There was no way she wasn't coming home with him. He braced his heart for the fallout that would take up a bunch of his time in the coming weeks, if not months. He just couldn't help it. He was powerless. She had a lure to her that he didn't understand. That he couldn't deny. It wasn't lust. In the traditional sense of the word. Not that that meant anything. It wasn't love either. Not that that meant anything either. It was a protective feeling combined with an annoying feeling, combined with a feeling in the loins, combined with a feeling that lacked description. Like he knew that she belonged in the world alongside he himself, which, if *that* was true, there was also this sense that their relationship was nothing if not toxic. He couldn't say no to her. He also couldn't say yes. She was like a sister. In one sense. In another sense, she was a wonderful lover. In a third sense, she was out of her mind and needed help. It was all very confusing to the Dishwasher. Toby was all-encompassing. He wasn't ambitious. Not in the general sense of what being ambitious meant. He had no designs on becoming the head cook at Altitude. He didn't even want to become a prep cook. Even though they had offered him the position many times. He just wanted to wash dishes until he figured some things out. He had some ideas. Where his life might take him. Toby, though—she was a monkey wrench in all of it. She was always somehow poorer than he was. Even though she would regularly bring in 200 dollars a night slinging steaks at the Cowboy. The problem was she hated working. She would rather just hang out and smoke pot. Maybe take a couple classes at the university to get her parents off her back. Her parents were nice people. The

Dishwasher had met them on a few occasions. They thought the Dishwasher was a good influence on her. This didn't take into account the kind of influence Toby was on the Dishwasher. She was adopted. Which gave her a stigma in this very conservative part of the world. She was also bipolar. She was also half Native American. Which, lucky for her that you could hardly tell, considering the amount of racism and disgust the locals felt towards such people. She was also raised Catholic, which, what can you say about that, but all of these things combined to make Toby a very odd bird. And because she was such an odd bird, the Dishwasher had a very big heart for her. Not to mention some other big things for her. One of which was very much on a crash course with her from the second she showed up half-drunk at the Altitude with her friend. She said:

"Hey Disher, what's with the shiner?"

"Oh, you know me, just a cool dude making things right with the world."

"Yeah, I'm sure. You still washing dishes?"

That was all it took. The Dishwasher didn't remember leaving the Altitude. The next thing he knew he was on his bed; the tights Toby was wearing were around her knees. The short skirt was around her waist. The smell of a night of dishwashing combined with the smell of a night of waitressing was intense. The Dishwasher didn't last very long. He fell down to the side. Toby said, "What about me?" The Dishwasher got her off with his fingers. They fell asleep spooning. His rotten jeans sweltering just below his knees. Toby's tights roughly in the same situation. He was holding her very tight. It was very sweet, in the grand scheme of things. Who knew what would happen in the morning. Maybe nothing. Or maybe things would get intense again. But at that moment. Things were going alright.

○

Sometime around dawn, the Dishwasher woke up. He had to

go to the bathroom. He pulled away from Toby and stood up. He kicked his velcros off. Let his jeans fall down. Kicked himself out of them. Went into the kitchen. Took a drink of water from the kitchen sink. With his hand. The roommates weren't up. They may not have even been home. He looked in the fridge. The 30-rack of beer they'd brought home was nearly empty. The box from the last beers was still in the fridge.

The Dishwasher went into the bathroom. Pissed. Flushed the toilet. Went to brush his teeth. He remembered breaking the toothbrush in half to teach his roommates a lesson. The top of the toothbrush was in the toothbrush holder. They had removed it from the trash. He couldn't believe it. That's not true, he could totally believe it, he was just a little stunned. He ran the hot water for a while. Until it was steaming. He ran the broken toothbrush under the water until he thought all the germs were gone. He put some toothpaste on the thing. Brushed his teeth with the half toothbrush. Got annoyed with the whole idea. Put it back. Turned off the light. Went back into his bedroom.

Toby was now under the blanket. She was naked. He found this out after taking his socks and shirts off. He snuggled into her. His erect thing nestled in between her butt cheeks. She pushed back. This led to him turning her onto her back and going down. The smells were insane. Both from her body and his body and the blanket and the mattress. But once his mouth and tongue were enmeshed in pubic hair and slippery things, he didn't mind so much. When she was finished he pulled her knees up to his shoulders and enjoyed the time they spent together. The sun was coming up. She looked him in the eyes and smiled. He smiled back. He thought, "Maybe this could work." The same way, a million times before, he had thought this same thought. But it never worked. In the back of his mind, he knew this. But at this very second it did work. And it felt good. And everything was alright with the world. And that was all anybody could hope for. Plus, there would be time now to sleep. Work was a long way off. He could deal with his roommates and Norman tomorrow.

Things happened.

Then Toby and the Dishwasher slept like dead people.

———

Sometime after noon, they woke up. Hungover. Toby was putting her clothes back on. The Dishwasher said:

"'You doing today?"

"Oh, I don't know, stuff I guess."

"You work tonight?"

"Nah, the Cowboy is closed on Sundays, remember?"

"Oh, right. Good for you, I guess."

"Yeah, I am thinking I'll quit soon."

"Yeah, but you make good money though."

"Don't you owe me twenty dollars?"

"I don't remember that."

"You do, that night at the Buckhorn, you said you'd pay me back."

"What night was that? I don't remember that at all."

"Of course you don't, you were drunk as shit."

"I don't know what to say, then. You got a receipt?"

"Fuck you. Give me your wallet."

"It's in my jeans, good luck." Toby took the Dishwasher's wallet out of his jeans.

"What the fuck is this?" She held up a condom.

"What's it look like?"

"Why do you have it?"

"I don't know, I think it was something funny I got from the Buckhorn bathroom or something."

"Like hell, who the hell have you been fucking?"

"Toby! Look at it! It's fucking purple, man!"

"Bullshit! Who you been fucking?"

"Seriously. Open it up. You'll see. That shit wouldn't fit a dog's dick." Toby opened the purple rubber. The Dishwasher stood on his knees and put his erection out for Toby to try it out. After a couple failed tries, she gave up. The Dishwasher said:

"While you are at it..."

———

○

Things were okay again for a few moments. The Dishwasher put his ruined jeans on. They smelled like mildew and rotten food. He buttoned the jeans. Went into the kitchen. Toby followed him. She said:

"Make me some coffee."

"There is no coffee."

"How about an omelet then?"

"All I got is some beer and water. You want a beer?"

"*Reeb*, no thanks. What's up with your roommates, they paying rent?"

"I mean, I don't know how to answer..."

"Hey fuckers! Wake up! Why you fucking with this guy?" Toby went into the roommates' room. Berating them. The Dishwasher was glad about this, but also slightly embarrassed. She came back. "They said they got it. That one guy, he has a big one, I just saw it. Why don't you kick those freeloaders out?"

"It's complicated, Toby."

"Fuck that! If I were you, I would kick them out yesterday. Why don't you have any coffee? Hold on, I got to pee." Toby went into the bathroom. She yelled from behind the door, "You're out of toilet paper!"

She came out of the bathroom. Dressed in her cowboy outfit. The Dishwasher couldn't help it. He grabbed her and kissed her. He was alert as could possibly be. Grabbing her ass. The fabric of her skirt riding up. She stopped him. "Not now, I gotta go." She yelled over her shoulder, "Make those fuckers pay the fucking rent! I'll be back tonight. Leave the door open."

Toby left. The Dishwasher stood there with an erection. The first roommate yelled, "Your girlfriend sucks!" The Dishwasher went into his room. Shut the door and masturbated. Thinking about Toby's giant tits swinging and whacking his face as she rode him. Trying to bite her nipples as they came by. Afterward, all he could think about was what a mistake he had made. This would spell trouble. He was in it now.

He didn't know if he should get up or just go back to sleep. He decided to try and take a nap. There was no rush on anything. Plus, Toby was right. The roommates had to go. But then what? He thought about having Toby move in, but that would be a nightmare. She was so terribly lazy. And she spent her money on the stupidest things. How she managed to keep the apartment she was living in was confusing. The only reason the Dishwasher could think of was that either her parents paid her rent, or her rent was so small that she could afford it without working. Either way, having Toby move in would just mean an extra headache without much benefit. Although, it might be nice to have her around.

Suddenly the Dishwasher was very confused. He couldn't take the nap he wanted to take. He decided to get up and go get a cup of coffee. Luckily the condom that led to the blow job meant that he still had some money in his wallet. He had to double-check. Maybe Toby had both found the condom and taken the money remaining. She had not. There were still twelve dollars inside of it. He put the wallet back in his front pocket. Put on the T-shirt he was wearing yesterday. Found some cleanish socks. Put them on. His velcros. He put his hoodie on. Left the apartment. The first roommate yelled, "We need toilet paper!" as the door closed.

The Dishwasher got onto the street. His hangover kicked in. He was suddenly attacked with anxiety. Intense anxiety. Agoraphobic anxiety. He had to hold on to the side of the building. His arms and hands started to tingle. He wanted to run away. The light was too intense. He needed water. His blood felt thick. The sounds around him seemed vague and distant. His mouth was dry. He thought he might pass out. He decided to just walk and walk until his blood got flowing again. There was no up or down. Just sideways. He chewed on his tongue. Looking for danger. There was no danger, just isolation. He tried to think straight but instead he just heard voices. The voices were nothing but ghosts. He thought about going back into the apartment and closing his eyes. That would be the easy thing to do. He could easily ignore the fear. He chose to embrace the fear and walk. Fast as he could, he walked to the train tracks. He took a left. Walked over to the viaduct. Up the stairs. He ran up the stairs. Hoping his heart would kick in. It didn't. He was surrounded by cotton. An acute silence. A nothingness. A train passed under him. He stood there for a second. Thinking he might jump off of the foot bridge. When he didn't, he felt a little better. He walked on. Faster and faster. There was no end in sight. He would just walk until he couldn't think anymore. It was the only way. To get so thirsty that he would have to run back home and drink a gallon of water. To clean out his veins. For some dumb reason, he lit a smoke. Which amplified his anxiety to a fever pitch. He dropped the cigarette as soon as he'd lit it and taken the first drag. He almost lay down. Hoping the earth would hug him. Instead he just walked and walked. Depressed by the sights he was seeing. The other side of the tracks. Where the even-poorer people lived. He was poor, and destitute even, but he didn't live on the other side of the tracks. Where people were desperately poor. Who were not part of the university's umbrella of poor-for-now-but-soon-to-be-middle-class thing that allowed the voting public to ignore how awful life was for a huge part of society. He walked and walked and walked until his hangover finally wore off. By that time he had come to a gas station that was kind of in the middle of nowhere. He looked around. Slightly confused because he had been so very focused on his anxiety. He crossed the street and went inside.

7

The Dishwasher was thirsty. He was also sleepy now. His body was worn down from processing the panic. He thought a coffee would fix things. He poured coffee into a medium-sized paper cup. Dumped some nondairy powdered creamer in. Some sugar. Stirred it with a skinny red straw. Licked the straw. Threw it into the trash can next to the coffee station. Put a lid on the cup. Looked around a little. Grabbed about two inches of paper napkins from the napkin dispenser and put them in his hoodie pocket. He would have gone back for a second grab, but he heard a noise behind him.

He walked up to the counter to pay. Manuel was behind the counter. The Dishwasher knew Manuel from the bar. Not the Buckhorn. The Dishwasher had never seen Manuel at the Buckhorn. There was a different bar a couple blocks over that sometimes was a dance hall. On the second floor. Above a real estate business. Across from the bank. His name was Manuel, but everyone called him Manny. Or at least that was what he told the Dishwasher. The Dishwasher had no reason not to believe him. But, the few times they had met, the Dishwasher never met a single person that Manuel knew. Or at least he never introduced the Dishwasher to any of his friends. If he even had friends. He didn't seem like he had any friends. In fact, he kind of seemed desperate for friends. And it came out in a really weird way. Which intrigued the Dishwasher, in a curious way. It also repulsed the Dishwasher in a more practical way. The Dishwasher would never be friends with Manuel. Not because Manuel was a bad guy. He just had some ideas that were not very easy to ignore. As much sympathy as the Dishwasher had for Manuel, he just couldn't get past his ideas.

Manuel's ideas were not really ideas in the real sense of what ideas were. They were more like suggestions combined with actions. The first couple times they had hung out at the Balcony, which was the bar that was sometimes a dance hall above the real estate office across the street from the bank. The first couple times that they hung out. Well, the first couple times that Manuel and the Dishwasher had *sat near each other* at the Balcony, drinking beer and listening to the DJ, Manuel was a nice enough guy. He told the Dishwasher all about the gas station and working there and how he lived across the tracks and what life was like there and what sort of stuff happened. The Dishwasher found him fascinating in some sense. Mostly because he didn't speak very good English and because it seemed so strange that he would come over to this bar in particular to hang out. Alone, it seemed. That he would just strike up conversations with complete strangers like the Dishwasher. And that he would share so many details about his personal life with a complete stranger.

Because of this, the Dishwasher was very glad to see Manuel the third time he saw him at the Balcony. He bought him a beer and sat down next to him on a very disgusting couch that was on the dance floor. This night in particular, there was no DJ so nobody was dancing. There was music playing, but it wasn't dance music. There was a little table in front of the couch. You could smoke in the bar. The Dishwasher lit a smoke and offered one to Manuel. Who declined. They got to talking, like normal. Then Manuel started to go into this weird story about digging around in the dumpster outside the gas station. He said he had found over one hundred porno tapes. He said he could find more if the Dishwasher was interested. He could get him all the porno tapes he wanted. He said he also found a lot of magazines that had nude pictures in them. This was all strange, but the Dishwasher was happy about where he thought it was going. He thought Manuel was just going to tell him about all the fucked up things he saw. Instead Manuel started to get really worked up. He kept saying, "I like to get really horny. Do you like to get horny? You wanna come over and get horny with me?" Then because he was so fond of sharing details about his life he did a play-by-play about how he got horny. He said, "I like to pull it out, ya know? Like to pull it out? Do I make sense to you? To pull it out? And then I just sit there getting really horny. I like to get horny. Do you want to come over and get horny with me?"

The Dishwasher was at a loss for words. He did not want to get horny with Manuel. The idea of going to Manuel's apartment and sitting on his couch with him while watching gas-station-dumpster porn and playing with his erection did not seem appealing at all. And the thing that the Dishwasher couldn't understand was, what was the point? He didn't get the impression that Manuel wanted anything more than to just sit there on the couch and play with his own dick while the Dishwasher himself sat on the couch and played with his own dick. It was very confusing. So confusing in fact that when Manuel stood up to get a pen and paper from the bar to write down his address the Dishwasher just sat there waiting for him to get back. Even though he had no plans to continue this conversation, or go over to Manuel's apartment at any time to get horny with him.

When Manuel came back, he handed the Dishwasher the piece of paper with his address on it. In an act of good faith, the Dishwasher took out his wallet and put the paper inside. Then, by luck or bad luck, whichever way you want to interpret things, Toby showed up. This was before she had punched the Dishwasher in the face while he was sleeping. They were a couple. Well, Toby thought they were a couple. They were still hanging out while the Dishwasher was actively trying to break up the relationship, which Toby refused to accept. He took the opportunity to stand up and get the hell out of the bar. Making a note to not talk to Manuel the next time he saw him.

In the end, though, he was curious about Manuel and his perverted life. He had been meaning to go to the gas station he worked at, ever since that conversation. If only to see what the place was like. To see Manuel in his element. He said:

"Hey, Manuel, how are things?"

"Manny, my friends call me Manny."

"Oh, sorry. Manny. How are things, Manny?"

"Hello, dishwasher guy, you never came over to my housing."

"Yeah, well, I still got your address."

"Come by this week, yeah? I found some new stuff to watch for us."

"Yeah, okay, we'll see."

"You come by. I will make a good rice to eat. Then we can do the videos. All day."

"Yeah, okay."

"You promise me?"

"I don't *not* promise—this is a busy week for dishwashing, man. But I will try."

"Oh, no, I don't think the dishes are too important. This is pretty important."

"I'll try."

"What happened with you and the va-voom girl? The red one." He did a maneuver with his hands in front of his chest that meant big tits.

"Toby? I don't know, I guess we went back to my place, I don't remember."

"Oh, I bet you don't remember. Haha. I remember pretty good."

"I am sure you do. What do I owe you?"

"Don't you worry about it. Just come by this week and bring a few beers. We can watch these new videos. I will make a good rice."

"I will see what I can do."

"You better, you promised."

"I'll see what I can do. I can already feel the dishes stacking up."

"I'll be waiting. You come by any time. If I am not there, I am here."

"Okay, Manny. I'll talk to you later."

The Dishwasher left the gas station. He looked at the dumpster where Manny found all the pornos. He was a little confused as to why people would just ditch pornos at this gas station in particular. Maybe that was something people did? They had a porno they didn't want anymore, so they just went to a gas station across the tracks and ditched it there? He kind of wanted to get inside and see if he could find anything. The Dishwasher was in fact curious about the collection of pornos that Manny had. If it was half of what he claimed it was, the collection would have to be massive. The problem, though, was with what Manny would want to do when they were checking the pornos out. They would eat a good rice. Then drink a couple beers. Then, he guessed, they would sit down on the couch and pull their wieners out and watch pornos? For hours? It sounded like Manny just watched the videos and played with his dick and then nothing else happened. Like, did he never come? Or did he just play with it for hours until some crescendo that happened right before bedtime? He would finish. Stand up. Stretch and yawn. Saying, "Okay, see ya later dishwashing guy, it is time for bed." None of it seemed very plausible.

The Dishwasher walked a few blocks away and just stood there on the corner, watching cars and trucks go by while he drank the coffee. Nobody slowed down to call him a faggot. In fact, there was no menace at all on this side of the train tracks. Just people going about their business. Nobody really paid any attention to him at all. He was starting to think that maybe he should move to the other side of the tracks. The rent was probably cheaper. He could probably get a better apartment that he wouldn't need roommates to afford. The idea was sounding pretty good. Then he thought about it for real. About raising enough money for a deposit. About getting his stuff in order, so he could qualify for a lease. Then he thought about how he didn't have a car. About how the life he was living was kind of easy, with his apartment being so close to work and all. About how if he had his own apartment Toby would want to move in. Not pay rent. Just sit around smoking pot all day. Probably get a cat. And then give him the grief all night every night until he went insane and had to take a bus to Denver or something to get away from her because she refused to let him break up with her.

Suddenly his anxiety was back. He looked around for a trash can, to throw his empty coffee cup away. He didn't find one. He lit a smoke. Kind of stood there for a second. Then he walked back home.

————

The apartment was still a mess. The roommates were gone. He went into their room. The place was a total pigsty. There was food and cigarette butts and empty beer cans everywhere. It smelled like rotten feet and dirty asses. He didn't know why he'd gone in there. Just to see. He supposed. The living room wasn't much better. It was all very depressing.

He went into his own room and checked on his jar of change in his closet. All the quarters were missing. His roommates had stolen them. Probably they'd found the jar when they were looking for the toothbrush. He hated them. He really did. There was nothing to do about it, though. He needed to call the first roommate's brother and tell him what was happening. Which he would have done at that very moment, but he didn't have any quarters. The Dishwasher realized he was being stupid. He dumped some change out on his bed. Found a dollar in dimes. Put the rest of the change back into the jar. Went into the closet. Decided that putting the change jar on the shelf above the shirt pole would hide it better. He shoved it into a corner. He stepped back. To get some perspective. He couldn't see it. Then he pretended to be his idiot roommates and tried to find it by accident. He found it by accident, but it took a little doing. For a second he thought about taking the jar outside and burying it in a chunk of dirt somewhere, but that was ridiculous. They had already taken the quarters, so what was the point? He jangled his pocket to make sure the dimes were still there. Started to walk out the door before his insides stopped him.

He went into the bathroom. Made use of the toilet. Used a single napkin that he took from his hoodie pocket. Flushed. Went over to the sink. Rinsed his hands. Looked in the mirror. He was not looking too good. All the late nights working and the limited sunshine made him pale as a doughball. His face was splotchy. He needed to shave. Even though his hairs were just random thin wires. He smiled. His teeth were alright, though. He looked at the broken toothbrush in the toothbrush holder. He hated his roommates again. He brushed his teeth with the broken toothbrush. Choking back disgusting thoughts. He spit. Rinsed the thing. Put it back. He walked back out of the apartment. Down the stairs. Onto the street.

The Dishwasher walked over to the gas station where he'd bought smokes the day before. He went to the pay phone out front. He checked the coin return to see if there was any change. There was not any change. He took the receiver off the cradle. Listened for a dial tone. Reached into his jeans pocket and brought out three dimes. He plugged them into the coin slot. He heard them register. He dialed the first roommate's brother's number. The phone rang three times. Then he picked up. He said:

"Yel-low?"

"Hey, dude."

"Oh hey, Disher, shit, what's up?"

"I'm sure you heard."

"Yeah, I don't know what to tell ya, I'll call my mom I guess."

"Yeah, okay. I'm fucking—I don't even know, man."

"Yeah, I know. Same thing. Can you cover it this month? I don't know. He said there was still a check coming. Maybe keep an eye out?"

"Nah, man. I am razor thin."

"Can you call the landlord?"

"I don't want to, but I guess I can. I don't think he knows you moved out, though."

"Oh, right. Listen, hang tight. I will call my mom."

"Okay. Thanks. 'You doing tonight? Anything happening?"

"B is having a kegger, I guess. Not sure. Something dress-up, I guess. Fishnets and something. First Week party."

"Shit, it's First Week already?"

"It's September, dude."

"Yeah, sure."

"You going?"

"I might. I don't think I will wear anything, though."

"Okay." The automatic operator came on. She said, "Please deposit ten cents for another minute." The Dishwasher said, "Hey, dude, my time's out, I gotta go."

"Okay, maybe see you later."

"What time you think you would go?"

"Nine, I guess." The automatic operator said, "Please deposit ten cents for another minute."

"Shit. Okay." The line went dead.

The Dishwasher didn't see a reason to call back. He could have paid the extra ten cents but he didn't want to. There was no point. The conversation was moot. Either the first roommate's brother would call their mom or he wouldn't. He could keep an eye out for an envelope from the university, but that wouldn't solve anything. It would if the first roommate paid rent with the check, but the Dishwasher didn't believe he would. He would probably just spend it on beer and weed and video games. That was out of the Dishwasher's control.

He hung up the phone and walked back towards the apartment. He had the next two days to do nothing. Well, he had today and tomorrow to do nothing. He was annoyed by the thought that there was no food in the apartment. That if he bought some his roommates would just eat it. That there was no toilet paper and his toothbrush was now broken in half and was being used by the entire household. He was not happy being stressed out about rent. But there was nothing he could do about that. The first roommate's brother would have to deal with that. There was a pretty good possibility that they would all just be kicked out at any moment. The Dishwasher didn't know what he would do if that happened. He could take his last 200 dollars and move to Denver or something. He did have another paycheck coming this week. This kind of made him feel a little free. If he didn't have to pay rent and he got a full paycheck, he was doing alright, as far as money was concerned. Maybe he could go sleep under the viaduct for a couple weeks. Work the whole time. Then he would have 600 dollars. Probably more. That was plenty of money to move to Denver with. He could just sleep in the park until he found a place to stay. Then he could get a dishwashing job there. The pay would be better. Then Toby wouldn't be coming around all the time, giving him the grief. Refusing to break up. Being a pain in the ass everywhere they went. Punching him in the chops when he was trying to sleep. Telling him that his roommate had a big one because she saw it when she went into their room to give them shit about being shitty roommates. In the end, Toby was the biggest problem in his life. She took up all the time. The energy. She was inertia incarnate. The Dishwasher loved her, but she was just too much. Half the time he couldn't think straight when she was around because it was nothing but fighting and good sex. But when she was gone, he felt like he spent all of his time avoiding her because she was nothing but constant chaos.

The Dishwasher was hungry now. He would have to do something about that. He thought about going into the gas station to get something to eat. But that would be a waste of money. He instead walked over to the Hardee's that he knew was selling 25-cent hamburgers as a special. They always hurt his guts, but at the moment it was worth it. He walked out of the gas station parking lot and onto the main street.

He got about a block down before a large truck showed up. Slowed down. The guy in the passenger seat yelled, "Yo! Faggot!"

and threw a plastic bottle at the Dishwasher. It bounced off the sidewalk in front of him. Chewing-tobacco spit sprayed up into the air. The Dishwasher barely avoided being hit by it. The truck slammed on its brakes. Luckily there was a car behind it. The car honked. The truck pulled into the gas station. Surely it was turning around. The Dishwasher took this opportunity to run across the street and dodge into the Hardee's. He stood by the lobby windows and watched as the truck drove by slowly. The Dishwasher waved at the truck. He could see the guy that threw the bottle of spit at him yelling out the window. He couldn't hear anything, but the guy's face looked like he was yelling *Faggot!* The truck kept driving. They could get him next time. There was always a next time when it came to getting faggots.

The Dishwasher went to the counter. The manager stood there, ready to take his order. The manager said, "I wish you wouldn't antagonize those guys before you came in here. I have a business to run, you know." The Dishwasher didn't take the bait. He ordered four hamburgers to go. The manager said, "You know the hamburger deal is only for college students. Can I see some ID?" The Dishwasher did know this. It was insane that the manager IDed him for hamburgers, but this had been going on for quite some time. The Dishwasher took out an ID he had found on the street by the dorms. The picture looked nothing like him. The manager said, "This looks nothing like you." The Dishwasher said, "Freshman fifteen, I guess." The manager said, "You lost the freshman fifteen?" The Dishwasher said, "C'mon man, I just want some burgers." The manager said, "Yeah, fine. Next time I am calling the cops." The Dishwasher said, "About hamburgers?" The manager said, "No, about you harassing people on the street." The Dishwasher said, "Are you kidding me?" The manager said, "$1.04, with tax." The Dishwasher paid the manager with a dollar he took from his wallet and ten cents he took out of his pocket. The manager gave him six cents back. Turned around and went into the back. When the employee brought him the hamburgers she said in a low voice, "Fuck that dick. There are a couple extra for you in there." The Dishwasher said, "No shit. Thanks! Come work at the Altitude. The pay is better." The employee made a bright face. The Dishwasher said, "Seriously, I will get you a job." The employee thought about it. Went back to doing stuff.

The Dishwasher yelled, "Fuck you very much!" The manager was running back to the counter. The Dishwasher was out the door before anything happened.

On the street, the Dishwasher looked in the paper bag. There were six hamburgers. He was happy about that. He ran across the street. No big trucks caught him. Nobody yelled faggot at him. He got back to the apartment and went into his room and shut the door. He ate two hamburgers, lying down. Saving the remaining four for later. He hid them under his dirty pile of clothes. He wadded up the papers from the two hamburgers and stuffed them into a dirty sock. He didn't want his roommates to smell the smell of hamburgers. They sucked. They were also bullies. He didn't think they would come into his room and forcibly remove the hamburgers from him, but they would, most likely, come into his room and pressure him into sharing the wealth. Which was a very annoying thought, to the Dishwasher.

The Dishwasher read for a little while. Then he fell asleep. Then he woke up. Then he thought about Lisa and her tight black nylon pants and her small breasts. Then he wiped himself up with the dirty sock that had the hamburger wrappers in it. Then he lay there. Thinking about what to do. About going to the party at B's later. About Toby saying she would come over later. About rent. About the roommates. About moving to Denver. About staying in Laramie. About washing dishes. About Norman wrestling him in the alley. About Dong Smells and The Slippery Wrist. About having time off. About fall leading into winter. There was a never-ending string of anxiety that wouldn't go away. But all of it really just hinged on what Toby would do next. She was such an unknown that the Dishwasher couldn't even allow himself to think about it.

He got up and went into the kitchen. He opened the fridge. There were a few beers left in the cardboard box. He took one out. Opened it. He drank it while pacing back and forth. Trying to think. He opened another one when the first one was empty. Then he lit a cigarette. He knew the roommates would be home at some point. They would give him shit about drinking their beer. But fuck them. He would deal with that when it happened. He drank more beer. Pacing back and forth. Then he felt guilty. So he started washing the dishes again. Placing them in the cupboards still wet. Using the last of the dish soap. All the while, drinking beer and smoking cigarettes.

When he was done, the kitchen felt better but the Dishwasher was out of things to do. The beer was now gone and he didn't feel like smoking anymore. He went into his bedroom and took a hamburger out of the bag that was hidden under his dirty clothes. He put it in his hoodie pocket. He hid the bag of hamburgers again. He went into the kitchen. He found scissors. He cut a hole in each of his hoodie's wrists. So his thumbs could go through. The nights were getting cold. Soon he would need to start wearing gloves. For now, though. This would do.

He walked out of the apartment. Turning off the lights first. Night had come. The roommates would be pissed that he drank all their beer. But they could fuck off. He was a little confused by the fact that they weren't around anyway. Maybe they had moved out. He hoped. That would make things easy.

He was a little afraid that Toby would show up at any moment. He went out onto the street. The clock tower rang eight times. That meant that he could make his way to B's, if he walked slowly enough. These parties usually started midafternoon, but they would pick up when it got dark. And nobody would think twice if he showed up early. Everyone would be drunk anyway. But he didn't want to be there alone. Although, B was pretty fun any time you hung out with him, so the Dishwasher just walked normally on the way to the kegger. Eating the hamburger from his hoodie pocket. There was no reason to delay. He would know somebody at the party. He thought about calling Dong Smells, but there was no pay phone on the way. Plus, he would have surely talked to the first roommate's brother. They were close friends. Whether or not The Slippery Wrist would get a heads-up was unknown. He had a girlfriend, so that usually meant he had only one night out a week. And that night was last night.

The Dishwasher stopped thinking about who he should try to get to the party around the second he crossed the main street. He needed to piss. He was looking for a good tree.

8

____

It was quite obvious that he didn't need to worry about showing up to the party early from the moment he turned onto the street where B lived. The party was already spilling out onto the street. Loud and drunk college students were doing obnoxious things that, had this not been a college town during the first week back from summer, they would probably have either been thrown in jail for, or at the least been given tickets and told to go home. If you did the numbers, this was probably one of a hundred or so parties like this happening at this very moment. Even if it was Sunday. Classes wouldn't start for a week. For most students. This entire week was almost essentially devoted to keggers and blowouts.

The parties would continue for the rest of the semester, but for the most part they would be localized and mostly considered calm compared to what was going on now. There were kids puking. Fighting. Destroying things. People making out in full view of the public. With nudity. Kids just drinking in the street. Smoking weed. It was all just very gross, mostly. There was some element of fun involved. Everyone was horny. That made things interesting. The beer was mostly free. If there was a keg. Nobody was depressed about grades yet. Or housing troubles. Or running out of food money. The weather was still nice. The first freeze was a few weeks away. In a way, it was a celebration. An optimism for the future. For some of these kids, it was their first year away from home. For others it was their second year, which gave them a bit of confidence—knowing the ropes. For the much older students, it was the last chance to let loose before they had to finish school and get jobs, or maybe travel or go to grad school. But there was something looming. It seemed important. Mostly. To most of them.

Not so much for the Dishwasher, though. He didn't care. None of it made a bit of difference to him. The only real thing on his horizon was work on Tuesday and maybe getting enough money together to move to Denver to get away from Toby. Who he assumed would hunt him down there; then he would have to move even further away. Somewhere out East. Like New York or something. Chicago wasn't far enough away. In his estimation, she had about a thousand-mile radius to her radar. He was about 100 percent sure she would sniff him out at this party when she went to his apartment and he wasn't there. She had done it before. He thought about this. About last winter, before he was working at the Altitude. Before he moved downtown to take over the apartment that the first roommate's brother was moving out of but still had a lease for that needed to be run out.

The Dishwasher had been living with his younger brother. Over in the WyoTech neighborhood. Renting a little back room. There was his brother, his brother's girlfriend, and two cats. It was nice. The Dishwasher didn't have a car so he had to walk to the campus, where he was working. Not the campus proper, but the fast-food taco place by the campus. It was a twenty-minute walk. Which was pretty awful in the winter. Sometimes if the timing was right he could get a ride, but mostly it was always walking. Walking while wearing his fast-food uniform. Which was very embarrassing. In the winter it didn't matter. Because of coats. But during the fall days he would either have to take a long walk around campus to avoid the students, or just suck it up and walk through. Feeling like a failure. He could have just put his uniform in a backpack or something, but that seemed ridiculous. Eventually he stopped caring. But for quite some time he was embarrassed.

One night, after he had finally ended it with Toby. The week before. It was late December. He had gone out drinking with his brother and Dong Smells and The Slippery Wrist. They were in the Buckhorn drinking beer. Shooting stick. He felt something. A presence. He had been avoiding phone calls and all situations that might involve running into Toby. For the most part, he had been successful. There were a couple close calls. He'd been able to ditch before anything happened. What he meant by *anything* was up for debate. He just didn't want to have a public fight or confrontation where he had to explain to her one more time how they just didn't work and their relationship was doomed. Which always led to crying and screaming and things being thrown.

But that night. At the Buckhorn. There was something in the air. The Dishwasher felt it. He froze. Looked around. He couldn't see her, but he knew she was in the bar. She must have come in the alley door because she wouldn't have gotten through the front door because there was a bouncer and she was not of age. The Dishwasher handed his brother his beer. Said, "Wish me luck." His brother seemed confused. It was very cold outside. Like below zero. He found his coat and walked around to the side, where the band was playing. Mixing in with people he didn't know. They kind of pushed him out of the way because he was invading their space. He didn't care. He held tight. Then a large group of people moved from the back to the front. He could see the top of her redheaded head mixed within the crowd. He made a run for the alley door. Got outside. Ditched to the left to avoid the front windows of the bar. Went around the block. Took as many side streets as he could to get back to Tech. Assuming she would understand that he had bailed when his brother couldn't lie to her. The Dishwasher didn't blame him. He knew how persuasive she was. Nobody was really afraid of her, but she was very intense.

The Dishwasher finally made it home. Got inside. Locked the door. They never locked the door. He didn't even have keys. His brother did, so he wasn't too worried about him not getting in. He was more worried that Toby would just bust in. To do what, he didn't know. He didn't want to find out. He stood in the kitchen drinking a beer. Hoping she'd just given up looking for him. Or hadn't bothered coming to look for him. That she just left the bar and went home to smoke pot or do whatever. He was wrong. There was a sudden knocking on the door. Then a banging. Then a pleading, "Disher! Just let me in! I want to talk." He stood there. Frozen. He wished he had not turned the lights on. But there was nothing he could do about that now. He stood there. Wondering what to do. The banging got worse and worse. Then it stopped. He sighed. Thinking she had left, he snuck into the front room where his bedroom was. It looked down on the street. Her car was still there. Then he heard some noises above him. Then the sound of footsteps on the roof. At that moment he panicked and ran down the stairs. Unlocked the door and ran out of the house. He didn't have his coat.

He went over to the first roommate's brother's house and hung out for a few hours. They played chess and drank beer and smoked cigarettes. After enough time went by, he walked back home. It was a long, cold walk. Toby's car was not in front of the house. He went inside. The door was unlocked. He brushed his teeth and went to bed. Nobody was up.

The next day he heard what had happened. Apparently Toby had caught wind of the Dishwasher. When she couldn't find him, she indeed accosted his brother and Dong Smells and The Slippery Wrist. They tried to play dumb but she wasn't having it. She had run out to her car. Hoping to catch the Dishwasher on his walk home. The windows had frosted over. Instead of scraping the windshield or waiting for the defroster to do it for her, she had rolled down the window and driven down the back streets with her head out the window. At one point, she hit a huge pothole or something and broke the front axle on her car. Somehow she kept driving. Got to the house. Somehow did some gymnastics maneuver to get onto the roof. Got to the other side. Managed to open a locked window and get inside. When the Dishwasher wasn't there, she waited for the Dishwasher's brother to get home. She told him something was wrong with her car. He went outside and had a look-see. Told her that she had broken her front axle and shouldn't drive the car anymore. She had said, "Fuck that." And then drove off into the night.

This is what was going through the Dishwasher's mind as he walked towards the party. She would either be there. Or come looking for him there. She would probably call the first roommate's brother, looking for him. He would have to lie, or hopefully he would not be at home when she called. She would probably call Dong Smells or The Slippery Wrist. His brother. Maybe even the Altitude. She would run out of quarters and come looking for him. Her car was fixed. It had been fixed since right after she broke it. Her parents paid for it. From what the Dishwasher understood, it was pretty expensive.

The Dishwasher didn't know if Toby knew B or that group of friends. They were old friends of the Dishwasher's older brother, who was no longer going to school there. Or living in Laramie. But because the first roommate's brother and the Dishwasher were slightly older, they bridged the friend gap.

It was a good thing that there were so many parties happening. Maybe Toby would just wear herself out looking in the normal places and give up. After that, it was anyone's guess what would happen. The Dishwasher had very much invited her back to his apartment. Maybe she would just be waiting in bed for him. Which on the one hand gave him a little jolt in his loins, on the other hand filled him with inertia. The relationship just wouldn't work. The relationship just gave him anxiety because it wouldn't work. Yet it was impossible for him to get out of it. In his mind he'd thought maybe he would meet somebody else tonight and could use that as an excuse to end things. But how would that go? Not well, he decided. He resigned himself to whatever was coming.

He took his cigarettes out of his pocket. They smelled like mildew. He really needed to wash his pants. They were getting disgusting. If he had any notions about finding a hot babe tonight, they kind of got dashed when he realized that he probably smelled like the slip mats from the Altitude. He became embarrassed by his poverty once again. Which was no way to enter a party. But he had his cigarette, and everyone seemed really drunk when he got to the opening of the chain-link fence that led to the back of the house where the party was taking place.

He looked around to see if he recognized anyone. There were a few. The naked guy was back. He was always back. There wouldn't be a party in the next few months where that guy wouldn't be milling around naked and doing keg stands. He wasn't really a friend, though. You couldn't have a conversation with him because he was always naked and always drunk. B was going around. Getting people riled up. Half-drunk himself. Or so it seemed. He saw the Dishwasher and put his arm around him. He said, "You made it! Welcome! Have a cup!" He handed him a red plastic cup. "The keg is inside!" Then he moved on to the next guy. Saying the exact same thing. There were a few other people the Dishwasher knew. Nobody he wanted to talk to. There were people everywhere. Mostly dudes. Mostly white dudes. Calling each other faggot. Saying, "What's your major?" Followed by, "Oh, an egghead!" Or, "Well I guess you picked the right school, because we like to partaaay!" Or something just as stupid. There was very loud and very lousy modern rock playing. Songs that randomly the whole crowd would start singing the chorus of—"Only Wanna Be with You" or some such nonsense.

The Dishwasher pushed into the house. He stood in line for the keg. When he got to the front, somebody handed him the spout. He filled his cup with foam and moved to the side. He decided to just stand next to the keg and try and get drunk watching things happen. He took over as the pumper of the keg. Making small talk with people as they came and poured beer into their cups. He got the air just right. Or so he thought. To keep people from getting nothing but foam. A few people told him the best technique. He argued with a few of them. A couple girls came around. He tried to flirt but they wanted nothing to do with the Dishwasher. He pumped keg for about three beers before he felt social. Decided to drink one more beer. When that was done, he filled his cup up again to the rim and took it outside. Trying not to spill it. Which was not easy.

The crowd was just a throng at this point. Someone yelled behind him. He turned around. The naked guy was doing a naked keg stand. People were chanting. "ONETWOTHREEFOURFIVESIXSEVENEIGHT." Then, "Eight seconds, everyone!" The crowd cheered. They put the naked guy down. He threw his hands in the air. Everyone cheered again.

The Dishwasher was now drunk. He managed to get a cigarette out, and light it. He stood in the middle of the throng, being jostled. Smoking his cigarette. Drinking his beer. Randomly, people would yell in his ear. He would yell back. Someone would bum a cigarette and then ask for a lighter. He would yell, "You want me to smoke it for you too?" Then the person would look confused. Then the Dishwasher would yell, "Oh, never mind!" This went on for a while. He eventually pushed his way back inside to get more beer. Then the keg went dry. The party started to rebel. Yelling, "FOUR MORE BEERS! FOUR MORE BEERS!" Then a couple guys showed up with another keg and the crowd went wild. Cheering. Someone yelled, "We got liftoff!" The crowd went wild again. The Dishwasher included.

None of his friends ever showed up. He never met a hot number that would save him from Toby. Eventually he was too drunk to drink and he just kind of swayed with the throng. By that time, he had to piss so bad that he couldn't avoid it anymore, so he stumbled to the front of the house. Past the chain-link opening. Found a spot behind a car. Pissed for about an hour. Kind of felt a little wobbly. Then threw up all over the street. Some guy came over and said, "You alright, man?" The Dishwasher held up a thumb. The guy, who seemed very drunk himself, said, "Don't worry man, it gets better." Then he started throwing up too. The Dishwasher could see the puke hitting his pants and his shoes. He tried to move over but it was too late. They both stood there, bent over, puking.

Eventually the Dishwasher was able to get upright again and stumble down the block. He was confused about what direction he needed to go, so he sat down on a stone wall near the corner of the street. Somebody yelled at him, "Hey! You can't sit there, you faggot!" Whether or not it was the owner of the house was unclear. The Dishwasher didn't question it. He stood up and stumbled downhill. Which he assumed was the way home. He tried to walk as best as he could. He was a little sad because the puke was mostly beer but he also could see some of his hamburgers from before. He wished they would have stayed inside. Somebody walking by asked him if he was okay. He said, "I'm not okay, but those hamburgers were good." The person kept walking.

Somehow the Dishwasher managed to get to the main street and cross it without getting hit by a car. He somehow managed to get to the apartment without getting arrested for being poor and drunk downtown. The cops must have been out busting parties. Or maybe because it was Sunday they weren't so worried about downtown. He got into the building. Barely made it up the stairs. Got into the apartment. His roommates were playing video games. He looked at them as he went into the bathroom. They laughed at him. He took another piss. Stood there for a second. Then a second wave of vomit came out. He puked until he couldn't puke anymore. Then he felt better. He flushed the toilet. Went to the sink. Brushed his teeth with the half toothbrush that he had broken in anger and rebellion. He was still pissed about it. He drank some water from the faucet. Walked into the kitchen. The first roommate said:

"Rough night?"

"Oh, fuck off."

"Your girlfriend is here. I don't like her—she is not nice."

"Good for you."

"You owe us for those beers you drank."

"Rent is due."

"Fuck off, dude."

"The feeling is mutual."

The Dishwasher stumbled into his bedroom. Toby was naked on his bed. He took off all of his clothes. Fumbled with his velcros. Kicked them off. Kind of keeled onto the mattress. He lay there next to Toby. She was awake. She didn't say anything. Started playing with his naked genitals. Stuff started to happen. Eventually she got kind of loud. After a while, there was the sound of his bedroom door slamming. He had left it open on accident. This made the Dishwasher laugh. His mouth was somewhere hairy. The roommate must have had to see his naked ass on full display. The laughing just made the noises louder. "Fuck those guys," the Dishwasher thought. "Roommates suck."

In the morning, Toby was gone. The Dishwasher tried to piece the night back together. He could only remember a few things. The naked keg stand. The puking on the street. Kind of the party in general. He remembered the sex with Toby. Mostly because he could smell her on his face. He remembered the hamburgers under his dirty clothes. He reached over and pulled the bag out. He lay there, slowly eating a hamburger. He was very hungover. He wondered where Toby had gone. If she would be back. He was very horny. He had a headache. He wanted some water. Maybe she was getting some food. A pop would be nice.

He lay there eating the hamburger. He was on top of the blanket. Fully erect. He heard a noise in the kitchen. Then the door to his room opened. Toby stood there with a long sandwich and a pop in a paper cup with a straw. She put the things down and said, "What are you eating?" The Dishwasher said, "Hamburger. Want some?" She took her clothes off.

After a while, one of the roommates banged on the wall. Yelled, "C'mon!" That just made things louder.

When they finished, Toby crawled over to grab the sandwich and the pop. The Dishwasher could see her butthole and tickled it with his finger. She yelped. Then threw her hand behind herself. Said, "Stop that!" The Dishwasher said, "You nearly pinched my finger off!"

Toby fell back onto the mattress. She took the sandwich out of the bag and laid it out. She reached over and handed the pop to the Dishwasher. He said, "Dr Pepper, interesting." Toby said, "They were out of Diet Pepsi. I hope you are happy."

The Dishwasher took a drink. He was happy. He was hungover but there was food and sex. He knew that every minute he spent with Toby meant another minute of extraction, but what could he do? He was in it now. They could eat the sandwich. Take a nap. Then have some more sex. Then, who knows what? She had a car. Maybe they could go to the mall or something. Drive up to Vedauwoo and climb around or something. The Dishwasher wasn't opposed to having a girlfriend. He just didn't like the one he had. Or more like he loved the one he had, he just knew it would never work so he was actively trying to get out of the relationship. For now, though. It was kind of nice.

They ate the sandwich in silence. Then she asked him where he was last night. She did not like his answer.

9

"And you knew I was coming over! I waited for hours!" The Dishwasher didn't understand why he hadn't just lied. He could have said anything. Anything other than the truth. Anything. This was a big problem with Toby. She had a way of making you tell the truth when you didn't want to. When you knew it would bring you nothing but grief. Not that she wouldn't have figured out the lie was a lie. She wasn't stupid. Quite the opposite. But a vague half truth would have done. Like, maybe the Dishwasher went to visit his brother and lost track of time. But then, also, she would have called over there. She would know that was a lie.

In the end, the real problem was that she was very canny in an uncanny way. You couldn't lie to her because she knew what was happening at all times. She asked too many questions. Was too curious. Could put together all the details and come up with the only single explanation. The true one. In this way, she was a scientist. An award-winning, bad-girlfriend genius scientist. And she *was* a bad girlfriend. A horrible girlfriend. A girlfriend that took up all the oxygen. Turned everything into a drama. Punched you in the face when you were sleeping. Chased you home from the bar in a car with a frosted windshield. She would show up uninvited and unwelcome. Create a scene. Make everyone miserable. And because the Dishwasher was the opposite his feelings always got hurt. He would feel bad for everyone and sacrifice his own feelings for the good of the group. Which always led to late-night fights that lasted for hours. Early morning fights that lasted for hours. Early afternoon fights that lasted for hours. Fights that felt like a huge brokenhearted breakup. Every single time. Fights that made the Dishwasher feel awful. He would try his hardest not to say mean things, but mean things came out. Then Toby would cry and he would feel bad. But he would try to stick to his talking points. But the tears would keep rolling. Toby would take on the appearance of a wounded bird that needed help. That needed coddling. Needed triage. But then when the Dishwasher would let his guard down she would attack, and the screaming and hitting and throwing things would happen again. The whole operation was exhausting.

"I really don't understand why you think you can treat me this way! I would never treat anyone the way you treat me!" The dirty clothes were flying all over the room. The Dishwasher had to jump into the way of a drinking glass as it flew towards the window. It smacked him right in the forehead. He stood there looking like he might murder her. She ignored the threat. More clothes. Then, "Why the fuck do you have a bag of hamburgers in your dirty clothes?" She threw the bag at him. He caught it.

The Dishwasher was upset now. This was not working. He put his clothes on. His shoes. His hoodie. She said, "Where are you going?" He didn't answer. "Where are you going!" He didn't answer. "Where the fuck do you think you are going?!" He walked out of the bedroom. Out the door to the apartment. Slammed it. Ran down the steps. Then ran as fast as he could to the end of the block. Turned right. Ditched down the alley. Ran two blocks. Ran past the back entrance to the Altitude. Kept running. Got to the next block and hid behind a dumpster. He waited. Peeking around the corner of the dumpster whenever a car would drive by.

It was five minutes before Toby drove by. He ducked back behind the dumpster. Held his breath. "She must be driving by the Altitude's back entrance by now," he thought. He slowly stood up and peeked. She was indeed driving slowly behind the Altitude. After she passed, she sped up. He decided to wait another five minutes, in case she came back around to try and catch him unawares. She didn't come back. He stood there annoyed. "What the fuck do I do now?" he thought. She had him trapped. He couldn't go back home. She would surely catch him there. He couldn't go to anybody's house. She would surely be making the rounds. He needed to go to the bathroom. He was annoyed with Toby, but he was more annoyed that she had yelled at him about the hamburgers hidden in his dirty clothes. He was certain his idiot roommates were in his room at that very moment looking for that bag. They would be gone when he got home. If he could manage to get back home without incident.

It was Monday. The bookstore would be open. They had free coffee and a bathroom. He plotted out his escape route. Ran through it in his mind. Made sure he hadn't overlooked anything. Slowly moved out from behind the dumpster. Took a look around. Listened for any cars coming. When the coast was clear, he made a break for it.

The route was tricky. It involved crossing the street, with all the traffic, twice. Once to get to the university side of town, and then crossing it again when he got past the Hardee's. This would be tricky. Double tricky. He would be avoiding Toby as well as any assholes in big trucks. Plus, the traffic would be pretty bad right now. He would have to wait for a lull in traffic and then keep an eye out while he crossed, and also make sure he had another escape route just in case he caught a glimpse of Toby's car. Then when he got to the next crossing he would have to do the same thing over again. It was all so very stupid. But he had no choice.

Why hadn't he just gone home after work on Saturday? He could have just yanked his chain to Lisa's tiny butt in those black nylon pants. Got to bed at a decent hour. Woke up fresh on Sunday and lived his life. Instead he was playing dodgeball politics with a menace to society. He was done with it. He wanted it to be over. All of it to be finished. Yet he was too much of a coward to really do anything about anything. Not that Toby would take no for an answer suddenly. But still, she would just have to accept it. He would just have to put his foot down.

He thought about that for a second. Remembered the time she banged on his door for four hours straight, when he wouldn't answer it. When she stopped, his heart filled with hope. He thought that surely she must have gone home. Oh, but no. When he finally opened the door, she was just standing there waiting. A whole mouthful of insults and pleading waiting for him.

There was just no way around any of it. She was there for keeps. He only had two choices. Marry the girl or move to a new town. A town very far away with millions of people. Millions of people she didn't know a single one of. His fantasies of moving to Denver were starting to get crushed, when he thought about this. She knew too many people there. She would seek him out and find him. She would seek him out and find him and make his life miserable.

As he snuck his way down a sneaky street that nobody really drove down, he started to fantasize about moving out East. He just needed some money. He thought a thousand dollars would do it. He could get an apartment. A job washing dishes pretty much anywhere. They had to pay better out there. It was more expensive. He could start all over again. Nobody would know him. Nobody would call him Disher. Or Dishrag, as the jerks at the Altitude called him behind his back. Which he'd learned from Dong Smells. I mean, nobody called anyone Skillet, or Fry Basket or something. The Dishwasher got his nickname from washing dishes, though. Even Dong Smells didn't get his nickname from anything like that.

They didn't call him Dong Smells because he had a stinky dong. They didn't call him that because it was ironic either. Like he had a perfumed dong. They called him that because the Dishwasher's brother had a three-point plan to get everyone to call him Dick Stinks. Which was a hilarious and clever joke filled with perspicacity. Dong Smells' name was M Donnell. The Dishwasher's brother started calling him Dong Smells. Because Dong Smells rhymes with Donnell. Which was going to become Dick Smells at some point. And then, when that caught on, he was going to switch it up to Dick Stinks. And the joke was that everyone would think that his dick smelled bad. But because of the nature of nicknames, Donnell just became Dong Smells. And that stuck.

But the poor Dishwasher. His fate couldn't be avoided. The longer he washed dishes, the longer his loins smelled like mildew, the longer his velcros were covered in rotting food, his fingertips bloody from being dry, his face bruised from Norman wrestling him in the fryer oil in the alley. And now, the knot on his forehead from the drinking glass that Toby threw at him. The fact that he was broke and starving all the time. Had no ambition to get out of the dish room. Only really thought about what it meant to wash dishes and how that reflected on society. He would write a book about it one day. Or start a movement. Then everyone would see. They couldn't just push him around all his life. He would let the world know who they were fucking with. And they would soon regret it. As he was having these profound thoughts, he still had to make sure that Toby wasn't creeping up behind him in her car. Ready to pounce.

He got to the Hardee's. Snuck behind the drive-through ordering kiosk. The manager that had given him grief the day before was taking a bag of trash out. He yelled at the Dishwasher, "Hey you! Get out of there!"

The Dishwasher didn't have the luxury to stick around and fight back. He ran across the parking lot. There was a little lull in traffic. He got across the street. Suddenly he was very exposed. He ditched into a tiny alley thing, next to a building that had a business front for rent. He waited for a second. Trying to catch a glimpse at the traffic. There were no cars that looked like Toby's. No large trucks. He made a break for it. He got to the parking lot of the business mall where the bookstore was. He ran to the pizza place and stood under the awning. He looked inside. For some reason, the guy standing behind the counter started yelling something at him. The Dishwasher held up his hands. The international sign for "What?" The guy shook a pizza cutter at him. The Dishwasher flipped him the bird. The guy started coming out. The Dishwasher moved on. He looked down. There was a twenty-dollar bill just lying there. He picked it up. Crammed it into his pocket. Looked around. He was far enough from the road that, unless Toby came into the parking lot, she couldn't see him. He relaxed a bit. The guy came out of the pizza place and yelled, "Hey! What are you doing? Get lost, you bum!"

The Dishwasher was confused. He didn't care, though. He'd just found twenty bucks. He walked the rest of the way to the bookstore fantasizing about what he could spend it on. Forty hamburgers. Twenty Taco Tuesdays. He could buy a 30-rack of beer. Have some money left over to buy a couple packs of smokes. Anything, really. The Toby worries seemed to drift away. He was no longer interested in going into the bookstore to go to the bathroom and drink free coffee. He did it anyway.

○

The bookstore was a chain bookstore. Which made it odd that they weren't open on Sundays. It was even more odd that they would be closed on Sundays because they also rented videos. Which made it even more odd because you would have videos due on Sunday but you couldn't return them on Sunday because they weren't open, so you would have to return them to a drop box outside. Which was odd mostly because it created a bunch of misunderstandings and late fees. Which must have been on purpose. However, that just meant people didn't bother renting videos from this bookstore because their return policy was too confusing and ended up costing people extra money. Which meant that people only rented videos from there out of desperation. Desperation that led to stress. In the end, they just had a very lousy business model. The only thing that was redemptive about the business was that they gave out free coffee, in the hopes that the college kids would come study there and maybe buy a book or two. Plus, they had a bathroom. And a good art book section. The Dishwasher liked to go there sometimes and look at the art books and drink free coffee. Nobody bothered him, and the music they played was almost tolerable. Mostly the place was alright. Actually. They just needed to be open on Sundays. But they weren't. And since it was Monday, all of this was moot.

The Dishwasher headed to the bathroom. He had to walk through the music section. He saw a new album that he wanted to hear. There was a kiosk with headphones he could listen to it on. He made a note of that. He went in the bathroom. Nobody was inside. He sat down. Taking his wallet and his newfound twenty-dollar bill out of his pocket. As he did things, he put the twenty into his wallet. Put it back into his front pocket. In his jeans. The jeans that were wadded up on the floor around his ankles. He wiped. Looked at the toilet paper. Rolled about thirty rolls around his hand and broke it off. Tucked it into his hoodie pocket. Stood up. Flushed. Pulled his jeans up. Made sure his wallet was okay. Buttoned his jeans. Fastened his belt. Washed his hands. Looked in the mirror. He needed a shower and some sun.

He walked out of the bathroom. Started walking to the music kiosk of the new release that he wanted to listen to. Somebody was there already. He recognized the girl as one of the girls that were cute from the party last night. That wanted nothing to do with him as he stood there pumping the keg. He got embarrassed and walked around the other side of the music section and went over to the coffee station. He got a cup. Squirted some coffee into it. Added some nondairy powdered creamer. Some sugar. Stirred it with a skinny red straw. Threw that away. Took a sip. The coffee was weak but warm. He was thirsty. He walked over to an empty table and put the coffee down. He went over to the art section. Grabbed the Tom of Finland book that he had looked at a million times before and took it back to the table. He sat down and flipped through it. Drinking his coffee.

There was something relaxing about this book. Between this book and the Egon Schiele book that was usually his second choice to look at. All the nudity and eroticism. The sincere sexualization that came out of either book. Somehow both objective and subjective. Like masturbation incarnate. So very sexual that it wasn't sexual at all. Not impossible, but also not real. He looked at the pictures until he finished his coffee.

He got up and put the book back. Threw the coffee cup away. The music kiosk was available now. The girl that didn't care for him was long gone. By this time, he didn't care. Not so much about the girl—that kind of made him wonder what he was doing wrong—but listening to the music didn't seem like that much fun anymore. He had no plans to buy the album. Not only that, but he had no way to play it if he bought it. Not only that, but those kiosks didn't let you listen to the full songs anyway. It would just be a teaser. And, if anything, someone he knew would have the album anyway. He could have a listen when it came up. If it ever came up. There was nothing very urgent about any of it.

The Dishwasher walked out of the bookstore the way he came in. Nobody gave him any grief. Nobody thought he was stealing anything. That was another nice thing about the bookstore. They didn't give two shits about who came in. Even if they knew you weren't a college student. All of the employees were either college students themselves or were teenagers that had better things to do. Even the managers fell into these categories. That still didn't explain why they weren't open on Sundays, though.

The Dishwasher stood there looking at the parking lot. He lit a cigarette. He wondered if enough time had gone by that he could go home without running into Toby. There was no way of telling. He would just have to risk it. There was no way that she had gotten bored. One of two things might have happened. She either went back home because nobody she ran into had any information. That, or she needed to smoke some weed. Which was kind of Toby's thing in life. She liked to get high. She was like some stoned gestapo agent. Nothing better to do than get high and look for a guy like the Dishwasher who was breaking some unknown rule she had decided was the most important rule in the world at any given moment. The Dishwasher knew that this would only last for a certain amount of time because Toby would indeed get distracted eventually. And then she would calm down and he could avoid her grasp until the next time. But when her focus was at its highest. When she wouldn't stop until she got what she wanted. Those were the most intense moments.

The Dishwasher somehow sensed those moments had passed. He walked back home with only the large trucks slowing down to throw things at him and call him faggot as his real worries. Plus, he had that twenty dollars burning a hole in his pocket. He walked quickly but not fast. When he got to the gas station, he turned right and got away from the busy road. He was safe now. He got to the apartment. Went into his room. The place was in total disarray. He saw the bag of hamburgers. Walked over to check on them. The bag was empty. Like he thought it would be. He really hated his roommates. They really did suck. It was late afternoon now. He shut his door. Kicked off his velcros. Fell onto his mattress. Found the book he had been reading. Opened it. Read a few pages. Started to drift away. He heard the clock tower chime four times as he was falling asleep. That somehow made his brain constrict. By the time the fourth bell rang, his brain released. Pancake batter on a smoking cast-iron skillet.

It was dark when the Dishwasher woke up. He thought about getting up to get some water. He could hear the roommates playing video games. Drinking. Being loud and stupid. He didn't get up. He didn't feel like dealing with them. He was hungry. Once again, he found himself annoyed with his roommates. For eating his hamburgers. He didn't know what to do about it. He remembered he needed to check the mail. To see if a university check had come for the first roommate. The check the first roommate's brother said was coming. He would do that tomorrow. That is, if he could find the mail key.

The Dishwasher couldn't remember the last time he had checked the mail. This gave him bad feelings. There were probably some overdue bills in there as well. More money, always more money. Always needing it, never having it. No matter how much he worked, or how little he spent, he always needed more. And this idea that starving somehow made you work harder. That was not the case. That was never the case. The more he starved, the less he wanted to try. To work. Because what was the point? It always ended the same way. With the Dishwasher being broke. Needing to work more. To barely get by. He was starting to think that this idea that hunger made you more motivated was just something people with money said in order to pretend that the system worked just fine and that poor people were poor because they were stupid and lazy. To place the blame on them. To justify slave wages for jobs that required minimal skill but needed a human body to do them. Like dishwashing. Or bussing. Or fast-food jobs. Or janitor work. Or really any job that didn't require a college education. And then the people who went to college would think the same thing, because look at them. They had to take out loans to pay for college, so they should be paid more. Which justified paying "unskilled" labor less, because they didn't have loans they needed to pay back. And even though all they did, the college crowd, was just show up to classes and take a few tests and write a few papers, suddenly they had "worked very hard" to get where they were because they had gone to college. Even though that wasn't true. If just showing up meant "hard work," then the world was full of superhuman workers. All of whom deserved to be at the top of their fields. It was all just a bunch of nonsense. That pitted poor people against even poorer people. All as a distraction from the real problem. Which was that the system was fucked and only the very wealthy benefitted. Everyone else just got fucked.

It wasn't the most elegant of thought processes, but the Dishwasher wasn't trying to win any thought awards. He just wanted to figure out how to get himself out of the hole that society dug for him. Without going to college and becoming another actually lazy idiot who didn't know how to work but was really good at blaming other people for problems that were not problems they created for themselves. If being born poor was a choice, that was pretty dumb thinking. And the world did in fact need dishwashers. Busboys. Janitors. Fast-food workers. What the world didn't need more of was entitled idiots whose only skill set was blaming poor people for being poor.

The Dishwasher gave these thoughts a little bit of time before he started to daydream about what his future was going to be once he figured it all out. When he solved science, or designed a dishwashing machine that could do all of his jobs for him. The scraping, the scrubbing, the rinsing. The only thing he couldn't figure out was how to get it to take the trash out and put the dishes away. He didn't like the idea of the thing being a robot. He was more inclined towards some assembly line sort of thing. That the Dishwasher could just feed and everything would come out the other side. Clean as a whistle. With long tubes for the cardboard. Which would end up in the dumpsters in the back. The same with the trash. That would somehow take all the leftover food and make a tasty food log that could feed the poor. His machine got very intricate. Then it became sexual. Then he was thinking about Lisa being really proud of him. So much so that she couldn't help herself and came into the dish room and took off her clothes so he could send them through his machine. To clean them up. And since she was already naked. The Dishwasher thought that she had very black pubes. And then the fantasties were over. He reached over and found a sock. Cleaned himself up. Rolled over on his side and went back to sleep.

The night was long. The moon coming through the window. He would wake up every now and again. Listen to a train go by. Or crickets. Or his roommates yelling some nonsense. Like, "Goddamn, dude! You blew the wrong dude up! Go back for the ammo!" The Dishwasher must have been worn out because he would fall right back to sleep. Eventually he fell asleep hard. He slept through the morning. Through the late morning.

He found himself wide awake around noon. Well rested. He needed to go to the bathroom. He got up. He was naked. Hard as marble. He stood there for a second, waiting for the thing to go down. It didn't.

He went into the kitchen. Listened for his roommates. He heard snoring. He walked to the bathroom. He stood in front of the toilet, waiting. Nothing happened. He sat down on the toilet seat. Waiting. Still nothing happened. He pushed down on it. Hoping to cut the blood flow. Nothing happened. He let it fling back up. Smacking his stomach.

He got worried. Maybe he'd caught something somehow. Something that gave him an eternal boner. This idea was foolish. Kind of. He wondered whether Toby had been seeing other people. It seemed unlikely, but she was such a menace that anything was possible. She had cheated on him before. In ways that seemed bizarre. Not because she had been sleeping with other people when they were in fact going out. But because she was so possessive of the Dishwasher. He thought about this and kind of became angry. The amount of grief she gave him, compared to how awful a girlfriend she was, was astounding. Whether or not he had an STD that would make his erection last forever, he was done with her. He was starting to think that she was maybe abusive. She needed help. And he loved her with all of his heart. But she was not a good girlfriend. The Dishwasher knew she was trouble, but at what point was that *his* fault? He needed to end it for good. And the fact that he was considering moving to the East Coast to get away from her was starting to sink in. This was no way to live. He was surprised she hadn't come back last night. Somehow got into the building and into the apartment. But, then again, she had done that same thing the night before last. She was waiting for him when he showed up drunk. Somebody must have let her in. And it wasn't the roommates, because they really didn't like her. To their credit, for once, he assumed they weren't the people that let her into the apartment. Which means the neighbors must have done it. That, or the door to the building was left open. Which was possible. But still.

All this negative thinking made the Dishwasher's erection deflate. He was finally able to piss. Although it was gross. He had to cram the thing under the toilet seat and the head rubbed against the toilet bowl. But he pushed down on the bottom of the shaft, where the pubic hair was, leaned forward, and made his tubes work. He stood up afterwards. Flushed the toilet.

The boner returned. He walked out of the bathroom holding it. Hoping the warmth from his hand would help. It did not. He went back into his room and thought about the girl at the music kiosk that didn't want anything to do with him. Suddenly he was as soft as a baby goose's haircut. Which would have been fine, except that now he felt frustrated because he didn't understand why that girl found him so repulsive. Which led him down a dark thinking process that ended when he decided to take the twenty dollars he had found and use it to wash his clothes. Buy some dish soap. A new toothbrush. A bar of soap. Even though he hated his roommates with an unresounding passion, he was starting to think that fucking them over was kind of getting in the way of his well-being. He would just have to accept that they would use the soap, and the other soap, whether they contributed to the household needs or not. He couldn't just go around being smelly and without brushed teeth.

The Dishwasher dumped his plastic garbage bag out. What was left of his clean clothes. He had one T-shirt, that he hated. A pair of khakis that he never ever wore except on laundry day. He put both of those things on. Put his velcros on. Without socks. Went around the room gathering clothes. They were everywhere because Toby had thrown them everywhere. He needed to wash his blanket and his pillowcase. And his pillow. And his mattress. But only the pillowcase ended up in the bag.

The bag was very full when he finished. He sighed. It was too much. More than one load. Maybe he could fit it all in the oversized washer? He remembered the T-shirt in the bathroom. The one that was used as a towel. He thought about it for a second. If he washed it, the roommates would know he had done laundry and would come looking for his actual towel. Which was in the garbage bag. And would soon be clean. He decided to let them suffer. He would at least get a couple showers from a fresh towel before they caught on. But for now, if they did in fact shower, they would have to use the T-shirt that smelled like death. And since there would soon be a bar of soap in the shower, they would probably do that. This gave the Dishwasher some good feelings.

He checked his change jar for quarters. Knowing full well that there were no quarters. There was even less silver change now. His roommates had started taking his dimes. They really did suck. He took his wallet and his cigarettes and his lighter out of his jeans. The belt. He transferred the belt to his khakis, the wallet, the lighter and the cigarettes. He put the mildew jeans in the garbage bag. He slung the bag over his shoulder and walked out of his room. He walked out of the apartment, making sure he hadn't forgotten anything. He decided he hadn't. He walked down the stairs. Out onto the street. Took a right. And started walking.

The laundromat was over ten blocks away. He tried to get his cigarettes out while walking, but couldn't. He decided to wait. He would have a couple of hours to smoke. While he waited. He wished he'd put his book in the garbage bag. He hadn't. It was too late now. He walked slowly. The bag was heavy. He was hungry and wanted some coffee. It was a nice day. Early fall. He needed to remember to wash his hoodie. Which he was wearing. He assumed he would forget. He always forgot. Mostly because he would be cold and not think about it. Or, like the last time he washed his clothes, he would think it was too hot out and he wouldn't need it for a couple months. When he thought about this, he realized that it had been over two months since the last time he had washed his clothes. No wonder the girl from the keg and then the music kiosk didn't want anything to do with him. He must have stunk the joint up pretty good everywhere he went. He was pretty sure that if he met someone that he thought was cute but smelled like mildew and rotten food, he probably wouldn't be into it too much. This thought was pretty depressing. But it kind of made him feel better about washing his clothes. Not that that would change anything. He would still be living in a shitty apartment with shitty roommates working at a shitty job, but at least his clothes wouldn't stink. For a day or two. At least.

The walk was slow but nice. The bag was heavy but useful. When he got to the laundromat, he was the only one there. There were a few washers going. A dryer. The place was larger than it needed to be. There weren't many people that used it. Most people that lived around this part of town could afford to have a washer and dryer at home. The only people that used it were oil workers in town for the week, living in hotels, and people that lived across the tracks that lived in rental units without washers and dryers. There was usually a college student or two who would come around before they realized they could use their IDs to get into the dorms. But those kids would usually figure it out by October. And then you wouldn't see them again. Or at least that was what the Dishwasher figured. He figured this mostly because this was what it was like the two times he had come here to do his laundry over the last six months he had been living downtown. He was aware that his control group was meaningless, but he thought this nonetheless.

He found an extra-large washer and opened it. He crammed all of his very stinky and very dirty clothes inside. Embarrassed that most of his socks were covered in dried cum. That the smells were very intense. That he should do his laundry more often. He was so very sick of being poor. But what could he do? He was not about to get a second job. Even if he died from hunger. Even if he was homeless. He refused. He would not buy into the narrative that he should just work harder. Pull himself up by his bootstraps. Because, fuck that. He just wouldn't do it.

He crammed all of his things into the extra-large washer. He folded the plastic garbage bag. Went to put it in his hoodie pocket. Remembered he should wash that too. Took it off. Now he was cold. He sighed. He shut the door. He put the plastic garbage bag in his back pocket. It was hanging out, like ten inches. He took it back out and put it in his right front pocket. But then he needed to get his wallet. He got frustrated and just crammed it under his T-shirt. Which was some white thing that had the words, "Work Is a Four-Letter Word" on it. With some bear or something shrugging. It was an embarrassment. It didn't fit very well. Too large. Plus, it was cheap and had too-large arm holes and too short of a length. It barely came down to his khakis. Which were pleated and very much showed his genitals in a way that was not very flattering.

He adjusted some things and went to the change machine to turn his twenty-dollar bill into smaller bills. He took a five-dollar bill and turned that into quarters. He took a dollar from that and bought a carton of detergent. He knew this wasn't enough detergent, but he was too cheap to buy another one. He went back to the washing machine. Tore open the box. Poured the detergent into the slot marked #1. For detergent. He had a change of heart. He went back to the change machine and got another dollar in quarters. Bought another carton of detergent. Went back to the machine. Poured it in. It still seemed like too little. But he just couldn't do it. He couldn't buy another box. He plugged $3.50 into the machine. Made sure all the knobs were turned to a cold wash. Hit the button to start the machine. Watched the water flow in. There were bubbles from the detergent. This was good. It meant that at least some of his clothes would actually get clean. He waited a few more moments. The machine started agitating. And that was all he could do.

He looked around. Hoping somebody had left a newspaper or something. He didn't find anything to read. He went back to the machine. The digital display said 25. Which was meaningless. Twenty-five what? It didn't mean minutes. It meant twenty-five units of washing machine. He knew this because there was no direct correlation between time and the 25 that the display said. He had timed it before. It was closer to thirty-four minutes. Depending. And the last time he had gone there he had used a regular-sized machine, so the number now was even more meaningless.

He decided to go outside and have a cigarette. Maybe see if anyone cool was cruising the strip. Which was a dumb joke. That only the Dishwasher knew about. There was that one time he saw a guy cruise by in a ragtop Camaro. On the way to the interstate. Whose weird hairpiece had blown back when a gust of wind came up at the traffic light on the corner.

He smoked fast. There was nothing interesting outside. The Dishwasher went back inside to wait. He checked the numbers. It said 24 now. He was certain he had been outside for at least five minutes. He frowned. He sat down. Next to the door. In a plastic seat that was bolted to the floor. There was a television. The sound was off. The program was a soap opera. He was bored. And cold. He felt exposed. His arms were naked. And the khakis made him cross his legs. He didn't want anyone to see his genitals. Even though he wasn't standing up. He was just very aware of them now. Plus, he had the garbage bag. He kind of placed it on his crotch to make himself less insecure. This just made him feel like he was homeless waiting for his clothes to be cleaned so he could go back to the encampment under the interstate. Not that there was one. The cops would have chased anyone homeless out of town the second they showed up. But this was just how he felt. The Dishwasher.

About ten minutes later, a woman showed up. She looked like she was not from the college part of town. Meaning, she looked like a young mom that had come to the other side of the tracks to do some laundry. She was cute and smiled at the Dishwasher. He got self-conscious and recrossed his legs. Flattening out the garbage bag. He tried to ignore her. She got a wheeled basket and took the clothes out of the dryer that had been running. She pushed it over to in front of where the Dishwasher was sitting. The folding tables.

This was okay for a while. He pretended to watch the soap opera like it was the only thing in the world. But he was not watching the soap opera. He couldn't ignore the woman folding her clothes. He didn't know what to do. The Dishwasher. He tried to ignore her, but he couldn't. She was cute. Folding those clothes. It was mostly shirts and pants. Then she started folding underwear. Holding them up. Folding them at the crotch. She even smelled a pair before she put them down on top of the folded pants. The Dishwasher was trapped. He couldn't stand up. And get away. But he couldn't just sit there watching. He had to lean forward and just stare at the ground. It was all just too much.

Eventually she finished folding her clothes and put them back into the laundry bag she had. The Dishwasher managed to look up at this point. The woman smiled at him. The Dishwasher tried to smile back, but it came out like he was a maniac. The woman cocked her head. Not sure what to do. The Dishwasher fumbled with the plastic garbage bag until she left the laundromat. The

Dishwasher was such a pervert, he didn't know how he lived with himself.

When the woman was gone, the Dishwasher felt relieved. But only kind of. That image of the woman smelling her own panties while folding them was now burned into his mind. He couldn't put it out of his mind. It was like something photographic. He just sat there feeling ashamed. Hoping nobody saw him acting the way he did.

A few moments later, his washing machine buzzed. He walked over to the machine. The plastic garbage bag covering the front of his pants. He looked at his clothes. Yes. They were ready to be transferred to the dryer. He wasn't ready to transfer them yet. Though. He waited a few moments. Opened the door to appear like he was going to remove them. A few more moments went by. He was ready to remove the clothes. And put them into a rolling basket. He looked down. His khakis had a little wet spot from what was happening before.

The Dishwasher sighed. Nobody was in the laundromat, but it didn't matter. He was still very ashamed. He took the rolling basket the woman who had been folding her panties had used, and rolled it under the extra-large washing machine. Clawed all the wet clothes out. Into it. He wheeled it over to a dryer. Put all the clothes inside. Used the fifty cents in his pocket to start the dryer. The Dishwasher made sure it was on the hottest setting. He then went to the change machine and got another dollar in quarters. He plugged all four of them into the dryer. Looked at the time. It was now 1:23 in the afternoon. The dryers were reliable. Time-wise. His clothes would be finished at 2:53 in the afternoon. An hour and thirty minutes later. He figured an hour would be enough, but he didn't want to risk it. Overdried clothes were better than underdried clothes. Plus, he was hoping the dryer would get rid of the mildew smell on his jeans.

The next hour and a half was really boring. Some oil worker came in and transferred his clothes from the washer to the dryer. He seemed drunk. The manager came in and changed the television channel. To the weather. Then frowned at the Dishwasher. Who was doing nothing but minding his own business. The Dishwasher thought about going to the grocery store to get some soap and a toothbrush, but that would take too long. He instead just sat there waiting. He didn't even bother to smoke. He was in no mood for it.

There was something about the oil-field guy that kind of turned him off about just doing things to waste time. He didn't know how to express it, but that seemed like the worst kind of job. To do something so dangerous and terrible for money, but to also wash your clothes on your day off (so it seemed), while also getting drunk at some bar down the street.

The second the dryer buzzer buzzed, the Dishwasher took his hoodie out. Put it on. Felt all of a sudden better. Warm now. And confined. Even though you could still see his genitals through his khakis, and his T-shirt still didn't fit and had such an idiotic declaration. But still, he felt normal again. He crammed all of his clothes into the plastic garbage bag. He would fold them maybe when he got home. Or not. He just wanted to get out of there. He was on the street. A warm bag on his back before he could even really reason with himself.

He got back to the apartment. Opened the door. Looked at the mailboxes. Remembered the university check. The probably-bills. Thought he should find the mail key. Which was maybe on top of the fridge. It was late enough now that he needed to think about getting to work as well. He was hungry, but he thought he could eat at work. He should probably shower, but there was no soap.

He went into the apartment. The roommates were either not there or they weren't awake yet. Which was possible. Considering. He went into his room. Shut the door. Dropped his khakis to the ground. Kicked off his velcros. He wasn't wearing socks. His feet were sweaty. The smell was not good. He fell to the mattress. It took all of three seconds to go through the memory of the woman folding her panties and smelling them. He felt like a pervert. He just couldn't help it, though. That was just something burned into his memory. From now until who knew when.

He didn't have a dirty sock to clean up with. He took the shirt that said, "Work Is a Four-Letter Word" off. He wiped himself down. Threw the shirt to the side of the mattress. Onto the floor. He was naked now. He thought he should get up and get ready for work. But he didn't want to. He just lay there thinking. He wasn't thinking of anything in particular. Just thinking. And then, without warning. He started to cry.

———————

II

The Dishwasher cried for long enough to feel stupid from it. He felt sorry for himself. Mostly he just felt frustrated. How did shit get like this? He could have sworn he had a plan for his life. Some sort of ambition that would make up for his lack of luck in this world. He was going to do something with his life. Like make a name for himself, or get rich. Or maybe become famous. Anything really. He hadn't pictured his life turning out this way. Creaming his jeans over a twenty-dollar bill that he found in the parking lot of some strip mall. Playing hide-and-seek with a menace to society. With someone he both loved deeply and very much resented to the point of almost hatred. Washing dishes at some dumb college-town restaurant for a little more than minimum wage. Fighting idiot roommates over 200 dollars in rent. Who ate all his food. Drank all his beer. Never bought toilet paper or did their dishes. Who used his toothbrush and stole his change from his room. Who ate his hamburgers that he was saving for later that his non-girlfriend/girlfriend threw at him because he went to a party without her. Who also brained him with an empty drinking glass. Who also punched him in the face when he was sleeping. It was all just too stupid to bear.

After the crying was done, he had a feeling of catharsis. The plan for his life came back into focus. He was still on track. He just needed to get through a few more weeks of this stuff and then he could sort himself out. Make the real plan. There had to be a plan. He could feel it, deep down inside. Life had to be more than compromising principles for decent sex, and playing catch-up all the time. There had to be a bigger purpose. The Dishwasher believed in fate. Well, kind of. He believed in himself. Whatever that meant. He would do something great. He just knew it. Be on the cover of all the magazines. The newspapers or something. The talk shows with the interviews. Then it would all make sense. All the suffering. The being dirt-poor. The anger. The wasted life working for somebody else who could give two shits about him. Yeah, things were changing. He could feel it. He was going to do it. What that thing was was up for debate, but he knew that when he saw it he would be ready to do what was necessary to make it happen. He just needed some time and some money. A little breathing room. Then he could focus. Truly focus on what needed to happen to get the future moving.

This little epiphany gave the Dishwasher a boost of confidence. He felt better about going to work now. About the stupid idiot roommates. About Toby. About Norman wrestling him in the alley. About the cute girl from the keg not wanting anything to do with him.

He stood up and rooted around in the plastic garbage bag. Found his jeans. Smelled them. They still smelled like mildew. He put them on. Found a pair of socks that kind of matched. Put one of them on. He got about halfway down before his foot stopped. He reached inside. Pulled out the two hamburger wrappers he had hidden from his roommates. He sighed. Put the other sock on. Found a button-up white work shirt. Put that on. He put his velcro shoes on. Went into the bathroom. Used the half toothbrush to brush his teeth. Put it back in the holder. Why didn't his roommates have their own toothbrushes? He was baffled. They were just so gross. They made him feel sick.

He remembered that he needed to check the mail. If only he could remember where the mail key was. He looked around. On top of the fridge. He dumped his change jar out. Thinking maybe he'd left it in there. Nothing. He didn't bother putting the change back. What was the point? He went into his roommates' room. They were gone. Not sleeping. He kind of looked around. Got grossed out by everything and gave up. He decided to just go and see if he could open the mailbox without the key.

When he got to the mailbox, he noticed that the key slot was clogged. He looked closer. The key had been inserted and then broken off. Those idiots. They probably got drunk and decided to check the mail. Broke it off and didn't tell him. There was nothing he could do about that now. He tried to pull the whole mailbox apparatus down. He couldn't. He was able to peek in a little. There were some letters in there that he could see. Maybe if he could just get some chopsticks in there or something. Fish them out. That was impossible, he decided. He would have to catch the mailman coming in. Explain what happened. Maybe he would let the Dishwasher get the mail. The problem with that, though, was he didn't know when the mailman came around. Nor did he know the mailman. There was a possibility the mailman would tell him to get lost. Or maybe it would be a woman. And she would want to come into the apartment for some fun times. The Dishwasher had a little fantasy, standing there. He had to force himself to focus. There was no way that he could tell the landlord. He wasn't supposed to be living there. Nor were the other two jerks that lived there. He laughed to himself when he realized that Toby could get the guy to give her the mail. But then again, getting her involved would be a nightmare.

The Dishwasher had no choice but to decide to give it a try, if he could catch the guy sometime. He would tell the roommates to keep an eye out. They would probably say something stupid in response that would make the Dishwasher want to punch them. But what else could he do? Rent needed to be paid. Like, now. The Dishwasher couldn't cover the whole rent. Payday was coming up. His check would be about 450 bucks this time around. He had worked close to seventy hours the last two weeks. He was pretty sure he had about 360 dollars in his bank account. Which meant that he could cover all the rent by next week. But he really did not want to do that. He would never see that money again. And the idea of putting up with those two assholes as well as paying their rent for them... The fantasy of having sex with the mailwoman turned into a fantasy about kicking his roommates out. He was a coward, though. The Dishwasher knew it. He would pay their rent and just be really upset about it. They would continue to shit on him. He would do nothing. He was back to dreading going into work. What was the point?

The Dishwasher got frustrated. Yanked on the apparatus. It broke free. He looked around real quick. Feeling like a criminal. He grabbed the mail. Pushed the thing back up. It didn't latch. He tried to make it latch. It didn't. He had bent the piece of metal holding the thing in place. He said, "Whoops." Scurried up the stairs and into the apartment.

There was a thing from the university addressed to the first roommate. Which looked like it was a check. A gas bill and an electrical bill. A letter addressed to the first roommate's brother. From his parents, it looked like. A flyer for a new business down the block. A Place For Hair. The Dishwasher put the letter to the first roommate's brother on top of the fridge, left the university letter on the counter. So the first roommate would see it.

He opened the bills. Frowned. The electricity bill was a final notice before shut off. They owed 112 dollars. Due in seven days, or the electricity would be shut off. This hurt the Dishwasher's stomach. The gas bill was cheaper. Twenty-four dollars. But it was a warning bill. Due immediately. Both these bills confused the Dishwasher. Not because they were in the mailbox but because there weren't other bills too. From previous collections. It had been a couple months since he had even thought about the mail or the bills, but something must have come during that time. Which meant that his stupid roommates had gotten them from the mailbox and then just thrown them away or something. Used them as toilet paper.

The Dishwasher placed them on the counter. So the idiot roommates would see them. See the shut-off notice. Hopefully get the hint. He knew they wouldn't. But he could hope.

He sighed. Now he had to come up with 536 dollars as soon as possible. At the very least, by next Tuesday. The rent could be delayed until then. Mostly because the first roommate's brother would be on the hook for that. Which was good for the Dishwasher. In a way. He would have to pay his portion of rent for sure, but the first roommate's brother would have to come up with the rest. Which meant that he didn't really need to force the idiot roommates to pay it, because the first roommate's brother would get involved. But that didn't mean that they wouldn't all just get kicked out. That the first roommate's brother wouldn't just say, "Fuck it." And not pay rent and not care what happened. Which meant that the Dishwasher giving the first roommate's brother rent could just mean that he pocketed what he gave him and hung them all out to dry. Which seemed tragic to the Dishwasher. If nobody else was paying rent, why should he have to? Why did the first roommate's brother just get to pocket his hard-earned money? The electricity, on the other hand. That would just suck, if it got cut off. At this point, though, what did it matter? The Dishwasher refused to bring food home. Because the idiot roommates would just eat it. The same with beer. And frankly, the idea that those jerks wouldn't have any electricity to play their stupid video games or have cold beer. That kind of sounded pretty good, all of a sudden. All it would mean was there wouldn't be lights on in the apartment after dark. And considering that there wasn't much to do in the apartment anymore. Ever since the idiot roommates took over. It might not be such a bad thing.

The Dishwasher felt like shit after thinking all these things through. He didn't want to live this way, but he was kind of buoyed by the idea of having an extra few hundred dollars to his name, if things went this way. If he worked for another four weeks as much as he had been working, and didn't spend anything, he would have the 1,000 dollars he needed to get the hell out of town. If he worked an extra week, he could pay for the bus ticket and have some money to burn. Suddenly things weren't looking so bad.

He went into his room. Put his hoodie on. Transferred his wallet and his cigarettes and his keys and his lighter into his mildewed jeans. He was all out of emotions. It had been a difficult day. And now he was being rewarded by having to go to work. Which was kind of okay. He was hungry and wanted some coffee. He would be early enough to maybe eat something and drink something. He wondered if the new guy, Mike, would be coming in tonight. Tuesdays were usually pretty slow. But it was First Week, so who knew what kind of chaos there would be when he got there. But Mike seemed alright. Or at least the Dishwasher remembered him as being alright. There were just so many of them coming and going, he forgot to keep track. But the kid did seem unfazed by the whole operation, if the Dishwasher remembered correctly.

The walk to the Altitude was brisk. Fall was coming fast. Soon it would be time for long johns. The sun was already starting to go down. The Dishwasher squeezed a cigarette from his soft pack. Lipped it out of the package. There were enough of them still left that he didn't need to straighten the thing. It was already straight. He lit it. Smoked it. Walked. Was just finishing the thing when he got to the back door of the Altitude. He flicked the cherry off and threw the butt towards the gallon can that was supposed to hold cigarette butts. He missed. Opened the screen door. Took his hoodie off. Hung it from a hook. Clocked in. Found a clean apron. Put it on. Put a hairnet on. A paper hat. Walked through the prep kitchen. Norman was there. He scowled at the Dishwasher. The Dishwasher wanted to punch his stupid ugly face. But instead he kept walking.

The kitchen was slammed. The dish room was full to the brim. The Dishwasher had to look at the clock on the wall to make sure he wasn't hours late. He was early. Twenty minutes early. Ronito and Roger were yelling things. Dong Smells was running the fry station. There was a full roster of tickets. Lisa came through the kitchen to tell Ronito that the 10-top was threatening to leave. Ronito said, "I am working as fast as possible, Lease, I don't know what to tell you." She was sweating. Ronito was sweating. Roger and Dong Smells were sweating. Lisa looked at the Dishwasher and said, "Oh, thank God! Can you buss six and twelve? We're short a waitress and a bus just came from Fort Collins." It wasn't a question.

The Dishwasher went into the dish room and got a plastic bussing tub. He went out into the dining room. The room was pure chaos. People were standing everywhere. There were twenty drinks ready to be served that were just sitting on top of the bar. People were trying to sit down, but there were probably ten dirty tables. It looked like only Lisa and Mary were waitressing. There wasn't a hostess. Randy, the guy behind the bar who liked to lift weights, looked like he might pass out. Suddenly his macho energy wasn't so macho. The Dishwasher bussed as fast as he could. It hurt his feelings as he just shoved dishes into the dish room window without any real sense of order. He was cleaning tables as fast as he could. The dishes just kept piling up. When he got ahead of it all, he ran back into the dish room and started scraping. The Hobart wasn't even ready to go. They must have been slammed for over an hour. The Dishwasher plugged the machine. Ran the water. Threw a cleaning puck inside and ran the thing twice. When it was ready to go, he scraped and sprayed like some sort of whirling dervish. Spitting clean dishes out the other side. Running them to the kitchen. Running back. Scraping and spraying.

He got slightly ahead of the rush and then had to run back out and buss more tables. Randy screamed that he needed glasses. Which meant that the dishwashing machine at the bar was acting up again. The bartenders only panicked about glasses when this happened. The waitresses were usually the ones who were freaked out about glasses. And the waitresses had no qualms about asking the Dishwasher to shut down operations for them. But for Randy to ask him to run glasses, that meant something special was going on.

The Dishwasher drained the Hobart. Ran it twice. Threw a puck in. Ran three trays of glasses. Took them out, steaming, to the bar. Set them on top of the bottle coolers. Randy sucked the glasses up as quickly as he could. So quick that the Dishwasher just stood there waiting. Then he would run back into the dish room. Grab another rack. Run it back to the bar. Watch Randy put the things away. He did this until he had no choice but to switch over to plates again. Then somebody yelled, "Silverware!" Followed by, "Frying pans!" The Dishwasher had to stop bussing. He ran the sinks full blast. Both hot and cold. There wasn't time for soaking. He was able to drop ten minis on an open tray, which he sent through first before the next round of dishes. Which he pushed through without thinking, cursing himself because it clogged the line when he had meant to run silverware instead. A rookie mistake. He wiped his forehead and decided to do something radical. He dropped a flat tray on the soaking sink and emptied the silverware tub directly onto the tray. He took the frying pans out and superseded the silverware. The frying pans were steaming as he brought them to the kitchen. Ronito yelled, "Thanks! More!" The Dishwasher ran back into the dish room. He checked the silverware. Normally he would run them twice. He checked the water. It was still clean. He made a choice. He ran the next round of dishes. Which left the on-deck position empty. It didn't matter. He would have to sacrifice the tray. He took the entire tray of clean silverware to the waitress station and sorted them there instead of doing it in the dish room. Lisa scolded him. "You're clogging the area, man!" The Dishwasher could smell Lisa. She smelled like vagina for some reason. Vagina and sweat and vanilla. This combo of smells was the opposite of sexual. He made a note of it, though. He was kind of annoyed that she yelled at him. What else was he supposed to do? He was the fastest sorter they had. He sorted so quick that Lisa came back and said, "Sorry, Disher. It's just, shit…" Then she was off again. Holding three menus and two sodas. The Dishwasher looked up. There was no end in sight. He ran back to the dish room. Cranked another round of frying pans out. Ran those through. Ran another tray of dishes. Then another. Brought them to the kitchen still steaming. Ran back to the dish room. Started to run more dishes through when Norman showed up with a bunch of prep things. Cold half pans and some condiment bottles. He said, "Yo, Dish, these are ASAP." The Dishwasher looked at the dishes he was putting down. Looked at Norman. He was not sweating. His eyes were red. The Dishwasher nearly wrestled him. But he didn't. He said, "Sure thing, I'll get right on that." The sarcasm wasn't lost on Norman. He was about to start something when Ronito came in with a burning frying pan. He said, "Hot stuff! Coming through!" Norman backed up. He said to Ronito, "Dude, this guy just..." Ronito said, "Norman! Get your ass back in the back!" Norman slinked away. Randy yelled for more glasses. The Dishwasher drained the Hobart. Ran it twice. Threw a puck in. Ran it again. Threw a tray of glasses in. Scrubbed skillets while waiting. Pulled the tray out. Ran another. Took the steaming glasses to the bar. Randy sucked them up. The Dishwasher looked up. Still no break in the crowd. But people seemed happier. There weren't very many dirty tables. Maybe two. The Dishwasher ran back to the dish room. Took the glasses out. Ran another tray. Took the steaming glasses to the bar. Ran back. Did the same thing with the third tray. Then ran some more dishes. Someone yelled, "Silverware!" Then someone yelled, "Pots!" Then someone yelled, "Ice!" It was a waitress. Which made it more urgent. But still, they hadn't run out of ice in the front since maybe six months ago. The Dishwasher ran to the ice room and filled two five-gallon buckets with ice. Brought them to the bar. Randy slid the metal lids open. They were bone dry. Maybe just one scoop left. The Dishwasher was impressed. He ran back and grabbed two more buckets of ice. Then he did it again. This time, they filled the ice containers to the brim. He was trying to calculate how much ice that was. Thirty gallons. What thirty gallons of ice meant. How many drinks that was. But he got sidelined when he got back into the dish room and saw how piled up he was. He started running dishes through without thought. He had to stop at one point to refill the soaking sinks. There was a pile of kitchen things that was too ugly to look at. He was thirsty now and as hungry as he had ever been. When a little lull came, he asked Lisa for a pop. She brought him one. He sucked it down in one drink. Through a straw. She hadn't left yet and she noticed, so she got him another and then smiled. For some reason, he thought that suddenly she was attracted to him. He wasn't used to people being nice to him. The thought faded when his body absorbed the liquid and he took a look around. There was no love, right in front of him. Just dishes. Lots and lots of dishes.

The night went on like this for hours and hours. It was relentless. At eleven, they called it. Said the kitchen was closed. Even though more people were still coming in. They were still serving fried things, if people wanted them. Which meant that Dong Smells was on a delayed schedule. Which pissed Dong Smells off. You could tell by the frown on his face. That the Dishwasher noticed. Ronito and Roger felt bad about this, so they cleaned his station for him. This cheered him up a little. Plus, Randy brought him a beer. Which changed his mood pretty quickly. This did nothing for the Dishwasher, though. He still had a million dishes to do. And he now had to wait for the frying stuff. Not that he would get ahead of it. There was no way. The Dishwasher kept washing. More and more things kept coming in. Things from the bar that would have normally come in hours earlier. Other old things that normally the waitresses dealt with. Things the cooks didn't want to deal with. Even Norman found some old dishes in the back of a fridge that didn't need to be dealt with right now, but why not? Where was the *Dishwasher's* beer? There were three bags of trash that needed taking out. All the cardboard. All the prep room things. At one point, Dong Smells brought the Dishwasher a plate of chicken wings. Said, "You alright?" The Dishwasher was arm-deep in dirty water. He said, "Yeah, I am fine, thanks." The Dishwasher didn't bother wiping his hands off. He took a chicken wing from the plate and sucked it down. It was spicy. He threw the bones into the trash. He hadn't realized how hungry he was. This gave him a jolt of energy. He went back to work. Stopping every now and again to eat a chicken wing. To go out and get more soda. From the bar.

The place was still busy in the front. Eventually they called it on the fried food. Which meant that Dong Smells could finish working. Ronito and Roger were long gone. Norman had left at some point. Both Mary and Lisa had come into the dish room and put money in the Dishwasher's button-up white shirt's pocket. They both thanked him. The Dishwasher was glad about the money, but was not too happy about what it meant. They had each made a thousand dollars for the night. And tipping him forty dollars or whatever didn't mean shit. They tipped Dong Smells out too. Probably even Norman. Who didn't do shit. They didn't need to tip Ronito or Roger out because they made decent money doing what they did. And the Dishwasher was a little confused as to why Mike hadn't shown up. Or why they were short a waitress in the first place. In his mind, the Dishwasher had just worked a triple shift and was compensated with maybe an extra five hours of pay. That came from the labor of the waitresses.

This system didn't work. Not only that, but the restaurant had just had a 10,000-dollar night. Or so it seemed. And the people that worked the hardest to make that happen were the least compensated. That didn't seem right. The Dishwasher didn't blame the waitresses. They didn't need to give him money. That was wrong. And they shouldn't be giving the guy that stayed on to fry some extra cheese sticks money either. If anything, they should be paying the workers a decent wage that was adjusted for the extra work they were doing. Instead, it was nearly midnight and the Dishwasher still had at least an hour's worth of work to do. It would cost the restaurant seven dollars to clean the kitchen while the front of the house was still raking it in. Having 50 percent of every dollar go to profit. The Dishwasher forced himself not to think about this as he methodically finished his job. Eating chicken wings every chance he had.

When he was finally finished with the dishes, he took the trash bags out. They were very heavy and he was afraid they might break. Luckily they didn't. Then he did the cardboard. He pulled his cigarettes out of his pocket before he started breaking down the boxes. He'd never had a chance to take them out before he started working. They were smashed. He was afraid they were ruined from water. They were not ruined from water. Thankfully. He squeezed one out. Lit it. It was bent, but not broken. The filter was flat, though. The fall air was nice. Crisp. He didn't do very much thinking while this was happening. He just wanted to be done. He was exhausted.

He finished breaking down the boxes. Went back to the dish room. Washed the slip mats. Cleaned the dish room. Looked at his empty plate of chicken wings. Dumped the bones. Put the plate in the sink and sprayed it. Decided to make himself a sandwich. Which was complicated, but he managed to do it without making too many new dirty dishes. Normally he could get the cooks to do this for him, but they were gone. Dong Smells was at the bar. He could hear him. Getting drunk. The Dishwasher wrapped the sandwich in foil. Took it to the back door. Put it in his hoodie pocket. Took his apron off. Threw it into the hamper. Took his paper hat off. His hairnet. Threw them in the trash. Clocked out. It was 1:12 in the morning. He put his hoodie on. Made sure the sandwich was there. Walked through the kitchen. Turning lights off. Turned the dish-room light off. Walked out into the dining room. Sat down next to Dong Smells at the bar and ordered a beer from Randy.

12

"Well that certainly sucked. Cheers." The Dishwasher held his beer in the air, looking straight forward. A nod to exhausted workers the world over. Drank half of the pint. Put the glass down. Stared at it. Took another drink. Put the glass down. Stared at it. Picked it up again. Finished it. Randy looked at him. He nodded. Randy poured him another beer. The Dishwasher went to take the tips from his pocket. Randy knocked on the bar. The Dishwasher made a face that was both a look of surprise and a thank you at the same time. It involved some nodding and pursed lips. The first beer was kicking in. He was feeling better. Dong Smells ordered a shot of whiskey. Said, "Want one?" The Dishwasher just shook his head. Whiskey never ended well. That is, unless a million cigarettes, an empty wallet, and a horrible hangover meant ending well.

The place was almost completely empty now. The waitresses were finishing up. Randy was almost finished himself. This gave the Dishwasher sad emotions. He wasn't ready to be done. He wanted to drink enough to forget how miserable the job was. It looked like that wouldn't happen. It was too late to go anywhere else. The roommates maybe had some beers. But that would involve drinking with them. Something he did not want to do.

He couldn't go over to Dong Smells' because his girlfriend really didn't like the Dishwasher for some reason. That reason was never really clear. Aside from the fact that she got jealous that Dong Smells would hang out late in the bars and never invite her over. Even though she rarely came anyway. She had no real love for bars. Or pool. Or drinking, even. The Dishwasher was kind of just waiting for their relationship to implode because of this. Dong Smells' favorite things in the world were the bars and the pool tables. He also liked poker night with The Slippery Wrist. A thing that Dong Smells' girlfriend could not stand. There was nothing to do about it, though. The relationship would just have to run its course. Something the Dishwasher was hoping for, but didn't actively care about. He wasn't that close to Dong Smells. The Dishwasher's brother was. Nothing would really change if Dong Smells and his girlfriend broke up. But still. He hated to see him get so much grief for doing the things he loved to do. For no real reason. The Dishwasher also assumed that Dong Smells' girlfriend blamed the Dishwasher and The Slippery Wrist for Dong Smells' proclivities. Which were in no way their fault. Left alone, he would spend hours alone at the Buckhorn drinking and playing pool with whoever came around. How was that their fault? The Dishwasher tried to explain this to her one time. It didn't go very well. And was probably the reason that she didn't like him the most, of all of his friends. He was just being honest. He said:

"It's not my fault he's drunk." They were at the Buckhorn one night. Dong Smells was wasted. Slurring his words and playing terribly.

"Well, you guys brought him here."

"What are you talking about, it's the Buckhorn. We work like two blocks away. Not only that, but nobody broke his arm about it."

"But somebody must have suggested it."

"Yeah. Dong Smells."

"You could have told him to go home."

"I also could have told him to run a marathon, what's your point?"

"He wasn't drunk when he called me."

"Well, he is drunk now."

"Yeah! Whose fault is that?"

"I don't know. He wasn't drunk until you showed up."

"Fuck you, Disher."

"Hey, man. Don't shoot the messenger."

"Dong! Get your coat! I am taking you home!"

"Not yet, baby, I got two balls!"

"I hope you are happy, Disher."

"What the fu—how did I get blamed for this?"

And it wasn't his fault. Dong Smells liked to drink. Everyone knew it. That was just how it was. Sure, they all kind of liked to drink. And Dong Smells liked to drink more than they did. But still. Nobody was holding a gun to his head. In fact, the Dishwasher made sure not to take shots with Dong Smells on purpose. Aside from not liking it, he also thought that if he didn't encourage the behavior it would help. It didn't. But he thought it might. Even the Dishwasher's brother and The Slippery Wrist were cognizant of limiting the shots they took with Dong Smells for the exact same reason. But for whatever reason the Dishwasher got all of the blame. So be it. He'd decided. He would be blamed either way.

After that conversation, the two never really spoke anymore. And because of it the Dishwasher wasn't allowed to go to Dong Smells' house anymore. Not that he really wanted to. The place was too clean. Too domestic for his liking. He felt like he was doing something naughty whenever he was there. Like their parents might show up and catch them drinking or something. And when Dong Smells' girlfriend did show up at times, it was exactly like that. Everyone would be scolded and sent home. Or at least away. And poor Dong Smells would just have to stay behind and get the guilt trip.

The Dishwasher finished the second beer. Randy said, "One more for the road? I am closing up." The Dishwasher nodded. Randy wouldn't take his money. He fumbled for his wallet to get some ones. Randy put his hand out. Meaning, *don't bother*. The Dishwasher put the two twenties that Lisa and Mary had given him into his wallet. Put the wallet back in his jeans pocket. Took a drink of beer.

The Dishwasher and Dong Smells sat there in silence. There

was nothing to say. The Dishwasher wanted to complain about work, but it would fall on deaf ears. It was nearly two in the morning now. Which was when the bar had to close. There was probably a party somewhere but the Dishwasher didn't know where it would be, or if it would be worth trying to find. He was exhausted. It was late. Tomorrow would be another day. Another slog that would give him the same results as today.

He wondered what Toby was up to. Whether she would be out looking for him or not. She was probably getting stoned in her tiny apartment above the weird house on campus that he didn't know how she had. How she managed to pay her rent. Because it must be expensive. Due to the location. He wondered if he should go over there. She would probably be stoned, and in a good mood for once. Would probably be pretty horny. He got a little excited. Down below. She might even have some beer in her fridge.

But then he really thought about it. It wasn't worth it. It would just add more time to his account. The account made up of their time together. The minutes he put in that would mean minutes he would have to spend getting back out. But dammit. The sex. He thought about his plan to get 1,000 dollars and get the hell out of town. This gave him an idea that he had kind of been hatching for a little while. Even if he hadn't actually used his brains to think about it. He could get a job as a prep cook. That would give him an extra three fifty an hour. That would save him a lot of time. A lot less time than it would take if he was making the dishwasher rate. He mentioned this to Dong Smells. He said:

"You think Laura would take me on as a prep?"

"I don't know, you should ask Lisa. You can't be any worse than Norman. And I think that dude's days are numbered."

"It's eleven, right? Easier than washing dishes."

"You good with a knife?"

"What, like cutting up broccoli?"

"Well, I don't know—it's more complicated than that."

"Like frying chicken wings and cheese sticks?"

"Hey, you don't know what we do—I know it looks easy from the dish room, but I guarantee it is much more difficult than what you do."

"Yeah, I have noticed. Fry this thing for some minutes, add some cheese to that thing. You want fries with that? Or should I make you a salad? That sort of thing?"

"It's not my fault you make seven bucks an hour, dude. Talk to Laura about that."

"Yeah, yeah, yeah. I don't want to hear it."

"Talk to Lisa, that is all I can say."

"Sure."

"You realize that Norman would have to train you, right?"

"Right. Fuck."

"Yeah."

"Yeah."

That was the end of the conversation. The Dishwasher finished his beer. Dong Smells did too. They both stood up. Said thanks to Randy. Who was looking roughed up. It had been a long night. They walked together, out the back door. Dong Smells kept walking. Into the parking lot. To get to his car. The Dishwasher took out his cigarettes and squeezed a smoke out of the soft pack. He lit it. Donger turned around and said:

"Hey, give me some of that."

"You want one?"

"Nah, I just want a, you know..." He made his voice sound squeaky for some reason. He took a couple drags. Handed it back. "See ya tomorrow."

———

The Dishwasher walked down the alley. The air was cold on his crotch. Where his jeans were wet. He would have to put his long johns on, soon enough. Start wearing a jacket. And then a coat. And then a hat. And then gloves. Winter sucked. The wet coldness on his crotch made him rethink not getting a ride from Dong Smells to Toby's. She would surely warm him up. Down below. It wasn't worth it, though.

He felt the weight of the sandwich in his hoodie pocket. He could just go home and rub one out. Eat his sandwich. Go to bed. Maybe his roommates weren't there. Maybe they had left some beer in the fridge. Maybe they took the check from the university and cashed it. Maybe rent would be waiting for him. Plus, they'd bought toilet paper and toothbrushes and food. He kind of laughed to himself when he thought about these things. None of them would be true. There was a possibility that the university check got cashed. But that was about all. There was a small possibility that there would be beer in the fridge. He would have to hang out with them a little bit to drink one. But it wouldn't be worth how angry he would get.

He walked slowly. The clock tower chimed twice. It was now two. A dog barked in the distance. A train came by. The night was empty. Nobody was out. No cars. No people. Just lonely cold air. Streetlamps. Hollow steps ringing on empty buildings. He finished smoking at the same time he got to the front door of his building. He threw the cigarette butt onto the street. Found his key. Opened the door. The mailbox was still open. From when he yanked it earlier. He looked into his apartment's slot. There was no new mail. This didn't mean anything. He felt bad that he had broken the thing. But there was nothing to do about it.

He could hear his roommates playing video games from the bottom of the stairs. This made him sigh. He walked up the stairs. Bracing for nonsense. He was not in the mood, but it was late. He had a few beers in him. He opened the door.

"Dishrag!" The roommates yelled. The Dishwasher sighed.

"Hey guys, what's up?"

"Check the fridge, man." The Dishwasher walked to the living room. The roommates were sitting on the floor. Playing video games. Drinking beer. "Check it!"

"Check what?"

"The fridge!" The Dishwasher turned around. He opened the fridge. The entire thing was filled from the bottom to the top with beer cans. "Damn!" They yelled.

"Damn!" The Dishwasher was actually impressed. That was a lot of beer. "That's a lot of beer!"

"You know it is! Now check the bathroom!" The Dishwasher took a beer out. Went into the bathroom. There were two huge things of toilet paper. The roommates yelled, "Damn!" The Dishwasher was likewise impressed.

"Damn!" That was a lot of toilet paper. It looked like forty-eight rolls.

He opened the beer and took a drink. He turned around and went into the living room. He sat down on the couch. It smelled like butts. He shoved his hand into his pocket for his cigarettes. He pulled the soft pack out. Lit one. Looked for an ashtray. Found an empty beer can. Ashed in it. He watched the video game. It didn't make any sense. Just some guy going around and doing stuff. Shooting things. He was about to say something when the first roommate said:

"Don't even start. Here." He threw money at the Dishwasher. It landed on his lap.

"The bills?"

"Oh, what the fuck do I care?" He threw another hundred dollars in twenties at the Dishwasher. This made the Dishwasher happy. Another huge weight lifted off his shoulders. All of his scheming about not paying rent and heading out of town to get away just kind of slipped away.

He collected the money as quickly as he could. Afraid the first roommate would suddenly become belligerent and take it back. He didn't. He just stared at the television screen. Yelling things. The Dishwasher sat there drinking beer. Smoking cigarettes. Watching. There was no conversation. Just the video game. He got up to get another beer. The roommates both said, "Yes, please." He brought them beer. They drank it. The Dishwasher hung out with them. On the couch that smelled like butts. Drinking beer. Smoking.

Eventually he couldn't stand it anymore and he got up to go to bed. Nobody but himself noticed. He took a piss. Had to navigate the toilet paper. Brushed his teeth with the half toothbrush that he'd broke in half in rebellion that got thrown away and then got dug out of the trash. He sighed about this. Looked in the mirror. He looked very tired. He needed some sun. A few more meals. He felt the weight of the sandwich in his hoodie pocket. Walked out into the kitchen. Was about to say goodnight to his roommates, but decided not to. They would just ask him for more beers. He was exhausted again.

He went into his bedroom. Kicked his shoes off. Undressed. The buttons of his white work shirt annoyed him. He unbuttoned the top and just pulled the shirt over his head. He dropped it on the ground. Unbuckled his jeans. Slid them down his crotch. His penis was stiff with cold. His balls were tight. The smell of mildew came rushing up. He sighed again. He turned around and ended up ass-naked on his mattress. He peeled his socks off. They smelled like the rubber skid mats smelled. They were wet.

He got under the blanket. Warmed up. He was too tired to masturbate. Too tired to eat his sandwich. He could hear his roommates playing video games. Yelling at the television. A train came by. Then the sound of the clock tower chiming. It was now four in the morning. He closed his eyes. The stress in his life had deflated. Rent was paid. He would now have to pay it. Which meant going to the bank and then getting a check made. But he could do that easily tomorrow. He could also pay the electric bill and the gas bill. Plus, it seemed there would be extra money. Combine that with the forty bucks that Lisa and Mary had given him, and the money he found in the parking lot. He was doing okay all of a sudden. He slept well for the first time in weeks. It helped that he would have breakfast in the morning. The sandwich in his hoodie pocket.

13

The Dishwasher slept until what felt like one. He woke up rock solid. He had nothing in his memory banks from yesterday. The work last night hadn't allowed him to collect any fresh material. That didn't make much of a difference, though. He always had his go to. Lisa in her tight-fitting black nylon pants. This time, though, he invented a scenario where she summoned him into the back office. Laura was there. They needed to show him something. What that was was they needed him to figure out who had the hardest nipples. They both took off their shirts. Then stuff happened and he was finished.

He wiped himself up with a dirty sock. Started a new pile of dirty clothes in the corner. He had to pee but he didn't want to get up just yet. He reached over to his hoodie and took the sandwich from his pocket. He lay in bed eating it.

It was one of the best sandwiches he had ever eaten. This made him think. He hadn't been eating very much, the last few days. Usually he would have a full meal at work. Then he would get something to go. Plus any other food that they were going to throw out. But because his idiot roommates kept eating all his food he'd stopped bringing stuff home. So instead of two or three things of food a day he was eating like one and a half. And even that wasn't big meals. Just a hamburger here. That sandwich Toby bought. The chicken wings last night. Something needed to change.

One of the main reasons that he was even a dishwasher was because he got free food. If he didn't get free food, the job was mostly useless. He tried to think of a way around his roommates eating his food. He couldn't. They even ate his hamburgers that were hidden under his dirty clothes. Granted, Toby had found them and thrown them at him and they were on his bed when they found them, but still. It was almost the same as taking the hamburgers out of the garbage, as far as the Dishwasher was concerned. Although they did seem to have a buttload of beer at the moment. Maybe they would also be buying food, or would be too drunk to eat the Dishwasher's food. Although, it was more likely that they would eat his food even more, now that they could get drunk even more than they already did. The only thing worse than scavengers for roommates was drunk scavengers with no self-control. Not that they'd had any to begin with.

The Dishwasher got up to go pee. He put his mildewed jeans on. They were still wet in the crotch. He forgot to lay them out last night when he went to bed. So they stayed the night wadded up at the foot of his mattress. He was annoyed. Why was everything so gross all the time? He was really getting sick of it.

He went into the kitchen. Looked in the fridge. The idiot roommates had made quite a dent in the beer last night. He looked in the living room. It was a mess of beer cans and cigarette butts. He could hear them farting and sawing logs in their room. He guessed that they would sleep until dark and then get up and do it all again. That was very depressing. But then the Dishwasher remembered that he had to go pay rent and bills and then go to work. Which was somehow more depressing. He found himself envious of his idiot roommates. Not in any real sense. Just the idea that they didn't need to work. Could sleep until dusk. Checks would just show up.

The Dishwasher went into the bathroom. He moved the packages of toilet paper into the kitchen. Put them on the counter. There wasn't room in the bathroom. He would figure something out later. He went back into the bathroom. Pissed. Flushed the toilet. He wanted to shower. There was no soap, though. Not even dish soap. He made a plan. A plan that he promised himself he would complete. He would go get a check made for the rent. Pay the bills. Drop the check off. Go to the grocery store and buy a new toothbrush and some bar soap. Maybe he would buy two toothbrushes. One he could keep in his room. One that lived in the bathroom. He was feeling generous. The fact that the first roommate had finally paid some rent and the bills was helping. Plus all the beer and the toilet paper. The Dishwasher knew he wouldn't see too much of the beer. It was possible they would run out of it by the next morning. At the rate they were going. But the toilet paper was a godsend. Even if they all got the runs for days on days, it would last them at least a couple weeks. If not longer.

The Dishwasher went back into his room. Found a T-shirt in his garbage bag of clean clothes. A pair of socks that kind of matched. He put the things on. Put his velcro shoes on. They were still wet. They smelled like a dog that had been rolling around in burned grease and rotting vegetables. He was annoyed. Why was everything so gross? This was getting out of control. It needed to stop.

He put on his hoodie. Made sure he had his wallet. Cigarettes. Lighter. Went into the kitchen. Grabbed the bills. Looked at them. Folded them. Put them in his pocket. Took his wallet out. Counted the money. There was 326 dollars. He would need to go to the bank. He knew that already, but he wanted to know how much money he should take out. He decided 300 dollars would be a good amount. That would leave him with about a hundred dollars. Which was a good amount of money. To have.

He left the apartment. Walked down the stairs. The mailbox was still wide open. He looked in the apartment's slot. There was nothing new. He walked out onto the sidewalk. Felt the air. It was kind of chilly. He thought about going back upstairs to get a sweater. He walked over to a place that had sun shining down. It was warmer there. He decided that he would put a sweater on before he went to work. He didn't need it now, though.

He walked across the street. Down the block. Went into the bank. Filled out a withdrawal form. He knew his account number by heart. He had a good memory for numbers. That was only part of it, though. He rarely used his bank account, yet the numbers were burned into his brain. Like old phone numbers. The bank account numbers only served one purpose. To get money. So they were important. Plus, it was just a few numbers anyway. Sometimes for fun he would memorize a long series of numbers just to remember later. Like from a phone card or whatever. Then he would make a long-distance phone call just to test it. Then he would hang up before anyone could answer. Like his mom or someone.

The Dishwasher took the slip to the teller. She typed his account information in. Took his ID. Looked at it. Compared it to the information she had. Handed it back. Asked him how he wanted it. He almost said something really stupid. But stopped himself. Said, "Twenties, please." The teller counted out 300 dollars in twenties. Put them in an envelope. Slid the envelope over. Told him that they had this new thing where you could use a card to get money out of the machine outside. He said he knew about it, but he didn't have the 400-dollar minimum he needed in order to get it. She looked at his balance on her computer screen. Said, "Oh." Then frowned. Then she asked him if he wanted his balance. His face was red. He said, "Yes, please." She printed out his balance. Handed him the paper. He said thanks; she told him to have a good day. But there was something in her tone that meant the opposite. He looked at the paper as he was walking out of the bank. He had $89.03 left. He would get paid on Friday, so he wasn't too worried about it. But that didn't matter. He was far away from his 1,000-dollar goal of getting the hell out of town. He wadded the paper up and threw it in the trash. He put the envelope of cash in his front pocket. Careful not to lose it between the bank and the check cashing place that he needed to go to next.

The check cashing place was nice for a couple of things. Paying bills, and money orders. The bank could issue you a money order, but it cost ten bucks. The check cashing place only charged you a percentage of the price of the money order. And for such a small amount, 400 dollars, the amount for rent, it would only cost about a dollar. Which was a lot less than ten dollars. He never understood why the bank charged so much, or why the check cashing place charged so little. But that was just the way it was.

He walked to the busy street. Crossed against traffic. There were no big trucks coming around to call him a faggot. Or throw things at him. There wasn't very much traffic either. It was after lunch. Or, at least, that was what he thought was the reason why. The Dishwasher. He walked up the hill for a few blocks. Took a left. Got to the university's main road. The road that took you by the dorms. Walked uphill for about ten more blocks. Came to the business mall where the check cashing place was. Went inside.

There were three people in line. None of them white college students. In fact, none of them were white. Aside from the Dishwasher. He sighed. Not because nobody was white, but because the line at the check cashing place always took forever. Three people in front of you might as well be a million.

Maybe this was why it cost so little? Or why it cost so much at the banks. If you could afford to go to a bank, you probably didn't care that it cost ten bucks for a money order because you were probably rich enough that you didn't need that service, because you could afford to have checks. And if you were in a check cashing place, that meant that you needed money right now. And didn't have the necessary documents to get a bank account. And this was where the check cashing place preyed on the impoverished. Where they made their money. Because they took a lot of it when they cashed your check. Like 5 percent. Which sucked. But if you were in this line, it usually meant you didn't have a choice.

It was very unfair. And vulturous. But there was nothing you could do about it. The system was rigged for the wealthy. Or at least the people with all the papers and money. Anyone else, anyone that didn't have the proper documents, was stuck going to places like this. Which meant that every single check that they cashed needed to be confirmed before they would cash it.

There was no benefit of the doubt. No government backing that covered bad checks. You had to stand there. Every single time. Even if you had been there one thousand times before with the exact same check and they recognized your face and even knew your name, they would have to make a call and verify the check. Which meant that if you were third in line, you should expect to wait at least thirty minutes before you got to the front. And if you made the mistake of going in on a Friday. Payday. You should just cancel your plans. Because it would be a very long wait.

The Dishwasher stood there, waiting. Ten minutes went by. Then fifteen. He watched the clock moving slowly. The second hand just ticking away. The employees behind what looked like three inches of glass. Some of them doing things. Others just sitting at computers. Why they never had more than one person taking people never made any sense. But that was just how it went. Being poor was a full time job. Everything was a tax. Inertia was the only movement. Twenty minutes went by. Then, finally! The first guy was done.

The next person moved up to the window. The Dishwasher was hoping she would say that she just needed to pay bills. Instead she said, "I need to cash this check and get two money orders." The time just slogged on. Eventually someone else came in. The Dishwasher heard them sigh when they saw the line. Then another person came in. Said out loud, "Are you fucking kidding me!"

Everyone in line turned around. Including the Dishwasher. It was an oil field worker. You could tell by how he was dressed. He didn't turn around to leave, or just stand in line in silence like everyone else. He made huffing noises. Stomping a little every now and again. His work boots loud on the tiles. Saying things like, "C'mon, just go already! I don't have time for this shit. Am I right?" Thinking that people would join his rebellion.

Nobody did. Everyone had no choice but to be here standing in line. Eventually he got so impatient that he went out to smoke. When someone else came in, you could hear him yelling, "Hey!

I am in front of you, just so we're clear, you got that?" Then when he finished smoking he came back in and said, "You know I was in front of you, yeah?" The poor old man that had come in while he was smoking never questioned the oil field worker. But the oil field worker was very aggravated nonetheless. He made a big show of getting back in line. Then he couldn't stand it. He yelled, "Isn't there another guy? I've been waiting here for hours! What the hell kind of business is this?!" Everyone in line tried to ignore him. He was making things very unpleasant. The Dishwasher wanted to tell him, "Dude! You're not the only one in here waiting. Calm the fuck down." But he was a coward. He just stood there stewing. Hoping the guy would leave. Or at least shut up.

The second person in line finished. Then the next person walked up to the window. The Dishwasher was hoping he would say, "I just have a bill to pay." Instead he said, "I have a check to cash and I need a couple of money orders." The Dishwasher sighed. The oil field worker let out a huge grunt. He stomped his boots. Paced around a little bit. Said to the poor old man behind him, "Fuck this, I'm smoking. This is my space, hombre. *Yo comprehend-ay? Fumar.*" The poor old man did his best to not look at the guy. He went back outside. He paced in front of the building, smoking. Everyone was on edge at this point.

The second person in line finished their business. The third person in line walked up. The Dishwasher was hoping he would say, "I just need to pay this bill." Instead he said, "I have a check to cash and I need a couple money orders." The Dishwasher sighed. He was next, though. There would be an end. He didn't know how long he had been there at this point. He had lost track of time when the oil field worker came in. It was probably forty minutes at this point, though. He stood there, as patient as he could be. Wishing that it was all over. That he was back out on the street. Free of standing in line. He didn't even have his usual ability to daydream in these situations. Mostly because he knew the oil field worker would be back soon enough. And he would disrupt everyone's neutral feelings.

A few minutes went by and the oil field worker came back. Elbowed his way back in line. You could smell the cigarettes on him. This made the Dishwasher want to smoke. He'd forgotten to smoke on his way to the check cashing place. Which didn't mean that much. His smoking habit was constant, but not overwhelming. He could take it or leave it. Or so he thought. But standing in line for what felt like hours kind of made him wish he could smoke right now. Plus, the smell of cigarette smoke coming off the oil field worker didn't help. The Dishwasher was resigned, though. To his plan. He would pay these bills and get the rent check made. He would drop that off. No matter what. But his chances of going to the grocery store to get soap and toothbrushes was diminishing by the minute.

The third person in line finished their business. The Dishwasher walked up. Slid the two papers into the slot. The gas bill and the electric bill. He said, "I would like to pay these, please. I also need a money order." The woman behind the three inches of glass took the papers and typed some things into her computer. Then she said, "What's the money order?" The Dishwasher said, "Four hundred dollars." The woman typed some more things. Then said, "536 dollars." The Dishwasher slid 540 dollars into the slot. She took the cash. Counted it. Gave him four dollars in change. He put it in his wallet. She said, "Who do you want to make the money order out to?" He told her. She typed the information in. A thing happened to her right. She pulled the check out. Folded the receipt back. So it would fit through the slot. Slid the money order and the receipt through. Said, "Thank you." The Dishwasher said the same.

He took the money order to the little counter next to the wall. There were two pens there. Connected to wires. One of them didn't work. He tried the other one. It worked. He wrote the address and the apartment number on the memo line. Pulled the receipt off of the check. It was perforated. Folded them in half.

Put them in his front pocket. The oil field worker said something vile. Then, "See, this guy gets it." Meaning the Dishwasher. The Dishwasher just looked down. He didn't want to engage. He was starting to feel ill. All that waiting was taking a toll on his desire to do the things that he wanted to do in his life. The oil field worker was just making it worse.

The Dishwasher walked outside. He reached into his pocket and took a cigarette out. He lit it. It tasted gross. He felt gross. He took a couple drags then threw it into the gutter. It was kind of chilly still. He would have to put his long johns on. Maybe even before going to work. He wished he would have gone back up and gotten a sweater. There was nothing he could do about that now. He walked downhill until he got to the main road where the big trucks usually harassed him. Called him faggot. Threw things at him. There weren't any large trucks. The only logic for this was that school had started again. Or, at least, that was what the Dishwasher thought. Why they didn't attack during school didn't make sense. Because there were a lot more faggots now than during the summer. But maybe that was it? They were now outnumbered. Too many faggots on the street to do anything about. It really was a conundrum.

The Dishwasher crossed the street. Walked a few blocks. Went into the real estate building where he had to pay rent. The woman behind the desk looked at the Dishwasher and frowned. She said, "Yes?" He said, "I got rent I need to pay." She said, "Let me see." He dug into his pocket and took the rent check out. She had a face like she might shit her pants or vomit. He handed her the money order. She didn't want to touch it but she had to. She read the memo. Typed something into the computer she was sitting at. Made another horrible face. Printed something out. Signed it. Handed it to the Dishwasher. He said, "Thanks." She said, "Yeah, sure."

As he was walking out the door, somebody came into the front room.

They said, "Who was that?"

The woman said, "These fucking—" What else she said got lost behind the door.

These fucking *what?* The Dishwasher wanted to go back in and find out. But he was a coward. He just let it stew. There was no winning in this world. The bank would take your money, the landlord would take your money, but they didn't have to like it. Trash was trash. Losers were losers.

The Dishwasher was defeated at this point. He looked at the clock tower. It was now 3:45. He didn't have time to go to the grocery store to get soap and toothbrushes. He needed to be at work by five.

He walked back to the apartment. He went inside. When he got to the kitchen he did an inspection of the bottle of dishwashing soap. He decided he could at least try. He went into his bedroom. Took his clothes off. His velcros. He had a boner now. He didn't do anything about it, though. He rooted around in his plastic garbage bag of clean clothes and took the clean towel out. He wrapped it around his waist. His boner poking out. Went into the bathroom. Started the shower. Went back out and grabbed the bottle of empty dishwashing soap. Took it back in. Put the bottle on the edge of the tub. Took the towel off. Hung it from the towel holder. Knocking off the dirty shirt that smelled like death. That used to be the towel. Adjusted the water. Started to get into the shower. Realized he needed to shit. Sat down. Let things go. It was a glorious thing to wipe with toilet paper. He felt kind of proud of himself when he was done. He flushed. Waited for the water to return to normal. Got in. Rinsed. Milked every drop of soap out of the dishwashing-soap bottle. Using it mainly for his crotch and his ass and his armpits. There wasn't much. He didn't get very clean. He rinsed his face. He wished he had more soap. His feet were itchy. He wished he had more soap. His face was greasy. He wished he had more soap. The Dishwasher.

In the end, there was no amount of rinsing that could make a difference. He turned the water off. Took the towel from the rack. At least the towel was clean. It wasn't. It smelled like mildew already. Why was everything so gross in this world? It needed to stop. The Dishwasher didn't even bother drying his hair. What was the point? He left the bathroom dripping. The towel around his waist. He threw the towel on the mattress on the ground that was his bed. He stood there. Looking. What the fuck was life? He was suddenly very hard. He dropped down onto the mattress. The door to his bedroom was still open. He didn't care. He would hear the roommates if they were coming. He yanked his boner like it was something dangerous. Somehow angry with it. When nothing came out, he felt very sorry for himself. He got back up and got dressed for work.

14

The Dishwasher got to work early. He wanted to make sure that he had a chance to eat something before his shift started. He was nervous that tonight would be as bad as last night. That he wouldn't get a single minute to relax during his shift. He traded his dirty button-up white shirt for a clean one.

He had made a decision to just switch shirts out from now on. There was no reason to bring one home, even. He would wear a T-shirt to work. Change out into a work shirt and then, at the end of the shift, change back. Why he hadn't been doing this the whole time was a mystery. He kind of remembered someone telling him to bring two shirts home with him. But who that was and why was long forgotten. It probably had something to do with an old policy that had changed that nobody told him about. That, or somebody told him something at some point when he was very busy and he just didn't hear it. Either way, he would just switch shirts now. If they didn't have a clean one, he would just work in his T-shirt. And if they had a problem with that, they could have a problem with that. He was starting to find it absurd that he was in charge of keeping his work shirts clean. Mostly because they paid him such shit wages. And it cost money to wash the shirts. And they never gave him any checkered pants like they gave the cooks. Even Norman, that useless jerk, got checkered pants.

The job was really starting to get on the Dishwasher's nerves. He was very close to being done with it all. The job, Toby, the Altitude, Laramie, his roommates, the apartment, being destitute all the time. The Buckhorn. The long days of doing basically nothing, the long nights of doing basically everything. His

1,000-dollar plan to get the hell out of town was sounding better by the day. He would do some thinking tonight, if he had a chance. If there was time. If it wasn't too busy. But for now he just wanted to eat something. Get caught up with the afternoon dishes and get to work.

He clocked in, just in case. If it was super busy already, he would have to do this anyway. He could get something to eat while doing work as well. He left his wallet and his cigarettes in his hoodie pocket. Put a hairnet on. A paper hat.

He went into the prep kitchen. No Norman. Maybe he had quit. That would be nice. Good riddance. The cooks in the kitchen were Ronito and Roger. It was Wednesday. Dong Smells wouldn't be in until seven. He knew Dong Smells' schedule pretty well. But that would change soon when classes began in earnest. There was nobody in the dish room. Just piles of dirty dishes and dirty pots and dirty pans. The Dishwasher assumed they'd just stopped trying to hire new people. He wondered about Mike. What happened to him? He seemed like he might work out. Maybe he would come in later.

He started to organize the dishes. Get the sinks ready. Ronito came in. To drop off a smoking skillet. He said:

"Yo, Disher, what's the haps?"

"Same ol' bullshit."

"Tell me about it." Ronito started to leave.

"Hey!" Ronito stopped and turned around.

"YE-essss." Saying yes like that meant that Ronito was in a good mood. Which was nice.

"Can you guys make me a cheeseburger with fries? I got too slammed last night to eat anything and I need to make up for lost ground."

"You got it. Straight or curly?"

"Curly."

"Coming right up."

"Thanks, Ronito, you really know how to make a man feel good." Ronito smiled and walked back into the kitchen.

It was not busy. The Dishwasher looked through the opening. The place was almost empty. Lisa and a new girl waitressing. Randy behind the bar again. The Dishwasher hoped it would be a slow night. Not too slow—he had some thinking to do—but slow enough that it didn't suck.

He cleaned and stacked the dirty dishes. Emptied the sinks. Rinsed them out. Started to fill them with water and soaps and stuff. He cleaned the Hobart. Ran it a couple times. Ran the glasses through. Then the dishes. When the sinks were ready, he moved all the dirty pots and pans and skillets and whatever else into the correct sinks. Ronito showed up with the cheeseburger and curly fries. The Dishwasher thanked him. Took the plate to the bag-in-a-box of ketchup hanging from the wall, that the waitresses used to fill up ketchup bottles. He pushed the spout button. A very large glob of ketchup came out.

The Dishwasher stood there eating curly fries. Then he put the plate on the wire rack in the dish room. Took a bite of the cheeseburger and got down to the serious work. Scrubbing the dirty pots and pans and skillets. As well as the other stuff. He stopped periodically to take bites from his cheeseburger. It was very good. The curly fries were top notch. He did a tray of silverware. Ran some more plates and soup cups.

Soon he was entirely caught up. Which didn't happen very often. He took this opportunity to clean the dish room. Wiping down every metal surface. Emptying the sinks. He really gave them a scrubbing. He took some cardboard outside. It was too early to smoke. In the sense that he didn't feel like smoking. It was already dark out. And kind of chilly. He would need to put his long johns on soon. Probably tomorrow. He finished folding boxes. Throwing them away. He went back inside.

The night went on. Slowly it got busier. At one point the Dishwasher went to the front to get some coffee. This was nice. He liked to drink coffee. This made him want to smoke, though. Now was not the time to do that, though. He wished he would have thought this through when there was time to smoke. He ignored the impulse and tried to keep up with the dishes coming in. They started to come in faster and faster. Soon it was a full-on blitz. Dong Smells showed up. Came into the dish room to drop off some things. Said:

"Working hard, or hardly working?"

"Shove it."

"Buckhorn tonight? Your brother said he has the night off."

"No shit? Fine by me, it seems like a slow one."

"Yeah, I guess."

The slow one that the Dishwasher was talking about was a race for his sanity. He became severely inundated. But in a good way. Because he had caught everything up before the rush, he was on top of everything else. He had a system worked out that was running as smoothly as could be possible. He never had to jump glasses or expedite silverware. He had everything under total control. He washed dishes like the wind. Never losing a single moment. He was even able to take the trash out and smoke without causing himself too much grief. He was at the top of his game. One with the dishes. He even pulled off a couple completely empty moments, which hadn't happened since the slowest day back in July.

He was feeling pretty good about himself. So good that he let his mind wander. Playing out scenarios for how his life might go. About moving to the city to get away from Toby. About living on his own in an unfamiliar town. About getting a job doing something else. Somewhere else. About finally making enough money to not have roommates. Or dirty clothes all the time. Or no soap in the bathroom. Or food in the fridge. Not having to worry about his spare change getting stolen. Or having a full toothbrush that he didn't have to share with idiot jerks who he had to wrench the rent and bills out of. Of getting some time alone in the place that he lived. A place where he could bring girls over. And they could do naked things without interruption.

His daydreams only really gave him a hard-on that he had to hide. That was poking out from under his apron. He had to force himself to focus on work again. But something seemed to have clicked. Some idea of how to get out of town. He thought about his money. His rent and the next few weeks. Months, even. It was September now. Soon it would be winter.

Moving anywhere in the winter seemed difficult. But what else could he do? Denver had the same winters as Laramie, he decided. So, so what? What did it matter when he moved? But what about New York? New York scared the shit out of him. He would need more of a reason to go there. But, then again, Toby was a pretty good reason. He knew she would never follow him out there. Denver was different. Even if she didn't move down there, she would be able to find him. Come down for a day or two and absolutely destroy his life. But 1,000 dollars was not enough money to move to New York with. It was close. He figured he could find another place that had 400-dollar rent. He would need to give a deposit. That would mean that he would have 200 dollars to last him a month. He could do that. But, then again, he would want more. But that would mean sticking around in Laramie longer. But that would cause more problems. More situations that Toby could claw her way into. That the Dishwasher would have to claw his way out of.

In the end, he decided he could get to Denver then decide what to do. A month in Denver was all he would need. Then he could make a little money and think about moving to New York. He figured the pay down there would be higher. The rents would probably be close to Laramie rents. The problem, though, was that he would have to get an apartment, pay the deposit, then break the lease. Which meant he would be out 400 dollars. So that would mean he would need more time in Denver to get the money together to go to New York. And Toby might catch up to him if he spent too much time in Denver. The problem was so very complex. If things failed in Denver, he could always just hitch a ride back to Wyoming. If shit went sideways in New York, who knew what would happen. He could find himself homeless and broke, unable to get anywhere near Wyoming. Then what?

It wasn't like he could call his parents and ask for money. They were just as broke as he was. His brother was doing alright. But that was because he had a scholarship to the university and was working at the pop company nearly full time. That would be a pretty big ask, to rely on the hard work of his brother to get back home. No, the only thing to do was to move to Denver. Haul ass about it. Get some money together and hop on a Greyhound and get to New York that way. Then never look back. See you later, suckers.

He could write poems and sell them on the street. To tourists. Start a band. Make a million dollars. Join the movies. Do some modeling. He was handsome enough. Or so he thought. The ladies around Laramie might say otherwise, but the New York ladies would love his gaunt and pasty good looks. His juicy prose. His unquenchable desires. The Dishwasher pictured himself as incredibly ambitious. Somebody would see that. Take him in. Give him a good home. Help him become the person he was destined to be. Who that was was not clear, but the idea was there. He just needed to get out of Laramie. Ditch Toby. Ditch the Altitude. The roommates. He was still young. Things would happen for him.

He just needed to get 1,000 dollars. Plus a bus ticket. Plus maybe some spending money. Plus a good reference. He had never tried to get an apartment before. He knew that you needed things like that. References. He didn't have any. His parents had had to declare bankruptcy at one point, so they were not good references. Maybe his brother? But then if he decided to break the lease and ditch Denver for New York, what would that do to his brother? His finances? The problem just got more complicated, the more the Dishwasher thought about it. He went from being very excited to being very confused. He had to stop thinking. It was not helping matters.

He shook himself from his daydream and focused again on the dishes. Feeling sadder, but more grounded. Something was missing. In his thinking. He would figure it out. He knew he would. He just needed to buy some time.

The night went on and on. Nothing really changing. Not speeding up. Not slowing down. The Dishwasher drank a few pops. Was asked to buss a couple tables. Somebody messed up an order of fish and chips. Roger asked him if he wanted it. The Dishwasher said he did. To put it in a to-go container for him. This was nice. He would have food for later. But then he remembered about going to the Buckhorn with Dong Smells. Maybe he could get some tinfoil and wrap things up and put them in his hoodie pockets. Which sounded like a good idea.

The kitchen closed at eleven. Since most of the cardboard was broken down, closing stuff was quicker than usual. He was almost ahead of the kitchen when the skid mats came in. He was so fast, in fact, that he had to wait on Dong Smells for the last of the fryer stuff. And that barely took a minute to run through. Ten minutes later, Dong Smells came into the dish room. Wearing his jacket. A baseball cap. No checkered pants; he had taken them off. He said:

"See ya in a few?"

"I just gotta run these buckets and I'm out."

"Gnarl-town."

The Dishwasher ran the buckets. He made sure everything was shipshape. He ran the Hobart a couple times. Pulled the drain. Made sure the doors were open. Looked around. Saw the fish and chips in the to-go container. Took them to the kitchen. Got some tinfoil and started wrapping the fried fish and the french fries into smaller things that would fit in his pockets. He made sure the tartar sauce got wrapped as well. He didn't want it to burst open and make a mess in his hoodie pocket. Lisa came into the kitchen. She said:

"How did it go tonight?"

"Not the worst—I could use some help, though."

"Yeah, right. So, hey, Dong Smells says you might be interested in prep work, is that true?"

"Well, I mean, the pay is better."

"That doesn't answer my question."

"I mean, if you are asking me if I want more money, the answer is yes."

"Okay, well that would involve learning to do prep stuff. Are you interested in that?"

"Does it involve Norman?"

"Norman doesn't work here anymore."

"No shit, did you can his ass?"

"Let's just say that he doesn't work here anymore."

"Oh, boy. That is not good."

"What?"

"Can you not see these bruises?"

"Well, yeah, but, I mean, it's not your fault that he was a horrible employee."

"Tell that to him."

"I did."

"And…"

"Okay, but listen. The job is open if you're interested."

"Can I think about it?"

"Yeah, I mean, yes, but if you want it show up at three tomorrow, otherwise I am putting a thing in the paper."

"And who will wash the dishes?"

"I don't know, I guess we will figure it out."

"Oh, right, the old we-will-figure-it-out?"

"C'mon, Disher, you know what I mean."

"Yeah, I know exactly what you mean."

"Well, okay, I mean, it is what it is, but if you show up at three tomorrow you can start doing prep stuff."

"What's the pay?"

"Eleven."

"And then what? I do dishes?"

"Most likely."

"For eleven."

"No, the same."

"So how does that work? I just transfer my time card over?"
"Well, you would have two time cards."
"Jesus Christ, you guys really have some wacky ideas."
"It's up to you."
"Let me think about it."
"Sure."
"Yeah, sure."
"You did great tonight. Thanks!"
"Yeah."

———

The Dishwasher finished putting the fish and chips in tinfoil. He threw the to-go container away. He turned off the lights as he walked to the back. He took his apron off. Threw it into the dirty clothes bin. He took his work shirt off. Threw that into the bin as well. He stood there naked above the waist. A cool breeze came in. It hardened his nipples. Made his wet crotch cold. He put his T-shirt on. Getting his hairnet and paper hat caught in the process. He threw those away. He put his cigarettes and his wallet in his front pockets. Put his hoodie on. Crammed the fish and chips into the pockets of his hoodie. Zipped it up. Clocked out. Walked out into the alley. The smell of rotten frying oil and decaying food. The fart smell of cardboard. A train came by. Slowly. It was half past eleven now. He wished that he would have looked at Lisa's butt as she walked away. For later. But he'd forgot to. He was too distracted by her work offer. There was nothing he could do about it now. He tried to think of an excuse to go back inside. Maybe she was dealing with dressing or something. He could catch her bending over. That gave him creepy vibes. He instead squeezed a cigarette out of the soft pack and lit it. It was not bent. He didn't have to straighten it out.

He walked slowly down the alley. Kind of thinking about what Lisa had said and kind of thinking about what was coming down the pike at the Buckhorn. He was a little exhausted, but not as bad as last night. Which was brutal. Tonight he just wanted to have some beers. Maybe play some pool. See his brother. And hopefully Toby wouldn't show up. But at this point he wouldn't mind. The sex would be good at least. And if he decided to go into work early that would be a good excuse to kick her out of the apartment. Not that she would leave, but he could at least try.

A cool breeze came down the alleyway. His loins got chilled. The Dishwasher wondered if his crotch would rot off one day. Like soldiers' feet did sometimes during war. Trench foot. They called it. He was wondering if it was possible to get trench crotch from having too much moisture down there. He really needed a new pair of pants. Then it occurred to him that if he took the prep job he would finally get some checkered pants. And this, more than any other thinking about it he was doing, was the thing that changed his mind. If he went into work early tomorrow, he would get a pair of work pants. His days of gross, smelly jeans would be over. His mind was made up. He would do it. Even if it meant working two different jobs for vastly different pay. If he got work pants, it would all be worth it.

After these thoughts, he walked a little faster to the bar. He was kind of excited now. He wanted to see what Dong Smells thought about it. And he was excited to see his brother. Not only that, but the rent and bills were paid. Payday was Friday and he wasn't terribly broke and he didn't owe anyone money. The Dishwasher also had a little over a hundred dollars in his wallet. He could buy his own beers, without acting like a succubus to his richer friends and family. Things were looking up. Now he thought that maybe he should even call Toby. Tell her to come down. He walked past the Buckhorn. Walked under the overpass. Took a right. Ended up at the gas station. He fumbled around in his pocket. He had two dimes and a nickel. Luckily they registered. He dialed Toby's number. She answered before it even rang. She said:

"Who is this?"

"Hey, it's me."

"No shit. What the fuck?"

"Come down to the Buckhorn."

"Where is that at?"

"Shut it, Toby, don't be a dick."

"Yeah, we'll see."

"See you soon." She had already hung up. The Dishwasher immediately regretted making the call. She would be there in ten minutes. If not earlier. He should have waited. But he hadn't. Now it was too late. He just hoped she could get in. Otherwise it would be a wasted night. She would be kicked out and the Dishwasher would have to figure out how to ditch her without leaving the bar. It would be a whole thing. Fuck. Why was he so stupid? The Dishwasher walked as fast as he could to the bar. Maybe if he got a couple beers in before she showed up everything would be alright.

He walked into the bar. There wasn't a bouncer. His brother and Dong Smells and their friend Curry were playing pool. The Dishwasher said a fast hello and went to the bar. He ordered two beers. Got carded. Showed the bartender his ID for the millionth time. Took the beers over to the pool table. Drank the first one as fast as he could. Then stood there holding the empty can. Watching his brother shoot a terrible shot that Curry just laughed about. Curry said something arrogant and sank a ball. Dong Smells stood there waiting. Rubbing chalk onto his pool cue. The Dishwasher took a drink from his second beer and waited. He had one eye on the windows. He would have to come clean. Nobody would like it. But what could he do? The trouble he had asked for was on its way. And that's what it would be when it showed up. Toby was actually a lot of fun sometimes. Sometimes. Sometimes she was the opposite of fun. Only the Dishwasher knew that she was coming.

He chugged the second beer down. Looked at Curry and Dong Smells and his brother. They all seemed to have full beers. He went back to the bar. Ordered another. Gave the bartender the empty cans. Paid him. Walked back to the pool table.

He stood there watching. Waiting for the time to tell them. They were very focused on the game. The Dishwasher just stood there. His crotch wet. Now slightly drunk. He watched them play.

In the end, Curry won and the Dishwasher's brother and Dong Smells groaned. A loud song came on. From the jukebox. Curry yelled:

"Who's next?"

15

"How'd it go tonight?" Dong Smells had been kicked out of the rotation. The Dishwasher's brother was already losing the next game. Curry was acting like a jackass about it. Showboating. Hitting on any girl that came within whispering distance.

"Better than last night."

"Yeah, right? Did Lisa talk to you?"

"Yeah."

"And?"

"If I show up at three tomorrow, I got the prep job."

"Nice. I mean, you don't seem too excited about it."

"I'm not. It is just more work for roughly the same pay."

"Yeah, but you can work your way up."

"Yeah, and also do two jobs for the price of one."

"But eventually you'll make the good money, right?"

"I mean, I don't see myself sticking around until then."

"Why? Where ya going?"

"I don't know, anywhere but this stinkhole. Denver, maybe."

"What, move in with Troll and Bogart maybe?"

"Maybe. I mean, it would be better to get my own place. Ditch Toby, hopefully."

"Well, good luck with that."

"Yeah, I know. She'll be here shortly, by the way."

"What the hell?"

"I'm sorry! I can't help myself. A guy's got needs."

"Yeah, have you ever considered *our* needs?"

"Yeah, I know."

"So, you going to do it?"

"What? Denver?"

"No, tomorrow."

"Yeah, prolly. I think it's unavoidable."

"Oh, don't be so bummed, dude. It won't be that bad."

"Oh, I'm not so worried about that. I know it will suck—I'm just pissed at myself for inviting Toby over. I don't know what my problem is."

"Your problem is that you have a dick. I would suggest you get used to it."

"I suppose you're right. Beer?"

"Don't mind if I do."

Dong Smells and the Dishwasher went to the bar. The Dishwasher's brother and Curry played their game. Music played on the jukebox. The night was a nice night. Calm. The Buckhorn wasn't crowded. There were still a few days of First Week left. Parties were still happening. Parties not worth going to. Parties that kept people from crowding the bars. Soon it would be too cold for parties. Well, at least the big ones. There would be smaller parties all year. All semester. Keggers even. But the blowout parties would last through this weekend and then that would be it until Halloween. And that would be the very last of the big parties. Then the break. Then when New Year's came around the parties would start up again.

The Dishwasher went out to smoke. It was cold enough he could see his breath. He would need to put his long johns on soon. Start wearing a coat. His wet crotch got cold. One reason to take the prep job. To maybe finally get some checkered work pants. That way his jeans would stop getting ruined.

The Dishwasher smoked as fast as he could. He didn't want to get caught outside with Toby when she showed up. He would never make it back inside, then. She would either start something or say something or do something that ended with them going back to his apartment. Or worse, she would begin some fight that he couldn't get away from. That he would have to deal with. Right there. In front of everyone. Or, he would have to run away again and hide behind a dumpster somewhere until she got bored and went back home. Toby was a menace. A harbinger of chaos. Her chaos made the Dishwasher hard down in his loins and anxious in his heart. She was like a sex-addled mechanical bull. A mechanical bull that went from zero to maximum without notice. Without any lead-up. Without foreplay. Something like that. On or off. There was no in-between.

He caught a glimpse of her car careening around the corner. Another driver had to slam on their brakes. That car honked. Toby zipped by the bar. She waved and nearly hit a parked car. The Dishwasher ditched his cigarette. Ran inside.

Toby would have to park down the street. She was too young to drink in the bar legally. If she parked out front, they would card her for sure. If she didn't, there was a chance that she wouldn't get carded. There was no way to tell. It really depended on who was working. Since there wasn't a bouncer, she had a good chance of not getting harassed when she came inside. There was only one bartender at the moment. If she came in right now, she might just pull it off. Then, when the other bartender came back from downstairs or whatever, out back, she would be grandfathered in. That sort of thing seemed to work all the time. Whether it was on purpose was unknown. The bartenders didn't really care. They just didn't want to get busted. As long as they didn't personally sell drinks to minors, they had plausible deniability. Toby would just have to keep a low profile. Which was something she was not good at. But as long as she didn't actually go up to the bar and try to buy drinks, she probably wouldn't get carded.

Toby knew the drill. She was even clever about it. She came in wearing a very bright red coat. Then went to the corner where the pool cues were. Took the coat off. And came around the other side wearing a black sweater. If the bartender noticed her coming in, she didn't look the same when she came out the other side. She had even put her hair in a ponytail by the time she got there. Everyone else knew the drill as well. Nobody shouted her name or anything. Even the Dishwasher ignored her until she was standing right in front of him.

She smelled like vanilla. He would have dropped everything he was doing if she had grabbed his junk. Taken her back to the apartment. Dealt with the fallout there. She didn't. She said:

"Hey, nerds."

The Dishwasher was standing next to his brother. He had just lost the last game to Curry. Who was apparently on a streak. Dong Smells was now losing to him. The Dishwasher and his brother were just looking around. Seeing if anyone had noticed Toby coming in. If she was about to get carded. It was all very obvious.

Nobody seemed to notice. There were a few more people in the bar now. Where they'd come from was confusing. Aside from Toby coming in the front doors, nobody else had come in. Maybe they had been in the back smoking cigarettes. Which was something you could do. As long as nobody could see you smoking inside, it was still okay to do that. Even though it was illegal. The smoking rules were new. Not that new, but new enough. All the bars had this sort of agreement. If there was a back room. As long as nobody flaunted the rules, it was okay. The Buckhorn was unique, though. Because it had such large windows. In the front. Anyone walking by could look inside and see what was happening. The only way they could get away with smoking in the front was if they shut the lights off. Nobody wanted them to shut the lights off, though. Even the smokers. They were used to being told where to go and for what reason why. You could still chew tobacco and spit on the floor if you wanted. But you couldn't smoke in plain sight. You either had to go to the back or go outside. Mostly, people just went outside. Soon it would be too cold to go outside; at that point the back would be where all the smokers drank. For now, though, the ones that really thought it was necessary to smoke inside just went into the back. Leaving their drinks, so nobody would take their seats. Their stools. Everyone else just went outside.

Toby was short. With her hair in a ponytail, she looked even shorter. She had bangs and a wide face. Splotchy. Her hair was red, with clear hairs by her temples. She was built like a tent spike. Or at least that was how the Dishwasher would describe her. Maybe because he sometimes had the desire to bonk her on top of her head so she would just go away. He felt like a dick when he had these thoughts. He had them anyway. She was kind of built that way, though. Like a tent spike. Heavy on top and tapered down to tiny, cute feet. She wore tight jeans and loose-fitting tops. Tennis shoes. She had strong shoulders and almost a boy's-size waist and buns. Large breasts, in comparison to the rest of her body.

The Dishwasher found her red hair and red pubic hair very attractive. He thought she was very cute. Her breasts were a little too much for him. However, they offset her boyish ass in a way that kind of balanced everything out. Like if her lower body was boyish, her upper body was the opposite. Womanish. He didn't give too much thought to her appearance. That was the least of all things about her. But he did find himself describing her. For some reason. To people that asked. And that was what he would say. That she was a little like a tent spike. A redheaded tent spike. With nothing but personality. Then the Dishwasher would feel bad for describing her that way and he would say that she was a firecracker. Which made things worse. For the Dishwasher. He didn't mean to reduce her to such idiotic terms.

Ultimately there was just no way to describe Toby. Visually, she was like a redheaded tent spike. Emotionally and figuratively, she was a force of absolute chaos. The closest the Dishwasher ever got to really describing her was when somebody said, "Oh, shit, I was at that party, I think I met her, how would you describe her?" he had said, "Oh, you would know, she was the redhead there that was nothing but bad news." And the person had said, "Oh, right. She was the girl that kicked Jason in the shins when he said he wanted to play her bongos." The Dishwasher said, "Sounds about right."

"Hey, Toby, you get the classes you wanted?" The Dishwasher's brother started making small talk. Toby didn't do small talk.

"Yeah, maybe. What kind of lame-ass shit is this? How's Hermes?" Hermes was the Dishwasher's brother's cat.

"He got shot by the Techers."

"No!"

"The pellet went straight through, though."

"Is he okay?"

"We took him to the vet. He seems alright. Nat's been pretty good with him. I think he'll pull through."

"Those fuckers! How'd he get out?"

"I was moving some shit to the truck and he got loose."

"That's tragic. At least he came back."

"The neighbor kids found him under the porch."

"Those fucking assholes."

The Dishwasher's brother didn't want to talk about it. He went to buy some beers. Toby looked around. Then she said:

"What's your problem? Where'd you go the other day?"

"I had a thing."

"Yeah, I'm sure. What the hell?"

"I don't know what to tell you."

"Well, what are you doing tonight?"

"I don't know. Want to come over?"

"Are you going to ditch me again?"

"I got work tomorrow."

"Yeah, and...?"

"I don't know. What can I say?"

"I thought you wanted to go for a hike or something. What about my needs? You just want to stand around playing butthole brothers with your lame-ass friends, in some lame-ass bar?"

"Well, that guy is actually my brother, and I just worked a long-ass shift. Sorry I didn't get your permission."

"Your lies are like chicken thighs."

"Nobody's lies are like chicken thighs. Let's just calm down a little. I don't know what to tell you. Sometimes I got to work."

"Pshh!"

"I don't know why you think you are so cool. I don't know what you are talking about."

This very useless conversation was interrupted by the Dishwasher's brother bringing beers over. He handed a beer to each of them and then slinked off. Not wanting to get into the middle of it.

"See what you did? Now my brother won't even talk to me. He even bought you a beer."

"More reeb. Always the solution for you guys. Just a bunch of lame-ass nerds shooting stick all day long."

"I don't know what that has to do with anything!" The Dishwasher said this loud enough that everyone looked up. Focused their attention on the two. The Dishwasher looked over at the bartender. He made a face. Fuck. She was about to get carded. The Dishwasher led Toby to the wall, under the speaker that the music was coming from.

"Don't push me around."

"I'm not pushing you around," the Dishwasher said in a hushed voice. "You're about to get kicked out of here."

"What the fuck do I care about that? I got better shit to do anyway."

"Toby! What the hell?"

"What the hell? Don't what-the-hell me. I can do whatever I want. I just want to know why you keep ditching me all the time. I thought we had a good thing going."

"I don't want to talk about it. Let's just drink these beers and get out of here."

"Then what?"

"Oh, I don't know, look, we'll go back to my place and I will eat you out, okay?"

"Yeah, okay."

———

The Dishwasher was confused. He would have done that anyway. He didn't know what kind of game Toby was playing. Maybe she wasn't playing a game at all. Maybe he was saying something that he didn't know he was saying. The Dishwasher. Like he was giving mixed messages. But he didn't know how, though. Sometimes he wanted to hang out with Toby. Sometimes he didn't want to hang out with Toby. How hard was that to understand? Sure, he did hide behind a dumpster to avoid her. Sometimes. But that was because she had gone insane. And tonight, there was no insanity. Just a few friends hanging out, drinking beer and playing pool at the bar. How was that a threat to what Toby was? The Dishwasher didn't have any idea about how Toby thought. How she processed information. She was unpredictable. Always. Even her asking about the cat came out of nowhere. The Dishwasher knew that she loved cats, but so what? Why would his brother asking about classes lead to her getting pissed about being in a relationship with him? Was it always going to end this way? Was there anything he could have said that would have changed the course of the conversation? It was all so very confusing. The Dishwasher didn't really care. He was in it now. He would take Toby home and just see what happened. He would eat her out. Toby. And then they would have sex. Then they would probably eat the fried fish in his hoodie pocket. The french fries. Then they would go to sleep. The Dishwasher thought this was all very clear. At all times, these things were clear. But Toby always somehow made it difficult. Everything. Became difficult.

Toby and the Dishwasher stood under the speaker drinking their beers. There was no reason to say goodbye to anyone. Everyone already knew what was going to happen. They were glad when the Dishwasher finished his beer and started walking out the back way. Towards the alley door. This meant that Toby would be going too.

Curry looked up from the shot he was about to take. He watched the Dishwasher put his empty beer on top of the bar. Toby did the same. He looked over at Dong Smells and smiled. He said:

"Eight ball, corner pocket."

Dong Smells grimaced. He said: "Ah, man!"

The Dishwasher's brother let out a sigh. The tension in the bar deflated. Curry straightened himself and said:

"Who's next?"

16

Outside in the alley, the Dishwasher and Toby started walking to the Dishwasher's apartment. Toby realized she had forgotten her coat. They circled back around to the front of the Buckhorn. The Dishwasher went inside to get it.

Curry said, "Back so soon?"

The Dishwasher just pointed. Frowned. Curry handed him the coat. Everyone else kind of looked down. They felt bad for the Dishwasher. This was one of quite a few times when he had left the bar before he was ready because of Toby. They were powerless to stop it.

Curry was mostly oblivious. His relationships were mostly drama themselves. But that was because he would fall easily in love with someone, turn the thing into something bigger than it was, panic when it got too heavy, and then he would cheat on the girl. Which meant that at almost all times he was avoiding somebody. Either the girl he thought he was in love with, who wanted to kick him in the balls, or the girl that he had cheated on her with, who also wanted to kick him in the balls. Usually one of them would find him. He would be drunk. They would end up sleeping together again. Then the cycle would repeat. He was a horrible boyfriend. But he liked living in a college town because at any one point he would only have to wait a semester before the drama would subside. Then he could find a new group of girls that didn't know his reputation, and he could do it all over again. Pitting friend against friend. Sleeping with everyone. Pissing everyone off.

That he'd made it this far without getting seriously beaten down was surprising. The Dishwasher thought of himself as a coward. Watching Curry behave, however, made him understand what a true coward was. At least he didn't do that. But Curry was fun to hang out with. And for the most part everyone knew what kind of trouble he was. If anyone was hanging out with him, they were either looking for trouble or were willfully denying that he was trouble.

Curry was the kind of guy that women thought they could change. What they didn't understand was that he was broken. Deeply insecure. Afraid of every single emotion he had. Not only that—deep down he was very afraid of women. Something happened when his parents got a divorce that never got resolved. Like he could never forgive his father for leaving and, more important than that, he couldn't forgive his mom for letting him leave. And, ever since he became a teenager and then an adult, he was making up for those feelings of insecurity by destroying as many naive hearts as he could. Whether it was on purpose or not was unknown. He didn't really share his emotions with his male friends either. Who he considered competition.

Mostly, Curry was just tragic and small. When the Dishwasher came back to get the coat he didn't feel shame for the Dishwasher, he felt remorse for himself. Because that meant he couldn't hit on Toby and try and steal her away from the Dishwasher. Which would never happen. Toby knew what Curry was all about. She wouldn't touch him with a ten-foot, redheaded, bipolar pole. Which the Dishwasher respected about her. She knew bullshit when she saw it. But that wouldn't stop Curry from trying. He knew that she knew that he knew she knew. Which only made it more fun for him. Which made the Dishwasher's feelings toward Curry complicated. Because he knew he was broken. But he also knew he would try and sleep with his girlfriend every chance he got. Which was just the nature of things.

The Dishwasher handed Toby's coat to her when he got back outside. She put it on. Took her ponytail out. Put the scrunchie around her wrist. The Dishwasher lit a cigarette. They walked the couple blocks to the apartment. Not talking. The Dishwasher was feeling very anxious. What was he doing? Every second with Toby was two seconds. One to get in, one to get out. He tried to control his breathing. He might just have a full-on panic attack. Right there on the street. His hands were shaking. There was a little bit of blackness coming in from the corner of his right eye. He was feeling a migraine coming on. He threw the cigarette on the ground. Tried to focus. There was maybe beer inside. He could chug a couple. That would be good. He opened the door to the building. The mailbox was still hanging open. He looked inside. There was nothing new. They walked up the stairs. Into the apartment. The video game was blasting from the living room. The Dishwasher walked in. The idiot roommates were both passed out. With game controllers in their hands. The first roommate had pissed his pants. The Dishwasher looked in the fridge. There were about ten beers left. He offered one to Toby. She said:

"Reeb? No thank you! I thought you were going to eat me out?"

"Just give me a second, Toby, I am getting a headache."

"You got any food?" The Dishwasher pulled the fried fish and french fries out of his hoodie pockets. Handed them to Toby. "Can't you heat it up or nothing?" The Dishwasher scowled at her. "What is it?" She opened the foils. "Cold fish and fries. Yum." This was very sarcastic.

"Just go wait for me in the bedroom. Eat it if you want. It's all I got."

"Then you'll eat me out?"

"Take your clothes off, I will be in in a second." Toby made a face. A face like she liked being told to take her clothes off and he would be in in a second. The Dishwasher liked it too. It was an accident. He wasn't trying to be domineering. He was just trying to get rid of his headache.

Toby went into the room and shut the door. The Dishwasher stood there. Drinking the beer. He finished it. Opened a second one. Started to drink it. He wanted to turn the video game off. At least turn the volume down. But he didn't want to wake up his idiot roommates. He decided to leave it be. He chugged the second beer. His headache seemed to be going away. He was less anxious. He lit a cigarette. Opened another beer. Stood next to the sink. Ashing in the drain. He was now feeling a little drunk. He smoked fast. Finished the third beer. Ran water over the cigarette butt. Left it in the sink. Along with the empty beer cans.

He went into the bathroom. Took a piss. Flushed the toilet. Took the half toothbrush. Brushed his teeth. He needed to get a new toothbrush. Some soap. Toothpaste. He didn't have time now. Not since he was going into work early tomorrow. Maybe if he left a note for the roommates they would get some soap, at least.

When he had finished brushing his teeth, he took a good look at himself in the mirror. His face was splotchy. He looked gaunt. His teeth were nice and white, though. He pulled up his shirt. He was very thin. He thought about the fried fish and the cold french fries. Then he thought about Toby. Naked. In bed. He forgot about the note he was going to write. He turned the bathroom light off. The kitchen light off. The light in the living room had burned out weeks ago. Nobody had bothered replacing the bulb.

He went into his bedroom. He could see Toby leaning against the wall. Sitting. Her legs spread. Eating something. Either the fish or the french fries. It was too dark to tell. He peeled off his velcros with his feet. Dropped his jeans. Laid them out to dry. Took his socks off. His shirt and hoodie. His body smelled like old fryer grease and mildew. He was hard as a rock. He bent into the bed. Slid his loins along the mattress. Came to Toby's spread legs. She pushed her butt towards him. He spread her hairs with his right hand. Then used his tongue to find the slippery folds. For some reason she kept eating whatever she was eating. Then he did something that made her stop eating. Then she pushed down further. He had to back up. Now his ass was up in the air. He reached up and grabbed her breasts. Playing with her nipples. She didn't last very long. He started to stop licking. She whispered, "Again." The Dishwasher started all over again. This went on a few more times. Eventually he couldn't take it anymore. He turned her over and slipped it in. Toby didn't make any noise. Just pushed back. The Dishwasher lasted just a few pumps. Shot a rope up Toby's back. Fell down to the side of her. She fell with him. The cum squeezed between them. Between her warm back and his skinny cold front. He put his arms around her. She pushed her butt into his crotch. His dick deflated between her butt cheeks. Soon they were both asleep.

A few hours later, he had to peel himself away so he could get up to go to the bathroom. The Dishwasher went into the kitchen. Looked into the living room. The idiot roommates were still passed out. The video game was still very loud. He walked into the living room and turned the television off. As he was bending over, the first roommate sat up. His face went right into the Dishwasher's naked ass. The first roommate screamed and pulled back. This woke up the second roommate. Who said, "What the? What the hell is happening?" The first roommate said, "What the fuck, man!" The Dishwasher just laughed and ran into the bathroom. He sat down on the toilet and pissed. He could hear the idiot roommates trying to figure out what just happened.

"Man, that dude just put his butt on my face!"

"Why would he put his butt on your face?"

"I don't know, man, I guess the guy's a faggot or something!"

"Fucking faggots, man."

The Dishwasher left the bathroom. He didn't flush. The idiot roommates didn't hear him come out. He tiptoed to his bedroom. He listened for another second before he closed the door.

"What the fuck is up with that guy? I think it might be time to move out."

"I don't want no faggot putting his butt on my face when I am trying to sleep, I will tell you that!"

"That was so gross! I think I can still smell his butthole."

"Dude, I think he was trying to hump your nose with his anus."

"Fucking faggots. Why do they think they can just hump a guy's face when he's sleeping?"

"Should we call the cops?"

"I don't know, man. That seems like a lot of trouble. I need a beer."

"Get me one too."

"Get the game going. I think I was about to punish your ass."

"No way, dude. I had your ass in a sling, if I remember right."

The Dishwasher resisted the urge to go into the living room and punch each of his stupid roommates in the face. He scratched dry cum off of his stomach and got back into bed. He rearranged the blanket and lay with his back to Toby. She rolled over and hugged his back. He wished she wasn't there now. That she would get up and go home. The sex had been great, but the minutes were ticking. Another night. Another night he would have to spend extricating himself from her.

He thought about Denver. About what Dong Smells had said. That Troll and Bogart were living there. He had forgotten about them. He had only pretended to remember before, because he didn't want to admit that his plan was nothing but hot air. He started to fantasize about moving. Getting on a bus. He could be there tomorrow, if he wanted. Or maybe he could wait until Friday, get his paycheck, leave on Saturday. If he did that, he would be free of Toby at least. She was friends with Troll and Bogart, but so what? By the time she hunted him down, he could have his own place. Denver was big. Like, really big. Compared to Laramie, it was a city. Compared to anything, Denver was a city. They had buses and cabs and lots of people. Cool bands. He could get some job washing dishes at some cool café. Hang out at cool bars. Make a name for himself. Maybe sell some science equations on the street corner. He had this new idea about gravity that would blow people's minds. It was hard to explain, but it involved little wires that made up the universe. That things traveling around the sun would get ahold of the wires and be sucked into the sun. If only he could find a way to express these thoughts. He would need to go to the bookstore or something. The library. Get some math books. It wouldn't be so hard. Then they would see. Everyone would see how smart he was. He didn't need to be washing dishes in Laramie anymore. He could just go out into the world and make a new science. It would be a little uphill at first, but before long he would be on the radio. The hosts would have all sorts of good questions for him. They would be like:

"This is such radical science thought, how on earth did you think of it?"

"Well, you know, I do a lot of washing. The dishes just keep coming in. There is no way to stop them. And I got this idea thinking about the girls bringing me the plates. You know? They just keep coming. Whenever one plate comes, another is right behind it. You see what I mean?"

"I do! How interesting. And this led you to what you are thinking?"

"Yeah, I mean, there is no end in sight. You get a night like a Friday night, or a Saturday. And nobody is thinking about nothing, and there I am just slinging the trays. One gravity thing on top of another gravity thing. And then, just like that, they all come out on the other side. The only real problem is how does it get removed? I mean, how does the universe drain itself? Like, are the dishes giving the sun the food or whatever? Is the food itself the gravity particles?"

"You can't be serious. That is so revolutionary!"

"Tell me about it! You ever watch the water just drain down a sink? Like that. That is what the gravity does. I mean, I am sorry for being so science-minded, but it is simple. The gravity just drains down into the black holes or whatever."

This fantastic radio interview went on for a while. The Dishwasher eventually fell back asleep, very full of himself. He spent the night asleep, trying to get away from Toby.

In the morning, he was wadded up at the foot of the bed. Toby was turned over on her side. Her arms splayed out. When the

Dishwasher opened his eyes, he was face to face with her naked ass. Her pink butthole just inches from his face. He reached up and scratched it. Toby screamed and pulled up to a sitting position. The blanket covering her breasts. Her arms in front of the blanket. She scowled at the Dishwasher. He was still in a fetal position at the bottom of the bed. But now his arm was propping up his head. He smiled. Toby relaxed. Shifted her legs out. Presented her naked vagina. The red hairs glistening in the dark, fall, early morning light. The Dishwasher grabbed her by the butt and pulled her towards his face. She came. Then the Dishwasher fucked her missionary. Her large boobs pointing towards the walls. She made a point of looking him directly in the eyes as he fucked her. He pulled out and came on her bush. He fell to the side. She wiped the cum off of her bush with the blanket. She got up and got dressed. He asked her what time it was. She looked at her watch. Toby wore a watch. She almost never had a reason to be anywhere on time, yet she wore a watch. She said:

"It's ten. I'm getting out of here."

"Leaving so soon?"

"What the fuck does that mean?"

"It doesn't mean anything."

"You want me to stick around? We can finish your cold-ass fries for breakfast."

"What the fuck did I do?"

"Oh, I don't know, maybe your snarky remarks, dickhole."

"But you said you were leaving?"

"I didn't say shit."

"You said you were getting out of here."

"You'd love that, wouldn't you?"

"What the hell are you talking about?"

"I said I was going to use the bathroom."

"No you didn't! You said you were leaving."

"I just can't win with you, Disher. You want me to come over just to fuck and then you just kick me out like yesterday's news."

"I didn't say anything! I just thought you said you were leaving!"

"I didn't say shit. And now that you want me to leave, maybe I will just stick around. Ever think of that?"

"Toby! You are out of your mind!"

"I'm out of my mind? You think you can just fuck me and that will be that? You got another thing coming, butthole!"

"I never said anything like that. I just was giving you shit is all."

"If that is how you are going to treat me, I am leaving!"

"Don't let the door hit you on the ass."

"Fuck you, Disher! You're a piece of shit!"

Toby gathered all her things and stormed out. The Dishwasher lay there confused. He played the conversation out in his mind. He was certain all he'd said was he was confused she was leaving so soon. But who knows? Maybe she had said she was going to use the bathroom and he had heard her wrong? Either way, he was glad she was gone. That conversation sucked. He was just glad she hadn't thrown something at him, like last time.

The Dishwasher looked around for the food he had brought home last night. Toby had eaten almost all of it. He found a couple fries on the carpet. He wiped them off. Put them in his mouth. Stared at the ceiling. He had a few more hours of sleep. He wanted them. But the sleep wouldn't come. He was now too anxious. The idea of doing the prep stuff today was heavy on his heart. He wasn't ready for any new responsibilities. He felt broken because of Toby. He just needed to get those 1,000 dollars and get the hell out of town. He kept adjusting the money. Thinking about Troll and Bogart. Maybe they would let him live with them until he got a job? Then he could save some money. There. In Denver. Maybe they wouldn't charge him rent. He could live on their couch or something? Maybe they had a closet they weren't using? He could just live there. Bring his blanket. A pillow. The garbage bag of clothes. He wouldn't need much else. They would have pots and stuff. Plus, maybe they would want a third roommate. He could pay just a little bit. Like, fifty dollars or something. That would be a good amount of money to live in their closet. Right? Just for a month. While he got his feet on the ground. Maybe they worked at a nice restaurant that needed dishwashers? The Dishwasher tried to remember what he had heard about what those guys were doing there. In Denver. He couldn't recall anyone mentioning their jobs. Maybe he should call them? Write a letter or something? Maybe his brother knew? There was a short time that Bogart lived with them, over in the Tech part of town. Maybe they were in contact still? Bogart and the Dishwasher got along pretty well. She was from the same town as the Dishwasher and his brother. Troll too. They wouldn't let a fellow hometown guy struggle. Right? There was no way. He just needed to get them on the horn. Tell them what was up. They knew all about Toby and her ways. They would understand. Or at least he thought they would. The Dishwasher.

The Dishwasher lay in bed for a while. Thinking about his future. He thought he would call his brother later and get Troll and Bogart's number. Then the Dishwasher would call them. Maybe tomorrow. Or Saturday. When he had money. He would be able to make some promises. Like, with rent or whatever. Maybe they would say, "Come on down! As soon as possible! We need a third roommate!" And then the Dishwasher could hop the bus and get the hell out of town. Toby could go fuck herself. Shack up with Curry for all he cared. Then she would be his problem, not his. Then in a couple months Curry would call the Dishwasher up and say, "Dude! You got to come get Toby! She is driving me crazy!" And the Dishwasher would just laugh all the way to the bank. "Too bad, so sad, sucker!" He would hang up the phone and feel like a million bucks. The Dishwasher.

For now, however, the Dishwasher had some time to kill before going into work. He was starting a new job. He would need to be aware. He sighed and started to get dressed. Maybe he would go get a coffee. Maybe the gas station had soap to buy. He needed a shower. They might have toothbrushes as well. He had never thought of that. It would save him a huge walk across town. The

Dishwasher stopped thinking about his future. He focused on his present. Suddenly things looked very bleak again.

○

The Dishwasher went out onto the street. It was a nice day. Cool, but not cold. He would need to put his long johns on soon. His jeans were still damp. He zipped his hoodie shut. He walked down the street to the overpass. Walked under it. Turned right. The gas station was right there. He went inside. He looked around. Found a bar of soap. There were some other things that he needed. A toothbrush. Toothpaste. The prices were wrong. He couldn't bring himself to buy them. The soap, though. He was willing to spend the extra cash for it. He really needed a good shower.

He took the bar of soap to the coffee station. Made himself a large cup of coffee. Poured a bunch of sugar and nondairy creamer in it. Stirred it with a thin red straw. Licked the straw. Threw it in the trash. Put a plastic lid on the coffee. Took the coffee and the bar of soap to the counter. Paid for them both. Put the bar of soap in his hoodie pocket. Took a drink of the coffee. Said, "Thanks" to the cashier. Walked back outside.

A big truck was pulling in as he started walking away. He got about as far as the corner of the gas station before the guy in the truck yelled, "Leaving so soon, faggot?!" The Dishwasher's shoulders fell. He almost turned around and confronted the asshole. Thinking he would throw his hot coffee at him and then punch his stupid face. But he didn't. The Dishwasher just scooted away. He was a coward in the end. There was nothing to be done about it. He would just have to live with that shame.

The Dishwasher got to the underpass. He stood there for a second. Drinking the coffee. Listening to the cars drive by. Overhead. He drank the coffee until it was gone. He dropped the cup on the ground. Next to all the other trash that had been left there. He felt bad about it, but what could he do? They should have a trash can there, or something. He had a feeling in his guts. The coffee doing its work. He rushed home to deal with it.

When he got back to the apartment, he ran into the bathroom. Relieved himself. Started the shower. Flushed the toilet. Went into his room. Took his clothes off. His velcros. Took his towel. Wrapped it around his waist. Remembered the bar of soap. Got it from the pocket of his hoodie. Took it into the bathroom. The bathroom was filled with steam. He took the towel off. Hung it on top of the dirty shirt that smelled like death. Adjusted the water. Took the bar of soap out of the cardboard box. The soap was green. The box was green. He washed his body. His butthole. His face. His hair. When he was done, he rinsed himself off. He put the bar of soap back in the cardboard box. He rinsed his fingers. Turned the shower off. Got out. Dried himself down. Put the towel around his waist again. Took the bar of soap back to his room. Hid it under his mattress. He thought about this. There was nothing he could do. His idiot roommates would find it, or not. He didn't know if they even cared to shower. But what could he do?

He got dressed. Finding clean socks in the garbage bag of clean clothes. A fresh T-shirt. His new plan of just getting a fresh button-up work shirt was working out just fine. He put his clean socks on. His mildewed jeans. Buttoning them up. Feeling grossed out by them all over again. They were like a sloth's fur at this point. Never changing. Just getting worse by the day. He sighed about it. They stank. He was astonished that Toby put up with his smells. But then again, Toby had some smells of her own. Which the Dishwasher gladly put up with. He thought about them. Found himself on the bed.

A couple seconds later, he was done. He had thought about tickling Toby's butthole. One day he would put it in there. He was surprised he hadn't done it yet. She seemed into the idea. He just wasn't sure what kinds of things would transpire. He was afraid of *instances*. Things he wouldn't be able to get out of his mind. In the end, it was the Dishwasher's squeamishness that had prevented it from happening. However, he did like to think about the idea. Sometimes he licked Toby's butthole just for fun. But that was as far as it ever got. One day, though. But then, that was as far as the thought ever got. Yet, he still thought about it.

The Dishwasher wiped himself clean with a dirty sock. He finished getting dressed. He looked at his long johns. Soon. He would need to put them on soon. Just not today. Today was not the day to be adding heat down below. He had no idea what kinds of things would be waiting for him at work. He would have to learn new things. He would need to pay attention. He was already anxious about it. He was starting to regret drinking the coffee. The dark spots were showing up in the corners of his eyes. He would be lucky if he made it through the night without getting a migraine.

He was super anxious because of Toby. She really did a number on him. Why wouldn't she just let him go? He was done. They were done. The relationship was going nowhere. Maybe he should insist that she spend some time with Curry? Like they should go on a nature hike or something. Let him do his magic. The same magic that had worked on so many girls before?

The Dishwasher had already tried to convince her that she was a lesbian. That didn't go very well. She just ended up crying and crying and following him all the way across town in her car. Like, literally. Driving next to him for two miles as she bawled out the window. Screaming, "You have no idea how much I love you!" Followed by the Dishwasher screaming back, "Just leave me alone! I am trying to get to work!" And then, when he finally got to the campus, he sprinted all the way to the taco place. He was sweaty and out of breath. But there she was. Waiting in the drive-through line. Tears rolling down her face. He didn't know what to do, so he just went inside. He heard her crying through the speakers, "I'll take a number three with a diet pop." And then, when she got to the window, he could hear her pleading, "Just make him come to the window. Please!" The manager had to go over and say, "Toby, you just have to leave. You are holding up traffic." The sound of her yelling "Please!" still sent shivers up the Dishwasher's spine. She only left because she had no choice. The Dishwasher spent the entire day expecting her to come into the place and jump over the counter, just to talk to him. She didn't. And later that night he ended up taking her back. Mostly because he had no choice. She was waiting at the house. On the front steps. She had been there all day. The two tacos and olés, still in the bag. The diet pop, undrank. She was shaking. The Dishwasher couldn't say no. He took her inside. She cried herself to sleep. And then the next morning they fucked each other's brains out. Causing the Dishwasher's brother and brother's girlfriend nothing but embarrassed grief.

After that, the Dishwasher was kind of dulled. There was no end in sight. He knew that he either had to leave town, or he would have to marry Toby. Have kids and be done with his life. There was no other option. She was done taking no for an answer. Then again, maybe Curry could cure her of this problem? Anything was possible. The Dishwasher would just need to get Toby to let her bullshit meter down. Maybe the Dishwasher could give Curry some pointers? The problem, though, was that Curry didn't actually like Toby. He just liked the idea of taking Toby away from the Dishwasher. Which was a problem that couldn't be solved. The Dishwasher couldn't undo Curry's trauma. In the end, this was just a bad idea. The Dishwasher let it go.

17

The Dishwasher didn't know what to do with himself. He now had hours to kill. He was hungry but he didn't know what to do about it. He could get some 25-cent hamburgers. However, the jerk that ran the place probably wouldn't be serving him for a while. Which was too bad. Those burgers were cheap. He could go get some tacos. Up by the university. That was an option. He might run into Toby, though. Which was whatever at this point. He was so far in now, there was no way he was getting out anytime soon. He would have to leave town. That was the only option. That, or she met someone new. Which was very unlikely. The third option was the diner by the interstate. They had coffee, and biscuits and gravy. Cheap biscuits and gravy. It was early enough that they might still be serving breakfast. That is, if he left this very moment. He panicked. There was something he felt like he was forgetting. He brushed the thought off and ran out the door.

The Dishwasher took back streets for as long as he could. Avoiding the main road, and the large trucks that were surely cruising around looking for faggots to harass. He popped up near the laundry. Kept his head down as he walked the last few blocks. Bought a newspaper from the machine outside the diner. Went in. Stood there until a waitress showed up. She said, "Table for one?" The Dishwasher nodded. He wished that someone was with him. His brother or Dong Smells. Even the first roommate's brother would be okay. But there was no time to lure anyone in. The waitress led him to the back. Which was where all the oldsters hung out. It was late in the morning, though. There wasn't really anyone there.

He sat down. Turned a coffee cup over. The waitress handed him a menu and filled his cup with coffee. He said, "You still got biscuits and gravy?" The waitress said, "Let me check." She walked away. The Dishwasher, being the pervert that he was, checked out her buns. She was probably twice his age. That didn't matter. There was an indent from her underwear. A thing that if Toby was there she would call a VPL. Visible Panty Line. And she would point it out. Loudly. Which would have embarrassed the Dishwasher. Profoundly. But Toby wasn't there. Her voice still rang out in the Dishwasher's head, though. He found himself annoyed with her all over again. He poured some creamer into his coffee. Stirred it with a spoon. Took a drink. Looked at the paper. There was nothing of interest on the cover. Just sports and local politics. Something about how the university needed physics majors. He had started to read that article when the waitress came back. She said:

"You're in luck! They have one order left."

"Great. I'll take it."

"Anything else? Eggs, sausage, pancakes?"

"Nah, just the biscuits and gravy, thanks."

The waitress seemed saddened by him only ordering biscuits and gravy. What could he do? Eggs would maybe be alright, but sausage or pancakes? That was just too much. He decided he would leave a good tip in order to make up for it. Like two dollars. That would make things better.

He watched her buns as she walked away. He just couldn't help himself. She was kind of attractive to him. The Dishwasher. Not that he would ever do anything about it. Plus, she was probably married. Plus, she most likely wouldn't want to have anything to do with a guy like him. The Dishwasher. He imagined her life as being mostly surrounded by truckers and the oldsters. She probably went to bed at nine at night. Got up when it was still dark, to come to this job. As much as she didn't want to have anything to do with him, he equally didn't want to have anything to do with her. That didn't prevent him from checking out her

VPL, though. In fact, if he knew himself, which he kind of did. The Dishwasher. He would think about this later before he went to work. And because he was a pervert, he would keep a photograph in his memory specifically for this exact reason. He felt ashamed of himself. Went back to reading about how the university needed physics majors.

The Dishwasher hadn't got very far into the article before the waitress came back. He moved the newspaper to the side. She placed the full plate of biscuits and gravy on the table. Asked him if he needed anything else. He said hot sauce. She had a bottle in her waitress pouch. Put it on the table. Topped his coffee off. Walked away. He didn't check out her buns this time. Instead, he sprinkled salt and pepper on the biscuits and gravy. Took the lid off the hot sauce. Spurted hot sauce all around. Grabbed his fork and started eating. He tried to keep reading the article about the physics majors but it was too boring. The gist of it, though, was that the university was trying to get physics majors because they didn't have enough and the university was going to lose science funding, so they were offering scholarships for undergraduates if they would become physics majors.

The Dishwasher thought about this. Maybe he could become a scientist? That was a pretty good idea. He could maybe figure out how to prove his theory about gravity and how it relates to doing dishes. But that would mean he would need to learn some math. Get his GED. He was a high-school dropout. He had left school on his seventeenth birthday. Which was in early fall. So he basically had a sophomore-year education. That meant a lot of catching up would need to happen. The last math class he took was Math 2. Which ended with geometric proofs. Of which he still had no idea what they were. His math teacher was the football coach. As far as he could tell, Mr. Allred didn't know what they were either. He was not a good teacher. Not only that, but the Dishwasher had failed the class because of it. He was pretty certain everyone else would have failed as well, apart from the pretty girls. It was an open secret that if you flirted with Mr.

Allred he would give you a good grade. That, or if you played on the football team. Or were on varsity in any other sport. The Dishwasher was neither a good-looking girl nor a varsity goon. He hated football with all of his passion. Pretty much all of the team sports. He enjoyed swimming. But that didn't matter. He was on the swim team his freshman year. It hadn't ended well.

The Dishwasher had to force himself to stop thinking about high school. It was too upsetting. It was a long time ago. Not that long ago. But long enough that he didn't have to think about it if he didn't want to. They couldn't touch him here. He was his own man now. With a job and a future of his own. If only he could get 1,000 bucks, he could get out of town. Get out of Wyoming. Make a name for himself. Get away from Toby. That was all he needed to do. Then his life would finally come together. He didn't need to go to college. To become a scientist. He could do that in his spare time. Read some books. Teach himself some math. Then he could prove his theories. That would show them. Then the university would come begging him to become a student. He wouldn't even need a GED. He could solve the GED in his sleep. High school was nothing to him. Just training wheels for the real world. The Dishwasher was already living in the real world. In fact, he had been living in the real world for years at this point. All of his life, as far as he was concerned. He scoffed at the idea of going to college. Those elite morons don't know shit. Was his exact thought.

He stopped reading the physics article and turned the pages of the newspaper to the comics section. Read a couple. They were stupid. He spent the last few bites of his biscuits and gravy doing the word jumble. He solved all the words and the riddle without writing anything down. This made him feel better about himself. He scraped the last of the gravy with his fork. Licked it. Finished his coffee. Took his wallet out. Found two dollars. Put it on the table. Stood up. Left the paper behind. Walked to the front. The waitress rang up his order. He paid. Said, "Thanks." She smiled.

Her smile was forced. He forced a smile himself. He walked out of the diner.

———

The walk back was the same as the walk there. Except this time there was a bubbling coming from his guts. He remembered why he didn't eat there very often. This happened every time. He scooted quickly back to the apartment. Focused on not having an accident. He was sweating by the time he got to the front door. He fumbled with his key. Nearly lost the narrative. Scooted up the stairs. Got into the apartment. Got to the bathroom just in time. He let out an audible yelp when he sat down. His body jerked and squeezed and twisted. His eyes were wide open. The smell was quick and abusive. Never again. He thought to himself.

But he had thought that before. He had even said that before. Specifically the last time. When he had gone to that same diner with his brother and Dong Smells, after a very late night of drinking at the Buckhorn. That time he hadn't even made it out of the diner before the food kicked in. When he got back to the table he said, "Never again." Both his brother and Dong Smells laughed at him. But the look in Dong Smells' eyes said he wasn't really laughing, because he excused himself when the Dishwasher sat down. Then the Dishwasher and his brother laughed about Dong Smells until the same thing happened with the Dishwasher's brother. After that they all said, "Never again." But it wasn't true. It would never be true. Not as long as the diner was there and was serving cheap breakfast. There was just no way around it. Then again, the joke was always that someone would ask if you wanted to go rent some breakfast from the diner. The results were not a secret. But when you added a hangover to the mix. That was when things got out of control. Or OOC, as Toby would say. Her words ringing in the Dishwasher's ears yet again. He couldn't get away from her. She was the earworm of girlfriends.

But that was the thing. Toby would never eat at that diner. The few times she went there, she only ordered tea. She knew a nasty diner when she saw one. And more power to her, because she never got sick from eating there. The Dishwasher had a theory about this. It all stemmed from her working at a restaurant when she was in high school, as a waitress. There was one day when she served someone a plate of something, something with rice. And the customer had found a Band-Aid in the rice. That place got shut down not long afterwards. For good reason, it sounded like. However, the food they served was "ethnic." And the Dishwasher was pretty sure Toby didn't tell anyone about the Band-Aid incident, aside from the Dishwasher. Of course, the patron knew about it. And the owners. But still, on one hand there was a Band-Aid in the rice, on the other hand, Wyoming was racist. The real truth probably landed somewhere in between. Which only really meant that Toby knew better than to eat at the diner. She was the only one, though. Everyone else just assumed that getting the shits was a fact of life. Whether the food was "ethnic" or not.

The Dishwasher spent a good deal of time cleaning up. He was feeling very glad that the idiot roommates had bought all that toilet paper. Otherwise he would have had to take a second shower to make things right again. As it was, he might do that anyway. When he stood up, he had to move lightly. There was a good possibility he wasn't finished with his business. He rinsed his hands off in the sink and walked out of the bathroom.

The second roommate was standing in the kitchen wearing boxer shorts. He looked insanely hungover. His eyes were swollen. He looked like he might puke. The Dishwasher looked down. The second roommate was the one with the large thing, it turned out. It was pressing out of his boxers. This embarrassed the Dishwasher. He said:

"I wouldn't go in there."

"Dude, you don't even know."

The second roommate screamed when he went into the bathroom. This was followed by puking noises. Then toilet flushings. Then more puking noises. The Dishwasher chuckled to himself. But then he had to squeeze his butt cheeks closed. He almost had an accident.

He stood there waiting. Not knowing how long it would be. He started to sweat. The puking stopped. There was more toilet flushing. Then the sound of things coming out the other end. The Dishwasher couldn't stand it. The idea of going into the bathroom after that sort of nonsense was too much to handle. He went into his bedroom. Clamping his cheeks closed. He would just lay in bed for a while. Wait for things to clear out. He left the door open so he could hear what was happening. When the second roommate came out, he yelled:

"My god! What the hell did you eat?!" The Dishwasher yelled back:

"I told you not to go in there!"

The Dishwasher lay in bed. Keeping his buns tight. Trying not to think of anything. The first roommate came into the kitchen. The Dishwasher could hear him take a deep breath in and then hold it. He must have gone into the bathroom because the door slammed. The Dishwasher heard some screaming. Then what sounded like puking. Followed by a long silence. Which probably meant that things were coming out the other end. The first roommate was probably as hungover as the second roommate. Eventually, the first roommate came out. He yelled:

"Dude! You need to see a doctor!" The Dishwasher yelled:

"That wasn't just me, man!"

The Dishwasher waited as long as he could. He thought things had calmed down. He let his butt cheeks relax a little. That lasted just a second. He was wrong. He didn't know what to do. He really didn't want to go into the bathroom yet. It became apparent that he had no choice, though.

He managed to stand up and scoot his way from his bedroom through the kitchen and into the bathroom. The smell was OOC. Out of control. Toby's phrase ringing in his brain. The Dishwasher dry heaved. He wasn't hungover so he didn't pass the threshold. But he came close. If he was going to puke he would just puke in the tub, the Dishwasher decided. He sat down. He squirted and exploded.

After that was just gas. Lots and lots of gas. He didn't throw up, but his ass hurt from all the wiping. He scooted over to the sink. Rinsed his hands. Pulled his jeans up. Stood there waiting. Just in case.

When it was clear there was nothing left, he went back to his room. He got back in bed. Leaving all of his clothes on. His velcros. His hoodie. He figured he would need to shower again. Before work. Otherwise his ass would get so chapped that he wouldn't be able to sit after his shift. This was a fact he had learned from experience.

For now, though, he would just have to give his body some time to recover. Plus, the smell in the bathroom was just too much. There was no way he was going back in there unless he had to. And as far as he could tell, he didn't have to. The Dishwasher.

———

The Dishwasher fell asleep while waiting for the bathroom to air out. When he woke up, he was startled. He panicked. Stood up and hurried into the idiot roommates' room. They were both passed out. The second roommate had an erection. The thing was massive. This took the Dishwasher by surprise. He forced himself to focus. He shook the first roommate awake. The first roommate was annoyed. He said:
"What the fuck, man?"
"What time is it?"
"I don't fucking know, get a watch."
"Oh, you're no help."
"Suck it, loser. You owe us three beers."
"What?"
"I saw, you drank three beers. You owe us."
"My God, what?"
"You heard me."
"Yeah, okay."
The Dishwasher went to the television. Maybe he could find

out what time it was on some channel. It took him a minute to figure out how to switch the television from the video game. He cursed the idiot roommates. He did manage to get the thing working. The television. He pushed the channel button up and up and up. There were only talk shows on. He kept pushing. He found a channel that told people about the weather. As well as local stuff. Like lunches at schools. Businesses in the area. That channel told him it was 2:45 p.m. He was late. He didn't have time to take a shower. He rushed to the bathroom and brushed his teeth with the half toothbrush. Spat into the sink. Ran some water. Splashed it on his face. On his way out the door, he heard the first roommate yell:

"Hey! Turn off the TV!"

"Suck one!"

The Dishwasher ran down the stairs. Looked in the mailbox on his way out the door. There was nothing new. Ran down the street. Took a right. Ran down the alley. Got to the back of the Altitude. Went through the screen door. Took his hoodie off. His T-shirt. Found a white button-up shirt that fit. Put it on. Put his wallet and smokes in his hoodie pocket. Put an apron on. A hairnet. A paper hat. Then he stood there. Confused. Did he need to clock in? Or should he start a new time card? He thought about it for a second. Took out a new time card. Wrote:

Disher/Prep

Clocked in. That would cover it. Even if he didn't get paid the better rate for the prep work, at least he would get paid. He walked into the prep room. Looking around. There was nobody there. The place had a different feel than normal. Because it was early. The dish room was silent. The main line seemed calm. The Dishwasher walked into the kitchen. Ronito was busy getting the dinner stuff ready. Roger was there too. He looked angry. His hat was on backward. Which usually meant he was having a bad day. He looked up from the onions he was slicing. He sighed. Ronito said hello. The Dishwasher stood there like an idiot. He was about to go talk to Lisa when Roger said:

"Okay, I guess this is my job now."

He pushed past the Dishwasher. Walked into the prep room. The Dishwasher just stood there. Ronito looked at him. Then nodded with his head. Meaning, *go in there.*

The Dishwasher walked into the prep room. Roger was laying out half pans. He went to one of the fridges. He said:

"Okay. Look. You take the bacon and do *this.* Then you put it in the ovens and cook it for fifteen minutes. Can you do that?"

"I think I can."

"Okay, then do it."

"Until it's done?"

"Do all the bacon."

The Dishwasher put the first pan of bacon into the oven. He watched it for a while. Then he remembered he was supposed to time it. He looked at the clock. It was almost 3:15 p.m. He made a note. The bacon would be done at 3:30 p.m. He stood there for a second. Then he started to put bacon on a second pan. This was hard. The bacon stuck to itself. He couldn't get it looking as good as Roger had got it looking. He spent the next fifteen minutes getting it just right. When the clock said 3:30 p.m., he took the cooked bacon out. He didn't know where the oven mitts were, so he tried to use a wet towel. This burned his fingers. He screamed. Roger came in. Yelled at him:

"What the fuck are you doing?!"

"I am trying to get the bacon out!"

"You can't use that, you'll just burn yourself."

"I know! I did!"

"What the hell? You don't have the other pans in?"

"What do you mean?"

"You cook all the bacon at the same time! You can't just do it one at a time!"

"You didn't tell me that!"

"The fuck! I have to do this all myself? You're useless!"

"I don't know, what do you mean?"

"Goddamn it! Fucking hell. Let me show you!"

The Dishwasher just stood there as Roger cooked all the bacon. The Dishwasher didn't know what to do to help. He tried to take the pans to the dish room but Roger yelled at him:

"Dude! You have to drain those first! Let me show you."

Roger drained the bacon grease into a bucket. He got pissed and threw the pans at the Dishwasher. He said:

"Take those to the dish room. Come back and I'll show you how to store the things."

When the Dishwasher came back, Roger had already stored the bacon. He looked pissed off. The Dishwasher adjusted his paper hat. Roger sighed. He said:

"Maybe you can cut these tomatoes?" Roger went to the walk-in cooler and brought back a box of tomatoes. He said:

"Get the slicer and bring it over here." The Dishwasher looked around. He had no idea what Roger was talking about. Everything looked like a slicer. He knew all of the parts of everything in the prep room. He just didn't know how they went together. The Dishwasher brought over what he thought was the slicer. It was not the slicer. Roger screamed at him:

"Dude! Are you dumb, or what? You can't slice tomatoes on that. You wanna lose a finger?"

"I mean, I don't."

"Just look!"

Roger got the slicer and tried to show the Dishwasher how it worked. He even sliced a tomato to prove it. The Dishwasher was confused. He knew that the tomatoes needed to be washed first, but Roger hadn't washed the tomato he sliced. Roger said:

"See how it goes?"

"Should I wash them first?"

"Of course! Are you an idiot, or what?"

"I mean."

"You know what, just slice these tomatoes and then come get me, I can't deal with this shit right now."

"Okay."

The Dishwasher spent a good half hour washing the tomatoes.

He didn't know what to do with the clean ones, so he just left them in the sink. When he was done cleaning them, he started to cut them in the slicer. The stems kept getting caught in the blade. Causing the thing to make this whirring sound. Eventually Roger came back to the prep room and yelled:

"What the fuck, man! You have to remove the stems!"

"I didn't know!"

"And you can't just leave the tomatoes in the sink like that! They need to drain. What the fuck? You're making a huge mess! Give me that!"

Roger tore a tomato out of the Dishwasher's hand. The Dishwasher stood there watching Roger slice tomatoes. At this point, Roger just stopped talking to the Dishwasher. Who was really confused. Did he need to help out somehow? Should he be washing something else? The Dishwasher was pretty sure he wasn't an idiot, but suddenly he was thinking that he was. There was nothing for him to do but watch. Eventually Lisa came into the prep room and asked how it was going. The Dishwasher said:

"I don't know, pretty good, I guess." Roger said:

"This dude is useless, get him out of my face." The Dishwasher looked at Lisa. Lisa frowned. She said:

"Disher, just go to the dish room. We'll figure this out." The Dishwasher had a moment of sadness. It didn't last very long, though. He was not in any way meant to do this work. He was worse than Norman. He felt bad for aggravating Roger about it, though. But whatever. Roger was a bully. The Dishwasher had never really liked him. Part of him was glad, thinking that Roger would have to do two jobs. And the Dishwasher would only have to do one. He wondered if he should clock in again on his regular time card. The Dishwasher went back and clocked in as his usual self, just in case. The two hours he had spent being a prep guy would just have to be a loss. It was either that, or put some actual effort into the thing. Which, at the moment, didn't seem like such a good thing to do. Those two hours had sucked. What did he care about bacon or tomatoes? He was more concerned about those half pans with bacon leavings that were sitting unsoaked.

He walked into the dish room feeling suddenly refreshed. This was his place of business. Roger could suck it. They could get a prep guy pretty quick. The pay was good. Roger would just have to do that shit until Dong Smells showed up. Then he could be forced to cut stuff up in the back instead of frying things all night. Dong Smells wouldn't care. He would get paid all the same. Not only that, but how many bacons and tomatoes did they need? It seemed, to the Dishwasher, like the line cooks did all the work anyway. The prep guy just kind of smoked pot and grumbled all the time. But that was maybe just Norman. Which was maybe why he got fired. Not because he wrestled the Dishwasher, and gave him a black eye, but because he was just bad at his job? Which maybe explained why Roger was so annoyed with the Dishwasher. Because he just wanted somebody good to do that job. And the Dishwasher was clearly not that person. Either way, Roger was a dick and the Dishwasher was not the guy for the job.

He soaked the half pans like normal. Got the sinks ready, like normal. Ran the silverware and the glasses. Made sure the dish room was ready for the night. Mostly he was ahead of schedule. He thought, maybe he should show up early from now on. It would save him some work. He would have to clear that with Lisa, though. And maybe tonight was not the night to bring it up. Considering how horribly the prep thing had gone.

18

The late afternoon led into the evening. Things started to pick up. The Dishwasher was going along. Minding his own business. Staying on top of things. He was feeling pretty good about failing the prep job. The more he thought about it, the more he realized he had no desire for more responsibility. He was going to make his 1,000 bucks and hit the skids. That was a certainty now. All he had to do was get the money made. Make some arrangements. Get on a bus and get the hell out of town. He just needed to call Troll and Bogart. See if they were down. The thought was becoming exciting. Almost dreadful. The Dishwasher was scared about moving to the big city. He had never even been to Denver. Aside from going to Montana a few times, he hadn't even been out of the state of Wyoming.

He had to do something, though. Toby was becoming too much. His idiot roommates were already too much. Laramie was starting to stagnate. It was kind of exciting that school was starting again, but that was meaningless and would be less exciting as time went by. It had been some time since he had met anyone new. That he liked. Or wanted to get to know. He barely saw his brother. And when he did, it was like last night. Toby screwing everything up. The Dishwasher was to blame for that, though. He'd invited her. He couldn't pretend he hadn't.

Once again, he'd let his loins do the thinking for him. This shamed him. He was starting to have this thought about shame. That shame was more hostile than guilt. That you can live with guilt because you could always apologize if you had to. Shame on the other hand. Shame was forever. You couldn't apologize for being ashamed. There was no taking that back. And the way that he behaved when Toby was around was starting to add up. He was afraid that he would have to be ashamed about his behavior for the rest of his life.

This filled him with a gusher of anxiety. There was no way around it. If only he could just start over? Forget the past. Move forward. Hit reset on the idiotic life he had led up until now. Like maybe not get into a wrestling match with Norman in the putrid grease in the alley. That would be nice. The Dishwasher wondered if it would ever come to a head. The thing between him and Norman. Should he apologize? He hadn't done anything except state the obvious, but still, would Norman accept that apology? Or would he just smack the Dishwasher in the face? Keep the beef going? This thought really bummed the Dishwasher out. He didn't like the idea of having enemies. Not that Norman was an enemy. He just wasn't a friend. Not anymore. If he'd ever been one.

As the Dishwasher was minding his own business. Getting his work done. Lisa came into the dish room. She took a look at the Dishwasher and said:

"What are you still doing here?"

"Roger said I sucked."

"Did you suck?"

"I don't know, ask Roger."

"What the hell is wrong with everyone! I'm about to tear my hair out!"

"I don't know what to say. It didn't work out."

"But I got that Mike guy coming in to wash dishes."

"Well, maybe he's a good prepper?"

"But then he would be making more money than you. How do you feel about that?"

"You can always just give me a raise?"

"You know I can't do that. Ask Laura."

"I'll get right on that. When is she in—6:00 to 6:05 a.m. Sunday morning?"

"You could call her."

"What the—Ha! I hope you are joking."

"No, just give her a call. I will give you her number."

"And say what? Hi, it's the dishwasher from your restaurant. Can you give me a raise please? I do good work."

"You could try."

"I could also put a spatula up my butt. I would probably get the same results."

"Don't be gross."

"Well, that is ridiculous. I believe you, Lisa. I mean, I trust you, but things just don't work that way. I would appreciate it if you just lied to me."

"I am dead serious. You never know. Laura is a reasonable person. You have met her before. I'm sure she knows how good you work."

"I know that she comes in once a week to collect money and to make sure we are making a profit. Aside from that, I don't know shit about this thing."

"Yeah, well. I am sorry. What should we do about Mike?"

"I appreciate you asking me. Actually. But I don't know. I would ask Roger. I don't think he wants to talk to me."

"Well, if he doesn't want to train him, do you mind if he shadows you?"

"We can always use more dishwashers."

"That doesn't answer my question. I don't want any hullabaloo from your shit attitude."

"My attitude is top notch, Lisa!"

"Yeah. I'll write that on my tombstone."

"Yeah, I mean, I am okay training the guy. I just am going to do it my way, though. Take it or leave it."

"Yeah, sure. Why am I surrounded by children?"

"Hey, you do the hiring."

"Yeah, I am very aware." The Dishwasher made a face. Lisa laughed. "Need anything from the bar?"

"I'll take a pop when you get a chance."

"Sure thing. Mike should be here in a few. I'll go talk to Roger. Speaking of children."

"Don't let him hear you say that."

"Right?"

Lisa walked out of the dish room. Yelled, "Hey, Roger!" She walked into the prep room. The Dishwasher checked out her buns. The tight black nylon pants. Her skinny ass cheeks. He liked Lisa. He thought that maybe in a different world they could be girlfriend/boyfriend. Not this one, though. The Dishwasher was too much of a loser and Lisa had too much promise. Even if she couldn't hire decent people for the restaurant she mostly managed. Even though she wasn't the manager. She would figure it out at some point. Probably move on to a better job that paid better money. For now she would just get through the next little while, getting by on her easy way with people.

There was no future at the Altitude. Not for her or for anyone. The place was just a jumping-off point for the people working there. A place for Laura to rake money in. Doing absolutely nothing. Just being the owner. Getting everyone else to do her work for her. And, so what? That was the nature of business. You started with money. Got a business going. Got other people to run it for you. Then just let the money flow in. Easy as pie. The idea that hard work had anything to do with it was a joke. Or that you even had to have a good business idea. Or plan. The food at the Altitude was average at best. Junk mostly. It was mostly just burgers and fries and bottles of wine. As long as the place was open during business hours, the place would make money. As long as they had enough employees doing the work, the place would make money. As long as the people showed up with the sacks of potatoes and the tubes of beef and American cheese and the onions and the pop bags in boxes, the place would make money. It was almost impossible for the place not to make money.

The idea that the Dishwasher would have to get on the phone and call the owner in order to get a raise was a complete load of horseshit. Lisa was either lying to the Dishwasher, or she just didn't care. Or both. She just probably didn't care for Laura. The less interaction the better. Nobody liked Laura. She was an asshole. She had no business sense. She was constantly trying to make things cheaper. She was constantly trying to change distributors. Which would lead to shortages in things like potatoes and onions and tomatoes. And then when those distributors wouldn't work out, either Ronito or Lisa would have to call the original distributors and beg them to come back. Which Laura couldn't understand. She would come in on the weekend and make a big huff about it. Somebody would have to explain to her what happened. She wouldn't like it. She would go into the back office. Count money or whatever. Feel better. Disappear for a week. Things would go fine for that week. She would come back. Do some math or something. Get sad about the bottom line. Do the same shit again. Get some fickle second-rate distributor involved again. A bottleneck would happen. Suddenly there wouldn't be enough potatoes or lettuce or whatever. Lisa or Ronito would make a phone call. Beg the original vendor to come back. Laura wouldn't understand. Someone would explain it to her. She would count the money. Things would be okay for a while. Then she would get cheap again. Then she would start the process all over again.

The whole thing was exhausting to everyone except Laura. Who considered herself a good business person. But the idea of the Dishwasher calling her up and asking for a raise was just the stupidest thing the Dishwasher could think of. The second-stupidest thing would be to burst into the back room when Laura was there and demand a raise. That would mean the Dishwasher losing his job on the spot. He would probably be rehired the next day. But still. It would be stupid. And from what the Dishwasher had observed, the look on Laura's face when she would come through the kitchen. Holding her breath. Wearing pastel cottons. Khaki pants. Expensive shoes and haircuts. Her tiny frame looking like she just got off a yacht at Martha's Vineyard. If the Dishwasher rushed into the back room when she was there, she would either mace him or call the cops. Or both. That is, after she fired him on the spot. Which meant that Lisa wasn't really lying to the Dishwasher. She just knew the thing was hopeless.

When Lisa came back by the dish room, the Dishwasher looked up from scrubbing a pot Ronito had just brought in. She shook her head. Then frowned. She came back with a pop for the Dishwasher. He took it from her, with hands covered in soapsuds. He said, "Thanks." She said, "I guess you got Mike tonight. Let me know how it goes." The Dishwasher took a drink from the straw. He nodded. There was nothing to say. Roger didn't like the idea. Big surprise. Lisa went back to waiting tables. Managing things. The Dishwasher put his drink on the metal rack. Went back to scrubbing the pot.

◯

When Mike showed up, he looked even younger and smaller than last time. He was cute. Ready to work. His little paper hat askew. His hairnet popping out on the sides. He had a lot of smiles. Shy smiles. The Dishwasher didn't know what to do with him. He had worked himself into a one man operation. Mike was just dead weight. The Dishwasher would try, though.

He was in a good mood now. For no other reason than that Roger was now doing the prep work as well as working the line. The same thing the Dishwasher had been afraid of happening to him. He had tried to like Roger. From day one, though, Roger was one of those assholes that took the job way too seriously. He thought that he was a chef or something. He was always trying to come up with new menu items that nobody liked. Like quiches or duck. He would work really hard on some new menu item. Test it out on all the employees. Everyone would try to like it. But nobody would.

Roger would get really upset. Take it out on the Dishwasher. Like, purposefully burning things in skillets. Or waiting until the very last minute to bring the closing dishes in. Which was something that all the cooks did. But mostly they did it by accident. Because the line was usually very busy every night. But the Dishwasher noticed that Roger would do it on purpose. He would watch him carefully stack things out of his way. Things that he didn't need. That could have been brought into the dish room easily. At any point.

When the Dishwasher figured this out. He would wait for Roger to go to the bathroom. Or out back to smoke. He would run into the kitchen. Grab the things. Bring them back into the dish room. At first Roger didn't notice. Because he was busy too. Because he didn't need the things he had been stacking up in order to fuck with the Dishwasher. But when he finally did notice. He would freak out. Come into the dish room and scream bloody murder about it. Like, "You don't know what I need or don't need, you idiot fuck!" And then Ronito would have to intervene.

Eventually Roger started hiding things from the Dishwasher. Hiding things on top of shelves and under the line. Even in the refrigerators, sometimes. Which was just a truly dick move on Roger's part. But he did it. There was nothing the Dishwasher could do. He tried to complain to Ronito about it, but Ronito just said, "It's just dishes, Disher. You have to do them eventually. What does it matter when they come in?" The Dishwasher liked Ronito, so he didn't spell it out for him. But that didn't mean anything.

Roger was a dick. And it gave the Dishwasher pleasure to think of him working double time just to keep up. He deserved it.

○

The Dishwasher had Mike deal with the cardboard. That was something. Then he had him scrub everything that came in. Whether it needed it or not. Then he had him go out and get some pops. After that, there was nothing for Mike to do. Aside from just watching the Dishwasher work. Which led to the Dishwasher giving commentary on everything he was doing:

"Well, you see *this* guy? You only get him like once or twice in the night. I like this spoon. It has this cool bend. You see the bend? I don't think that Randy knows it, but it's his favorite spoon. He only puts it in the bucket out of desperation. I mean, if I notice it in there I will run it right away with the glasses and bring it back to him. He always seems surprised. But he smiles. I mean, there is another one like it, but it doesn't have that curve. I think it ended up in the prep mix last night. Judging by when it came in. But, if that happens, I just put it to the side and run it with the salad stuff as a reminder. But that is just me. You can do what you want to do with it when you are in charge. For me, though, I just like to have it on hand, just in case the better one gets lost in the bottom of the bucket. Which happens sometimes, if it gets really busy. Tonight is not that night, though. I'm surprised. It is Thursday. Usually Thursdays are ballbusters. I don't know what is going on. I guess there wasn't a game tonight. Usually there's a game on Thursday. I guess you didn't hear about a game tonight?"

Mike looked at the Dishwasher. He had no clue about a game tonight. Or any night, as it was. He just smiled and shook his head.

"Yeah, well, I don't think it matters. What is important, also, is *this* one. This guy gets the good treatment. It can barely stand up on its own, so you have to lean it against something tall. Which is usually a soup bucket that only comes rarely. I mean, you can use one of the water guys, but those things fall over if you aren't careful and then you have to run them twice. We used to have glass ones, but they kept breaking so they replaced them with these plastic jerks. I mean, those things run pretty good if you have a full flat of them, but if you have to run them alone, good luck, bub! You know what I mean? You won't be happy when that door opens again. I mean, ha! Good luck! Sometimes I forget about them enough times that I get angry and then that just gives me problems later because you can't get angry during the rush. No sir! You'll just end up with a headache and a whole bunch of dishes that needed to be out in the theater, like yesterday. I mean, sometimes I like to think about the floor as a theater because it is so dramatic. Ha! The waitresses are the actors. And, like the cooks are like the stagehands or whatever. Ha! Are you a theater major, Mike?"

Mike just smiled and shook his head.

"Well, good. That is a waste of time. Don't do that. I guess you're a dishwasher major now! Ha! Don't do that either. The pay stinks and the hours are horrible. Do me a favor and soak that pan. Who brought that? I didn't even notice. Quit talking to me, I am trying to focus, ha! But seriously, soak that pan."

Mike didn't know what to do with himself. He couldn't tell if he was learning how to do his job or if he was getting a comedy lesson from the Dishwasher. He did what the Dishwasher told him, though. As long as he was on the clock, it didn't really matter.

However, when the Dishwasher said, "Hold down the fort, I am going out for a smoke," Mike just stood there. He had no idea what he should be doing. Dishes kept coming in. He scraped them and stacked them. But the Dishwasher's very specific directions about what needed to happen next just confused Mike. Should he put them in a tray? Spray them down? Wait for the perfect dish to come? What the hell was that about Randy's special spoon? Did he need to look for that? Should he go tell Roger he was a jerk? Find a bag of potatoes to wash? Ask for a raise? Get some more pop? Mike really had no idea. He just kind of stood there, turning from side to side. Waiting for the Dishwasher to get back.

When the Dishwasher got back. He didn't even notice that Mike had done nothing. He just went back to his soliloquy:

"See, I don't even know how these ended up here. Did you mess around when I was gone? No worries. You are green. This is hard work. It requires a great deal of focus. Look at this. What time is it? Oh, it doesn't matter. We need to do a run-through. Now, pay attention, this will save your life! Ha! Just joking. But look, you see how dirty and greasy this water is. That is *no fresco*! Just joking. Ha! *No bueno*, that means 'no good.' You speak Spanish, Mike? I don't. Ha! But I know what no bueno means. It means no good. This water is not good. You see this? You pull this up. Yeah, I know, I showed you before, but look at this. This thing of grease, that is too much grease. I mean, ha! We have to do a triple run around the maypole this time! I mean, that is something they don't teach you in dishwasher school. How many times you gotta run this beast without any dishes. Imagine! Ha! Running the Hobart without any dishes. What a waste. Am I right?"

Mike was very confused about his training. But he was kind of getting into it. The Dishwasher was entertaining, at least. And in some ways he was actually learning. He started dealing with pots and pans as they came into the dish room. Without being asked. After a while, the Dishwasher said:

"You know what I think—now let me know if I am out of line—but I think we should get a couple reuben sandwiches for din-din. What do you think?"

Mike made a face that said, "That sounds pretty good."

Then the Dishwasher remembered that Roger hated sauerkraut. If he had Mike ask for reubens, Roger would probably spit in them. The Dishwasher said, "Now, hold on. Maybe we do the steak sandwich. I think it's on special tonight. What about that?"

Mike just nodded.

"Okay, go tell Ronito. Regular french fries or curlies?"

Mike shrugged his shoulders and smiled.

"Curlies it is! Go sock it to him!"

Mike left the dish room and went and told Ronito that they wanted steak sandwiches with curly fries.

○

The night continued without a hitch. Dong Smells showed up at some point and ran the fry station. At one point, he came into the dish room and said:

"How'd it go with Toby? You guys looked like you were about to break up. Again."

"Hey Smells, you met Mike?"

"Yeah, we met last time. How's the dishes?"

"Pretty dirty." Mike said. He meant it.

"Payday tomorrow, though. It will all be worth it."

"Yeah, right?" The Dishwasher said. Remembering that tomorrow was Friday.

"You break up, or what?"

"Nah, the same ol'. You can start dating her if you want, I wouldn't mind."

"You want your girlfriend to start dating Smells?" Mike didn't understand irony.

"I mean, I do, but I wouldn't wish that on anyone."

"Because she is a bad girlfriend?" Mike said.

"Well, I wouldn't say that. I mean, as far as girlfriends are concerned."

"But what does she do that makes you say that?" Mike said.

"I don't know, Mike. I guess you would have to meet her."

"But why date a girl you don't like?" Mike said.

"You got me. Smells?"

"Hey, leave me out of this," Dong Smells said.

"Buckhorn tonight?" the Dishwasher said to Dong Smells.

"Can't. I promised."

"Shucks. What are Curry and my brother up to?"

"Curry has a date and your brother spent his evening-out last night. Sucks you couldn't stick around. Curry was in rare form after you left."

"Shots?"

"No! Not even that! I'll tell you later."

"Yeah, okay."

Dong Smells went back to the fry station. The Dishwasher kept teaching Mike all the things that he knew. They had a good time about it. Whether Mike understood anything about the job or not was up for debate. But he was learning something. Mostly he just learned that the Dishwasher took his job way too seriously and there was comedy in it. That the job was just doing the dishes until they were done. It didn't really matter how they came in. They just needed to be clean when they went out. That nobody respected the Dishwasher. That everyone thought they could do the job better than him, but nobody really could. That he should be making more money than he was. That he would get out of there at some point. Make a name for himself. Solve the gravity conundrum. Maybe write a book about it. He would save a thousand dollars and move to Denver. Then nobody could tell him what to do. Or what to think. That his roommates were a couple of idiots. That one of them had a big wiener, that he'd seen. That *that* was a tragic waste of things. That Toby was a big jerk and he couldn't get away from her. That Roger, too, was a big jerk. The Dishwasher said this in hushed tones. That this guy Norman that used to work there gave him a black eye when they wrestled in the back in the rotten oils next to the dumpster. That later that day Toby had thrown a glass at him and hurt his face. The Dishwasher even complained about the idiot roommates using his toothbrush. That he had broken in half. That one of them had dug out of the trash, and now they were all using the same toothbrush but it was broken in half. In the end, Mike wasn't even sure he would be coming back to work at the Altitude. If so, he would need a great deal more training. But for now, he was entertained at least.

The Dishwasher had Mike take the trash out. Told him that he could clock out and be done for the night. Mike did these things. Came back and said goodbye. The Dishwasher told him he would put a good word in. Mike smiled. He bobbed his head. There was nothing to say. He walked out of the dish room. Out the back door.

The Dishwasher finished the rest of the dishes. Ran the

skidders through the Hobart. Put them back where they came from. Roger and Ronito had left half an hour ago. The Dishwasher could see Dong Smells sitting at the bar. He unplugged the Hobart. Watched the water drain out. Turned the light off. Went to the back. Took his apron off. Took his white button-up shirt off. Threw them in the dirty clothes bin. Threw his paper hat and hairnet away. Clocked out. Looked at his time card that said:

Disher/Prep

He sighed. He knew he wouldn't be seeing those two hours. Or if he did, they wouldn't be at the eleven dollars an hour they should be. But then again, those hours wouldn't be on the paycheck tomorrow. They would be on the next one. He would have to keep an eye out. But then, he would probably forget all about it by next week. But hopefully next week he would be on a bus. Heading to Denver. A thousand bucks in his pocket. Saying farewell to Toby and Laramie and the Altitude. Starting a new life. He could do it. He knew he could do it. He just needed to hold onto any money that came his way. He put his hoodie on. Put his wallet and his cigarettes into his wet front pockets. Turned the lights off as he walked through the kitchen and into the bar. He sat down next to Dong Smells. Ordered a beer from Randy. Smiled, at nothing in particular. Took a drink. Just like that, he forgot all about the night of work.

19

"So, how was it tonight?" Dong Smells was already a little drunk. He had to go home, but he wasn't going to go home sober. The Dishwasher wondered why everyone he knew had such a lousy relationship with their girlfriend. Or more specifically, why did the girlfriends choose such lousy boyfriends. They had the upper hand. There were more boys than girls in this town. The Dishwasher used those terms. Boys and girls.

Nobody he knew was an adult. They were all adult-aged, but nobody had anything figured out. Any real future planned. His brother was the closest one. Then again, he kept switching his major. First it was philosophy, then it was psychiatry, now it was business. A business degree from the University of Wyoming was about as vague as you could get. Short of a liberal arts degree. Donger was majoring in some kind of science. The Slippery Wrist was studying nursing or something. He had a decent girlfriend. In the she-actually-accepted-who-he-was sort of way. But they had been in a relationship since high school. But that didn't mean anything. The Dishwasher's brother also had a girlfriend since high school. And she did not accept him for who he was.

Even Toby had been in high school when the Dishwasher met her. But they were never high school sweethearts, as they say. Who *they* were exactly was unknown, but still. The Dishwasher thought that Toby accepted him for who he was, mostly. That wasn't the problem with them. The problem was that they shouldn't be together. The Dishwasher knew it. Toby refused to know it.

"Don't remind me. My ass is on fire."

"What, you ate something spicy?" Dong Smells said.

"Oh no, not that. I went to the diner before work. It did not go well."

"Ah, I see. You should have taken a shower before coming in."

"I tried! But then I fell asleep and woke up late. Stupid Toby got all worked up about some dumb bullshit and ruined my day. She really needs to go. I mean, I really need to get out of town. You wanna loan me a thousand doll hairs?"

"No, I do not. Why didn't you do the prep thing today?"

"I did! You didn't hear?"

"What do you mean? I mean, Roger was all pissed about doing prep shit, but I just assumed you had just decided not to do it."

"Yeah, that fucker. Shit." The Dishwasher looked up. Randy was listening.

"Oh, no worries. Everyone knows Roger is a dick. My lips are sealed."

"Well, that dick got pissed at me the second I got here. Then he kicked me out of the prep room. That's about it."

"What? You didn't do so good?"

"I did not."

"Well, I mean, if you can't do the job..."

"Yeah, I know. I mean, I was pretty bad at it. In my defense, I didn't try very hard."

"So what's the plan then? It's gonna take you forever to make a thousand bucks, at this rate."

"Well, I got about a hundo in the bank. Tomorrow is payday. If I don't spend a single dollar, I can maybe have a thousand in two weeks. But then rent is going to be due again. I don't fucking know. Hey! You got Troll and Bogart's number?"

"I got it at home. I can bring it by tomorrow."

"I thought you didn't work on Fridays?"

"I work some Fridays. Dude, didn't we work together last Friday?"

"I can't fucking remember."

"Tell me about it. Uh, I am not working tomorrow, but it's

payday, right? I can leave the number in the dish room or something."

"Great! I can call them on Sunday or something. I think it is cheaper then anyway. Plus I still got seven dollars on this phone card I bought."

"Well, okay."

"Indeedy."

They sat in silence for a while. They each drank a beer. Dong Smells ordered a shot. Another beer. The Dishwasher ordered another beer. He said:

"So what happened with Curry that you were saying?"

"Oh, that fucker. You remember that girl Dallas that he was hanging out with? Well..."

———

Dong Smells went on to tell this very convoluted story that involved Curry hitting on some guy's girlfriend, then the guy got really pissed and threatened to punch Curry's lights out, and then Curry was a dick about it, but didn't fight the guy, but then a while later Dallas showed up and started harassing the guy whose girlfriend Curry had hit on, for some reason, and the guy got really pissed and threatened to teach Dallas a lesson, which made all the men very agitated, and that led to the guy getting in a yelling match with the bartender, and the whole time Curry just stayed back and played pool, egging the whole thing on, then the guy took a swing at the bartender who called the cops and had the guy removed, and then for some reason his girlfriend stayed behind when her boyfriend went to jail and played pool with Curry and Dallas and everyone else, Donger and the Dishwasher's brother. And then, at the end of the night, both Dallas and the girlfriend of the guy that took a swing at the bartender ended up leaving with Curry to have a threesome.

"I really don't know how he does it." Dong Smells was in awe of Curry. He thought he led a pretty wild life. Compared to his. No commitments. He would fuck whoever came around. Do shit like this. Get a guy arrested, then have a threesome with his girlfriend. That was truly the life. According to Dong Smells. The Dishwasher had a different take. He saw Curry as damaged and lonely. A child that just needed attention. Nothing but drama and fits.

But this story was something that would be remembered. Curry would probably have to answer for it sooner or later. The Dishwasher guessed he wouldn't be seeing Curry at the Buckhorn anytime soon. The boyfriend would without a doubt come looking for him. And although Curry was a big guy who had been in a few fights, nobody liked to get punched in the mouth. Especially when they could avoid it.

Dong Smells and the Dishwasher had a good laugh about this story. The Dishwasher thought maybe that was the way to get rid of Toby. Get arrested at the bar and then have Curry do a threesome with her. But Dong Smells pointed out that she would never go for it. Not only that, but they were friends, so Curry wouldn't try and pull that shit. The Dishwasher pointed out that, in fact, Curry had tried to pull that shit before, it just didn't work. Dong Smells said, "Good point, but still."

But still. That was the motto for dealing with Toby. She was so very slippery. None of the rules applied to her. She was the exception to the rule. Unpredictable and impossible to pin down. Yet so very consistently persistent. Once again, the Dishwasher was wrestling with the fact that he would have to marry her if he didn't get out soon. There was no other option.

Dong Smells finished his beer. He was now quite drunk. He stood up from his bar stool and managed to knock the empty pint glass over. He reached for his wallet. Randy wouldn't take his money. The Dishwasher finished his beer. Stood up himself. He didn't knock his pint glass over. He didn't even try to pay. They both told Randy thank you. Dong Smells stumbled through the kitchen. The Dishwasher followed. They walked into the alley. It was very cold. The Dishwasher would have to put his long johns on soon. The cold air made his loins recoil. The front of his jeans were very wet. He reached into his pocket and pulled his soft pack out. He squeezed a cigarette out. Straightened it. Lit it. He took a drag. Handed it to Dong Smells. Dong Smells took a drag. Blew it out. Took another drag. Handed it back. The Dishwasher said:

"You good to drive?"

"Oh, I'm fine, Mom. It's just a few blocks."

"Yeah, but it's Thursday, man. The cops are out."

"Oh, I got a route."

"You want a smoke for the road, just in case?"

"In case of what?"

"Oh, you know, so they don't smell booze or whatever."

"I ain't getting fucking pulled over, man. Don't jinx me, man."

"Your funeral."

"I'm fine."

"Just trying to help."

"Well, go help your butt hump a dick."

"On that note."

"Hey! I'm just kiddin' you! Hand me that thing." Dong Smells took a drag. Handed the cigarette back. Stumbled to his car.

He got into it just as a cop car came around the corner. It drove slowly down the alley. The two cops inside were checking out the Dishwasher. The cop on the passenger side had his window rolled down. The Dishwasher stood there. Smoking. The cop car stopped. The cop with the window rolled down said:

"You work here?"

"No, I just like the smell of the oil."

"You can't be smoking in the alley like that."

"What?"

"Regulations."

"What the fuck are you talking about?"

The cops drove away. The Dishwasher could hear them laughing in their car. *What the fuck is wrong with people?* The Dishwasher thought. Fucking cops. He watched Dong Smells drive out of the parking lot. He didn't seem drunk. His driving, that is. He could hear music coming from the vehicle. It must have been quite loud because the windows were rolled up. Dong

Smells got to the alley. Where the street met it. He rolled his window down. The music was very loud now. Dong Smells yelled:

"Yo Disher!" He held his hand out. The middle finger sticking straight up. "Suck it!"

He peeled out. The Dishwasher cringed. He half expected to hear sirens. He wasn't sure what he would do then. Walk over to help out, or just walk home. Leaving Dong Smells to his own creation.

There were no sirens. The Dishwasher thought to himself, "Not my problem." He started walking down the alley. Smoking his cigarette. The cold air making his loins recoil.

It was early still, and he didn't know what to do with himself. Go home to his idiot roommates and do nothing? Go to the bar by himself, see who was there? Call Toby and see if she wanted to come over? He thought about Dong Smells. About how he was supposed to bring that phone number over tomorrow. The Dishwasher hoped he wasn't too drunk to remember. He thought that maybe he should call him tomorrow to remind him. But that seemed stupid. If he was going to call him, why not just get the number from him then? Everything was becoming a crapshoot.

The Dishwasher was horny, but he also wanted to drink more. He could go over to Toby's, but she wouldn't have anything to drink. Just weed. The Dishwasher didn't want to smoke weed. Not only that, but Toby was too young for the bar. She could get in, like last night, but it would be the same thing. Without the other guys there running interference, she would get kicked out the second she came in.

The Dishwasher was suddenly bored and annoyed. There was nothing to do and nobody to do it with. He could go to the bar and maybe try and hit on some girls. But his ass hurt from having the runs earlier and then working all night. Plus, his clothes stank. Nobody liked a guy that smelled like rancid oil and mildew.

Toby didn't mind. But she was the exception to the rule. Plus, she smelled like that too. Not all the time, but when she worked she did.

The Dishwasher was now horny and bored. Maybe Toby was working tonight. The Dishwasher had no idea what her schedule was these days. If he ever knew. She didn't tell him. He never asked. But maybe. Just maybe, she was working. He could get her to come over after work. Bring him some steak.

He could call her from the bar. The pay phone by the toilets was a nice pay phone. It even had a phone book. He could find the Cowboy's phone number. Call her up. Tell her to come over. Bring some steak. And he could sit around for a while, drinking beer and waiting.

This plan seemed perfect. The Dishwasher threw his cigarette butt to the ground and walked faster down the alley.

———

The Buckhorn was busy. There was a guy at the door checking IDs. He wasn't charging money. There was no band. Had he been charging money, the Dishwasher would have just gone home and dealt with whatever was happening there. His idiot roommates demanding that he give them back the three beers he drank last night. Or worse. They would be drunk and wanting to hang out.

The Dishwasher showed his ID. Got in. Went down to the bathrooms. Looked at the phone book. Found the number for the Cowboy. He reached into his pocket. He didn't have any change. He thought about what to do. He stuck his finger into the coin return. There was a quarter there. This was a good sign. He put the quarter in the slot. Dialed the number. Somebody answered. The Dishwasher said:

"Hey! Is Toby working?"

"Who's calling? She can't take personal calls."

"Oh, no. This is business."

"What kind of business?"

"Oh, I am from the beef council, this is beef-related." There was some talking from the other side.

"Hello? Who is this?" It was a different person.

"I'm from the beef council, I am looking for Toby."

"She's busy, what do you want?"

"I want to talk to Toby, it is beef-related."

"It's midnight, what kind of beef-related thing happens at midnight?"

"Hey, I don't know about you, but beef is important at all hours of the day."

"What?" There was some more talking that the Dishwasher couldn't make out. A big lug came down the stairs. Pushed the Dishwasher to the side. Went into the bathroom. The second person came back on the phone. She sounded irritated.

"Where did you say you are from?"

"Beef council! I need to speak to Toby!"

"Why are you calling, hey, I don't..." Toby's voice came over the phone.

"Who is this?"

"It's Disher, from the beef council!"

"What the? You can't call me at work! Are you trying to get me fired?"

"Hey! Don't hang up! Come over later, bring me a steak!"

"Why are you—? What?"

"When you're done with work. Come over. Bring me a steak!"

"You can't—What? Where are you calling from?"

"I'm at the bar. Come by after work. Bring me a steak. I'll leave the door open."

"I can't. What?"

"Toby!"

"I gotta go."

"Toby!"

The line went dead. The Dishwasher didn't know if he'd been successful or not. But he was proud of himself. He found out that Toby was working. Plus, he put the idea in her mind that she should bring him a steak. Plus, she would come over. He could tell by the way she responded. He would be able to have a few beers. Go home. Then later, hopefully, he would get some steak and Toby would want to hump. Things were looking up.

He hung up the phone. The big lug came out of the bathroom. Pushed the Dishwasher's head into the wall and called him a faggot.

The Dishwasher did something he wouldn't normally do. He reached up the stairs and pushed the big lug's foot to the side. In a very soft way. That the big lug wouldn't notice. Or so he hoped.

The big lug fell onto the stairs. Smacking his face. He stood up again. Trying to pretend it didn't happen. The Dishwasher could hear him say, "Watch that last step, it's a doozy," to the next big lug coming down the stairs.

The next big lug looked at the Dishwasher and said, "Gangway, faggot." The Dishwasher held up his hands and let him pass.

He walked up the stairs. The Dishwasher. He went to the bar. Squeezed in. Ordered a beer. Stood there drinking it. Looking around. The place was filled with college students and locals. There was high tension. But only from the locals. The college students were mostly minding their own business. Excited about college. Trying to get drunk. Trying to get laid. The locals were trying to hold their ground. This was their bar during the summer. Now that school was about to start, they were losing their hangout. Soon, if not already, they would either have to acclimate or go somewhere else. The locals. For now they held on. They were outnumbered, though. They would be until next summer, when everyone left. For the time being, though. The locals did stuff like push people around and call everyone a faggot. Hoping to get into fights.

Nobody fought them, though. They just got out of the way. Like the Dishwasher did. Because what was the point in fighting with a drunk lug? It was two different universes colliding. A bunch of jerks that just wanted to drink beer and get laid and a bunch of jerks that just wanted to drink beer and get laid.

The Dishwasher watched this play out. It wasn't good. It was idiotic. Everyone had the same idea. Yet still. Nobody could figure it out. Nor should they. Hatred was easier than understanding. The college kids had nothing to lose. The locals had everything to lose. Yet, so what? The stakes were all very low. There was a point where hanging out at the Buckhorn was just not worth it. Even if you thought you had something to prove. There was a point when you were just fighting yourself. The locals would eventually understand this. Even if they were the lugs and everyone else was a faggot. For a brief second, though, it was very interesting. And this was what the Dishwasher watched. Laughing to himself about tripping that goon on the stairs. It was a small victory. A victory nonetheless.

———————

20

One beer turned into three. Then a fourth. The Dishwasher got nervous about the remaining money in his wallet. Payday was tomorrow, at least. So what, though? He needed to save as many pennies as he could, if he was going to save a thousand dollars. He did some math in his head. His check would be about 450 dollars. Add that to the roughly hundred dollars he had in his bank account. Plus what was left in his wallet. This was not good news. If he did it right, though. Didn't spend another dollar for the next two weeks. Worked all his shifts. He could pull it off.

It would mean just ditching town. Abandoning the apartment. This would piss the first roommate's brother off pretty good, but what could you do? The lease was up soon anyway. In theory, he wouldn't even have a place to live when that happened. What was a couple months between friends?

Plus, fuck the roommates. Those idiots. Smoking the place up. Eating all his food. Drunk all day and night. Playing video games. Using his half toothbrush. Never doing the dishes. And that one with the big wiener. That was just a waste. How does something like that happen? The thought was so abstract that the Dishwasher couldn't even really comprehend it. In his mind, things like that were too phony to even exist. But Toby had seen it too. She even said something about it. The Dishwasher wondered what she thought about it. Then he started thinking about his own penis. Which was not good for his mood. Sitting alone thinking about his things, comparing them to other, larger things. His confidence shrank.

He had been checking a few college girls out, while drinking his beers. Now he just kind of stood there, staring in the mirror behind the bar. Looking at the people behind him having what seemed like a good time. Even if they weren't having a good time, they were certainly being loud about it. He finished the fourth beer. Thought about getting another one. Realized he was kind of drunk. He felt better than before. Before, when he wasn't kind of drunk. But he felt gross too. He could smell himself. The mildew. His wet jeans pushing against his average things. Shrunken with shame. The shame of not being huge.

He decided to not get a fifth beer. He looked down at his empty can. Made sure he hadn't left anything on the bar. Like his cigarettes or something. His wallet. He pushed through the crowd of very loud, drunk people. A couple of guys shoved him on his way out. Someone called him a faggot. He was used to it.

If Toby had been there, she would have said something. But she wasn't. She was still working. The Dishwasher thought about the steak she might be bringing to his apartment. This cheered him up.

He made it outside. Took his cigarettes out. Squeezed one out of the soft pack. Pulled it out with his lips. It was kind of bent. He lit it. Put the soft pack back in his pocket. The cold air cooled his loins. He would need to put his long johns on soon. He zipped his hoodie up. He would also have to start wearing a coat soon. Or maybe a sweater underneath his hoodie.

He walked slowly home. The night was quiet. He couldn't see a moon. He looked up. There were enough stars to make him feel lonely. But also something other than alone. Like it was a great big world or something. Maybe there was something else out there. He heard a train approaching. The whistle gave him a deep sense of profound oneness with things. He was enjoying himself. Half-drunk. Almost happy.

And then the sound of screeching tires.

Toby came barreling around the corner. The Dishwasher almost jumped for cover. She really was the worst driver. How she didn't get pulled over every time she got into the driver's seat confounded the Dishwasher. She pulled up next to him.

Slammed on the brakes. He watched her lurch forward because she'd stopped so hard.

He looked in the car. She was pulled tightly to the seat. The seat belt slicing her very large breasts in two. She could hardly move, the seat belt was so tight. The Dishwasher chuckled and shook his head. She tried to reach over to roll the passenger-side window down. She couldn't because she was stuck. She just kept reaching, though. Hoping the seat belt would release. It didn't. The Dishwasher walked over and opened the passenger-side door. There was a to-go container on the floorboards. It looked like it had probably once been sitting on the seat. He bent down and stuck his head in the car. It smelled like weed. He said:

"Toby, you should roll a window down if you are going to smoke in here. The cops would have a field day with you, ya know?"

"It was cold!"

"Your funeral."

"Get in! I'll drive you the rest of the way."

"It's half a block."

"Get in!"

"Fine."

The Dishwasher reached further down. Messed around with the to-go container. There were fries poking out. The box was at a weird angle. He tried to make it right. Toby said:

"I got you a steak!"

"Thanks." The Dishwasher opened the lid. There was in fact a steak inside. With fries. He closed the lid again.

"Thanks? That's all I get?"

"Thanks!" The Dishwasher was not being sarcastic. He meant it. He was just annoyed with Toby's driving.

"Well, if you don't want it, I can take it back!"

Toby peeled out. The passenger-side door was wide open. The Dishwasher was holding the to-go container of steak. Toby screeched around the corner. The Dishwasher just stood there.

A couple minutes later, Toby came screeching around again.

She pulled up next to the Dishwasher and slammed on the brakes. The passenger-side door shot forward and then came slamming back. Shutting itself. The Dishwasher opened the door. Got in. Put the to-go container on his lap. Toby drove the final half block to the apartment. She parked. They both got out.

The door to the apartment building was open. Somebody had left a newspaper on the ground so the door wouldn't close. The Dishwasher stepped over it. Assuming it was one of the idiot roommates that had done it. He looked in the mailbox. It was still hanging open from when he had broken the lock. There was no new mail. Not for their apartment at least. Other people had mail. He walked up the carpeted stairs. Toby right behind him.

He went into the apartment. The door was unlocked. The kitchen was a mess. The roommates had ordered food, apparently. There were all sorts of containers. It looked like Chinese food. But, because of the way they had torn into it, it was hard to tell. It smelled like Chinese food. The Dishwasher pushed a bunch of things to the side to make room for the to-go container of steak.

He went into the living room. There was only one roommate. The first roommate. He was playing a video game. A plate of food next to him. He was leaning against the couch. A cigarette hanging out of his mouth. He looked drunk or stoned. He kind of looked at the Dishwasher. Then he saw Toby was there, so he sat up straight. Then when he realized it was Toby, he slouched back down again. He said:

"Hey, man, did you bring us those beers?"

"What beers?"

"Those three you drank, don't you remember?"

"Do I remember drinking three beers?"

"No, man, you drank three of our beers, man, you owe us."

"Oh, right, yeah, I will get right on that."

"Dude, you promised."

"Well, I am working on it, you have to be patient."

"Dude! We are out of beer!"

"Where's your buddy?"

"I told you! We are out of beer."

"Tell him to get me some, you can have a couple of mine."

"Ah, man! C'mon. That is not cool. You know we don't got IDs."

"It's a cold world."

"Dude! Maybe you can get us some beer!"

"I'm not getting you beer. Plus, it's too late."

"Not yet! There is still time!"

"How the hell can I make it there on time?"

"What about *that* one? I know she has a car. I saw her driving the other day. Nearly got a dog." The Dishwasher looked at Toby.

"Who walks their dog in the middle of the street?" Toby said.

"It was a crosswalk."

"I didn't hit the dog."

"C'mon, dude! You owe us!"

"I don't owe you shit."

"You fly, we buy."

"Where's Jeff?"

"I told you, he's out looking for beer."

"Who's Jeff?" Toby said.

"The other roommate."

"Oh, wiener boy."

"Yeah."

"Wiener boy?" The first roommate said.

"Cough it up." The Dishwasher decided to help out. He kind of wanted another beer himself. The first roommate got up and rushed to his bedroom. He came back with a twenty-dollar bill. Handed it to the Dishwasher.

"Get as much as you can."

The Dishwasher and Toby went back downstairs. They got into Toby's car. She peeled out. The Dishwasher spent the next couple blocks trying to get his seat belt on. Trying to ignore Toby's driving. She zipped in and around corners. Driving too fast, then too slow. She ran a red light. Made a couple cars swerve out of the way. The Dishwasher was rigid the whole time. Expecting a crash any moment. When they got to the bar drive-through, Toby pulled up, just barely avoiding scraping the car against the side of the building. She had to back up and try again. The Dishwasher was certain the person at the drive-through would think she was drunk and not sell her booze. But the guy didn't care. He seemed drunk himself. He said:

"That was a tight turn there, toots. What'll it be?"

"A case of Coors cans!" the Dishwasher yelled from the passenger side. The cashier slid the window shut. He walked away. He came back with a case of beer. Sat it on the shelf in front of the sliding window.

"ID." The Dishwasher took his ID out and handed it to Toby. Toby handed it to the cashier. He looked at it. Handed it back. "Nineteen." The Dishwasher handed the twenty to Toby, Toby handed the twenty to the cashier, the cashier handed Toby a dollar back, Toby handed the dollar to the Dishwasher. He put it in his wallet. The cashier handed the case of beer to Toby, Toby handed the case of beer to the Dishwasher, the Dishwasher put the case of beer on his lap. The beer was cold and heavy. The Dishwasher yelled, "Thanks, man!" Toby smiled at the guy. The cashier said, "Watch those corners." He slid the window shut. Toby rolled up her window. Screeched out of the drive-through. Nearly got in a crash when she got onto the street. The other car honked at her.

A few minutes later, they were back in front of the apartment building. The Dishwasher was a little sick from the drive. He got out of the car. It was a little difficult with the case of beer. They walked to the front door. The newspaper was gone now. The second roommate must be back, the Dishwasher decided. He handed the beer to Toby. Who looked annoyed. The Dishwasher unlocked the door. Held it open with his foot. Took the beer back from Toby. Walked up the carpeted stairs and into the apartment. He used his elbows to move some more of the trash on the counters to the side. In order to put the beer down. He looked over.

The steak and the fries were gone.

The roommates had eaten the steak while he was out getting them beer.

He couldn't believe it. He really just couldn't believe it. He didn't know what to do. He was so angry that he almost started opening the beers and pouring them down the sink.

He instead walked into the living room and looked at the roommates. They both had chunks of steak in their hands. The fries were gone already.

The Dishwasher just stood there looking. He had been confused when they didn't come into the kitchen when he showed up. Normally they would have been thrilled. But they knew they had done something wrong. Like bad dogs. The look of guilt on their faces.

The Dishwasher just stood there. He wanted to punch their stupid faces. Their dumb eyes just looking up at him.

The Dishwasher went over to the case of beer. Took three of them. Took them back to the living room. Threw them at the roommates. Who barely dodged out of the way, just in time. He yelled:

"There you go, fuckers! The beers I owe you. I am taking the rest." The roommates made a *ooohnooo!* sound. Like he had just killed their puppy.

The Dishwasher went back into the kitchen. Grabbed the rest of the beer. Took it into his bedroom. Threw it on his mattress. Reached into his pocket and pulled out his soft pack. He squeezed a cigarette out. It was in the shape of a J. He lit it like that. The bend pointing down. Toby didn't know what to do. She kind of stood there, and then kind of made her way to the mattress. The Dishwasher paced back and forth. Smoking. Ashing on the floor:

"Those fucking sons of bitches, I can't fucking believe it, get me to buy them beer and then eat my steak. I, I mean, I, fucking hell, those fuckers. Those stupid sons of bitches."

He paced and paced. Toby just kind of sat there. She didn't know what to do. She hadn't seen the Dishwasher like this, ever, but it wasn't scary. It was just kind of funny. It was all just idiotic. The idiot roommates stealing his steak. The case of beer. What was he going to do? Drink it all before they got their hands on it? How could he manage that? Toby watched the Dishwasher fume. Trying to add some sort of comfort. Saying stuff like:

"Disher, don't worry, it will all be alright." Then he would explode:

"How can it be alright! These fuckers just fucking shit up! Of all the fucked up things!"

"It's just a steak. It's not the end of the world. We can get you another one."

"You don't know the half of it! It is not just a steak! It's everything! These fuckers, man! They are just fucking it all up! Can't you see it? Can't you see it! Am I the only one that can see it?!"

Toby didn't understand. She watched him writhing in pain, yet she didn't understand. It was just a steak. The case of beer was nothing. It took like five minutes to get. There was no reason the Dishwasher should be this upset. But he was this upset. He was melting down. He opened a beer and drank it as fast as he could. Then he did it again. Toby said:

"Disher! You can't drink all those beers! That is too many beers!"

"Oh, yes I can, watch me!"

The Dishwasher tried to chug another beer. Instead, a bunch of foam came up and he puked on the carpet. At that point he screamed. Claimed he couldn't do anything right. Tried drinking the beer again. Which just made him puke more. After that, he stopped trying.

He came to his senses. Looked around. Saw the puke on the

carpet. Toby looking confused on the bed. Her knees tucked under her legs. She had pushed herself into the corner.

At that point, the Dishwasher just started bawling. He couldn't take it anymore. The tears came like pigs in a pipeline at first. Spitting themselves out one at a time. For every single emotion he had crammed down inside himself over the last year. Then they started really flowing. Gushing. All the shame, all the hurt, all the embarrassment. Getting pushed around. Called faggot. All the shit at work. All the dirty dishes. The bullies in his life. Norman. Roger. Lisa. The Altitude. The apartment. The roommates. His poverty. The lack of any future. It all just came out. Like violent waters. It all came out. Turgid and corrupt. He cried and cried. Puking up foam. Screaming nonsense about steaks and cases of beer.

Toby sat there, watching. Tucked in the corner. Her feet tucked under her legs. She was unfazed. This was her natural emotion. And it was neither scary nor off-putting. She waited until the Dishwasher had finally purged himself of all of his emotions. Then he collapsed. Onto the mattress. Wet and limp. Shaking.

It was then that she pulled her feet out from under her legs and scooted up next to him. Holding the Dishwasher gently as he squeezed the last vestiges of emotion out of himself.

The Dishwasher could only see in black and white while the fit was happening. When he felt Toby's touch, he began to see colors again. They were soft colors. Mostly blues and yellows. He was embarrassed, but he didn't care. He didn't feel judged. Then red, then orange, then green. As he calmed down, the world became whole again.

He stayed shaking until he fell asleep. Toby played with his hair the whole time.

After the Dishwasher fell asleep, Toby got up and went into the living room.

The roommates were sitting against the couch. Playing video games. The first roommate said:

"Hey, cowgirl, where is your crying cowboy?" Toby was still

dressed in her western outfit from work. Minus the boots. She had taken them off during the Dishwasher's fit.

She walked over to the second roommate. Took the controller from his hand. Threw it on the floor. Stomped on it. Breaking it into pieces. She looked at the first roommate. He was holding the other controller up and over his shoulder. He refused to hand it over.

She just looked at him. Then put out her hand.

He didn't know what to do. He didn't want to hand it over. The look in her eyes told him he had no choice. He handed the controller to her. She put it on the ground and stomped on it. Breaking it into pieces. Then she went back into the Dishwasher's bedroom. He was still asleep. Snoring now. She cuddled up behind him and fell asleep herself.

21

Hours later, the Dishwasher woke up. He had to piss. He got up. He was still clothed. He felt dizzy. Still drunk. He was confused. He vaguely remembered his fit. Then he remembered that the idiot roommates had eaten his steak. Then it all came back to him. He felt gross. His body could have used the steak. He was shaky.

He went into the kitchen. The light was on. He saw the mess on the counter. He sighed. He went to the entrance of the living room. Expecting to see the idiot roommates. They weren't there. The television was off. He looked at the floor. The two broken video game controllers. He found this all very odd. He went into the bathroom. He pissed. Flushed. Was confused by the controllers again. Walked to the roommates' room. They were both sleeping. He went into the kitchen. Turned the light off.

He went back to his own room. Shut the door. Took his shoes off. His clothes. He draped his jeans over some things that were on his floor. Hoping they would dry. He knew they wouldn't, but he still hoped they would. He got into bed. Toby was naked. Under the blanket. He slid into bed. He was erect. He pushed himself into Toby's ass. She pushed back. He pulled back. Reached down and angled some things. Found himself in the right spot. The Dishwasher pushed forward. Toby pushed back. They rocked back and forth for a while. The Dishwasher holding Toby's hip. Some things happened and then it was over. The Dishwasher pulling out at the last second. The two of them fell back asleep on top of the wetness on the mattress.

A few hours later, they both were awake. The sun was out now. The light coming through the window seemed like early morning light. The Dishwasher was thirsty. He got up and put his jeans on. He went into the kitchen. Drank from the faucet. He looked into the living room again. He wasn't sure if the controllers being broken was a dream or not. They were still broken. He went back into the kitchen. Took another drink from the faucet. Went back into his room. Toby was on top of the blanket. Her legs spread. She was playing with herself. The Dishwasher took his jeans off.

A little while later, the Dishwasher sat up. He said:

"Those idiots destroyed their controllers last night for some reason."

"I did that."

"What?"

"I did that. They pissed me off, so I broke their controllers."

"Holy shit! No shit?"

"Yeah, I mean, they shouldn't treat you like that."

"Well, damn. I don't care what they say about you, Toby, you got some balls."

"What who says about me?"

"Nobody."

"But you said you don't care what they say, who are *they?*"

"It's just an expression."

"But who's talking about me?"

"Nobody."

"But you said."

"I know what I said, I just mean it's just something people say."

"About me?"

"No. About people, I guess."

"About which people? I want to know who is talking shit about me."

"Nobody is talking shit about you, Jesus! It's just something people say."

"Yeah, I know, but who said it?"

"What the fuck? Are you dense?"

"What? Because I want to know who is talking shit about me?"

"Nobody is talking shit about you!"

"But you said."

"I know what I said! Can we drop it?"

"I just want to know who's talking shit is all."

"Nobody is talking shit!"

"But you said."

"Arghhhh!"

The Dishwasher went from having really nice feelings about Toby to being trapped yet again. It was all some horrible loop. Some horrible game the universe was playing on him. He couldn't get a moment of peace. The longer he spent with this girl, the longer he had to spend getting himself untangled. And now that she had done something terribly awesome. In the Dishwasher's defense, even. He felt more trapped than ever. Like he had made some sort of agreement with some double-talking wish maniac. But not like a devil or something. It was more like a random jerk that was playing a joke on him. A jerk that had nothing but free time to fuck with him. At every turn, there was Toby. Doing something cool and then fucking it up by being an asshole. His luck was just bad. He just had bad luck. He got mixed up with the wrong girl was all. And there was nothing he could do about it.

He didn't feel like talking to her anymore. He wanted to be alone. But she wasn't going anywhere. He could tell. He was trying to think up some excuse to get rid of her, but he was out of ideas. It was too early to pretend that he had to go to work. He could say that he needed to get his check and go to the bank, but she would just want to go with him. Then he would have to go to the bank. He didn't want to go to the bank. He thought about making an excuse that he had to go help the first roommate's brother do something or other, but Toby, being Toby, would ask too many questions and his excuse would be exposed as a lie. Which would just make her angry and she would start a bunch of new shit. He was trapped. He decided to just ignore her. This didn't go very well. He thought that maybe he would take a shower. He was looking around the room for the bar of soap he had hidden. He thought it was under the mattress but he couldn't find it. Toby just talked. Asking questions about who was talking shit.

"Was it your brother? I bet it was your brother."

"Toby, not now."

"I bet it was your brother, he always talks shit, I just know it. Remember when he said that thing about my driving? I bet he says stuff like that all the time when I'm not there. Am I right?"

"Toby, please."

"I bet it's him. Him or his girlfriend. She was like that in high school, you know? She was always saying stuff like she was cool shit, and guess what, she isn't as cool as she thinks. Where the hell does she get off?"

"Toby!"

"What are you looking for?"

"I had a bar of soap."

"A bar of soap in your bedroom? That's kind of odd, don't you think?"

"It's not odd, you know my idiot roommates."

"They steal your soap too?"

"No! They don't steal my soap, they leave the soap in a puddle of water and it lasts like two days. I just don't want them using it."

"Then why don't you tell them not to use it? Were they the people talking shit?"

"Yes, Toby, they are the people."

"What! Fuck them! I'm gonna go fuck them…"

"Dude! They talk shit all the time, but they aren't the people talking shit."

"So it's true! People are talking shit!"

"Toby! Nobody is talking shit!"

"But you just said."

"Toby!"

The Dishwasher grabbed his towel that was kind of clean and wrapped it around his waist. He went into the kitchen. Slammed the door behind himself. Let out a huge sigh. The second roommate came out of the bathroom. He said:

"Trouble in paradise?"

"Don't fucking start."

"I wouldn't go in there if I was you." The Dishwasher's shoulders slumped. He was now stuck between Toby in the bedroom asking stupid questions about bullshit and the smells of his idiot roommate's butthole. "You owe us two controllers, dude."

"Take it up with the Better Business Bureau."

"What?"

"Dude, don't fuck with me right now. I'm not in the mood."

"Dude. Your bitch broke our controllers last night. You owe us."

"Look, fucker, if you call her a bitch again I don't think you will like what will happen."

"Oh, big man on campus. Whatcha gonna do? Cry into your dirty sock pile again?"

The Dishwasher was having a horrible morning. Had he not been standing there with a towel around his naked body, he would have done something. But, as it was, he had to just take the abuse. He couldn't catch a break.

He was now angry. He wanted to punch the guy. He wanted to do more than that. He wanted to really hurt him.

He went back into his bedroom. He dropped the towel. He put his jeans on. Buttoned the top button. Took a six-pack of beer. The same beer he had gone out to buy for his idiot roommates while they ate his steak. He marched into the idiot roommates' room. Before he knew what was happening, he was throwing full cans of beer at them both. One clocked the second roommate on the shoulder. He picked it up and threw it back. It hit the Dishwasher in the stomach. He took another beer and threw it at the second roommate. He dodged out of the way. It hit the window and broke it. The first roommate was still in bed, but had scooted to the side. He said:

"Duuude! You broke the window! You're gonna have to pay for that!"

The Dishwasher took the last beer and opened it. Dumping the contents all over the room. The second roommate tackled him. Then the first roommate piled on. Before long, they were all rolling around the room. Knocking over half-filled beers. Rolling over ashtrays. Smells coming from all directions. Dirty socks. Old underwear. A shoe got smacked into the Dishwasher's face. And then his face was ground into the carpet. He could taste the dirt. Then for some reason he had a Band-Aid stuck to his lips. Which made him stand up very quickly. Wiping his mouth like he had just been stabbed by a dirty needle. Someone kicked him in the balls. He fell back down. Tears running out of his eyes. A heavy pain in his lower body.

He looked over. Both the roommates had horrified looks on their faces. Things had gone too far. They knew it. The Dishwasher knew it.

He tried to stand up. It was too painful. The second roommate came over and picked him up by his armpits. Bouncing his ass on the ground. Trying to help with the pain. This did help. It was an old-schoolyard trick. When somebody got hit in the nuts. You bounced them on the ground. The science wasn't solid, but it did seem to make things better.

After a while, the second roommate let him go. The Dishwasher just sat there. Not really sure what had just happened. Things were getting out of control. And now the window was broken. The Dishwasher could have cried. He didn't want to pay for a broken window. That just wasn't in his budget if he was going to save the 1,000 dollars and get out of town.

He managed to stand up. He looked around at the mess. It wasn't that different from normal. The idiot roommates just kind of sat there staring. The Dishwasher didn't have anything to say. He left the room. He could hear them talking as he walked through the living room. Stepping over the broken controllers. They said:

"That dude owes us some new controllers."

"And the window."

"But hey, we got beer."

The Dishwasher heard two beers being cracked open. Then the word, "Foamy!" He went back into his room. Toby was dressed now. Wearing her cowboy outfit. The Dishwasher got excited. He didn't mean to. The outfit just turned him on for whatever reason. Toby, strangely, was okay with it. They made out for a second. While they were making out the Dishwasher was grabbing her ass under the miniskirt. Then he pulled her tights and her panties down. A second later the Dishwasher was behind her. Toby's butthole staring up at him. Her face down in the mattress. Then, that was that. The Dishwasher confused again. He just couldn't help himself. Their relationship was not normal. He knew that. He wasn't sure if Toby knew that. She pulled her panties back up. Her tights. Stood by the door while the Dishwasher lay in the bed. Naked. His things off to the side. Growing soft. She said:

"See you later?"

"I guess."

"What's that mean?"

"I don't know, Toby, it has been a hard morning. Cut me some slack."

"Oh, yeah. Maybe I will come back later and fuck Wiener Boy."

"What the fuck!"

"I don't know. You tell me!"

"Yeah, you do that. See where it gets you."

"Maybe I will."

"Maybe you should!"

Toby stormed out. The Dishwasher felt a huge weight lifted off his shoulders. She was just too much. Toby. Always and at every turn. The thought of her coming back to fuck the second roommate was just fine with him. The Dishwasher. At least then he could be done with it. And if she thought doing that sort of thing would make something better, more power to her. No skin off his neck. If she wanted to be with some dude that just sat around playing video games and getting drunk all day, that was on her. The Dishwasher had plans. What those plans were wasn't clear at the moment, but he had them. And he would be spectacular when they happened. Wiener Boy aside.

The Dishwasher waited long enough to know that Toby wouldn't come back. He took his kind-of-clean towel and wrapped it around his waist. He went into the bathroom. There were no smells aside from the usual, mildew and dirty bathroom. The bar of soap was sitting in a puddle of water. Disintegrating. The Dishwasher sighed. There was no winning. He turned the hot water on. Sat down on the toilet. Watched the bathroom fill up with steam. New smells mixed with old smells.

After a while, he stood up. Flushed. Waited for a second while the toilet tank filled up. Got into the shower. Adjusted the temperature until he could stand underneath the spray. He didn't know what to do. He just stood there. Trying to think.

The morning had been awful. Everything seemed like it was falling apart. He had no desire to get clean. What was the point? He would finish the shower, and then what? He had hours to kill before work. He didn't feel like going to work. But it was payday. But so what? All that money needed to be saved. And now the broken window. And the controllers. Did he really have to replace those? At first he loved the idea of Toby smashing them, but now that he had some time to think he felt different. That was kind of a lousy move on her part. Then again, she had done it to defend him. The Dishwasher. Didn't that count for something? If so, what? How was he in love with somebody that he kind of hated? Someone that was just a pain in the ass at all times. Did he have to be loyal to her? Like, did he have to fight her battles the way that she apparently fought his? Were they really a thing, though? Half of the time, yes. The sex was great, and when they were alone and nothing was giving Toby issues. That seemed to be nice. But all the other times? Her paranoia? Starting a fight with everyone whenever she felt like it? She was a full-on piece of work. A full-time job. And there was no future. There was just no future. He knew it. The Dishwasher. But did Toby know it?

The Dishwasher cleaned himself. The disintegrating bar of soap getting much smaller. Slimy and excessive. Why didn't anyone understand the thing needed to dry out between uses? It couldn't just stand in water for hours at a time. That was just a waste of a bar of soap. Why was he so alone in this way of thinking? The Dishwasher. What was he missing? It wasn't even funny, it was just annoying. You get like six showers out of a soap? Then what? You just buy another? The idiot roommates seemed to understand that you needed more than one roll of toilet paper, how come they didn't understand that soap got used too? Or toothpaste? Or toothbrushes? It was all just exhausting. Even if there hadn't been money involved. It was all just wasteful.

The Dishwasher was clean when he got out of the shower. The towel made him dirty again. He dried off as best he could. He brushed his teeth with the half toothbrush. Wiped the mirror steam with his hand. Looked at his splotchy face. He really needed some sun. He smiled at his reflection. His teeth were doing okay, though.

He left the bathroom. Went back to his room. Took the towel off. From around his waist. Tried to hang it on the windowsill. That didn't work. He took it to the door. Opened the door. Hung it on the door. Shut the door. The towel keeping the door from shutting completely.

The Dishwasher got back into bed. Everything was dirty. The bed felt like sand. Like he was laying out on the beach. Lots of little things clung to his moist body. He rolled himself up in the blanket. Pulled it over his head. He was tired. He would have been hungover but the morning had been such nonsense that he just felt tired. Dehydrated. Hungry. He had no idea what time it was. He didn't really care. He would take a nap and see what happened. He was depressed. Nothing was going right. Maybe he would sleep through work and get fired. Then he would be forced to make some changes in his life. As it was, he was just going along with the flow. His daily life, an annoying waste of time. Everything was a bummer. He was sick of bummers. He just kind of wanted to sleep and be done with it. Sleep until things became something worth doing. The Dishwasher really felt bad for himself. No end in sight. Just the same ol' bullshit. He just needed to sleep. To sleep for a mile. A mile of life. Then things would look good again. He had the time. He was young. Somewhere in these thoughts, the Dishwasher fell asleep.

22

The Dishwasher woke up in a panic. He had been dreaming of work. He sat up. Looked around. He almost ran into the living room to see if he could figure out what time it was. Then he looked around again. It was still light out. There was no way he was late.

The panic wore off. He now felt like a goon. The thing with the idiot roommates and Toby was terrible. Ridiculous. A horrible waste of time. And, frankly, emotions. There were just too many emotions going around.

He needed to get out of town. And quick. If only he could get the thousand dollars and hit the skids. He stood up. Got dressed. Thought about putting his long johns on. He didn't. It wasn't time yet. Maybe tomorrow? He was not looking forward to winter. The winters in Laramie were the worst. The place was situated at the bottom of a canyon that blew cold air down the Rockies. It was also at like 7,000 feet. Pretty much on top of a mountain. When it got cold, it stayed cold. And then it got colder. Frozen even. Once winter settled in, the weather would suck for the next six months at least. The idea of being holed up with his idiot roommates for the winter, going to his stupid dishwashing job. It was all too much. Too much to even think about. So he fought it. In his way. By denying it was even happening. Keeping his long johns off. Folded up under his stack of winter clothes that had been sitting unmolested on his carpeted floor ever since he took them off last spring. When it got warm enough to not need them. But they were there. Mocking him. Waiting to be unleashed, like some portent of discomfort. Of gloved hands and coats. Sweaters and two pairs of socks.

Never being really warm again. Just the dumb stupid winter and its icy sidewalks and unpredictable snows. Everything just a little bit harder.

He put his velcros on. Looked at the rest of the beer that his idiot roommates had him buy while they ate his steak. There were sixteen left. Plus the one that he opened but couldn't drink because he was puking from the one he had drunk before that. Normally he would have saved that beer. Put it in the fridge. Drank it later in an emergency. Instead he just left it where it was. On the carpet. Next to the wall. Next to his pile of dirty clothes.

He didn't know what to do with the case of beer. There was no way the idiot roommates were getting their grubby meathooks on it. He would pour it all in the toilet before he would let that happen. Every single drop. But sixteen beers was a lot of beers to hide. No matter where he hid it, they would find it. He thought about drinking a bunch before work, but that seemed stupid.

He had gone to work drunk before and it was awful. His job was hard enough as it was. And being sloppy just caused him grief. Strangely, though, a hangover made him better at his job. Forced him to concentrate. And there was something about working hard through a hangover in such a sweaty environment. Even if he didn't try, his hangover would be gone by the end of his shift. The heat. The noise. The endless glasses of pop. These were probably the biggest benefit to working as a dishwasher. That and the fact that he never had to worry about food. He could always eat. Always eat and get rid of hangovers. These were really very tiny benefits for working a $7.50 an hour job, but they were the benefits that existed. Plus, he never had to be up before noon if he didn't want to be. That was a benefit. But then again he had to work until midnight, so that kind of balanced out.

The Dishwasher dumped his clean clothes out of the plastic garbage bag they were in. He put the beers inside. He would just take them to work with him. The idiot roommates couldn't get them there. He was having a little fantasy about leaving mousetraps around his room for when the roommates came looking for the beers. Like, they would get their fingers snapped whenever they lifted something up. "Oh, maybe they're under here?" Snap! "My fingers!" He chuckled to himself. He didn't have any mousetraps, though. Then he went a little insane and thought about rubbing shit everywhere. So they would get covered in shit when they came looking. But he sobered up about that when he thought it through. He didn't want to rub shit all over his things. Even if it would make life miserable for those two assholes.

He went into the kitchen. Looked at the huge mess on the counter. Reached down and gathered as much of it as he could. In his arms. Took it into the living room and dumped it on the couch. His idiot roommates were nowhere to be seen. They were probably out buying new controllers. Or something equally as stupid. Dumping all the trash on the couch made him feel better for a second, then he realized it would probably end up on his bed.

But then he realized that he didn't care. It was all the same. In his mind, they had already done that. With each microaggression they perpetrated. Them leaving that shit on the counter in the first place was the same as leaving it on his bed. Them eating his steak while he went out to buy them beer was equal to them shitting on his bed. The broken toothbrush, the melting soap, the never-paying-rent until it was way past due.

Everything they did made the Dishwasher furious. He started to walk into their room to take a piss on their beds, but then he sobered up again. That would mean something more than the normal passive-aggressive bullshit. That would start something that wouldn't stop until somebody got really hurt. And because there were two of them and only one of him, he would lose.

He went into the bathroom. Pissed. Brushed his teeth with the half toothbrush. Looked at himself in the mirror. His splotchy face. He really needed to get some sun. He looked tired and gaunt and sad. He stopped looking at his face. He went back to his room. Made sure he had everything. He checked his smokes. He needed a new pack. Very soon. He figured he could get through the night. Then tomorrow. He grabbed the plastic garbage bag filled with the beers. Walked out of the apartment. He didn't lock the door. There was never a reason to. The only thing to steal was the video game thing and maybe the television. But since the idiot roommates were basically using both at all times, whatever thief came around would have to fight them for them. It would be a good thing if somebody stole them. It would be a great thing if somebody came in and beat the idiot roommates and stole them. Maybe the thief would have a gun and make them shit their pants? That would be cool.

When the Dishwasher walked outside, the cold air hit his jeans. They were still damp. His things shriveled up. He was regretting not putting his long johns on. It was time. He couldn't ignore that fact any longer. Even if it was only mid-September, it wasn't going to get warmer again. It was just going to get colder and darker and more miserable. There was no reason to suffer more than he already was. He had lost.

There was no winning. Not this battle about the long johns, or really any of the battles he was fighting. He still was waiting for Norman to show up and beat him down. That could happen at any moment. Maybe even today. It was payday. He might be at Altitude waiting for him. The Dishwasher.

The battle with Toby was just bonkers. She needed to go. But there was no getting out. Even her threat of coming around while he was at work to fuck the second roommate was just wishful thinking. The Dishwasher would love nothing more than to have a full-on and tight excuse to kick her to the curb. But she would never do it. It was an empty threat. Sadly.

The battle with the idiot roommates was just annoying and needed to be done with. The more he thought about it, the more he realized he didn't care one iota about just ditching the place without notice. Let those fuckers sweat it out. Shit, the amount of grief they had given the Dishwasher over these last few months. It was really something else.

The battle with the Altitude needing to pay him more, the Dishwasher, well, that would never go anywhere. And why should it? They didn't care about him and he didn't care about them. Shit, he could just not show up to work one day and they wouldn't even notice. Well, that wasn't true. They would notice acutely, but not the owner. It would just mean that everyone would have to work harder until they found a replacement. Which was a risk they really didn't mind taking. Because what did they care if everyone had to work harder? Just as long as the place stayed open. This last thought sent the Dishwasher's mind into overdrive. Nobody cared. Really, nobody cared. He could come or go and nobody would give a shit. For a while, he'd been feeling guilty about the idea of just ditching town. Moving to Denver or wherever. When he finally scored the 1,000 bucks. But if they didn't care and he didn't care, what was there to worry about? Nothing. That's what there was to worry about.

The Dishwasher squeezed a smoke out of his soft pack. Bent it straight. Lit it. He was suddenly in a very good and pleasant mood. He had a bounce in his step, even. The plastic bag of beers hanging from his other hand. The flat smoke hanging in the original hand. Suddenly he didn't feel guilty for thinking about his future. There was nothing holding him back aside from his own shame. Which was kind of a lot. But he could push past that. He walked to work feeling quite strong and empowered. He even smiled at a bird.

When he got to work, he went in through the back door like always. The screen door. He put the garbage bag of beers on the metal shelves. For a second, he got paranoid that someone would mistake them for trash. But then he realized that he was the one that would have to think they were trash because it was his job to deal with the trash that collected on those metal shelves. He went over to the time cards. His paycheck was hanging off of his time card. He took the envelope off. Leaving the paper clip on the time card. He opened the envelope. There was a note inside. It said:

Troll and Bogart 303-647-6519

Dong Smells. He came through. The Dishwasher took his wallet out. He put the number in the wallet. He looked at the check—$456.21. Not bad. Not good, but it was what he thought it would be. Almost to the penny amount. He put the check back into the envelope. Folded it into thirds. Put the thing in his wallet. Put the wallet back in his jeans. He looked at the time. It was early. He had another thirty minutes before his shift started. He stood there for a second. Looking at paychecks. Norman's paycheck was there. The Dishwasher frowned. He didn't want to see him. He decided to go out and find a pay phone and call Troll and Bogart. The nearest one was at the laundromat. Which sucked. That would mean crossing the main, busy street. He wasn't really in the mood for assholes in big trucks calling him a faggot. Not that they ever did anything to him. Aside from throwing shit and calling him names. It was still very unpleasant. He decided to risk it. The Dishwasher. It was worth it.

He walked to the busy main street. Waited for the cars to go by. Ran across. No trucks came by. He got to the laundromat. Somebody was using the phone. He waited. Trying to not be invasive. He thought about lighting a cigarette, but he had to conserve. Otherwise he would run out before the end of his shift. And that would be tragic. He could always bum one if he had to, but he preferred not to. He stood there for a second, thinking about how there was a gas station a few blocks away that he never really went to. That he could buy some smokes and use their pay phone. He made a decision. He took off.

The closer to the interstate he got, the more he regretted making that decision. There were all sorts of assholes hanging around. He would be lucky if nobody harassed him. He almost turned around. The Dishwasher. But he was excited. He wouldn't let these goons ruin his excitement.

He got to the gas station. Went inside. Either nobody noticed him come in, or they just weren't in the mood to spit vitriol at him. He bought a pack of cigarettes. They only had soft packs. He paid. Counting the money in his wallet. This made the guy behind him get impatient. He said, "Move it or lose it, faggot." The Dishwasher made a face. He looked at the cashier. The cashier made a move with his head that meant, "Get lost."

The Dishwasher put his wallet away without counting his money. Took the cigarettes and went outside. He put the soft pack in his front pocket. Took the other soft pack out. Squeezed one loose. Bit it with his lips. Straightened it. Lit it. Put the soft pack back in his front pocket. Next to the new soft pack. This felt like too much stuff. He took it back out and put it in his other pocket. He went over to the pay phone. Picked it up. Dialed the 800 number that he had memorized. When the voice told him to, he entered the pin that he had memorized. When prompted he dialed Troll and Bogart's number, which he had also memorized. This made him feel smart. He was good with numbers. Well, at least he was good with memorizing numbers. The robotic woman's voice said he had twenty-three minutes left on the card. There was a double click that meant the call was going through. The Dishwasher sighed.

This was a long-distance phone call. The Dishwasher had a joke about that. He tried it out on a few people. Nobody really cared for it. It went like this:

"Why did the Dishwasher need so many quarters?"

"So he could make a *long-Dishtance* phone call."

The joke was kind of dumb. And not entirely true. When the Dishwasher made local calls, he used change. Because it was cheaper than using the phone card. He had these numbers committed to memory for emergency use. Or to call home. At some point, his mom had gotten an 800 number in case he needed to call home. Which made his memorization of the phone-card number moot. However, it was useful at this very moment. He had the card in his wallet if he forgot the number. But he didn't. Plus, he only had twenty-three minutes left on it. He would need to buy a new one soon. And then he would have to memorize a new number. But for now, he was doing alright.

The phone rang a few times and the Dishwasher was thinking

that nobody was there. Should he leave a message? What kind of message would that be? "Hey dudes, you can't call me back, but can I come live with you?" The Dishwasher was suddenly filled with shame about everything. Embarrassed with where his life had taken him. Not sure who to blame. The phone rang two more times and finally a voice came over the line:

"Yel-low?"

"Troll? This is Disher, from over here in Laramie." The Dishwasher sounded like his father. He wanted to bury his head in shame.

"Disher! No shit! How the fuck are you?"

"I'm okay, ya know, living, I guess. How's Denver?"

"Fucking wild, man! What are you up to?"

"Hey, I have a thought, do you guys need roommates? I mean, I'm thinking about ditching Laramie and all…" There was silence on the other end. "Troll?"

"Yeah, sorry, Bogart's loading a bowl, I got distracted. What was that again?"

"Roommates. You guys want a roommate?"

"You mean you?"

"Yeah, me. I am thinking about ditching town. Make a run of it in the Mile High City or something."

"I don't fucking know, hold on." Troll held the phone down. "Hey Bogart! You want a roommate?" The Dishwasher could hear Bogart in the background. "A roommate? Who?" Then Troll said, "Disher!" Then Bogart said, "Seriously? I don't fucking care! We got a couch." Then Troll came back on the line, "I don't care! Bogart doesn't give a shit. We got a couch!"

"No shit! I am thinking of leaving in a couple weeks."

"I mean, man! It would be great to see you!"

"Well, fuck! It's a deal then!"

"Holy shit, fuck yeah it is! Come on down!"

"Well, holy fuck! Let me get my shit straight. I'll call you back in a few days!"

"Well, okay then."

"No shit, okay! Fuck, this is the best news I got in years!"
"Fuck it, dude. Come live in Denver. Get your ass down here!"
"I'm gonna do it!"
"Do it!"
"I am!"
"Well shit, then."
"Shit, indeed! I'll talk to you soon!"
"You got it."
"Tell Bogart hi!"
"Bogart! Disher says hi!" Bogart yelled, "Hi, Disher!" in the background. "She says hi back."
"Okay, then."
"Right on, man."
"Right on, indeed!"
"Later."
"Late."
That was that. The Dishwasher hung up. He was elated. He figured he'd only spent five minutes on that call. The thing took an extra ten minutes for every call you made, so he figured he had eight minutes left. The Dishwasher. That would be enough to get their address. Then he could look on a map. Figure out where they were living. Figure out where the bus went. Maybe walk to them. Or, if they had a car, maybe get a ride?

The logistics didn't matter. They said yes. That was what mattered. If the Dishwasher didn't spend a single cent, worked for two more weeks, and then bought a bus ticket, he would have nearly a thousand bucks in his wallet. That was perfect. He would just need to make it through the next two weeks without letting Toby know about it. Or the Altitude. He could tell Dong Smells and his brother. He didn't know what to do about the first roommate's brother. The lease and the apartment. But so what? The first roommate was an asshole. He could suck it, for all the Dishwasher was concerned. And, so what? The lease was up in January anyway. It wasn't like he would be causing too much grief. If anything, the first roommate's brother owed it to him for having to deal with his lousy brother all this time. Eating his food. The Dishwasher's. Using his toothbrush. Not paying rent. Eating his steak while he went out to buy them beer. There was no reason to feel bad.

The Dishwasher was elated. Truly elated. He lit another cigarette and rushed back to the Altitude. He was now late for work. It didn't matter if Norman was coming around. He needed to get to work. He crossed the busy main street. Nobody called him a faggot.

He got to work. Went through the screen door. Hung up his hoodie. Put his wallet and his smokes in the pockets. Found a clean button-up white shirt. Put it on. Put a hairnet on. Put a paper hat on. Tied an apron around his waist. Went to clock in. Norman's check was gone. Which was good news. He wondered if there was any drama when he came to pick it up. The Dishwasher clocked in. It was ten minutes after five. He walked through the prep room. There was a new prep cook. She was kind of short and had tattoos. Black hair. The Dishwasher said hi. She looked at him and nodded. He felt intimidated.

He rushed past her and into the dish room. The place was a complete mess. It must have been a busy afternoon. The Dishwasher got to work. Running sinks. Cleaning plates. Getting ready for the night. He was insanely happy. Things were looking up. He fantasized about moving to Denver. About what life would be like. He didn't even notice when it started to get really busy. He was just so very focused.

He eventually snapped out of his fantastic inclinations, when Mike showed up. Mostly because he was now training Mike to replace him. Even if nobody else knew about it. Mike would have to learn the ropes. And fast. Things were changing. The Dishwasher went into his usual spiel about how to keep the dish room operating. About the soakers and the leavers. The scrubbers and the scrapers. The easy spoons and the soup cups. How much chemical you should use. When to drain the Hobart.

Mike was confused. He thought he had already been trained. He didn't know why the Dishwasher was being so intense.

Around nine, the Dishwasher ordered an open-faced steak sandwich. Mike got the fish and chips. The Dishwasher stood there eating the steak with a knife and fork while Mike ran the dish room. His fish and chips getting cold. The Dishwasher was kind of being an asshole about it. He said:

"You see, you got to be able to just forget about your food. Sometimes it gets cold. There is nothing to be done about it."

"But we're ahead. Why can't I just eat?"

"You got to learn, man. There is no other way."

"But, I'm hungry."

"You can eat when you are dead."

"Oh, fuck off. I'm taking a break."

"Your funeral."

Mike took his fish and chips into the prep room and ate it while talking to the new prep cook. Something the Dishwasher would have never done. Which was maybe why nobody liked him very much. That and the fact that he would do shit like make the new dishwashers jump through needless hoops to learn the job. Plus, his dumb dishwasher jokes. And his piss-poor attitude about the job in the first place. Complaining that he did all the work and nobody else did shit. It was true that nobody would miss him if he left. Even if he did it the way he was thinking. Mostly they would be better off. The job wasn't nearly as complicated as he made it out to be. And it was probably true that he scared off new employees because of that.

The Dishwasher stood there eating his steak sandwich. Watching the plates pile up. He felt happy and smug. Soon this would all be over. And then they would be left to their own devices. These morons.

Lisa showed up. Asking him to get the trash behind the bar. He just nodded. Chewing on a fatty piece of steak. She made a face that meant, "What the fuck are you up to?"

The Dishwasher thought he was being clever. He put the knife and fork down. Followed Lisa out of the kitchen. Checking out her tiny buns in their black nylon pants. He was such a pervert. He couldn't help it. He was already thinking about masturbating to that image later.

He was suddenly overcome with shame. He didn't understand why he had pushed things to this limit. Arrogance was not a nice fit on him. He felt dirty.

He took the trash out of the bin. Tied it. Reached down. Got another trash bag. Whipped it full. Put it in the bin. Randy told him thanks. He lugged the full trash bag to the back of the kitchen. He watched Mike hitting on the new prep cook. She seemed to be enjoying it.

The Dishwasher went outside. The cold air hit his wet crotch like a brick of ice. He really needed to put his long johns on. This was the last night. He couldn't stand it anymore. He threw the full trash bag in the dumpster. Slipping on grease. He nearly fell down. He caught himself on the side of the dumpster. Now his hands were covered in putrid oil and other things.

He went back inside. No longer in a good mood. He went to the dish room. Cleaned himself with the sprayer. Then cleaned the sprayer with its own water. After that, he went to work, scraping plates and running dishes. Things were busy again. He worked as fast as he could.

23

The night dragged on, like all nights that drag on. The Dishwasher wanted to think. He couldn't, though. Because of Mike. Mike was everywhere. If he juked right, there Mike would be. Scrubbing something or scraping something. If he juked left, there Mike would be. Taking dishes out of the Hobart, or something else that was annoying. Getting in the way. The Dishwasher tried to take a break to smoke a cigarette, have some time to himself. But Mike came out with boxes. Breaking them down. Talking about nonsense.

"I think I might ask the new girl out."

"Are you so sure about that?"

"Why not? She's cute. We seem to hit it off okay."

"Yeah, but it's work, man."

"So what?"

"Oh, I don't know, what if it doesn't work out? Then you have to work with her. You think of that?"

"Oh, no, not really."

"Yeah, well there are quite a few things you haven't thought about."

"Like what?"

"I mean, what if she says no? Then what? You have to live with that shame. That's what."

"Oh, I don't think she would say no."

"Yeah, we'll see."

"You're just jealous."

"Jealous of what? Embarrassing shame?"

"Dude, just because you are well past your prime doesn't mean the rest of us have to pull our puds every night."

"You think I pull my pud every night? Dude, if you only knew how much sweet tail I get whenever I want it, you wouldn't even say that."

"Whatever, dude."

"Whatever, dude, right back at ya."

"I don't care what you say, I'm gonna ask her out."

"Fine by me."

"I am."

"Well, invite me to the wedding, won't ya?"

"You're a dick, man."

"Don't say I didn't warn you."

"Fuck off."

Mike went back inside. The Dishwasher had been a dick. What the fuck did he care if Mike and the new girl hooked up? Maybe he *was* jealous.

This thought filled the Dishwasher with shame. Everything was filling him with shame lately. Shame on top of shame. He thought about the fight he had with the idiot roommates earlier. The broken window. The bag of beers. The steak, and Toby smashing their controllers. The trash he threw on the couch that would be on his bed when he got back home. He couldn't take it anymore. He needed a new life. The sooner the better. It was cold now. He could see his breath. His loins were ice cold. The breeze blowing on his apron. Tomorrow. Tomorrow he would put his long johns on. Even that filled him with shame. He hadn't washed them since he took them off in the spring. Or had he? Did he wash them with the clothes he just washed? He couldn't remember. But that wasn't something he would normally do. Thinking ahead. Even for a minute. His whole life, he always just went from moment to moment. Minute to minute. Never really thinking things through. Not in the way most people did. Most people. Who are *most people*? He felt confused. The Dishwasher. Nothing was adding up anymore. The job sucked. Toby sucked. The apartment sucked. Laramie sucked. Winter sucked. Winter sucked and it wasn't even winter yet. And all this shame. Sliding down his insides. His thoughts. His desires. Just filled with shame.

He thought about his credo again. How shame was worse than guilt. With guilt you could at least ask for forgiveness. Shame lasted forever. He thought about dying. Lying on his deathbed. No guilt. Just shame. How could he ask for forgiveness for all the shame he experienced in his life? Who would abolish him of those things? Was that what life was? All the shame from a past life just piled on, the minute you were born? And then it was your job to have an ounce of courage to break the cycle? And if you couldn't break the cycle then that shame added to the other shame, so that when you got born again you had just piles and piles of shame. Shame so deep that even the most courageous fool alive couldn't get through it in a million lifetimes.

The Dishwasher decided he would apologize to Mike when he went back inside. But on his way through the prep room he saw that Mike was being handed a piece of paper by the new prep cook. He assumed it was her phone number. She was smiling. Flirting. The Dishwasher was overtaken with jealousy. There was no way he would apologize now. Fuck that guy.

The night was reaching an end. The Dishwasher was working as fast as he could to stay ahead. Mike came back. The Dishwasher tried to ignore him. Mike said:

"I got her number."

"Good for you."

"I think I might call her later tonight."

"Just let me know when to rent the tux."

"Oh, I will. I most certainly will."

"Dude, just deal with those scrubbers, would ya."

"Goin' to the chapel and we're gonna get married...."

Mike sang this. And then he whistled the tune. For the rest of the night, he whistled the tune. At first it was on purpose, then it became second nature. The sound was very grating on the Dishwasher's nerves. He just wanted to think. To do some thinking. But no. He had to deal with this bullshit. He tried to ignore it. He tried and tried. Eventually he started whistling it himself. Eventually they became in sync. Finishing the night as a team. By the time the kitchen closed, they were well ahead of everyone else. Just waiting for the last of the utensils and rubber mats. The Dishwasher let Mike go. He was about to apologize, but then Mike said:

"Wish me luck on my date!" The Dishwasher rolled up a wet rag and snapped Mike's bottom. Mike spun around like he was about to punch the Dishwasher. The Dishwasher jumped back. He hadn't meant to connect. He felt bad about it. That was going to leave a welt, he thought. He said:

"Dude! I am sorry, I didn't mean to connect!" Mike just looked at him with annoyed, tired eyes. Eyes that said, "It's not worth it."

This filled the Dishwasher with shame. He wasn't even worth punching in the face. Not even by a little dork that could barely hold a candle to him. Dishwashing-wise.

Mike walked away. The Dishwasher waited for the last rubber mat. Ran all of them through. Replaced them to where they had come from. Cleaned the Hobart. Drained it. Ran it twice. Drained it again. Turned off the light. He went to the back. Clocked out. Took his white button-up shirt off. Threw it in the hamper. His apron. He threw the paper hat in the trash. The hairnet. Put his hoodie on. Looked at the plastic garbage bag of beers. Sighed. What the hell was he going to do with them? He picked them up. They were heavy. Dong Smells wasn't around so he didn't want to go have his shift drink. It was Friday. The Buckhorn would be packed. There would be a cover and a band. School started on Monday. It might be fun, he thought. The Dishwasher. There would be some babes at least. Maybe even some people he knew. Most likely there would be people he knew, but would it be worth seeing anybody? He had nothing to say. Nothing new had happened. He had the garbage bag of beers.

He went out to the alley. The cold nearly knocked his dick off. How did it get cold so quick? He wished he had a sweater. He zipped his hoodie up. Took a soft pack out of his jeans pocket.

Squeezed one out. Bent it straight. Lit it. The flat smoke drifted into the cold air. He found this interesting. That smoke would have the same shape as the cigarette. He blew smoke out of his nose. The smoke didn't look like nostrils. It just looked like smoke.

He was on the fence. It was not even midnight. The bar would be open for another two hours. He didn't want to go home, but he wasn't in the mood for the bar either. He walked across the parking lot. Took a left down the train tracks. Came to the metal viaduct that the workers used to cross the tracks during busy times. It was supposed to be off-limits to pedestrians, but sometimes people would go up on it to smoke weed. Or throw rocks at trains. There were no lights pointed on it. Which made it a perfect hangout. He climbed the metal stairs. Walked to the middle. Sat down. Stared off into the distance. Down the train tracks.

To the left of him was the poor part of town. To the right, the business district. He didn't need to worry about cops on the left side. They wouldn't be patrolling that part of town. He only kind of needed to worry about the cops on the right side. It was Friday, so they would be busy pulling over drunk drivers.

The Dishwasher opened the garbage bag full of beers. Took one out. Opened it. It foamed everywhere. He said, "Shit." Then hung it over the tracks to finish foaming. He took a drink. It was warm. The beer. But so what? The Dishwasher drank it. Looking out down the tracks. Things were peaceful. A train came down the line. Slowly. The lights blinding him. He waved at the conductor. The conductor waved back. He threw his empty can of beer on top of a train car. Then he reached into the garbage bag of beers and got another one. He opened this one more carefully. It only kind of foamed. He drank it slowly. Trying to think.

There was nothing to think about. His mind was made up. The call with Troll had done it. He would get on a bus to Denver. The real question was when. He had work tomorrow. Then he had Sunday and Monday off. He could go tomorrow to the bus depot and figure out the schedule. Or he could just call the people. That would save him a trip. Find out the price. Or, even better yet, he could go down to the bus depot with his things and just wait it out. The bus depot was out past the gas station where he had made the phone call earlier. Nobody would be looking for him out there, if he did that. Not Toby or the idiot roommates or the Altitude. He could just put his stuff in the plastic garbage bag and be gone. See you later, suckers. I hope you choke on it.

But the thought filled the Dishwasher with shame. He should tell the Altitude he was leaving. Give them notice. But fuck them. What did they ever do for him? Seven-fifty an hour for the best wash in town? Bullshit. He didn't owe them anything. He thought about the broken window in the idiot roommates' room. The smashed controllers. He had the same reaction. Fuck them. Both those fuckers. Eating his steak when he went to buy them beer. The broken toothbrush. But Toby? What did he owe Toby? I mean, she was very nice about his meltdown. But so what? If anything, she somehow caused it. Not only that, but they were destined to fail as a couple. It was just a matter of time.

The biggest problem was what to do when he got to Denver. He had no address to go to. He forgot to ask. Not only that, but he didn't know Denver at all. How could he get his hands on a map before he left? The bookstore would have one. He would just need an address. Although, maybe he could call Troll and Bogart when he got there. Have them come pick him up. The bus depot in Denver must be in the middle of the city, right?

It turned out the Dishwasher had loads of things to think about. He dropped the second beer can on the tracks. Opened another one. Carefully. He was now very excited.

He lit another cigarette. Thinking about the new life he would lead. The new job he could get. Living in a city. With good roommates instead of idiot roommates. Not only that, but he had another week of pay coming to him. The way the pay system worked, there was a week delay. That meant another 300 dollars coming his way. Add that to the check he had in his wallet. He would be doing pretty good. Nearly a thousand dollars.

The only problem was he needed money for the bus ticket. He would have to wait until Monday to get it. When the banks were open. He could empty his account. But that meant waiting until Monday. Suddenly he wasn't very excited anymore. That was three days. A lot could happen in three days. For all he knew, Toby would move in over the weekend. So she could gain access to the second roommate's unnaturally large things. This filled the Dishwasher with a new jealousy. A jealousy he didn't want to confront.

He dropped the third beer can on the tracks. Opened another one. Not caring if it spilled foam everywhere. He drank it. Faster than he meant to. He sat there burping foam for a while. Trying not to puke. He managed to keep it down. Mostly. He put the can down. He stood up to piss on the tracks. Nearly vomited while he was doing it. He held it in, though. He kicked the nearly empty can onto the tracks. Bent over. Picked up the garbage bag full of beers.

The Dishwasher walked to the end of the metal viaduct. Climbed down the ladder. He walked through the parking lot. Looking at the Altitude's back door. The lights were on in the prep room. He tried to remember if he had shut them off. It didn't matter. He wasn't going back in. Even if he forgot.

A cop car turned down the alley. Slowed down. A spotlight came on. Pointed at the Dishwasher. Holding the garbage bag full of beers. He froze. The cop said:

"What are you doing?"

"Walking."

"What's in the bag?"

"Stuff."

"You'd better come over here."

The Dishwasher fought every urge in his body telling him to run. He had a route mapped out in his head. The cop would have to go around the corner or back up before he could chase him.

He could probably get to the corner before they caught up to him, and then he could either hide somewhere or make a run for it.

He was about to do this when something else kicked in. He wasn't doing anything wrong. He was old enough to be holding a bag of beers. The cops couldn't do anything to him. He was within his rights. Or at least he thought he was.

He didn't run. He walked towards the cop car. Towards the spotlight. He got close enough that the cop said:

"Okay, don't move. Open the bag." The Dishwasher opened the bag. Pulling it up to show the beers. "Beers?"

"Beers."

"You old enough to be drinkin'?"

"I got beers, don't I?"

"You better adjust that attitude, boy."

"They're my beers, sir."

"How many beers you got there?" The Dishwasher looked in the garbage bag.

"Twelve, I guess."

"Why do you have twelve beers in a trash bag?"

"I don't know, how many beers am I supposed to have?"

"Where were you just at?"

"Walking."

"I know you were walking, but where were you walking at?"

"I don't know, from where I came from, I guess."

"Jesus, kid, just tell me why you are carrying twelve beers in a garbage bag."

"You really want to know, sir?"

"I said as much, did I not?"

"Well, it all started last night when I got home from work."

"Oh, Jesus Christ, just get yourself home. I don't want to see you around here anymore."

The cop drove away. The Dishwasher was glad he hadn't run. That would have been stupid. The cops would have chased him and he would have probably ended up in jail, or worse. His nerves were tight. The Dishwasher's. He was shaking. He fumbled around and lit a cigarette. Not sure what to do.

The cops were a menace. He hated them more than the assholes with the big trucks. At least the goons in the trucks just called him a faggot. The cops could easily beat him down. Or throw him in jail for doing nothing. He didn't know why he was always a smart-ass when he talked to them. But they were bullies. They expected weakness. When they didn't get it, they became confused. So maybe it was smart to act that way? There was no telling. He figured they must have better things to do than harass him. The Dishwasher. But that was not apparent.

He wondered if he should ditch the garbage bag of beers in the entrance to the Altitude. He could pick them up tomorrow. But, then again, he was hatching a plan to drink them at the Buckhorn. He could pay at the door and then just drink the beers. That would save him like a million dollars. And because they were the same beers that they served, nobody would notice. He would just have to be discreet about it.

The Dishwasher walked down the alley. Smoking his cigarette. Walked by the alley door of the Buckhorn. Some asshole was pissing behind the dumpsters. He shook his dick at the Dishwasher. Said, "Want some lemonade, faggot?" The Dishwasher looked down. Not wanting to engage. When he turned the corner, the place was a madhouse. People on the sidewalk. People inside. People in line. Everyone as loud as shit. Drunk. He pushed forward. Got to the bouncer. Showed his ID. Paid the five dollars. Got a stamp. Pushed his way inside.

The bar was a throng. The band was not very good, but they were playing the hits. The Dishwasher went to the back. Reached into the garbage bag of beers. Took one out. Opened it as discreetly as he could. Foam went everywhere. He just let it do what it was doing. Looking around to see if anyone saw. Nobody did. Nobody cared.

He saw a few people he knew. The Dishwasher. Nobody he wanted to talk to. He watched the band. They played music.

Stopping every now and again for applause. The Dishwasher finished his beer. He didn't know what to do with it. If he went to the bar and left it there then someone would know that he was out of beer. He let the empty can fall to the ground. He kicked it into the crowd. Watching for somebody to step on it. It just bounced around for a while. Then it was out of sight.

He opened another. The Dishwasher did. The bag was getting lighter. He was now drunk. There were cute girls everywhere. He wanted to talk to some of them. Every now and again, though, he would smell the mildew coming off of his jeans. This made him self-conscious. Plus he kept finding steak in his teeth. Now he was afraid that he smelled bad and had food in his mouth. He tried his hardest to have fun, but his heart wasn't in it.

Most of the people there were college kids. Making the best of their last days before classes started. A cute girl came up to him and started dancing close. She was about to say something and then made a face. She walked away. There was no denying it. He smelled like fryer oil and mildew. Even as handsome as he was. The Dishwasher. As handsome as he thought he was, there was no getting away from his job. He was regretting that you couldn't smoke in bars anymore. He could have easily avoided the shame of a cute girl coming up to dance with him and then recoiling in disgust. The Dishwasher thought this was funny, at first, but then the shame of it all sent him spiraling into insecurity. He finished the beer. Dropped it to the floor. Kicked it into the crowd. Then walked towards the alley door. Pushed it open. Was met with a guy pissing. The guy shook his penis at the Dishwasher. He said:

"Hey, faggot, want some lemonade?" The Dishwasher sighed. He didn't want any lemonade. He didn't want any lemonade at all. He just wanted to go to sleep and be done with everything. He walked down the alley. Hoping that the cops wouldn't come around the corner and give him shit for still being out with his bag of beers.

He made it back to the apartment without incident. When he opened the apartment door, the trash was on the counter again. From the couch. The idiot roommates hadn't put it on his bed like he had assumed. They were in the living room again. Sitting on the floor. Their backs pushed against the couch. The Dishwasher walked to the doorway. Next to the bathroom. Next to the kitchen sink. They had new controllers. They were smoking. Both of them. The Dishwasher threw the garbage bag of beers on the floor between them. He said:

"Merry Christmas."

"Oh! No shit!" They both reached inside to get a beer. The first roommate said:

"It's warm. What the hell?"

"Yeah, well."

"Dude, you owe us a window. And that bitch of yours..."

"Hey!"

"Your *girlfriend* owes us controllers."

"I'll get right on that."

"We're serious, dude, I think we might sue," the second roommate said.

"Call my lawyer."

"We will! I hope you have money!"

"I'm going to bed."

The Dishwasher went into the bathroom. He pissed. Brushed his teeth with the half toothbrush. Turned the light off. Took a drink from the faucet. Listened to the idiot roommates play their video game. He guessed that Toby hadn't come over and started having sex with the second roommate. Like she threatened. Because she wasn't in his room when he got there.

The Dishwasher undid his velcros. Kicked them off. Took his jeans off. Laid them out to dry. Took his hoodie and shirt off. Got into bed. The mattress was cold. He was naked. He pulled the blanket over his body. Got an erection. Played with his things for a moment. Thinking of Lisa's cute little buns in their black nylon pants. Like he had predicted. Finished. Wiped himself up with a dirty sock. Curled up into a fetal position. Listened to a train go by. Then disappeared from this earth. Tired, drunk, and confused.

24

The Dishwasher woke up early. Early for him. Early for him on a day when he had to work. Not really noon, but around noon. He had some business to attend to. He got up. He didn't follow his usual routine. He thought about this as he walked into the bathroom. He wondered if he would regret it. If he would spend the day distracted.

At the moment, he felt fine. He wasn't hungover. He went into the bathroom. Remembered the towel. Went back to his room. Grabbed his dirty towel. Smelled it. Frowned. Mildew. Everything was mildew. His heart felt like mildew at this point. Not pure anymore. But not rotten either. Just something growing that he couldn't clean. Shameful and unpleasant. He was thinking, it seemed like some sort of metaphor. But he couldn't quite piece the idea together in the right way to make it clever. It was just some sort of dumb poem running around in his head.

He started to write the poem: "This wet and humid heart / That can not dry / It stinks / To high heaven."

He used the toilet. The shower was hot by the time he was done. The bathroom steaming. He got into the shower. The bar of soap nearly disintegrated. Just sitting there in a pile of film. Scum. The Dishwasher was annoyed. He ignored his annoyance. He got out. Dried himself off with the stinking towel. Wrapped it around his waist. Brushed his teeth with the half toothbrush. Wiped the mirror down. Removing the fog. He looked at his splotchy face. He needed to shave. He needed some sun. He needed to eat more. His teeth were looking good, however.

He left the bathroom. Looked into the living room. There were empty beer cans and cigarette butts everywhere. He would be glad to be done with this nonsense. These idiot roommates. He heard a loud fart come out of their bedroom. Then some giggles. He laughed. One of the roommates yelled:

"You owe us some new controllers and a window, butthole!"

The Dishwasher went into his room. He thought about things. He was in a rush though. He got dressed. Thinking about putting on the long johns. He didn't. He looked out the window. It was bright and sunny. He would be fine. Tomorrow, he thought. He rooted around and found a clean T-shirt and some clean socks. Put them on. Walked back into the kitchen and then the living room. Grabbed the plastic garbage bag that had held the beers. Looked inside it. For holes. There were no holes. He took it back to his room. Put his velcros on. His hoodie. Made sure he had his wallet and smokes. Walked out of the apartment. Down the carpeted stairs. He looked in the open mailbox. It was still not fixed. There was nothing. Not for him, at least.

He walked out the front door of the apartment building. The cool air hit his loins. His things shriveled. Maybe he should have put his long johns on, actually? He walked down the street. Under the overpass. Turned right. Walked down the main, busy street. Keeping an eye out for big trucks. None came by. Nobody called him a faggot. He got to the parking lot of the shopping center. Walked to the bookstore. Went inside. Went straight to the coffee station. Made himself a coffee. Pouring sugar and imitation powdered cream in the cup. He stirred it with a thin plastic straw. Licked the straw. Threw it into the trash. Walked over to the map section. Found a map of Colorado. Took it to a table. Set it down. Set his coffee on the table. Sat down himself.

The bookstore was mostly empty. There were some tunes playing over the loudspeaker. He opened the map book to the Denver pages. He tried to make sense of it. What was what. Where was where. He noticed that there was a street called Colfax that ran east to west. There was a street called Colorado that ran north to south. Aside from that, it was all just a bunch of neighborhoods he didn't recognize. Not that he recognized *anything*. It was a big city. He studied the map for some time. Got up and made himself another coffee. He thought he found where the bus station was. But that was about it.

He finished his second cup of coffee. Got up. Put the map back. Went into the bathroom. Took a leak. Went back to the table. Grabbed the empty coffee cup. Threw it in the trash. Walked back outside. He took his nearly empty soft pack out of his jeans pocket. Squeezed one out. Straightened it. Lit it. Watched the cigarette shoot square smoke. Blew smoke out of his lungs. He looked around. For a pay phone. He saw one over at the chain diner. Walked across the parking lot. Dialed the 800 number. Dialed the pin. Waited. Dialed Troll and Bogart's phone number. Waited. Soon there was ringing. A few rings later, Troll picked up. He sounded like he had been sleeping. He said:

"Yel-low?"

"Hi Troll, it's Disher over here in Laramie, Wyoming." Once again he thought of his dad when he said this.

"Oh, hey, man!"

"Hey! Sorry to wake you."

"Oh, no prob, dog. Just waking up."

"Hey, what is your address? I am thinking of coming up sooner than later."

"Oh, no shit! Um..." Troll told him the address. The information meant nothing. To the Dishwasher. He memorized it, though.

"Well, okay then!"

"When you thinking of coming?"

"I don't know, Monday maybe?"

"Well, shit, soon. Nice. Just give us a call from the bus station, we can pick you up."

"No shit?"

"Yeah, I mean, if it's Monday. I don't work and Bogart gets off early. When does the bus come in?"

"Don't know, about to find out."

"Well, okay." A voice came over the phone. Saying there was one minute left on the card.

"Hey, man, I gotta go, the thing said my time's up."

"Right on."

"Right on, in—" The phone cut off. "Indeed" was what he was going to say. There was nothing to do about it, though. The Dishwasher thought about buying another phone card, but he didn't have very much money left in his wallet. He took it out and double-checked. He had some money. Not enough, though. He would have to go to the bank on Monday. Cash his check and maybe close his bank account. He wasn't sure if they had his bank brand down in Denver. Plus, he would need all the money he could get. So he could buy the bus ticket and not have to worry about getting money when he got there. And really, if he needed to, he could open a new bank account in Denver. He supposed. Although he had no proof of that. But so what? He would just have all the money he owned in the world on him at that point. He thought about the last paycheck from the Altitude. He could deal with that when he got it. They must have check cashing places there too, if needed? He supposed.

He stood there for a second in front of the chain diner. Hanging up the phone. Thinking. He was about to go back to the bookstore and look at the map again, but then he thought that if Troll and Bogart were going to pick him up when he got to Denver, what was the point? It's not like he would be able to walk to their place anyway. Denver was huge. He was hit with a sudden panic. The idea of being in a big city without any idea about anything. He confused himself. Almost decided not to go. He felt ashamed. What had been his plan in the first place? If Troll hadn't said they would pick him up from the bus? Was he going to take another bus? A taxi? He hadn't thought this through. It didn't matter now, though.

The Dishwasher started walking. Hoping the feelings of shame would go away. He walked down the busy main street. Not paying attention to anything, aside from his thoughts. He got to the streetlights by the gas station where he usually bought coffee and cigarettes. A big truck pulled up next to him. Slowed down. The passenger-side window rolled down. A paper cup came flying at him. He barely dodged out of the way. The asshole that threw it yelled:

"Suck on that, faggot!"

The cup exploded next to his feet. Chewing spit went everywhere. Up his jeans leg. The Dishwasher dry heaved. It was visceral. Grotesque. The truck peeled out. Shooting gravel from the rear tires. Shooting tiny rocks at the Dishwasher. The Dishwasher sighed. He wasn't so ashamed anymore. He was glad to be getting out of this shithole. He walked and walked. All the way to the interstate. Then he took a left. Walked up a grassy hill. Looked around. He could see the bus depot. But he couldn't figure out how to get there. The Dishwasher. He thought for a second about running across the interstate. But that was too stupid. Even for him. The Dishwasher.

He walked back down the grassy hill. Took a left. Under the interstate. Walked for about half a mile, then crossed an on-ramp. He had to go around a little pond, and then down onto a weird side street that didn't really make sense until he finally came to the end of it. There was a hill and then the road led down onto a highway. The highway led to the bus depot. He was confused about why the bus depot was in such an odd place. Kind of in the middle of nowhere. He didn't understand why it was really only accessible to vehicles. Like, why did they assume you would have a car if you were taking a bus? He didn't have any answers for himself. The Dishwasher. He then thought about why he even knew the bus depot was where it was. Then he remembered taking a trip out to Vedauwoo. With Curry and Dong Smells, to spend the night taking mushrooms and playing guitar. When Curry had made up that song he wrote that was just the word:

Bouillon.

Over and over again. But he sang it in a singsong voice. Bouillon. Like: Do dee doo. Bou-li-on. He had noticed the bus depot as they got onto the interstate. The Dishwasher. He must have put it in his memory banks. The bus depot.

The Dishwasher walked down the highway until he got to the bus depot. He went inside when he got there. There was nobody in the lobby. There were no buses waiting. There was a pop machine and a snack machine. A bench. A kiosk. There was a man behind the kiosk desk. Standing. There was a thing behind him that said:

Billings: 10:20 AM
Salt Lake City: 11:14 AM
Chicago: 3:07 PM
Denver: 5:09 PM
The man behind the desk said:
"Can I help you?"
"Oh, I guess not. The bus leaves for Denver at five?"
"5:09 p.m."
"Every day?"
"Every day."
"How much?"
"Sixty-nine, anytime."
"What do you mean?"
"Sixty-nine dollars. All the time. That is our motto. Anywhere in the U.S."
"Wait, what? I can take a bus anywhere in the U.S. for sixty-nine dollars? Even Alaska and Hawaii?"
"Well no, not Alaska. You can't take a bus to Hawaii."
"Even New York?"
"Yeppers."
"Whoa."
"Pretty good, right?"
"I mean."
The Dishwasher stood there. He was out of questions. He said:
"Okay, then."
"Okay."
"Oh! Can I just show up and get a ticket when I get here?"

"You can—as long as the bus isn't full, you can get on it."

"And does that happen? The bus being full and all?"

"Depends on the bus. Denver and Chicago, yes; Billings, not so much."

"Shit. Okay."

"You got somewhere to be?"

"I was thinking, on Monday, of going to Denver."

"Yeah, Monday, I think you'll prolly be alright."

"Well, okay then."

"Okay."

"See ya then!"

"You got it."

The Dishwasher processed this information while he walked back to the underpass of the interstate. Sixty-nine, anytime. That was kind of a great motto. How could they do that? It made sense to go to Denver with that price, but New York City? They must be losing tons of money. Like, what if you took a bus from Maine to Los Angeles? That would be a cheap trip. He wondered if anyone did that. Just because they could. He wondered if maybe that was what he should do instead. See the country. That would be wild. Basically a free ride. He tried to calculate mileage versus money. He knew the U.S. was 3,000 miles coast to coast, but at an angle like that? Or better yet, Seattle to Miami. That had to be like 4,000 miles. Divided by sixty-nine dollars? That would be like something like 60 cents a mile. Or something.

As he was doing these calculations, he got confused about what the dollar amount meant. The Dishwasher. Was 60 cents a mile a good thing or a bad thing? Or maybe it would be 0.06 cents a mile? That would be better. Maybe it was even less than that?—0.006 cents a mile. Had he not divided by 100 enough times? The Dishwasher was good at some math, but these kinds of problems always stumped him. All he knew was that it would be a good deal to go from Maine to Los Angeles or from Seattle to Miami. The trip to Denver wasn't such a good deal, though. It was like a two-hour trip. But whatever. At this point he would pay a hundred bucks to get out of town, if that was what the price was. He had made up his mind. He would do it. And that would be that.

He suddenly got really afraid. This was such a big decision that he couldn't even process it. He had to stop under the underpass to get his bearings again. But then the sound of cars and trucks passing over just made him more anxious. The hair stood up on his arms. He thought he might pass out. Maybe he was hungover? Dehydrated.

He started running. Trying to get away from what he assumed was death. He thought he was dying. He could barely see. He got to the laundromat before he calmed down again. He wasn't dying. His heart was racing now. He was shaking. He wanted to lie down and die. Or at least sleep for a while. His whole life was suddenly right in front of his face. Too close to look at. Toby and Denver and the Altitude and the idiot roommates and Norman. Norman. He didn't know why he was thinking about Norman again. But he was. The Dishwasher. He was starting to realize that he wanted to punch Norman's stupid face for being a big jerk. For making him feel like shit. The Dishwasher. He didn't usually hold grudges. But now that he thought about it, Norman was an asshole that needed to be roughed up. He started thinking about punching Norman in the face. The Dishwasher. This relieved him of his anxiety attack.

Before he knew it, he was back in front of his apartment building. Then he was walking up the carpeted stairs. Then he was inside the kitchen. He was home safe now. Exhausted from his outing. He took a drink from the kitchen faucet. Wiped his face. Then he wiped his wet hand on his jeans. He went into his room to have a look around.

———

The Dishwasher stared at his possessions for a while. He didn't have much. Just clothes and a blanket. The mattress had come with the room. All of his clothes could fit into the plastic garbage bag. He would leave some behind, though. Make room for his coat and his sweaters. He looked around for his long johns. He found them. Smelled them. They smelled normal. Kind of like a butt, where his butt lived when he wore them. But nothing gross. He checked out his change collection. There was nothing silver anymore. Just pennies. He could leave them for the idiot roommates. Like a going away present. But that was it. All that he owned was basically a tramp's handkerchief, except in a black plastic garbage bag.

There wouldn't be a stick. And he would have to carry the blanket. He could leave the pillow behind. Also for his idiot roommates. They could drool all over it, for all he cared. Maybe they could tape it to the broken window to keep the cold out. Then again, they would need to get some tape to get that done. Which seemed like a hard thing for them to procure. But whatever, they did manage to get all those beers that one time. And they did manage to get new controllers for their video games. So, who knows?

The Dishwasher lay down on the mattress. He read his book for a while. Fell asleep. Woke up a little while later. Very hungry. He wasn't sure what time it was, but he didn't care. He got up. Went into the bathroom. Brushed his teeth with the half toothbrush. Looked at it. Thought about it. He would take that too. That and the toothpaste. This thought gave him pleasure. The idea that those assholes wouldn't even have a toothbrush when he left. That they would just be sitting around playing video games with a broken window, no toothbrush, the bar of soap just a whisper of scum. They wouldn't know what hit them. He would be gone and they would be fucked.

He made sure he had all his things, and left the apartment. He was afraid he was too early now. When he thought about it. When he got outside. When he realized that his idiot roommates weren't in the living room when he left. But the sun was going down. So who knows?

When he got to the Altitude, he was early. But only kind of. It was fifteen minutes before five. He looked at the clock, turned around, and went back outside. He squeezed a smoke out. From his soft pack. Straightened it. Lit it. Stood there smoking. Standing in putrid grease. Next to the dumpsters. He was feeling pretty good. The Dishwasher.

The sun was setting. Fall was turning into winter. Kind of. It was still September, but the cold was blowing in from the mountains. A train went by. Blowing a sad song. Or at least it seemed sad. The Dishwasher was feeling kind of nostalgic.

This would be his last night of work. If he played it right. He wouldn't tell anybody. He couldn't. They would just beg him to stay. He decided. He wasn't sure. Or certain how anyone would feel when he left. They would just be annoyed that he left. Leaving them with no dishwasher to do the dishes. But fuck them. He thought. They didn't care. If they cared, they would pay him more money for doing his job. The job that they were certain anyone could do. They didn't care that he was good at his job. The Dishwasher. Even though he proved it every night. Every single night. They would see. See how much they needed him when he was gone. And they only had Mike to do their bidding. Mike, or some other goon that would sleep with all the prep cooks and then brag about it. Making everyone else feel jealous. Like he was. The Dishwasher.

The Dishwasher stopped his thinking in its tracks. He was confused by jealousy. He didn't really feel it the same way that other people did. Or, he assumed he didn't. He wasn't jealous that Mike could get the new prep cook's phone number. He was jealous that the new prep cook couldn't see how awesome the Dishwasher was. That was different. It was her loss. Not his. If only she knew how much Toby liked the way that he made sweet love to her, then she would understand that she was missing out. He had some good moves. Moves that all the ladies loved. Even if he smelled like mildew all the time. That wasn't his fault. It was the job's fault. Not only that, but he had an idea about how the universe worked and one day he would write a whole book about it. The Dishwasher would. He would solve all of life's problems and it would be rather glorious and the new prep cook would be filled with regret for not picking the Dishwasher over that little pip-squeak Mike.

The Dishwasher finished his smoke. Went inside. Hung his hoodie up. Put his wallet and the unopened pack of smokes in the pocket. Found a button-up white shirt that fit him. Put it on. Put an apron on. A hairnet. A paper hat. Clocked in. Walked through the prep room. The new prep cook was there. The Dishwasher blushed. Said hi. She nodded. Went back to placing bacon on half sheets. The Dishwasher went into the dish room. There was a medium amount of dishes. The Dishwasher started running the sinks. Ronito came in. He said:

"Yo, Disher, what's the good word?"

"Oh, the usual. Hey! You busy?"

"Not yet."

"Can I get a reuben with curlies?"

"You got it, dog."

"Thanks, man."

Ronito went back to the line. The Dishwasher scraped some dishes. Made sure the Hobart was clean. Ran the rest of the sinks. Went to the bar to get a pop. Came back. Got to work. A while later, Ronito came into the dish room with the reuben and curlies. The Dishwasher thanked him. Went around the corner and poured ketchup onto his plate from the waitresses' refilling bag that was hanging from the wall. He put the plate of food on the metal shelves in the dish room. Had a few bites from the sandwich. Drank some pop from the straw. Went back to scraping plates and running dishes through the Hobart.

Soon after, Lisa came in to ask for him to go down and bring a jar of olives up. He said he would. She thanked him. Walking away. He watched her tiny buns in her black nylon pants. Suddenly he was overwhelmed with thoughts. He regretted not taking care of things earlier. Now he was very distracted. He walked to the back of the restaurant. Down the stairs into the dry storage cellar. He was suddenly very hard. It took all of his effort to not take it out and empty himself out.

He grabbed the olives. Ran back upstairs. Holding the jar of olives over his erection. He was very ashamed. Luckily he was soft again when he got to the bar. Randy thanked him for the olives. The Dishwasher went back to the dish room. He had a few more bites of his reuben. Dipped a couple curly fries in ketchup. Went back to doing dishes.

25

Around six, Mike showed up. He was chipper and annoying. According to the Dishwasher. He didn't tell anyone this. He just thought it. The little pip-squeak. With his good haircut and charmful charms.

Mike wasted no time before giving the Dishwasher grief about the new prep cook. He said: "Oh, hey Disher. Sorry I'm late, I was just in the prep room making plans for later. I must have lost track of the time."

"The joke's on you—you're early."

"Oh, I don't come early, unlike you."

"That doesn't even make sense."

"Ask the new prep cook, she can explain it to you."

"Dude, she can probably hear you."

"Well, your mom can hear *you*."

"Well, your mom can't hear nothing because her legs are behind her ears."

"Low blow, man. My mom is dead."

"Shit! I am so sorry!"

"Nah, just joking."

"What the fuck?"

The Dishwasher and Mike were heading into bad territory. Something had shifted in their dynamic and Mike was acting like a real asshole about it. The Dishwasher would have been very agitated about this, normally. But tonight was different than most nights.

It was his last night of work. He had decided. And he was the only one that knew it. It was a secret. His secret. The Dishwasher's.

He took some pleasure in slacking at his job, seeing if Mike could keep up. This annoyed Mike. He just thought the Dishwasher was fucking with him. When he would slow down, Mike would slow down. Things would pile up. Then the Dishwasher would laugh about how Mike couldn't actually handle the job. And Mike would laugh, thinking he was getting back at the Dishwasher. In the end, they both suffered. It was a stupid game. Played by a couple of idiots.

At a certain point, the dishes started really flying into the dish room and they both had to focus. By the time the actual rush started, they were backed up to a degree that they never really recovered from until the night was finished. A thing that kind of made the Dishwasher sad. He'd wanted to go out on top. Now he couldn't. He would have to work his ass off, for no other reason than he'd wanted to fuck with Mike.

At one point, he traded jobs with Mike. The Dishwasher. Scrubbing pots and dealing with the clean dishes. Dong Smells came into the dish room. Dropped some dirty frying pans off. Talked to the Dishwasher. He said:

"Stick tonight? The Slippery Wrist is coming by at closing."

"Total."

"You get that number?"

"I did. Thanks."

"You call them?"

"I did, I'll tell you about it later."

"Oh, really?"

"I mean, yeah, keep it on the down low."

"Right on."

Dong Smells went back to the fry station. Mike overheard the conversation. He was curious. He said:

"Keep what on the down low?"

"None of your business."

"C'mon man! I am your work buddy. You gotta tell me, it's the code, remember?"

"What the hell are you talking about?"

"The dishwasher's code, didn't you tell me about the dishwasher's code?"

"I don't think, I mean, oh, you're joking." Mike was smiling. It was true that the Dishwasher had a dishwasher's code, but he would never tell anyone about it. Not because he didn't believe in it, it was just that nobody would take him seriously. Especially a little worm like Mike.

"Dude, just tell me the hot gossip. This job is so very boring."

"Mind your own business."

"Mind your mom's business."

"Oh, grow up."

The Dishwasher and Mike made it through the night without really speaking any more to each other. At one point, Mike went into the prep room to flirt with the new prep cook. This was a nice break for the Dishwasher. Even though he was jealous about it. The Dishwasher.

He made an excuse to take some trash out, even though the bag was only half-full. So he could eavesdrop. But he couldn't hear their conversation when he walked by. He could just see them flirting, while chaos controlled the kitchen. He threw the trash bag in the dumpster. A cold breeze went by. Freezing his wet loins. The Dishwasher's. He would need to put his long johns on sooner than later. His loins recoiled from the cold.

He went back inside. Trying again to catch a little bit of conversation. He heard nothing. He went back to the dish room. Put a new trash bag in the garbage can. Hurried through some new dishes. Scraping and spraying. He was trying to ignore the fact that he was jealous. He didn't understand the jealousy. What did Mike have that he didn't? The Dishwasher. I mean, he was just some short jerk with a nice charm and good looks and a nice haircut. Wimpy macho. The kid was on the soccer team. He knew that. The Dishwasher. Was that what the girls wanted? A soccer kid with a nice haircut? A charming wimpy macho kind of guy? What was it that he had that the Dishwasher didn't have?

Then he had a shameful flashback to the girl from last night, who wanted to dance with him at the Buckhorn. Who turned around and walked away when she smelled him. The shame was unbearable. He once again had the thought about shame and guilt. How guilt was easy, you could always ask for forgiveness, but shame, shame lasted forever. There was no way to rid yourself of shame. It was bone-deep.

He made a promise to himself to clean up his act when he got to Denver. To stop working as a dishwasher. To get a job where he could have clean clothes and not smell like mildew and putrid grease all the time. Maybe an office job or something. Something that didn't involve working your ass off for peanuts. That you could have pride in. Like accounting or something. But the Dishwasher would need to go to college for that. Or at least get a GED or something. At the moment, he kind of only had one option. Work in a kitchen washing dishes, or starve to death. Two options, he guessed. And starving to death wasn't much of an option. Even if it was a reality.

This thought sent panic into the Dishwasher's heart. He was about to be unemployed with only a few hundred dollars to live on. In a big city that he didn't know. He got so scared that he almost called the whole thing off. It wasn't too late. He could just deposit his check on Monday and forget all about going to Denver. Nothing would change if he did that. That would be the easy thing to do.

The Dishwasher tried to push through these thoughts. To get his courage back. The panic started a thing in his brain that he couldn't process. Suddenly he was seeing flashing lights out of the corner of his eyes. This was it. The big one. He thought. Amplifying the migraine that was about to happen.

He started shaking. Trying to ignore his eyes. He was certain he was about to die.

The light got brighter. Suddenly he could only see out of his left eye. Which was his bad eye. The eye that couldn't see very well. The eye that was getting worse as he got older. That would mean he needed to get glasses or something. Contacts.

His arms started tingling. He became insular. He had cotton in his ears. He lost focus. He panicked. Not sure what to do. Was he about to pass out? Was he having a stroke? Did he need to go to the hospital?

He took some glasses and ran out into the dining room. Trying to put them away. He was doing a bad job of it. Randy asked him if he was okay. The Dishwasher just blinked at him. Randy looked confused. The Dishwasher put the tray of glasses down and ran out the back of the restaurant.

When he got out into the alley, he puked behind the dumpster. Reuben and curly fries and pop. He stood up. Swallowed. Bent over again and puked more reuben and curly fries and pop.

He straightened up. Wiped his mouth. Swallowed again. Breathing heavily. The lights were gone. In his eyes. The Dishwasher's. His teeth hurt. Not from the stomach acid but from his sinuses. They felt like they might just pop out. Squeeze out. From pressure. His teeth. The Dishwasher's. He had a headache now. His arms were still tingling. He needed some pain medication.

He went inside. Went to the medical kit hanging from the wall in the prep room. He opened it. Grabbed the box of painkillers. Took three packets out. Put the box back. Put the three packets together and ripped the tops off. He dumped the pills into his hand. Wadded up the packages. Put them in his jeans pocket. Put the pills in his mouth. Walked into the dish room. Took a drink of his pop. Swallowed the pills.

His anxiety was gone. Now he was just trying to not vomit anymore. He focused on scrubbing pots. Spending more time than normal on them. Hiding the fact that he was in pain from Mike. Mike, who he assumed would just give him shit for it. And he wasn't wrong. Had Mike known that he just puked in the alley, he would have said something inconsiderate and stupid. Being a wimpy macho dude who played soccer. He would have said something like:

"Game face, bro." Or other such nonsense. "Push through the pain." Or, "Pain is just weakness leaving your body."

Mike was an idiot. The Dishwasher knew this. He didn't even need to hear such bullshit from him to know this.

After a while, the painkillers kicked in and things went back to normal. For the Dishwasher. He did his job, washing dishes. Putting dishes away. Scrubbing things. Breaking down cardboard. Throwing out trash bags full of wasted food. A little after eleven, the kitchen closed. The dish room became swamped with things. Mike and the Dishwasher busted ass. Their lousy game of chicken from earlier really coming back to haunt them now. The kitchen was empty for a good thirty minutes before they finished. Doing their last bit of work while standing on a pile of dirty rubber skid mats that needed to be run through the Hobart. Had it been a normal night, the Dishwasher would have sent Mike home. But he didn't want to finish the work alone. It was too much and he wanted to be done with it. The Dishwasher. He could hear the bar in the dining room hopping. He didn't bother looking out to see what was going on. He didn't want to know. He would be done soon enough. He could smoke a cigarette and then have some beers. Play some stick with Dong Smells and The Slippery Wrist. Forget all about this stupid job, and Mike and his stupid new girlfriend, and whatever else.

The Dishwasher felt a little bit of shame for calling the new prep cook stupid. He didn't mean it. Even if he'd just thought it. She was fine. Or she was just fine. He didn't know her. She seemed fine. Her only problem, as far as the Dishwasher was concerned, was that she found Mike charming and wanted to hang out with him outside of work. Which hurt the Dishwasher's feelings. For reasons he didn't care to understand.

Around midnight, they were done. The Dishwasher and Mike. Mike looked exhausted. Which gave the Dishwasher pleasure. Sure, it was a hard night. But still. It was just a normal night. Mike would have to learn. And on Tuesday, when the Dishwasher didn't show up for work, Mike would get a crash course in what the reality of washing dishes was really about. Yes, Mike would finally learn what an asshole he really was. The Dishwasher thought. Knowing full well that Mike would probably have a backbone and just tell the Altitude to fuck off. The kind of backbone the Dishwasher didn't actually have. As much as he pretended to. Because Mike didn't need the job. He had a future. He was working towards that future. The soccer and the college. Not the Dishwasher. He needed that job. As much as he hated it, it was all he had. But still. Seeing the sad and tired eyes of Mike as the last rubber mat went into the Hobart. Begging to be let go. To just be done with it all. It gave the Dishwasher pleasure.

The Dishwasher let Mike go. He told him, Good luck. Which Mike didn't understand. He thought the Dishwasher was just saying good luck with the prep cook. He said:

"Yeah, I am sure it will go well." Which the Dishwasher then misunderstood as Mike knowing that the Dishwasher was quitting and he would be just fine.

"I am sure you will figure it out." The Dishwasher said.

"What do you mean?"

"I don't know, what do *you* mean?"

"Man, you're a weirdo."

"Yeah, well, it takes one to know one."

"Yeah, okay, I'm out."

The Dishwasher walked to the back of the restaurant. Took off his apron. Put it in the dirty clothes bin. He took off his button-up white shirt. Put that in the dirty clothes bin. Threw away his paper hat. His hairnet. Reached into his pocket and threw away the wadded up empty packages of painkillers. He put his hoodie on. Transferred his wallet and the full soft pack of smokes into his jeans pockets. Went out into the alley. Squeezed the last cigarette out of the old soft pack. Straightened it. Threw the empty package in the dumpster. Lit the cigarette. Square smoke floated into the night air.

A breeze came up. His wet loins recoiled. Shrinking. He felt exposed. He would need to put those long johns on tomorrow.

He decided. He didn't know why he resisted this so much. The long johns. *I mean, I know.* He thought. If you put them on too soon, you have to take them off again. You can't just decide something like that on a whim. If every time you got cold you put your long johns on, *then* what? You're out there sweating your balls off, that's what. Too much, too soon. It somehow seemed like a metaphor. A dumbass metaphor for certain, but a metaphor nonetheless.

The Dishwasher smoked until the cigarette was done. A cop car drove by. It didn't stop. To harass him. This was a good omen. The Dishwasher decided. Then again, it was a quiet night. The last Saturday before school started. Most of the kids would be at parties. Not downtown drinking at the bars. Or, the Dishwasher supposed. There was no real logic in his thoughts. He thought that it should be busier outside. With drunks and assholes making loud noises. Pissing on things. Maybe it was too early for that? But it was midnight.

The Dishwasher didn't have an answer. He smoked his smoke. Watched a train go by. Slowly. Some guy out East had spray-painted: SMELLS on the side of one of the cars. That made him smile. He wondered who these guys were that spray-painted things on the sides of train cars. He kind of wanted to be one of them. But how do you get into that business? He supposed you could just buy some spray paint and do it, but where? And when? Omaha? Chicago? New York? He never saw anyone in Laramie doing it. But, then again, it must happen in the night when there was nobody around. But then, when were there just trains sitting around doing nothing that you would have the time to do such a thing? It was all very confusing. To the Dishwasher.

He finished smoking and went back inside. He clocked out. He hadn't meant to delay clocking out, he'd just forgot to. He wasn't sure if there was a secret camera that recorded people clocking out or not, but he assumed there was. He looked around. He flipped the bird to the imaginary cameras. A last bit of rebellion.

He looked at his time card. He had five days that weren't

crossed out. He counted the number of hours. Decided he had 375 dollars coming to him. He would need to figure out how to get that money in a couple weeks. Maybe Dong Smells could send him the check? He really didn't want to have to call and get Lisa or someone to mail it to him. She would probably be pissed off at him. Ronito and Roger would be pissed off too. Randy wouldn't care, but so what? It was unlikely that he would get Randy on the phone at some random point during open hours. He would have to get Dong Smells to do it. That was the only way. He decided he would ask him tonight. Just to be done with it. Otherwise the check would end up at the apartment. He supposed. And then what? There was no way he would see that money if his idiot roommates were involved. They would probably somehow cash the check and use it to buy themselves beer or controllers or a window or something. Those idiots. He thought.

The Dishwasher put the time card back. Walked through the kitchen. Turning lights off. He looked into the dish room. Said a somber goodbye.

The smell of bleach came into his nostrils. He was suddenly nostalgic. All those dishes he had cleaned. All the glasses and pots. The soakers. The leavers. The scrubbers and the easies.

He found himself saddened by this. All the thought, all the work, for nothing. Just to disappear into the ether. The one thing he was good at. To be gone, just like that. It was a stupid thought. But he had it. Maybe he was being dumb? Like he was giving up too soon? Like, maybe there was actually a future here. For him. The Dishwasher? He could just do it. Commit. Work his way up the ladder. Take the prep job. Then the fryer. Then the front line. He could do it, right? Have a job. Make some money. Get his own apartment. Free of lousy assholes. Shit, he could even get his GED. Go to college. Who knew? Let the science people know about his theories on gravity. He could get famous for his thoughts. Write a book about them or something.

His thoughts dissipated when he heard the crack of the pool table outside of the kitchen. He was ready for a beer. He admitted he was as tired as Mike had looked. If only to himself. Tonight was rough. It was time to be done with work. He walked into the dining room and ordered a beer from Randy. He took it up the steps into the room with the pool table. Dong Smells was getting his ass kicked by The Slippery Wrist. The Dishwasher shook his head. Dong Smells said:

"What? You think you could do better?"

"I couldn't do worse."

"Yeah, we'll see."

"Eight ball, side pocket." The Slippery Wrist finished the game. He looked up at the Dishwasher. "Scared, or what?"

"Sloppy dunk like that? I hope you like grass, because your ass is about to eat some."

"Your mom said that last night and, boy, was she satis-fied."

26

The Dishwasher lost within minutes. Went and got another beer. He didn't have enough money to pay, so he asked Randy to open a tab for him. To put against his next paycheck.

Normally that would be a horrible idea. The beers at the Altitude were expensive and when you weren't keeping track of them, your paycheck would disappear like the beer itself. There was nothing worse than renting beer against your rent money.

But tonight was different. The last night. For the Dishwasher. Or at least that was his plan.

Dong Smells was the only one that knew about his plan. And even he didn't have any of the real details. Dong Smells just knew the Dishwasher was planning on moving to Denver. And soon. Soon like maybe two weeks, not two days. Not on Monday.

The Dishwasher thanked Randy and went back up the little stairs that led to the pool table room.

The three of them stood around making lousy, crude jokes. Shooting pool. Drinking beer. Dong Smells was drinking shots whenever he went to get more beer. He got drunker faster than the Dishwasher and The Slippery Wrist.

After a while, Dong Smells wanted a smoke. He and the Dishwasher went out back. The Dishwasher opened the new pack. Threw the cellophane in the dumpster. Handed one to Dong Smells. Lit it for him. Lit one for himself. They stood there looking around. Up the alley. Sometimes at the parking lot. Dong Smells was strangely silent. Eventually he said:

"Dude, I have to confess something."

"Yaass?" The Dishwasher thought he was about to tell him his butt smelled, or something dumb and drunken.

"Um, I ran into Toby last night. At the Firelight. Your stupid brother lured me out."

"Shit! Why didn't you come get me? I was right here!"

"I know—it was a last minute thing, I'm sorry. But that's not what I have to confess. Um, I was talking to Toby and uh, um, I kind of let it slip that you were thinking of moving to Denver. Sorry, man."

The Dishwasher collapsed. Not his body. Or his face, even. His soul. His soul collapsed. Shit. This was the worst possible news. He said as much:

"Shit, man. Fuck. That is the worst possible news."

"Yeah, I mean, I am so sorry! I didn't mean to, but you know Toby, man. That chick should be a detective."

"Tell me about it. Shit, I am surprised she didn't come over. Was she drinking?"

"I don't remember. I mean, I was two sheets and kind of only a little bit remember talking to her. It dawned on me when I came to work tonight. When I saw you."

"Well, okay. That changes some things, I mean, I guess. Shit. Thanks for the heads up. Shit!"

"Yeah, sorry man."

"Fuck. Fuck. Fuck."

"I am sorry!"

"Oh, really, no worries. I mean—I once had a thought about her friend Lindsay, you know Lindsay? The one with the long hair?"

"Yeah."

"Well, I kind of had some thought that she had a nice ass, one time when we were hanging out together, and I don't fucking know how she did it, but fucking Toby managed to find this out and make a huge fucking deal about it. I mean, that girl is fucking Houdini. I'm surprised she didn't already know. I mean, about me leaving. How did she take it?"

"She wasn't happy. If I recall."

"Well, what can you do? More beer?"

"Don't mind if I do."

They threw their finished cigarettes into the alley. Dong Smells slipped on grease and nearly landed on his ass. He managed to catch himself on the dumpster. Getting putrid grease all over his hands. He cursed. Kicked the dumpster. The Dishwasher said, "Instant karma, dude." Dong Smells said, "Fuck you."

They went inside. Dong Smells went into the dish room to wash his hands. The Dishwasher got another beer. The Slippery Wrist was waiting. All the balls were waiting too. V-shaped. He said:

"Care for another pounding?" In an English accent.

"Wipe that smile off your face, man. Your luck is about to run out."

The Dishwasher lost. Dong Smells lost. Then the Dishwasher again. Then Dong Smells again.

Eventually they were notified that the bar was closing. All three of them were drunk by then. Dong Smells was wasted. The Slippery Wrist said he would get him home. The Dishwasher signed his tab. Without looking at it. He didn't want to know. Not that it mattered. Half of him thought he would never even see that last paycheck anyway. He had meant to ask Dong Smells to get it for him in a couple of weeks, but it was too late now. He would deal with that later. The Dishwasher.

They stumbled through the kitchen. Out into the alley. Dong Smells and The Slippery Wrist went to the left. To where the Slippery Wrist was parked. The Dishwasher went right. Towards his apartment. He was drunk enough that he didn't feel compelled to go and check out the Buckhorn. But he wasn't so drunk that he'd do it anyway.

He lit a smoke and walked slowly home. Wondering what Toby was going to get up to. He really hoped she wasn't waiting for him outside his apartment. That would be too much. He didn't have it in him to fight with her tonight. Or any night for that matter. But tonight of all nights, he just wasn't into it.

He wanted to get some sleep and make some plans for

tomorrow. Maybe pack. Maybe take a nap. Swing by the taco place and get some Soft Shell Sundays. He kind of wanted to go and talk to his brother. Tell him he was leaving. But that would be a lot of walking. Maybe it would be nice out. Or maybe he could call him and have him come get him. They could go get tacos together or something. He really didn't like the idea of leaving town without telling his brother. But he was nervous about Toby. The less people that knew, the better. Even if it was his brother. His brother would tell his girlfriend. Who was friends with Toby.

No. The Dishwasher wouldn't call his brother. He hoped he would understand. He could call him from Denver. When it was safe. Maybe leave the details vague. Just in case.

The Dishwasher was feeling like a coward. How did a nineteen-year-old girl scare him so much? What was the worst she could do? Show up? Physically keep him from getting on the bus? Well, no. He thought. The Dishwasher. But she could make a huge stink. Yell and cry and hit him and who knows what else? Stab the tires of the bus? Drive her car in front of it? Block it from leaving? She was really capable of anything.

He wondered if he could avoid her before he left. For the next thirty-six hours or whatever. That would be best. Then there would be nothing she could do. Aside from driving down to Denver to come looking for him. Which he didn't put beyond her. That was something she would do.

That was something he would eventually have to deal with. But hopefully by then he would have his own place and she wouldn't be able to find him. Although that would mean he would have to have a job, and it would get out about where he worked. She would find him and it wouldn't be pretty.

He couldn't think about that right now, though. The Dishwasher. He just needed to focus. To focus on getting out of town. He needed to go to the bank. Empty his bank account. Cash his check. Pack all of his shit up. Somehow get to the bus depot without getting caught by Toby. And then it was clear pastures for him. The Dishwasher. He could start a new life. A life without grief. A life without the Altitude. Or Roger and Norman. Without Toby and the idiot roommates.

He was hit with a sudden guilt. About the first roommate's brother and the broken window and the lease and the rent and the bills and whatever else. He pushed this shame deep down into his cowardly heart. Promising to deal with it later. To himself. He made a promise to himself. The Dishwasher. He would deal with it later. There was nothing he could do about it now.

This was an emergency. Getting out of town was an emergency. He decided. He had to do it. There was no other way. If he didn't get out of Laramie as soon as possible, he would be stuck there forever. Forever washing dishes for barely above minimum wage. Teaching pip-squeaks like Mike how to wash dishes while they flirted with girls like the new prep cook. Who, for whatever reason, just didn't find the Dishwasher sexy or whatever. Who liked macho wimps that played soccer or whatever.

By the time the Dishwasher got to the apartment, he was exhausted from thinking. There was nothing but anxiety and shame left in his heart. He just wanted to get into bed. Think about Lisa's tiny buns and then hit the sack.

There was no Toby waiting outside. The mailbox was still open. Not fixed from when he broke it. The Dishwasher. He walked up the carpeted stairs. Walked into the apartment. Expecting to run into the idiot roommates. They weren't there. Even the lights were turned off. This felt like a luxury. He felt along the wall. Found the switch. Flipped it up. The lights came on. The kitchen was almost clean. There was a note on the counter:

Yo Scum Nuts went to Worland for the weekend don't drink or beer you owe us for window and contolls

The note was written on a paper bag. *Or* instead of *our*. *Contolls* instead of *controls*. Or *controllers*. *Scum Nuts*was nice.

It made the Dishwasher look in the fridge. There were two

twelve-packs of beer. He ripped the side of one of them and took a beer out. He opened it. Took a drink. This was the first time in all the time he had lived there that he didn't have to worry about those assholes being assholes, or even coming around.

He went into the living room. The place was kind of cleaned up. There weren't any cigarette butts or empty beer cans. The broken controllers were gone. The game thing was gone as well. As well as the new controllers.

The Dishwasher went into the idiot roommates' room. He turned the light on. The place was disgusting. They had taped some cardboard to the broken window. To keep the cold out. There was a large bump in one of their bed things. The Dishwasher looked under the blanket. It was the game thing and the new controllers. They were truly morons. Did they really think he wouldn't find it? The two jerks that stole every single piece of silver money from him. The Dishwasher. Who stole his soaps and toothbrushes and food? Did they really think they were hiding something from him?

He didn't care. The Dishwasher. He didn't want their stupid game thing. He didn't want anything that they had. Well, the beer was a nice touch. Why they bought a bunch of beer and left town without hiding *that* seemed pretty stupid, but maybe they just wanted to keep it cold? And since they were idiots maybe they thought their little note would keep the Dishwasher from drinking it? They were idiots. That was all that could be said about them. How they'd managed to get through life up to this point was a great mystery.

The Dishwasher made a face as he took another look at their room. It was really something else. It made the Dishwasher's room look spotless and inviting, in comparison. There were socks so filled with cum they could stand up on their own. Cigarette butts everywhere. Empty beer cans. A few glasses that must have had milk in them at one point, or something. Green with mold. The room smelled like a fart pushed through a diarrhea shit that had rotten meat floating in it. Plus the smell of cigarette butts and something else, something that the Dishwasher couldn't put his finger on, but was cum-soaked socks and unwashed feet and bad breath. The smell of drool on a pillow. On a pillow without a pillowcase.

He would have shut the door when he left, except the room didn't have one. It was like some dirty murder room that gave anyone that looked into it the chills. To think about the horrors that happened in there.

He shut the light off. Walked out of the living room. Stood in the kitchen, drinking the beer. He wanted to drink all the beers. Out of spite. But he couldn't. The Dishwasher. He was exhausted. It had been a hard day.

He slammed the rest of the beer. Put the can in the empty sink. Went into the bathroom. The half toothbrush was still there. They hadn't taken it. Which was something he assumed they would have done. But they were gentlemen. This thought made the Dishwasher make a slanted smile. It was funny in a way, because it was halfway true. They were not gentlemen, but they probably thought it was a noble thing to leave the toothbrush behind. Like, as a favor. Thinking that would mean the Dishwasher would respect their wishes to not drink their beer or something.

The Dishwasher brushed his teeth while he took a piss. He flushed the toilet. Went over to the sink. Spit toothpaste out. Ran the sink. Put the half toothbrush in the toothbrush holder. Looked in the mirror. He looked exhausted. Splotchy. He needed some sun. And more food. He'd only eaten once today. He was getting skinnier.

He frowned. Left the bathroom. Turning off the light behind him. He locked the front door. Thinking it would keep Toby out, if she got stoned later and wanted to come get in a fight or something. He turned the kitchen light off. Went into his room. Kicked off his velcros. Took his jeans off. Laid them out to dry. He sighed about this. His jeans were ruined. There was nothing he could do about that. But maybe he would get a different job. One that didn't keep ruining his jeans. In Denver. He peeled off his shirt. Taking his hoodie with it. Peeled off his socks. Got into bed. His skinny naked body was shivering against the cold blanket. He played with his thing until it became hard. He thought about Lisa coming down into the dry cellar to help him with the olives. It took maybe ten seconds. He reached over. Found a dirty sock. Cleaned himself off. The moon came in through the window. A train came by. Blowing a lonesome whistle. He curled himself into a baby shape and fell asleep.

———

In the late morning, the Dishwasher woke up feeling like a criminal. He was hiding. He was hungover. He had a headache and had to piss. He remembered the idiot roommates were gone.

He stood up with a very hard erection. Swinging it in the breeze. Without shame. He went into the bathroom. Sat down on the toilet. Waited for the thing to go away. It didn't. He slid back and pushed it down onto the toilet seat. It wouldn't fit in. He stood up. Pissed into the bathtub. Fully erect. When he was done, the erection went down. "Typical," he said out loud.

He went to the kitchen sink. Drank some water from the faucet. He found himself luxurious. The Dishwasher. He went into the living room. Sat down on the couch. The scratchy cushions gave him a little thrill on his naked butt. He got hard again. The couch smelled like ass. This added to his excitement. He yanked his erection while his balls bounced on the cushions.

He fell back when he was done. Then he felt gross. The couch fibers were sticking to him now. His back was itchy. His ass. He stood up. Things dripped to the floor.

He went into the bathroom. Started the shower. Waited. Got in. He rinsed himself. Went to get the bar of soap. It was just a puddle of liquid now. He scooped some of the liquid under his fingertips. Spread it around his body. His things. The ejaculate became a stiff mess. Getting caught in his pubes and on his leg hairs. He had to scratch it out. Which kind of hurt because it pulled on everything. He scooped some more soap. It didn't help matters. He made a note of this. Don't take a shower with a stomach full of cum. He should have wiped up first.

Eventually he gave up. Turned the shower off. Got out. There was no towel. He had forgotten the towel in the bedroom. He walked into his bedroom. Naked and dripping. Dirt clung to the bottom of his feet. He left puddles of water on the kitchen floor.

When he got to the carpeted room, he found the towel and dried himself off. The smell of mildew. He wondered if he should bother packing the towel. He knew he had to. He wondered if there was a way to isolate it first. Put it in another bag or something. There was no way. It would just sour all of his stuff. So be it.

The Dishwasher got dressed. He thought about putting his long johns on. He didn't. It looked nice outside. Sunny. He found a clean pair of socks. Put them on. Put his jeans on. They were still wet. They stank. Like mildew. He found a clean shirt. Put it on. Put his velcros on. His hoodie. He wondered what time it was. It seemed like noon. He went into the bathroom. Brushed his teeth with the half toothbrush. Spit into the sink. Looked at his reflection. He looked hungover and tired and splotchy and skinny. He took his wallet out. Looked into the folds. He had six dollars left. Enough to get some food, at least.

He walked out of the bathroom. Tried to open the apartment door. It was locked. He said, "Oh, right." Unlocked it. Walked down the carpeted stairs. Looked at the open mailbox. Sighed. Went outside.

The cold air hit his loins. His penis shriveled and got stuck on a pube that was glued to his dick with cum. It was itchy. He looked around. Nobody was looking. Nobody was on the street. On the sidewalk. There were a couple of people down the block. But they were looking in a store window. He reached into his jeans and plucked his penis from the pubic hair it was glued to. He pulled his hand out of his jeans. Smelled it. It smelled like soap. He started walking towards the campus.

The day was nice but cold. Bright but windy. He crossed the

busy main street and walked uphill. The Dishwasher was too hungover to smoke. He kept his head down. Rolling with the sidewalk. The places where the trees had grown up out of their roots and buckled things. He tripped a few times. When he wasn't paying attention.

The Dishwasher got to the campus. The sidewalk got busy. He dodged in and out of families saying goodbye or going to the university store to get T-shirts or textbooks. He was annoyed by this. The Dishwasher. He didn't want to deal with emotional parents and idiot students at the moment. He was hungover and just wanted to eat something. He passed the check cashing place. A church. The bar that sucked. That all the students seemed to love but was nothing but trouble for the locals because it was expensive and carded everyone, even when nothing was happening.

The Dishwasher kept walking. Got to the fast-food taco place. Went inside. It wasn't busy. He saw a clock. The clock said it was a quarter past noon. He ordered two Soft Shell Sundays. Thought about it for a second. Did the math. Ordered a third. And a small drink. They had free refills. There was no reason to order a medium drink. What was the point? The cashier gave him a number. On a teepee-style plastic thing. Which was pointless. It was only him and one other guy in the place.

He took his number and his empty cup to the pop thing. He filled his pop cup up. With pop. He didn't get ice. The Dishwasher. He needed fluid. He put a lid on his cup. Got a straw. Pushed the straw through the paper covering. Grabbed the paper with his mouth. Pulled it off. Put the straw through the lid. Put the paper in the trash. Took a little plastic cup. Filled it with Super Hot. Went and sat down. He put the plastic teepee number in front of him. Stared at it. 19. He was number 19. He looked out the window. The wind was blowing the pine trees. It was very sunny. He was hungry.

A very young and plump girl came out into the lobby. She put the tray of tacos in front of him. The Dishwasher. Took the plastic teepee with the number 19 on it. He said thanks. She pursed her lips. Walked away.

The Dishwasher opened the paper wrapping. Dumped some Super Hot on top of the liquid meat, where it met the shredded cheese. Closed the taco. Took a bite. It was the best. The meat and the cheese and the lettuce and the flour tortilla. The Super Hot sauce and the regular mild hot sauce. A perfect combination. He took more bites. Taking drinks of pop in between. He ate five of the tacos. He had to get up and get more pop and more Super Hot while he was doing this. Also looking out the window. Watching the wind blow on the pines.

People started pouring in at one point. Before long, there was a line out the door. The Dishwasher put the last taco in his hoodie pocket. For later. He took his tray to the trash. Threw his wadded-up wrappers away. The empty things of Super Hot. He put the empty tray on top of the other empty trays. The Dishwasher. He filled his pop cup up with more pop. He had to fight his way to the pop machine to do this. Not because people were using it, but because they were standing in the way.

He pushed his way out the door. He got back outside. The wind was really blowing now. He made sure the last taco was secure in his hoodie pocket. Secure against the wind. He walked back downhill. Past the church and the lousy bar and the university store and the check cashing place. He rolled with the sidewalk. Only tripping a few times on the roots of the overgrown trees.

He got to the busy main street. Crossed it without incident. Nobody called him a faggot. Got back to the apartment building. Went inside. Up the carpeted steps. Went inside of the apartment. Nobody was there. Not Toby or the idiot roommates. The luxury of this made him rethink hauling ass out of town. If only life was like this all the time. He thought. He went into his room. Fell down onto his mattress. And closed his eyes.

He could hear the wind really going now. This was not a good sign. A storm must be coming. He thought. The Dishwasher. So what, though? He just needed to make it to the bus tomorrow and things would be different. The five o'clock bus. He could haul ass to Denver and be done with it all. He lay there for a second, thinking. Thinking he might take a nap.

A few moments later, the tacos kicked in. He clenched his butt cheeks together and stood up. He scooted towards the bathroom.

27

The bathroom was unpleasant and explosive. After a while, though, it ended.

The Dishwasher did his best to clean up. He stood up. Pulled his jeans up. Flushed the toilet without looking. Walked over to the bathroom sink. Rinsed his hands off. Looked in the mirror.

There was something in the look in his own eyes that gave him a sudden panic. He looked both scared and depressed. What was he doing? Was he running away from something? Was he running *towards* something? Part of him wished there would be a knock on the door and Toby would be standing there, begging him to stay. Saying she couldn't live without him. Or maybe the landlord. Telling him that he had to fix the window and pay rent in advance for the rest of the year. That he had to sign a new, yearlong lease. Or maybe even Lisa showing up. Declaring her everlasting love. Taking her black nylon pants down. Showing him what he needed to stick around for. This last little fantasy switched his thinking. He went straight to his room. Dropped his jeans and fell down on top of his blanket.

The Dishwasher found his attraction to Lisa very confusing. Maybe that was what was attractive about her? The confusion. The impossibility of it all. There was no way in a million different scenarios that they would ever get together. But she was nice and cute and the Dishwasher had a thing for her. Even if it only came out in little bursts. She had her shit together. The Dishwasher did not. She wasn't *exactly* the opposite of the Dishwasher. Lisa. But she was close enough. Maybe he could settle down or something. Work his way up to the front line. They could open a restaurant together or something. She could manage it. He could cook and do the dishes. Or whatever.

The Dishwasher grew tired of this idea. It was stupid. Pointless. A waste of energy. He didn't want that thing. Not now, probably not ever. But still, if she showed up and knocked on his door at that very moment, he would consider the possibility.

That didn't happen, though. Nor did Toby knock on the door. Nor the landlord. Nobody knocked on the door. The Dishwasher just lay there. Feeling a certain freedom knowing that the idiot roommates were out of town. Plus, there was beer in the fridge. A taco in his pocket. And tomorrow he would get on a bus and haul ass out of Laramie.

The Dishwasher tried to take a nap, but he was too excited. He would shut his eyes but instead of sleeping he would start thinking about his new life. Free of the Altitude. Free of Toby. Free of Laramie. Free of large trucks and assholes calling him a faggot. No more Buckhorn. No more Norman or Curry. No more Mike. And especially, no more idiot roommates. Eating his food. Using his toothbrush. Stealing his change. Ruining his soaps. Taking up all the space in the apartment.

It occurred to him that he was indeed running away from something. A life he was sick of. A life that was stagnating. A life that was dictated on everyone else's terms, not his. The Dishwasher's. He had no idea what Denver would be like, but it had to be better than this. It just had to be. He would have almost 600 bucks. Plus the other $300 coming to him. $300 minus the beers from last night. Which he assumed were roughly forty dollars.

This filled him with sudden guilt. Sudden shame. Why did he waste all that money last night? It was too much money. Money he needed. He found himself very upset with his actions. The Dishwasher did. The shame. For shame. Shame, the thing that was worse than guilt. At least with guilt he could ask forgiveness; with shame, it lasted forever.

He would never get that forty dollars back. It was gone. He

had a vision of himself homeless and begging for money on East Colfax. Holding up a sign that read: *I spent my last $40 like a moron. Please help.* He laughed about this. To himself. He decided he would rather have that future than the one he had here. Staying here. Doing the same old shit. Day in, day out.

The Dishwasher got up. Giving up on the nap. He took a look around his room. Deciding what to do. He gathered the pile of dirty clothes and took them into the living room. He threw them on the couch. He went back to his room. Gathered all the clean clothes and took them to the living room. Throwing them next to the pile of dirty clothes on the couch. He went back to his room. Looked behind the door. All the winter stuff was there. He gathered that up and took it to the living room. He threw it on the floor in front of the couch. He went back to his room. He grabbed his change jar and took it to the kitchen. Placed it on the counter. He went back to his room. Grabbed his book. Brought it into the kitchen. Placed it next to the jar of change. He went back to the room. Took the blanket off of the mattress. Wadded it up. Placed it in the closet. Threw his pillow on top of the blanket. Flipped the mattress up. Leaned it against the wall. That was it. There was nothing else. Nothing else aside from the black plastic garbage bag. He grabbed that. Took it into the living room. Threw it on top of the clothes.

He went back into his room. Took a look around. It was depressing. There were little bits of trash here and there. An empty beer can. He grabbed the beer can. Took it into the kitchen. Put it in the sink. It clanked the other empty beer cans. He lit a cigarette. He went back into his room. There was nothing else to do in there. He went back into the kitchen. Stood around for a while. Smoking. Ashing in the kitchen sink. He finished the cigarette. Put it out by running some water over the cherry. Put the butt in an empty beer can. He took a drink from the faucet. He went into the living room.

The Dishwasher took the black plastic garbage bag and put the dirty clothes in it. He was trying to figure out a way to keep the clean stuff away from the dirty stuff. He couldn't think of a way. But then he thought about his towel. The towel was just as gross as the dirty clothes. Even if he wanted it to, it wouldn't separate the clean clothes from the dirty ones. It would just make the clean clothes dirty. The whole operation was hopeless. The Dishwasher just gave up. He would have to do laundry at some point in the near future. Until then, he would just have to smell things to decide if they were clean or not.

He found a clean shirt, a pair of clean socks. He looked through all the stuff until he found the long johns. He smelled them. They smelled okay. The butt kind of smelled, but not too bad. He put them with the clean shirt and the clean socks. Tomorrow, he decided. He would put them on tomorrow. But maybe not. It still seemed too soon.

As he was thinking about this, a gust of wind rattled the windows. He heard a clanking noise. He went into the idiot roommates' room. The cardboard was flapping against the window. He looked outside. Little flakes of snow were blowing by. Sideways. That was not good.

He didn't want there to be a snowstorm. He was worried about the buses. Normally he loved a snowstorm. It was the kind of thing that would slow everything down. People wouldn't go out. Work would be slow. He wouldn't feel obligated to do things. But if a storm came through *now*. That would not be helpful. It would easily put a kink in things.

He worried about his nerves. The Dishwasher. Things were fickle. There was very little that was keeping him from just giving up on his idea to ditch Laramie for Denver. He needed to keep his spirits up. His courage.

He was a coward. He knew this. Everyone knew this. He assumed, at least. He was just a coward wrapped in shame and guilt. With no prospects and a shitty job in a shitty town with a shitty girlfriend and shitty roommates. His friends were alright. But he had known them for ages. His brother too.

He suddenly felt very guilty, thinking about his brother. About leaving town without telling him. But what could he do? He needed to get out of town before Toby found out. Although, according to Dong Smells, she already knew. But who the hell knew what exactly transpired between Toby and Dong Smells. For all he knew, the Dishwasher, Dong Smells had made the whole thing up in his mind. He did have a very large capacity for drinking. Maybe it was just imaginary.

The Dishwasher tried to make this thought true, but in his heart he knew it was a lie. He knew that Toby knew. That he would be very lucky to get out of town without running into her. He could feel her right now, circling like some menacing vulture. Just waiting for the right time to come down and start chewing on the Dishwasher's bones. The Dishwasher rephrased this in his mind. Toby was waiting to come down and start chewing on his flesh. After *that*, she would start chewing on his bones.

New shame came to the Dishwasher. Toby. What to do with Toby. He was aware of how badly he treated her. In a sense. She treated him just as badly. But still. They were an item. Supposedly. Even though the Dishwasher had tried one million times to break up with her. She did do that thing with the idiot roommates' controllers. That was nice. And she was there for him when he had that massive panic attack. That was nice. But still. They shouldn't be together. It just wasn't correct. The Dishwasher didn't want it. He knew that. He just wished that Toby could understand that. And maybe she would. Eventually. Eventually she would get over him. That, or she would move down to Denver and make his life miserable until he had to move to Chicago or something. New York City. Or, who knows, San Francisco?

The Dishwasher couldn't take any more shame. He went into the kitchen. Opened the fridge. Took a beer out. Opened it. Started pacing in the kitchen. Trying to think.

The wind kept blowing. The windows, rattling. The Dishwasher would go every now and again to look outside. The snow was just dust. Which was good. He drank more beer. Paced around. Packed the rest of his clothes into the black plastic garbage bag. He left his coat out. Just in case. He drank more beer. Pacing. Thinking.

The day started to darken. The Dishwasher paced. Thinking. He drank more beer. Smoking. Pacing. Thinking. Listening to the wind. The tiny snowflakes pelting the windows. He heard a train go by. Blowing its whistle. The streetlights came on. He looked out the window. The dusty snow blowing through the streetlights. Nothing was collecting, though. The snowflakes didn't seem to be getting bigger. The Dishwasher paced. Thinking. Drinking beer. He was getting excited now. The more he drank. The more he smoked. The more he paced. He got hungry. Took the taco out of his hoodie pocket. Ate it, standing next to his book and jar of change.

When he finished the taco, he dumped the change on the counter. He spread it out. It was nothing but pennies. The idiot roommates had cleaned him out. He already knew this, but he wanted to double-check. He also wanted to leave the change on the counter. To let those fuckers know that they were assholes. Hoping they would feel some sort of guilt or something. After a while he found himself stacking the pennies into piles of ten. Then he stacked the tens into hundreds. Eventually there were nine stacks of a hundred pennies. Nine dollars. What a waste. The Dishwasher wondered if he should take the pennies to the bank tomorrow. But then that seemed like way too much trouble. The idiot roommates could use it to replace the beers he drank. He decided.

The Dishwasher paced and paced. Drinking more beer. Smoking. Going to the bathroom. Looking in the mirror. He was looking more happy now. Or at least he thought so. His face had colored. He seemed handsome. His haircut was looking alright. He was either more handsome and doing better, or he was just kind of drunk.

Either way, it didn't matter. Tomorrow he was leaving. Tomorrow he was getting on a bus. He would be in Denver before midnight. Troll and Bogart would pick him up from the bus station. He would live there now instead of here now. Things would be different. He would have a new life. A life of new freedom. With new friends and a new job and no Toby and no Altitude and no Norman or Mike or Lisa or Curry or the Buckhorn or whatever else, no assholes in big trucks calling him a faggot. No idiot roommates with their demands for whatever it was they thought he owed them. The Dishwasher. Yes, things were looking up. If he could just get out of town tomorrow. If he could get to the bank, clear his account, get back to the apartment, grab his shit, walk to the bus depot, buy a ticket to Denver, get on the bus and drive away to greener pastures or whatever. All of that without once running into Toby. Something about it seemed tricky. But he was excited for the trip. The new life. The difference.

As the night went on, the pile of empty beer cans in the kitchen sink got taller. At a certain point the Dishwasher was drunk. He thought it was hilarious, how many beers he drank. The idiot roommates were going to be pissed. He thought it would be funny to leave them a note telling them how much they sucked. He took their note. The one they left behind, telling him not to drink their beer and that he owed them money for the controllers and the window. The Dishwasher wrote:

Dear ButtFucks,
I am not sorry I drank your beers. I bequeath you my pillow and my $9 in change. Good luck being idiots.

love Disher
p.s., eat a butt

The Dishwasher thought this was a hilarious note to leave. He stood over it for quite some time, laughing to himself. Smoking a cigarette.

Something kicked in that made him suddenly very drunk. He

stumbled into the bathroom. Took a piss. Didn't flush. Stumbled to the bathroom sink. Brushed his teeth with the half toothbrush. Stumbled out of the bathroom. Stumbled into his room. Threw the mattress on the carpet. Went into the closet. Grabbed his pillow and blanket. Threw them on the mattress. Kicked his velcros off. Took his clothes off. Got into bed. He managed to wrap himself in the blanket. Wadded the pillow under his head. Listened to the wind. The dusty snow blowing against the windows. He fell asleep.

———

The Dishwasher woke up hungover. There was some light coming into the room. It was a dark light, though. He got up. He had to piss. The mattress was wet. He sighed. He must have pissed the bed. The Dishwasher was ashamed. That was gross. He looked out the window. There was snow on the ground. It was still snowing. The snowflakes were larger now. They seemed wet and heavy. He sighed again. He went into the kitchen. He saw the note he had written. The lights were still on. He hadn't turned them off. He chuckled when he read the note. He went into the bathroom. Pissed. Flushed the toilet. He went back to his room. Took the blanket off the bed. Flipped the mattress over. Got back on it. Grabbed the blanket and the pillow. Put the blanket over himself. It was dry. He must have been lying face down when he pissed the bed. He wadded the pillow up. Under his head. He went back to sleep.

A few hours later, he woke up again. It was daytime now. He pushed himself up on his elbows and looked outside. It was still snowing. He groaned. Falling back down. Nothing he could do about that. If it was going to snow, it was going to snow. He could only do what he could. He was still hungover. Now he had a headache. He lay in bed for a while, trying to think about what to do. He needed to get up. But he didn't feel like it. He was still tired. He had to piss again. He played with his loins for a while. But that didn't help. He had to piss more than he had to do other things.

———

He got up. Walked into the kitchen. Looked at his note. Chuckled again. Looked in the kitchen sink. All the cans just filled him with shame. What the hell had he done last night? That amount of beer was too much. He thought he might have to throw up. He went into the bathroom. Took a piss. The feeling of vomit passed. He started the shower. The Dishwasher. He went into the living room. Rooted around and found the stinky towel. Took it back to the bathroom. He hung it on the towel rack. Got into the shower. Got wet. Scooped some soap out of the area where the bar of soap once lived. Some of it got caught under his fingernails. He rubbed his hands around his crotch, his butt; he tried to wash his feet. His face.

The shower was mostly nothing. There just wasn't enough soap. But when he was done he felt a little better. He dried off with the stinky towel. Getting dirtier by doing so. He didn't try to dry his hair, though. Not wanting to transfer the smell of mildew to his hair. This left him dripping.

He walked out into the living room. He looked down at the clothes he had set aside. He frowned. He went into the idiot roommates' room and looked out the window. The snow was really coming down now. He frowned again.

He went back to the couch. He grabbed the long johns. He was still wet. He struggled as he put them on. Pulling them up and over his loins and butt.

And so it was. The long johns went on.

He felt a new sadness because of it. Like the long johns meant something. But that was stupid. Long johns don't mean anything. He decided.

He pulled his socks on. Then he pushed the tops of his socks down. To allow for the long johns. He put the clean T-shirt on. Walked into his bedroom. Put his mildewed jeans on. His hoodie. He sat on the mattress and put his velcros on. He stood up. Took the blanket from his bed and went back to the living room. He threw it on the couch. He went back to his room. Looked around. The naked pillow sat there on top of the naked mattress. He wanted to light it on fire. Throw it out of the window. But he didn't. He just left it as it was. He took the dirty pair of socks and the dirty T-shirt. Walked out of the room. Closed the door.

The Dishwasher went to the living room. Put the dirty pair of socks and the dirty T-shirt in the black plastic garbage bag. Folded the blanket. Tried to cram it inside the black plastic garbage bag. It didn't fit. He put the blanket on the couch. Started tying the black plastic garbage bag. Then stopped.

He went into the bathroom. Brushed his teeth with the half toothbrush. Spit into the sink. Took the half toothbrush and the toothpaste. Put them on top of the things in the black plastic garbage bag. Tied it shut. He was ready to go.

He took a drink from the kitchen sink faucet. The water clanking on the pile of shameful empty beer cans. It was loud. The sound hurt his feelings. The Dishwasher's.

He went into the living room. Grabbed his coat. He put it on. It was fluffy. It smelled like stretched-out oils. A thing that only the Dishwasher could describe. But something he couldn't define. Like something animal, dog-like, but also dirty, like burnt hair. A collection of last winter's smells. He poked around in the pockets and found nothing but trash. Old cigarette packages and receipts. Even a few cigarette butts. He sighed again. He didn't want to think about last winter. Touching those pockets felt like touching hot lava for some reason. He pulled his hands out as quickly as he'd put them in.

He walked out of the apartment. Touching his jeans pockets. Making sure he had his wallet. He walked down the carpeted stairs. He looked in the broken mailbox. The mailbox he broke. It wasn't fixed. There was nothing new. Not for him. It was Monday. There was no reason for there to be anything new anyway. He looked anyway.

He walked out onto the street. The snow was coming down gently. The wind wasn't blowing. His head got cold. He put his hood up. From the coat. The hood from his hoodie was crammed at his neck. He had to adjust it. Then instead of putting his coat hood on his head, he just put his hoodie hood on his head. Letting the feathers from his coat hood collect snow. His loins were warm. He was glad he had put his long johns on.

The Dishwasher zipped his coat up. Walked out further into the falling snow. He walked the few blocks to his bank. Went inside.

He went to the station that had the papers for deposits and withdrawals. He took his wallet out. Took his paycheck out. Signed it. He stood there for a second, thinking. Water started dripping down. He pulled the hoodie hood back. He wasn't sure what he needed to do to empty his account, so he filled out a withdrawal form and left the amount blank.

He went and stood in line. There were a couple people in line in front of him. The Dishwasher. He was feeling tired but excited. He also felt like a criminal. He was about to empty his bank account. He had no reference for what that would mean. Would they have to call the cops or something? Let the government know? He didn't know how this stuff worked. When he got to the front of the line, he said:

"Hi, I am, uh, I need to cash this check and like, uh, close my account or whatever."

It was the same woman from the last time. That had given him shit for being too poor to have a bank card. There was a thing of glass between them. He wasn't sure if she could hear him very well. She said:

"Hi, sir, can you say that again?"

"Yeah, I mean, I need to cash this check and then close my account, I have this withdrawal thing. I mean, I filled it out, but I didn't write the amount."

"You want to cash this check?"

"Yes."

"Okay, and you have an account here?"

"I do."

"And then you want to close that account?"

"I mean, yeah, I mean, kind of."

"Okay, let me see your ID."

The Dishwasher took his ID and slid it to the woman behind the glass. The check and the withdrawal form as well. She looked at all three things. Typed something into the computer. Looked at the Dishwasher. Frowned. She said:

"We can close your account, but we can't cash this check."

"Huh? But why? I cash these checks here all the time."

"Yeah, but you don't have enough to cover the check. You can deposit it, and once it clears you can withdraw it, but until it clears, you are out of luck."

"Really? Shit. How much money do I have in the account?"

"$89.03."

"And when would the money from the check become available?"

"I don't know—two days, three."

"But it's from just down the street. Can you call them, or whatever?"

"Sir, the check needs to clear before we can give you the cash. Your account doesn't have enough in it to cover the check."

"But I really need that money right now."

"I don't know what to tell you, sir. You can deposit the check and come take it out when it clears, or..."

"Don't you know the Altitude, though? They are just down the street."

"I am sorry, sir, that is all I can do."

The Dishwasher's heart was broken. What could he do? He could take all his money and buy a bus ticket, but that would leave him barely twenty dollars to get by with. He could find a check cashing place—shit, he could even go to the one up the hill, but they would charge him an arm and a leg to cash the check. Things were not looking good.

He tried to think. What could he do? He felt ashamed. The guilt of his hangover was pushing down on his soul. Why had he drunk so many beers last night? The note he wrote to his idiot roommates was mocking him at the moment. Why was everything so complicated all the time?

"Shit. Okay, how about this—just give me the money and I will keep the account open?"

"All the money in your account? The $89.03?"

"Yeah, I guess."

"And then deposit the check?"

"No, I'll just take that."

"You don't want to close your account?"

"I don't really see the point."

"You know there is a minimum balance of $50?"

"Yeah, but so what? I won't have any money. You can't charge me for money I don't have, right?"

"Not now. When you go to cash that check, though, you will be charged a fee."

"Seriously?"

"That is the policy."

"So if I don't deposit that check now and in the future I do, because I don't have any money in my account you will charge me money for depositing my check and then taking it out again?"

"Yes."

"What the—? Seriously? That is bullshit."

"Sir, please don't use that language. Do you want me to withdraw this money from your account or not?"

"Yeah, I guess."

"And you don't want me to deposit this check?"

"I guess not. I suppose I will figure it out."

"Okay, then fill the form out."

"$89.03?"

"$89.03."

The Dishwasher filled the form out. He slid it to the bank teller. The bank teller slid the paycheck back. The Dishwasher put the paycheck back in his wallet.

This sucked. He was wondering if he should walk up to the check cashing place. He figured he had enough time. But still. It was ridiculous that his bank wouldn't cash his check for him. He took the cash from the teller. Put it into his wallet. He put his ID in his wallet as well. He made a face to the teller. She made one right back at him. He didn't say thank you.

He walked to the doors of the bank. Looked outside. The snow still coming down. He put his hoodie hood up. He couldn't decide if he should go to the check cashing place or not. He had enough money to get on the bus. That seemed okay. He could find a place to cash the check there. In Denver. Or not. He was very frustrated. He just stood there, looking at the snow. Through the glass doors. He felt defeated.

At that moment, Toby drove by in her car. This startled the Dishwasher. What was she up to? She must be going to his apartment. Fuck. He thought. Fuck, fuck, fuck. What the hell? His plan about leaving town had just got really kinked. Between the check and the snow and now Toby, things were looking dismal. He tried to gather his thoughts. The Dishwasher. He looked at the clock on the wall behind him. It was barely noon. He didn't know what to do. He just stood there, thinking.

Eventually a guy in a suit came over to him. The Dishwasher looked over. The guy was large and had an expression on his face that said, "Get lost." The Dishwasher almost yelled at the guy. But then he noticed another guy just off in the distance. The bank teller herself was looking at him. It was all just too much. There was a conspiracy against him that he just couldn't get ahead of.

He walked out into the snow. Through the glass doors. The Dishwasher. He stood there thinking. Taking in all the doom. He made a face and listened to the snow. The silence on the street. His head was under a hood. The snowflakes were silent.

28

The Dishwasher didn't know what to do. He wanted to know what Toby was up to. He also wanted to cash his check. The idea of going to the check cashing place was hard to wrap his mind around. He had time. Lots of time. But he didn't feel like walking there. He didn't feel like standing in line. He didn't feel like paying the ten or so dollars that he would have to pay to get the check cashed. That part was inevitable, though. The paying of the ten dollars.

He was trying to think this through when he heard a car coming around the corner. He panicked. Ran around the corner of the bank and hid in the bushes. The car wasn't Toby. He felt embarrassed. He looked around. Nobody saw him. Or at least he thought nobody saw him. He snuck back out of the bushes. Walked down the street. Came to the corner. Stopped. Peeked around the corner. Looked down the street.

Toby's car was parked in front of the apartment building.

He stood there staring. What an idiot he was. Toby! The Dishwasher hadn't thought to lock the doors to the apartment. Toby was inside. At that very moment. Looking at the black plastic garbage bag. The note on the counter. The empty beer cans in the sink. The empty room. The jig was up. There was no way he was getting out of town without some sort of confrontation.

He began to shake. This was a nightmare for the Dishwasher. He was a coward. Confrontation was to be avoided at all costs. He tried to make himself just get it over with. Just walk over to the apartment. Have it out once and for all with Toby. Be done with it. He felt a severe panic attack coming on. His vision was getting smaller. Thinner. His heart was pounding. He thought he might just drop dead. Right there in the snow on the street corner. He was holding on to the building. Hoping it would keep him where he was. Safe from death.

He tried to focus. He found himself walking towards the apartment. Against his own will. There were pins in his arms. He was sick to his stomach. The sounds around him were insanely loud. He was so jumpy that he couldn't breathe. He just needed some water. He reached down and grabbed a handful of snow. He sucked on it. The snow turned to ice. It hurt his hand. The pain was good. It helped him focus. He reached down and grabbed another handful. He sucked on the snow. Looking straight ahead as he walked.

Just then, Toby came bouncing out of the apartment building. Her hair in a ponytail. She looked like a sporty redheaded cheerleader, from afar. She got into her car. Spun out in the snow. Nearly crashed into the car parked in front of her. Skidded down the street. Nearly spun in a circle. Somehow pulled it off. Turned left. Then she was out of sight. The Dishwasher froze. Thinking. He waited a beat and then ran towards the apartment building.

When he got there, he opened the door to the building. It wasn't locked for whatever reason. He stopped briefly to check it out. The lock was broken. Someone must have yanked too hard. He had a feeling it was Toby that had yanked too hard. He also had a feeling she had *just* done it. Moments ago.

He ran up the carpeted steps. Ran into the apartment. Grabbed the black plastic garbage bag. Looked at the blanket on the couch. Said, "Fuck it." He could get one in Denver. He didn't need to be hauling that thing around. He looked into the bathroom. Nothing. His room. Nothing. He went into the idiot roommates' room. Nothing. The cardboard was on the floor now. From the broken window. Snow was coming in. He said, "Whoops."

He went into the kitchen. Looked around. The pile of empty beer cans in the sink filled him with immense shame. He took a drink from the faucet. The water clanking on the empty beer cans. He looked at the note again. Had a good chuckle. Reached into his pocket. Pulled out his keys. Put them on top of the note. Looked around one more time. Said, "Suck it, fuck-faces." A little bit of nostalgia crept in. But then he remembered the last nine months and wanted to burn the apartment to the ground.

He left. Shutting the door behind him. He ran down the carpeted steps. He got to the street. Looked around. Making sure that Toby wasn't hiding somewhere. He didn't see her. He took his black plastic garbage bag and himself, and ran to the busy main street.

He waited for a clearing. He ran across. He took a right. Then the first left. He was taking the back streets to the check cashing place. He walked fast. As fast as he could without running. He got to the street that he thought the check cashing place was adjacent to. He took a left. Walked the two blocks. Took a right. Looked around. No Toby. He went inside.

The line was two-people long. He looked at the clock on the wall. It was a little after one in the afternoon. He stood there, waiting. Snow melting off of his winter coat. A small puddle of water collecting under him. The Dishwasher.

He waited. Ten minutes went by. He looked out the front windows. There was traffic and snow. No Toby, though. He waited.

Another five minutes went by. The first customer was finally finished. He walked over to the shelf on the wall and messed around with some papers. He looked familiar. It was the horny guy from across the tracks. The one that worked at the gas station. Manuel, or Manny as he liked to be called. The Dishwasher hid his face. Praying that the guy wouldn't recognize him. He didn't. Thank God. Manny left the check cashing place. A gust of wind came in when he opened the door. It sent a shiver through the room.

The Dishwasher waited. Another ten minutes. Then twenty minutes. The woman in front of the line was doing something extremely complicated. The Dishwasher's nerves were on edge.

He kept looking out the windows. Keeping his eyes peeled for Toby. She didn't drive by. Another customer came in. Sighed. Stood behind the Dishwasher. Melting.

A little while later, the woman in front of the line was done. The man behind the Dishwasher said, "Finally." The Dishwasher made a face. To himself. He had been there for thirty-five minutes already. This jerk had been there maybe three minutes. What was he complaining about?

The Dishwasher stood there until the cashier told him to come forward. He slid the check and his ID through the slot. The cashier looked at the check. The ID. She asked him if he had ever cashed a check there before. He said that he had not. She said, "Okay, we are going to have to verify this—it could take a second. Could you go stand over there?" The Dishwasher frowned. He obliged, though. The cashier stood up and took the check to the back. Handed the check and ID to another person sitting behind a desk. He was on the phone. He looked at the check and ID. Put them down. Kept talking on the phone.

The impatient man behind the Dishwasher got to the cashier and said, "Quite the operation you got going here, I mean, I don't have all day to be spending in line." The cashier ignored him. The Dishwasher wanted to strangle the man. He was an oil worker. Cashing a check. The Dishwasher watched as he received his money. There were forty-two hundred-dollar bills and four twenties and four ones and some coins. The man complained about how much it cost him. The cashier informed him that there was a bank just down the street that he could open an account at. This just pissed him off. He spit on the floor. Put the money in his giant Texas-style wallet. It had two metal buttons holding it together. The Dishwasher was surprised it wasn't connected to a chain.

He wondered how he would get out of there alive. And not get mugged by the time he got back to his truck. Or at least that was what the oil worker's face looked like when he looked around after putting his wallet back. The Dishwasher made a face at him. The oil worker made one back. He said, "Fuck you very much." Under his breath. Which was supposed to sound like, "Thank you very much." He walked to the door. Held it open for the woman that had taken twenty-five minutes to conduct her business. He nodded and said, "Ma'am." What a fucking phony. The Dishwasher thought.

The Dishwasher stood there waiting. Another woman came in. Paid some bills. Left. A college kid came in and tried to cash a university check. The cashier wouldn't take it. She said she couldn't because of rules. The college student nearly cried. He looked hungry and confused. He was not having a good day. School had started that morning. He was probably one of hundreds of very confused college kids out on their own for the first time. The parents were gone. And now they had to do things on their own that they weren't used to doing. Like getting checks cashed or opening bank accounts or whatever other easy bullshit that they never taught kids in high school. The Dishwasher felt bad for the kid. But there was nothing he could do for him. He would have to learn it on his own.

Another ten minutes went by. The Dishwasher was getting nervous. It was now after two in the afternoon. He looked out the windows. No Toby. Just snow and traffic. Another person came in. An old woman who needed to send some money to Mexico. The Dishwasher watched the transaction happen. Keeping an eye on the guy in the back. Behind the desk. He was done with his phone call. He was looking at the Dishwasher's check. His ID. He picked up the phone again. Dialed some numbers. Said some words. Nodded. Nodded some more. Read something to the person on the other end of the phone. He wrote some stuff down. Frowned. Then hung up the phone. He put the check and the Dishwasher's ID on top of his desk. Reached down and pulled some sort of book out. Thumbed through it. Got to the page he was looking for. Wrote something.

The old woman's money transfer was a go-ahead. She seemed really nervous. She was wringing some red leather gloves that she had been wearing when she came in. Her eyes were open very wide. She was speaking in Spanish. The cashier spoke Spanish back to her. Something happened and the old woman was very relieved. She was very thankful. The cashier was smiling when she finished the transaction. The old woman went to the shelf on the wall and sorted the papers she had brought in. The cashier looked at the Dishwasher and frowned. She told him to come over. She said:

"Okay, you are good to go. How do you want it?"

"Oh, I don't know. Hundreds I guess." The cashier counted out four hundred-dollar bills, two twenties, a five, a one, and twenty-one cents. The Dishwasher got distracted. He was thinking of the oil worker's stacks and stacks of money. He kind of felt ashamed that his check was so small. Maybe he should get a job in the oil fields? But then he thought about it. For, like, a second. The assholes he would have to work for. It wasn't worth it. By the time the cashier was done counting, he had lost track of the money. He just assumed she was right.

"There you go. Anything else I can help you with?"

"Oh, not today, thanks."

"You're welcome. Have a good day." She half smiled at him. The Dishwasher. He half smiled back. Took the cash to the shelf on the wall. Took his wallet out. Put the money in his wallet. Put the wallet in the front right pocket of his mildewed jeans. Lifted his black plastic garbage bag. Everything he owned in the world. Looked out the windows. No Toby. Just snow and traffic. He walked out onto the sidewalk.

———

The Dishwasher didn't know what to do now. It was 2:35 in the afternoon. He had about two and a half hours to burn. Before he could get on the bus. The snow was getting heavier. It was almost dark out. Not because it was late, but because the storm was really hitting now. He decided to make his way to the bus depot. He would buy his ticket and then do what, he wasn't sure. He was hungry. He was still hungover. He wanted to smoke but he was afraid it would trigger a panic attack. He was kind of glad about the snow. It would mean that maybe Toby was rethinking hunting him down. That maybe she would just go back to her apartment and get stoned and forget all about the Dishwasher ditching town. It was unlikely, but he could hope.

The Dishwasher pushed his way through the snow. Carrying his black plastic bag over his shoulder. He must have looked like a vagabond. In every sort of way he actually was a vagabond. He was on the move. Getting out of this lousy town. Moving on to better, more pleasant places. Denver. The Mile High City. He was kind of very excited now. Even if he had to avoid Toby. He was excited. He kept an eye out for any erratic cars screaming around the corners. It was hard work. He was paranoid. She was everywhere. Every street corner. Every car without its headlights on. Every slammed brake and honk. She was there. Waiting for him. To pull over and start screaming at him. Begging him not to go.

He got to the gas station by the interstate. The Dishwasher. He went inside. He pulled his hood down. Snow fell on the already-wet floors. He slipped a little. The Dishwasher. He looked around. The place was warm and cozy. He wanted a coffee and something to eat. He found a burrito that was called something like The Bomb. He looked at it for some time. Read the ingredients. Then looked at the front again. It actually said, Tha Bomb. He put it in the microwave. Hit a button that said "Burrito" on it. One minute and forty-five seconds started counting down. He went over to the coffee station. Filled up a large styrofoam cup with coffee. Poured some sugar and some nondairy creamer in the cup. Stirred it with a skinny red straw. He threw the straw away. Put a lid on the coffee. Left it sitting there at the coffee station. Went over to the microwave. Opened the door. The burrito was puffed up like a pillow. He turned it over. Shut the door. Hit the "Start" button again. He looked around until he found some chips he thought he would like. He took them back to the microwave. The thing dinged. He took the burrito out. He took it to the coffee station. He looked around. He put his black plastic garbage bag down. With all of the things he owned. There was no salsa. Only salt and pepper and mayo and mustard and ketchup. He grabbed some mustard packets. Put them in his winter coat pocket. Some napkins. Somehow managed to grab the coffee and the burrito and the bag of chips and the black plastic garbage bag. Took them to the cashier. She rang him up. He had to adjust some things to get his wallet out. Then he had to sort through all of the cash to find what he was looking for. He paid. Somehow gathered everything again.

He went outside. Stood next to the trash can. Put his burrito and coffee on top of the trash can. Set his black plastic garbage bag down. Put the chips in his winter coat pocket. He would eat those on the bus. He took a drink of the coffee. It was good. It warmed him up. He stood there next to the trash. Looking out at the snow. The mountains and the interstate. He opened the burrito. Steam came barreling out. He took a packet of mustard out of his winter coat pocket. Ripped a corner off with his teeth. He squirted some mustard on top of the burrito tip. Took a bite. The thing was smoldering. He opened his mouth so the steam could come out. He blew. The first bite was good. He squirted more mustard on the burrito. The next bite had a bunch of meat filling. It was even more smoldering than the bite before. He breathed steam. He took a drink of coffee.

People came and went from the gas station. He nodded at some of them. The traffic on the interstate seemed slow. The snow was really coming down.

The sun was going down at this point. It turned the mountains purple. It was actually very beautiful. Not that the Dishwasher cared. He would shit on those mountains, if that were possible. The Wyoming beauty was more annoying than anything. It mocked him somehow. How could something so pretty be such horseshit?

He stood there eating his burrito next to the trash can. The Dishwasher did. Squirting mustard on every bite. Glowering at the landscape. He kept an eye out for Toby. He couldn't see the bus depot, but it was just there, over the interstate. He would finish his burrito and make his way there. That was the plan.

———

The Dishwasher finished his burrito. He threw the plastic wrapper it came in into the trash. The plastic swinging door was disgusting. A million ketchup-slathered hot dog foils had left their mark. It seemed like nobody in the history of the gas station had bothered to wipe it down. He took a napkin out of his winter coat pocket and wiped his lips. He threw that away. He chugged the rest of his coffee. He threw the cup away.

He sighed. The Dishwasher. He picked up his black plastic garbage bag with everything he owned in the world and walked towards the interstate. He looked over at the diner across the street. Thought about the waitress and the biscuits and gravy that had nearly put an end to him. He wondered if he should go over there and ask the waitress if she wanted to go into the walk-in cooler and have some sex for good luck. Like a departing gift or something. Then he felt ashamed. He would never in a million years do something like that. He did put the thought in his memory banks for later.

The Dishwasher kept walking. The snow was thick now. He was leaving tracks on unwalked sidewalks now. He crossed the exit ramp without incident. Walked under the overpass. It stopped snowing for a while, while he did this. He crossed the entrance ramp without incident. Took a left. Looked around. No Toby.

He walked up the hill. Came to the bus depot. Went inside. Shook the snow off. Looked around. There was nobody there. Nobody aside from the guy behind the kiosk. The same guy from before. The one who had told him how much the bus to Denver was. He walked up to the kiosk. He said. The Dishwasher:

"Hi, one ticket to Denver, please."

"You got it."

———

"Hey, is the bus on time, or what?" The guy was busy typing something into the computer.

"What's that? Sixty-nine dollars." The Dishwasher put his black plastic garbage bag down. The bag with all of his belongings in the world. He took out his wallet. Found seventy dollars and handed it to the guy.

"The bus, you think it's on time, or—?"

"One dollar in change. Um, yeah, this storm is just around here at the moment. The bus coming out of Big Piney isn't experiencing snow at all."

"Cool. Cool."

"There ya go. Have a good one!"

"Thanks, man."

"You got it."

The Dishwasher put the dollar in his wallet. He looked at the ticket. One-way to Denver. He felt a sudden burst of excitement.

He picked up his black plastic garbage bag and went over to a bench and sat down. He looked outside. The sun was setting now. It was getting dark. He looked at the clock. Then he looked at the bus schedules. He had an hour and a half to kill. He felt exposed. The lights in the bus depot were glaring. He could hardly see outside. He wondered when Toby would show up.

He didn't want to be caught off guard. The Dishwasher. But it was too cold to go hide outside. But maybe not. He was wearing his long johns now. Maybe he could go hide behind the bus depot until the bus showed up? Why not? Maybe it would do him some good to suffer for a while. Plus, if Toby showed up and he wasn't there, maybe she would think he had taken another bus. An earlier bus or something. The bus to Chicago or whatever.

The Dishwasher didn't know what to do. He just sat there, thinking. Nervous whenever he saw a headlight on the interstate. He was a sitting duck. He knew that. There was no way around it. All he could do was hope. Hope that Toby was finally seeing things like he saw them. The Dishwasher. That they had no future. He and Toby. That there was nothing to do about it. That they were doomed, together. She and him. It couldn't last. It only made sense that he should move on. Get on the bus to Denver. Haul ass out of town. Start something new. Make something with his life or whatever. Either way, it didn't involve the Dishwasher and Toby being together. These thoughts only made things worse. The dread he was feeling was OOC as Toby would say. Out of control. He really didn't want to fight her on this. He just wanted to get on the bus and get the hell away. As he thought, sitting there on that bench waiting for the bus, the coffee kicked in. The Dishwasher got up and went into the bathroom. Taking his black plastic garbage bag with all of his possessions with him.

The bathroom was gross. He spent a few moments putting toilet paper on the toilet seat before he sat down. The Dishwasher. Things came out fast and loud. He wasn't hungover anymore, or at least he didn't think he was, but his body was acting like it was. It took a lot of wiping to clean himself up. He stood up. Pulled his long johns up. His mildewed jeans. Flushed the toilet without looking. Went to the sink. Washed his hands. Took his black plastic bag back out into the bus depot lobby. He sat back down on the bench and waited.

An hour went by. He thought about getting his book out, but he couldn't focus. He was nervous. Waiting like that. Knowing that Toby would be by at any moment. What would she say? What could she say? There was no turning back. He had the ticket. He had his stuff. He was moving to Denver. He would have to be firm with her. She didn't control his life. She was just a thing. He wasn't even sure what kind of thing that was. They spent some time together. That was certain. But still. What was the relationship? The humping was really good. But so what? Half the time they were fighting. The other half of the time he was working. They spent almost no time together outside of his apartment or the bar. But the humping was good. And he had to admit that the drama she created kind of turned him on. She was a force of nature. Whether it was a force for good was debatable, but she was really something else. But still! She couldn't come to Denver. She had to stay behind. There was no way it would work. The Dishwasher had shit to do. There was a future for him. He could feel it. Even if it was just piddly shit like getting a job in Denver. He would write that book or whatever. Start a band or something. Write the physics ideas down. He could do it. He had time. He was young. Right? He didn't need any ball and chain dragging him down. Right? And Toby deserved better. As insane as she seemed. She deserved a guy that treated her well. That hung out with her outside of the bars or humping all the time. She was a good person. The Dishwasher decided. Even if she was a huge pain in the ass.

The Dishwasher sat there waiting. No Toby. The hour was closing in. Soon the bus would be there. He checked his winter coat. The bag of chips for the bus was still in his pocket. He remembered a book he had read about this kid that had a sandwich in his pocket that he kept checking to make sure was there. He felt like that kid. Nervous and uncertain. Abused, even. Even though he didn't know where the abuse was coming from. The Dishwasher. Another twenty minutes went by. The Dishwasher was shaking with excitement. Maybe he was okay? Maybe Toby would just get the message. That she should stay away. Leave him alone. Move on with her life. As the minutes slowly disappeared, the Dishwasher was feeling very lucky. No Toby. Even the snow seemed like it was not falling as thickly as before. He felt so lucky that he went outside. Leaving his black plastic trash bag behind. The bag with all of his belongings in the world.

He stepped outside. Took his soft pack out. Knocked a cigarette out of the package. Lit it. The snow was falling even harder than before. It was an illusion, inside. He frowned. Pulled his hoodie hood up. Walked away from the door. The snow was cozy, though. The wind seemed to have stopped.

A car drove up into the parking lot. It wasn't Toby. A woman got out. Then an older kid. Maybe her son. They were talking as they got out. Continuing the conversation they'd been having in the car:

"And you will call me when you get there?"

"Yes, Mom."

"And you have that cashier's check in your wallet?"

"I already told you!"

"And you will call me when you get there?"

"Mom!"

The Dishwasher got out of the way as they walked into the bus depot lobby. They walked to the kiosk and started talking to the guy behind the desk. The Dishwasher lost interest. He kept smoking.

A little while later, another car showed up. A guy got out. Told the driver, "Thanks." Slammed the door. The car drove away. The guy looked annoyed. He was underdressed. Wearing just a windbreaker. He started to light a cigarette. But then the bus showed up. He said, "Oh shit!" And threw his cigarette to the ground. He needed a ticket.

The Dishwasher panicked. His bag was still inside. He threw his cigarette butt next to the full cigarette that was just hanging out on top of the snow. He went inside and grabbed his bag. The black plastic bag with all of his belongings in the world in it.

He stood there, not knowing what to do. A few people came inside. From the bus. Whose destination was Laramie. Apparently. The bus driver came inside.

The clock said that there was still ten minutes before the bus was leaving. The Dishwasher didn't know what to do. He very much wanted to get on that bus. The bus that now said "Denver" on its face. In bright yellow letters. Denver. But the bus door was closed. The driver was inside the bus depot. Ten minutes and counting. He was going to get there. He would get out without any drama. No Toby. No blowout. No nothing. Nothing doing. He couldn't believe his luck. The Dishwasher.

He was starting to relax now. He double-checked to see if he still had his bag of chips. In a couple hours, he would be in

Denver. Seeing the sights. Living the dream. Troll and Bogart would pick him up from the bus depot in Denver. He would start living a beautiful life of pure whatever. Excitement. Possibilities.

The Dishwasher stood by the doors. The doors of the bus depot. Waiting for the bus driver. He went out a couple of times. Bringing things back in from under the bus. Not opening the doors.

Eventually the guy in the windbreaker and the mom and son stood behind the Dishwasher while he waited. They were ready to get on the bus as well. The mom had stopped asking questions and was silently weeping. The son looked very annoyed. He kept saying, "Calm down, Mom, it's just a short trip. I'll be fine." The mom was still worried, though. She kept weeping silently. Saying racist things every now and again. Telling the son to watch his back. The son just stood there. Trying to be stoic. Embarrassed by his mom. The windbreaker guy really wanted that cigarette. Eventually he revolted and said, "Fuck it!" He went outside to smoke. Leaving his duffel bag in the line behind the Dishwasher.

The Dishwasher was confused. He hadn't meant to start a line. He was just waiting to go out and get on the bus. But now that he was at the front of the line, he was kind of annoyed with the windbreaker guy for going out to smoke when they were about to board the bus.

Eventually the bus driver came back. He opened the doors of the bus depot. Putting the little legs down to keep the doors open. He said:

"Denver bus! All passengers must show tickets! Leave your baggage under the bus! Denver bus! All passengers must show tickets before boarding the bus! Denver bus!"

The Dishwasher started walking out the open doors. He looked down at his black plastic bag. He didn't want to put it under the bus. It was everything he owned. Plus, it looked like a trash bag. He was afraid that they would just throw it away. Thinking it was trash. He stopped at the bus driver and said:

"Do I have to put this under the bus, I am afraid that..."

"All luggage under the bus!"

The Dishwasher walked to the side of the bus. He put his black plastic bag down. Double-tied the top. Hoping that would help. He really didn't want to put it under the bus. But he did it anyway. There was no way to make anyone know that it was his luggage. He wished he had a handkerchief or something. To wrap around the top. To let people know. He didn't. He placed the bag on top of a suitcase. Sighed. Turned around. Started walking towards the door.

Suddenly a car came out of nowhere. Came screeching to a halt. It was Toby. She burst out of the door like something on fire. She yelled:

"Dude! What the fuck? You are just leaving!?"

The bus driver, who was just seconds ago a solid rock of unchanging commitment to protocol, suddenly recoiled. His eyes were wide. The Dishwasher's heart fell into his long johns. The timing was amazing. He was stunned. He stood there.

"Toby, I…"

"What the fuck, dude. What the holy fuck, dude! You can't just leave like this, man! Who do you think you are?"

"Toby, I…"

"You can't just leave like this! Are you kidding me? I don't get it! What are you doing? You have to tell me! How can you just leave me like this? I don't think I can take it! What the hell? What the hell!!!"

"Toby, I…"

The guy in the windbreaker smirked as he got on the bus. The mom told the teenager, "See, you see how these maniacs are?" The teenager was elated. He couldn't believe it. He ignored his mom until she pushed him onto the bus. The bus driver didn't know what to do. He stood there staring. The Dishwasher looked over. His eyes said, "Help me." The bus driver just stared. Toby moved in towards the Dishwasher. Screaming at him. Yelling:

"You can't just leave me like this! I don't know what to do! You just can't!"

The bus driver kind of scooted between the bus and Toby and the Dishwasher. He slammed the doors on the side of the bus closed. He scooted back. He said, "Denver bus, last call." But he only kind of meant it. He wanted to get out of there. As soon as possible. But he knew the Dishwasher had a ticket. So he kind of kicked his feet around, not knowing if he should get inside or not. Toby grabbed on to the Dishwasher. She screamed:

"I don't get it! I just don't understand!" The Dishwasher panicked. He said the first thing that came to his mind:

"Toby! It's just temporary! You can come visit me in Denver! I am just getting out of town for a while, I swear!"

"You mean it? You really mean it?"

"Toby! I swear! You can come visit me! I'll call you the first chance I get!"

Toby's eyes were broken. She didn't look normal. She was crying and grabbing on to the Dishwasher's winter coat like if she let go, she would die. The Dishwasher was backing into the bus door. He didn't know how to get her to let go. He was pleading with her now:

"Toby! I swear! Just let me go! It will be alright! I will call you! I swear!"

"You swear! Tell me you swear!"

"I swear! Toby, I swear!"

The Dishwasher managed to get up and onto the bus. Toby let go of him. The bus driver was inside. Sitting in the driver's seat. He looked like he just ate a plate of gravel. He kept moving his mouth around and around like he couldn't figure something out. Toby tried to get inside. The bus driver said:

"You need a ticket, miss." Toby just cried. She fell onto the steps. Bawling. The bus driver didn't know what to do. He just waited. Eventually she stood up and walked away. The bus driver closed the door. He was shaken. He looked around. He double-checked that the door was closed.

The Dishwasher walked to the middle of the bus. There were two seats side by side that were empty. He sat down. Slid to the window. Looked out. Toby was sitting in her car. Crying. The amount of shame that went through the Dishwasher was too much. Too much shame. He almost stood up and ran to the front of the bus. Guilt, you could ask for forgiveness, but shame, shame lasted forever. He watched Toby crying in her car. The bus driver said over the intercom. His voice slightly shaky:

"This is the, uh, 5:15 bus to Denver, making stops in Fort Collins and Greeley. If you are on the wrong bus, tell me now. Please respect your neighbors. The arrival time in Denver is expected to be 8:05 p.m."

The bus driver backed out. Out of the Laramie bus depot parking lot. He went around the bus depot and headed into Laramie proper. Under the interstate overpass. He took a left. Heading to the highway. The Dishwasher relaxed a little. He was still nervous that something bad would happen. That somehow Toby would take over the bus and force him to come back to her. He looked out the window. The snow was still falling. He didn't know how he felt. As the bus got to the edge of town, he let himself relax even more. In a couple hours, he would be in Denver. Starting a new life. Troll and Bogart would pick him up. They would get drunk. Have a good laugh about the olden times. He would start his new life. Or something. Something would happen. After buying the bus ticket he had 463 bucks in his pocket. No job. No girlfriend. No Altitude. No idiot roommates. No Norman. No Lisa. No nothing. He was looking pretty good. And now he had an empty bus seat next to him and a bag of chips to look forward to.

About a mile out of town, he looked down at the highway. He couldn't believe it. Toby was driving next to the bus. Trying to get it to stop. He heard the bus driver yell:

"What the holy hell!"

The Dishwasher watched as Toby rolled down her passenger-side window. Screaming into the snow and wind:

"Pull over! Pull over!"

Or, at least that was what it looked like she was yelling. The bus driver didn't pull over. He just kept driving. They passed the Cowboy and the fireworks stand and the place you could buy porn. Toby had to pull back every time a car came down the highway. She didn't give up, though. When they crossed the Wyoming/Colorado border, the highway patrol was waiting. There were suddenly flashing lights. The bus pulled over. The highway patrol came up and talked to the bus driver. The bus driver just said yes and no a bunch of times. Then he closed the door. Pulled out onto the highway. After that, there was no more Toby. She was either in handcuffs or was driving back to Laramie or was bawling on the side of the road. The Dishwasher felt so guilty that he couldn't even eat his chips. Then he felt guilty for even thinking about eating the chips. Then he felt guilty for leaving the way he did. Then he felt guilty for moving to Denver. Then he felt guilty for the black plastic garbage bag under the bus with all of his belongings. Then he felt guilty for feeling guilty. Because he could ask for forgiveness with guilt. Not shame. Shame lasted forever. He felt guilty for not feeling ashamed. The Dishwasher.

Acknowledgements

Thanks to:
Miette Gillette
Teresa Hartmann
Michael Jung
George Truman
Tina Satter
Scott Gillette
Jack Warren

About the Author

Joey Truman is a writer and artist based in New York City. He performs with the bands UM, Escalators, Bronko Dilater, and Soft Inserts.

Other titles by Joey Truman:

Hilarious (a serial, 2023)
Moveable Rooms (2022)
Sequestered (2021)
Donkey (a serial, 2021-2022)
Etiquette (2020)
Cooking Cockroach (2019)
Killing the Math 2 (2019)
Parlay (2018)
KinderRinder (2017)
Killing the Math (2016)
Postal Child (2016)

About the Publisher

Whisk(e)y Tit is committed to restoring degradation and degeneracy to the literary arts.

We work with authors who are unwilling to sacrifice intellectual rigor, unrelenting playfulness, and visual beauty in our literary pursuits, often leading to texts that would otherwise be abandoned in today's largely homogenized literary landscape. In a world governed by idiocy, our commitment to these principles is an act of civil service and civil disobedience alike.